SLEEPLESS FLAME

SLEEPLESS FLAME

BOOK ONE

ODIN V OXTHORN

ISBN: 978-0-9998349-0-9 (Ebook)
ISBN: 978-0-9998349-1-6 (Paperback)
Library of Congress Control Number: 2018903794

Edited by Valorie Clifton.
Cover Art by Karolina Jędrzejak (RinRinDaishi).
Formatting by Serendipity Formats.

To Alex, for dealing with my inexpressive bullshit.
Love you.

And to Jess and Tina, for being amazing Morale Officers and pushing me through.

ACKNOWLEDGMENTS

These awesome individuals deserve recognition for supporting me through this roller coaster of a journey. Thank you so much:

Jessica Nesler
Valorie Clifton
Nicole McDonough
Mag Made Bijoux
Mary Macdonald
Andrea Watkins

sound, trying to drown the noise out with her anguish. But the sound was relentless, engulfing her senses as the abyss claimed her.

Darkness swallowed her vision, leaving her alone with the pulsating screech as it tore her awareness apart.

##0.2##

BEEP. BEEP. BEEP. BEEP. BEEP. BEEP.

THE ALARM CLOCK berated her with its infernal shrieking, drilling into her brain with a maddening tempo.

"FU-*UCK*!" Nara bellowed as her fist slammed the source of the annoyance. She rubbed the crud from her eyes, letting out a dismayed grunt as she slowly gained awareness of her surroundings.

Flashes of the dreams replayed through her brain, flooding her with disgusted bitterness. A grimy revulsion crawled over her skin as she unwittingly reflected on the semi-sentimental themes. She loathed her psyche. The lack of control left an unclean, violating taint over her thoughts, as if an outside observer was toying with her mind for amusement, forcing her to think in ways aberrant to her nature.

She barely had time to curse out her heritage before her NetCom shattered her attention with a demanding buzz. As the device's persistence intensified, she laboriously rose from her bed to respond to the call, letting off a sharp growl as she lurched toward the living room.

"What do you want, Annon?!" she snapped as she jabbed at the device.

"Good morning to you too, Sunshine," a dry, masculine voice hissed through the speaker. "I'm calling about your contract. I assume you were able to complete it?"

Oh, yeah. Nara rubbed her face vigorously as the jumbled pieces of her thoughts slowly clicked into place. *Been holding on to that thing for a while now, haven't I?*

"Yeah, I have it." She sniffed, rooting around the apartment for her clothes. "And I assume you want it?"

“That would be lovely,” the voice on the NetCom quipped. “I expect you to be at my office this afternoon. The client is quite eager to receive his product.”

“Yeah. Sure. Whatever. I’ll be there.” She cut off the channel, walking back into her bedroom.

She idly picked up the glittering object sitting on top of her end table, a gold ring with outlandish characters carved along the thick band. In the center was a large ocean blue jewel, shining with an odd brilliance in the dim light of her flat.

Nara had grown attached to the jewel and briefly lamented having to part with it. But it was unhealthy to double-cross the people she routinely worked under for the sake of frivolous knowledge. If she were only a few years younger, perhaps she would have cared enough to deal with the consequences.

She let out a wistful sigh as she pocketed the trinket, absentmindedly rubbing the inscriptions as she headed for the front door. The sour bite of the crisp night air invaded her nostrils as she made her way outside, the desolate streets welcoming her with bitter notes of metal and carbon.

The sun could not penetrate this deep into the city, and any life inhabiting the decaying streets thrived in scant quantities. Despite the dangers of being alone and out in the open, Nara walked with confidence. Few in the Undercity were foolish enough to bother a creature of her stature. She could conceal a sizeable arsenal inside her loosely-fitted attire, creating a risk of uncertainty that most malefactors would not take.

There are, however, exceptions in every group of criminals, especially if those exceptions recognize her from a distance.

A smirk distorted her lips as she discerned the pattering of noisy humans trailing behind her, inadvertently broadcasting their presence to her sensitive ears.

And who will it be today? She mulled over the possibilities. *Venom Clan? Eh, too quiet. Intia-Tech? No, they’re too small a company to worry over. Phylox Synthetics? Hmm.*

She led her quarry around in a maze of alleys, moving through decayed structural playgrounds, abandoned corporate buildings, and crumbling domiciles. She casually strolled through the shrapnel carpeted ground, stretching out her wrists as she navigated through the garden of concrete mounds and jagged wire beams.

She continued making spontaneous turns on her journey, and the ungainly tracks of her pursuers magnified in chaotic notes as they struggled to keep up with her. Her smile widened as she walked onward, leading them to a favorable stomping ground.

Their hushed curses and hasty stumbles aided her awareness, and she pinpointed the location of the pack using the tiny echoes they cast into the street. She counted six clamorous shadows tailing her, but deeper inspection unearthed one softer intrusion murmuring further back. Number seven advanced in contrast to the rest of the group, stifling their movements as they meticulously progressed through higher ground.

"Okay, I think we've gone far enough," Nara addressed the air. "You may come out now."

She listened to the hesitation, stretching her arms out and rotating her neck as the pack uncomfortably shifted in their hiding places. She let out a soft chortle, feeling the tension above her bubble over as the raiding party deliberated their move.

"It's either that or I come up and get you," she taunted, glancing down at her nails.

Five figures emerged from the shadows, typical lackeys that infested the city with their shiny guns and smug bravado. But number six preferred a more dramatic entrance, gliding toward her with elegantly tailored clothing and a wolfish grin. His smugness was haloed by a shock of golden hair, greased back into a rigid ponytail that pulled his forehead taut.

Her smirk began to fade as she regarded the creature. The Face archetype of thugs annoyed her greatly. They were usually armed as well as they were dressed, but they rarely lifted a finger in conflict, instead hurling their haughty voices around while the meatheads did the dirty work. And they took advantage of their speaking privileges by any means.

She ignored the garish entry of the smirking goon, concentrating on the muffled disruption in the distance. Number Seven had not entered the arena, dawdling behind the raiding party in the safety of the ruins. The movements of the mysterious individual were cautious, yet clumsy, as they navigated through the fragmented floors of the buildings nearby.

"Galavantier sends his regards," the sharply-dressed thug called out to her.

"Oh, how *very* nice of him." Nara smiled widely, baring her fangs.

##0.3##

That was too close for comfort, Garrett thought. *I need to find a better means to get down here. Baran isn't going to cover for me much longer.*

The descent into the Undercity filled him with childlike delight, even though his thoughts inevitably delved into macabre existentialism. The leisurely expedition inside the glass elevator calmed him down from the strain of his hasty retreat, soothing him with the marvelous view.

The light surrounding the vehicle warped as it traversed through the misty Haze, the perpetual sickly purple cloud that divided the bright and glowing Uppercity from the cold, polluted heart of Under. The noxious air that shrouded the buildings was responsible for Undercity's weather, or more accurately, whether it rained or not.

At this level, the glittering windows of the megascrapers owned by Uppercity corporate forces were replaced with solid blocks of foundation, the habitable areas constructed stories above the taint of the Haze. The condition of the buildings deteriorated the deeper the elevator descended, unsightly chunks carved out of the material in erratic patterns. The decay matched the aesthetic of the crumbling Undercity buildings, remnants of an era hardly known to any Upper citizen.

The elevator descended into the craggy claws of Undercity's decomposing structures, sinking into the welcoming grasp of bony steel and eroded concrete frames. With a gentle hiss, the vehicle slowed its engines, easing its way through the visceral ruins as it delicately settled onto the ground. A swirl of thick cool air curled inside the chamber as the glass doors slid open.

Garrett stepped out into the shadows, sliding his hood over his face as he paused to let his eyes adjust to the lack of light. Shifting a cautious glance at his surroundings, he sent the elevator back to his Upper home.

The massive towers dwarfed everything around him, a concrete forest eternally bound to nightfall. His eyes traced over the jarring stylistic shift between Upper and Undercity architecture, picking out his landmarks from the collection of deserted outposts and bunkers as he headed to his first stop.

The H.U.D. was a drinking establishment and inn that was easy to spot from a distance. It was one of the only intact buildings in the vicinity. The tavern was erected from fresh materials imported from Upper instead of the makeshift structures hastily welded together from chunks of ruin. A beacon on the roof radiated vibrantly through the gloominess of the environment, accurately projecting the name of the bar, unlike its derelict neighbors, whose signs commonly spelled out obscene phrases with strategically burnt-out consonants.

Rumor had it that the keeper, Darius, was once a noble from the Upper districts, but the details regarding his arrival to the underground remained a mystery. Some of the wilder stories claimed he was a deranged criminal hiding from the police, while others said that he was a revolutionary, running a war behind the front of the bar. Others painted him as a social worker, bringing the comforts of the Uppercity to the downtrodden. And still many more said he'd grown weary of the bright lights and drama, wanting nothing more than to settle down in a contrasting environment.

It was quiet at the inn this time of day, but the ashy cloud of smoke from weeks past always managed to linger inside the walls. Darius kept a tight ship, and apart from the heady atmosphere, his bar was by far the cleanest in the Undercity. The wood-paneled flooring and burgundy wallpaper were kept stain-free, and the tables were always found upright. Fights were quickly dispersed before they erupted into chaos, and any resulting property damage was swiftly repaired.

"Garrett, my young friend!" The stout, bearded innkeeper greeted him warmly, pouring his guest a drink. "What news from the sky do you have for me?"

"Nothing lately, I'm afraid. Still the same old boring life," Garrett replied, accepting the offering. "Why do you think I'm down here all the time?"

"My charisma, perhaps?" Darius flashed a cheeky grin.

"Hah, or the free drinks."

"Don't abuse my hospitality. Just because I know you'd actually *pay* your tab . . ." Darius waggled a finger at him. "And what are you up to this dreary afternoon?"

"I am looking for a place to soak up a bit of culture. Maybe purchase a few unique items you normally wouldn't find in a vending machine?" Garrett expounded, taking a sip.

"The black market up on Verner's Row has moved to this quadrant this time of year. That seems to be the best place to go if you are looking for intergalactic goods," Darius offered with a pensive chin rub. "Though be careful that what you buy doesn't end up back there right after you purchase it."

"Any dealers, in particular, I should be looking for?"

"Nope. Good deals tend to find you before you find them. Just avoid looking like a fuckin' tourist when you encounter it, and you'll keep all of your limbs." A wry smile etched across the barman's lips. "But that's nothing you can't handle, right?"

"Of course," Garrett evaded, tossing his head back to finish his drink. He was still shaken by the piercing gaze his guardian had cast on him before he snuck off. It pained him to see Baran so disappointed, but remaining a prisoner inside that suffocating house had forced his actions. Each trip he risked endangered both him and his friend, but Garrett hoped that when his plans fell apart, he could shoulder the repercussions alone.

Darius contemplated the young man's distant stare. "What's eatin' you?"

"Nothing. It's just . . ." Garrett sighed as he rubbed his temples. "I'm not sure how many excursions I can take in the immediate future.

It's getting harder to bribe the butler to cover for my departures. I need to think of another way to get down here quietly."

"Why not just move down here permanently?" Darius offered, toying with the bottles behind the bar.

"Would you move out of an impenetrable fortress if you knew you didn't have to?" Garrett shot him a stern look. "Besides, I am not exactly the most skilled at fighting, especially down here."

"I suppose not. But a man thrown amongst the wolves tends to learn real quick how to fight 'em off, else he gets eaten."

"True." Garrett frowned, resting his head in his hands. *But on the other hand, if my disappearance is noticed, I will cause trouble for a lot oj people. Probably start some unnecessary wars.*

"Oh!" Darius suddenly snapped his fingers. "Speaking of interesting artifacts, a customer of mine gave me this little trinket."

"What is it?" Garrett asked as he watched the man extract a glittering object from his pocket.

"Not sure. It was in exchange for his tab. I only took it because it wasn't likely that I was going to get any real money out of him," Darius admitted as he passed it over. "Said it was a protection talisman from some random civilization across the galaxy, and it supposedly could summon great powers to aid the wearer."

"Fascinating!" Garrett beamed as he delicately placed the trinket into the palm of his hand.

He traced over the elegantly crafted coin-sized medallion, pinching the twisted chain between his fingertips to assess the durability of the links. Unfamiliar characters were engraved along the circumference of the piece, jagged and swirling flourishes from a language he had never encountered. In the center was a relief of two weapons crossing, fluid hybrids of plate armor and blades. Metal knuckles on the curious devices extended into vicious edges, giving the weapons the appearance of spiked praying mantis legs.

"I'm all for respecting other people's beliefs, but I leave the superstition to others." Darius shrugged. "I figured you would value its cultural significance more than I would. I get plenty of culture here after a full night."

"It's certainly something I've never seen before," Garrett

commented, tilting his head as he tried to decipher the mechanics of the menacing implements.

"Maybe it could summon a great demon to help you out when you are getting the shit kicked out of you down here." Darius paused, letting a chuckle slip from his throat. "Or up at your place. I don't know what kind of discipline you're in for when they find out you're down here."

"I . . . sure." Garrett ignored the remark, too engrossed with the alien object. "I will definitely investigate further."

"If you find more about it, cool. If it's worth something, and you sell it, just think about your ol' friend Darius here." The man smirked as he wiped off the counter.

"I won't forget. Thanks for sharing with me." Garrett winked as he pocketed the piece. "I'd better head out. I only have a few hours before anyone gets suspicious."

"All right then, don't get killed out there, you hear?" the barman warned.

"I'll try my best." Garrett smiled and headed out of the building, setting off to find adventure.

To the foreign observer, the Undercity was nothing more than a haggard web of decaying buildings cast in constant darkness. But to Garrett, the underground was a place of history, remnants of a thriving empire that spanned over horizons instead of skies. On his more fortunate expeditions, he could find traces of this glorious past buried in the debris piles left ignored by passersby. He had unearthed fascinating artifacts, recordings of personal journals, audio scraps of popular music, and even the occasional shred of painted canvas.

Garrett let his mind wander as he approached a set of crumbling high-rises, climbing up the precarious levels to avoid the perils of walking alone on the road. He hauled himself through a gaping hole in the wall, yanking his clothing from the jagged edges of cracked tiles as he crawled across the floor. Wedging himself behind a slab of concrete, he projected a map from the NetCom on his wrist to collect his bearings.

Undercity was composed of a series of concentric circles, the boundaries of the territories within shifting based on the movement of the various dangers that threatened the citizens. At the very center was the Civilized Zone, the most sterilized area of Under where bold tourists from Uppercity descend from government-controlled public elevators to embark on an exciting escapade behind the safety of the corporate police checkpoints.

From there, the borders blended into Uncivilized Space, where the locals of Under could live their lives in peace without meddlesome Uppercity politics infecting their business. Though it was the quietest area of the city, a trusted weapon, or several, and a spare set of eyes were necessary for journeying to the hidden gems of supply vendors and nomadic marketplaces.

Beyond this precarious region was the Fringe, where only the most armed, or luckless, individuals dwelled. Gangs of varying sizes, influence, and technologies squabbled over scraps of land, and disgraced street doctors performed unsavory experiments on the hapless wanderer. Their cruel medical procedures were often cut short by a stray bullet, an unintentional act of mercy.

The deepest reaches of Under were sealed off by No Man's Land, a physical border of swirling blue fog that coated the remainder of the planet's surface. Rumored to have been created by a combination of lax environmental control and corporate curiosity, the exact purpose of the caustic shielding is unavailable to the public, sealed off inside digital archives built generations ago. Crowdfunded expeditions run by The Cartographer's Guild had attempted to study the enigma with inconclusive results, leaving the greater part of Arcadia's earth uninhabitable.

A stir below him disrupted his navigation, a crunch of a footstep across the crusted carpeting. Garrett lowered onto his stomach, slithering toward a jagged pit torn into the floor. Peering over the edge, he spotted a man dressed in dark colors on the level below him, creeping forward in a hunched posture while fixated on the street outside.

Garrett hoisted his torso up to window level, squinting through a gap in the shattered pane to get a look at what the man was staring at. He spotted another figure strolling nonchalantly across the road, a giant compared to the average human, cloaked in a hooded calf-length leather coat that obscured their features. The mysterious brute seemed to have an air of confidence about them, as if they knew they were being followed, or blissfully oblivious to the ambush.

Garrett edged closer to the window while his common sense tugged at him, urging him to seek shelter from the backlash of conflict. But his burning curiosity fueled a dangerous mood, tempting him to observe the engagement.

He watched the giant stop in the center of a parking lot, stretching their arms out as they heaved an exaggerated breath of air. They called something out into the street, then stood patiently on the asphalt. On their summons, the man beneath Garrett emerged from the building and into the road, advancing on his target with hands in pockets. More men appeared from out of hiding, surrounding the figure with self-satisfied smiles.

Frustrated with the inability to hear the conversation, Garett slipped through the window, planting a careful foot onto the rusted fire escape that tenuously clung to the face of the building. He cringed as he eased outside, treading forward in dainty steps over the rickety metal.

Despite his vantage point, he still could not make out the exchange in the street. Squatting down in slow, controlled movements, he slipped his feet into the rungs of the half-attached ladder, ignoring the shuddering of the cantankerous balcony as it argued with his shifting weight. He awkwardly descended in timid steps, pushing back his anxiety that relentlessly questioned the stability of the structure.

Having given up on eavesdropping, Garrett turned his grip in the ladder, determined to witness the scenario behind him. He pleaded the force of gravity for mercy as he turned his shoulder around, leaving the tenuous stability of the wobbly ladder as he adjusted his view.

##0.4##

Ah, yes, Galavantier, Nara grumbled. *Should have guessed that one first. He only sent seven this time?*

"You have been inconveniencing him greatly," the haughty leader addressed Nara.

"Take it up with my agent. I don't need a pack of dogs yapping at my ankles," Nara chided. The men chuckled synchronously at her insult.

"Pleasant, as always." The leader paused to bask in his wit. "My employer has suffered substantial profit losses due to your . . . *antics.* He is requesting compensation for the damage you have caused."

"I would hardly call my work 'antics.' And despite our previous history, it's just business. Nothing personal." As she brushed her coat sleeve, the henchmen twitched, synchronously snapping their arms up to reach for their weapons. Nara glanced around at the posturing display, her lips curling into a sneer. "However, your presence is certainly making it personal."

A subtle scratching sound hit her ears, a metallic squeaking from the buildings behind her.

What the hell is Number Seven up to? she mused as kept her face stone, masking her perception from the mob. *They can't belong to this crowd. Probably a scavenger waiting to pick up the leftovers.*

"You see, *someone* has to pay for the damages done. You are the only annoyance that consistently disrupts my employer's production." The leader dramatically folded his arms.

"And I was severely overcompensated, considering how easy it was to break into that compound," Nara scoffed. "He should have paid me to protect his shit twenty years ago before he decided to unleash his foaming hounds on me instead."

"As if he would have given you the option." The man laughed derisively as his supporting goons exchanged eager glances.

The obnoxious scraping amplified as Number Seven fidgeted in their hiding spot. Nara unlatched the holster on her wrist, sliding a pistol down her sleeve. Civilian or not, the observer was not worth the risk to her.

"Whatever. Are we going to do this or not?" Nara griped, loosening her shoulders with a slow rotation. "I have places to be, and your squeaky voice is irritating."

With a cacophony of discordant laughter, the goons advanced.

A skin-shriveling screech tore through the air as the rust-seasoned ladder gave a final protest of Garrett's fidgeting, drowning out the pained screams from the mob behind him. The piping lurched toward the pavement in a spray of sparks, causing a yelp to burst from his throat as he clawed at his fleeting support, wrapping his limbs around the grimy metal.

An explosive crack disrupted the air, breaking his concentration on his dire predicament as an invisible force violently shoved him forward. Metal clanged through his ears as his forehead smacked against a ladder rung, only to be overshadowed by a lance of pain that tore through his shoulder, sending searing lashes across his chest. Stunned by the sensation, his numbed arms unfurled, letting gravity pluck him into its embrace.

He blinked rapidly, fighting back a pressure swirling around his brain as he struggled to process the events. He watched in awe as his garments shifted color, darkening with a slick crimson hue.

Funny, his morbid thought process proclaimed, *gunshots didn't hurt this much in the simulations.*

He somehow mustered the strength to cough out a weak laugh at the absurdity of his farce, the storm in his head amplifying to a percussive agony.

The pitiful moans of the two thugs writhing on the ground did not drown out the sickening thwack of Number Seven's body hitting the concrete. Nara tightened her grip around the throat of Number Three, ignoring the distraction while she watched the movement of the pack leader.

"It's not fair to bring another person on your team," the cocky man taunted, maintaining his gaze on her as he kept his smoking gun pointed at the street. "The odds aren't exactly even as it is."

Seven didn't belong to them, she thought. *Interesting.*

The flagellating spectacle of another henchman disrupted the atmosphere as he babbled unintelligible curses, terror flickering through the light of his augmented eyes as he fixated on the buildings behind. He staggered back to the leader, who snarled in warning as they collided. The muttering soul could not hear the reprimand, frantically reaching an arm behind him to seize the man's attention.

"What the fuck is wrong with you?!" the leader barked, dodging the frightened man's desperate smacks. The grunt gathered the courage to turn around, leaning in to the leader's ear. Upon hearing the whimpering words, the color drained from the leader's face, his expression stretching to horror. "What has gotten into you? You're so full of—"

"Enforcers!" Another thug shouted, leaving his comrades behind as he bolted into the streets.

Shit, Nara growled as she dropped her hostage, shoving them away. *Not what I need right now.*

As the thugs picked themselves up and dashed from the scene, Nara ran in the opposite direction, taking shelter amid the debris of the building where Number Seven had fallen. She slid under a slab of concrete, pulling the body out of sight, and waited for the ominous patrol to appear.

An ethereal hum resonated through the street, announcing the arrival of a squadron of towering black-cloaked figures. They glided to the center of the arena, systematically situating themselves to form a perfectly proportioned square barrier around the scene. The hum waned as the last unit slid into their designated space, and the collective stood in pensive silence, analyzing the pavement for their indiscernible purpose.

The Enforcers were the ubiquitous remnants of a law enforcement system that had served centuries ago before the divide of Upper and Under. With their infrastructure long since dissolved, the remaining active units drift amid the desolate streets, hunting for perpetrators against an unknown power. No one has deciphered their motivations, or dared to try, but fearful speculation painted the blame on them for innumerable disappearances of Under citizens.

Nara remained frozen inside her derelict fortification, releasing her breath in soft, controlled wisps. Despite their ill-omened presence, the Enforcers possessed a notoriously short attention span, allowing her to wait patiently from a safe distance while they collected their arbitrary data. She turned her attention to the body next to her, questioning the sanity of an individual who would spy on a conflict this deep inside Uncivilized Space.

A glint on the pavement stole her curiosity, and she traced her eyes over a golden chain trailing from the human's pants pocket. She stretched her arm out, delicately hooking the necklace under a finger. With a gentle tug, a coin-sized focal playfully jumped out of hiding, revealing its regal inscriptions.

What the fuck? Her eyes widened as she regarded the familiar medallion, gingerly placing it in the palm of her hand. She traced over the engravings in disbelief, a perplexing resentment warming her skin.

Panic churned through the fragments of Garrett's consciousness as his brain struggled to process reality. His body was frozen, numbness binding him to the pavement as the tearing agony spasming across his chest stifled his movement. Macabre thoughts of mortality coursed through his mind, swelling with the torrent of dizziness as he struggled to stay awake. He twitched as he felt a tickling sensation slide over his leg.

Shit, I can't die now, he fretted, sending his heart thundering through his agonized body. *Baran would find me and kill me again. Why did I come here? I'm so fucking foolish.*

"Shh," a voice softly chastised.

Oh gods, is he here already? his paranoia babbled. *Fuck! Lay still. Maybe he won't find me.*

He peeled open his eyelids to discern the source of the warning, only to be welcomed by the horrifying visage of a scarlet-skinned demon, their animalistic eyes alight with an icy fire. The massive figure scrutinized him with a cold, unfeeling expression. Fear crippled his thoughts as he beheld the emissary of Death, permitting the creeping fog of darkness to overtake his consciousness.

Nara fervently examined the suspicious human, uncertainties grinding at her discomfort as she questioned the identity of the upstart Upworlder. She poked her head out of her shelter, watching the drove of hooded ghouls depart with a silent flutter of tattered gossamer. When peace had settled in the streets, she slung the human unceremoniously over her shoulder, shifting her glance before heading back toward her apartment.

What the fuck am I doing with my life? she scolded, adjusting the body in her grip. *This tool had better have some damned good answers for me when he wakes up.*

CHAPTER 1

##1.0##

Garrett's senses were stirred by a strange aroma, not unpleasant, but definitely unfamiliar. The sensation was quickly overshadowed by a wave of castigating pain flickering across his shoulder. He looked down at the wound, neatly bandaged beneath his torn and bloody clothes.

Right, that wasn't a dream. I'm in so much shit, he thought. *Where the hell am I?*

He cringed as he gingerly shifted in the cushions of an unusually long couch, craning his tender neck to examine the darkened room. Everything appeared to have been created from the same gunmetal material, the utilitarian furniture built with only durability in mind, embellished with a scattering of empty shell casings and liquor bottles. The few windows in the room had been obstructed by metal bars and rails, while the metal-paneled walls were reinforced with orderly rows of cabinets and racks, exhibiting an impressive array of blades, guns, and other objects of violence unrecognizable to him.

The enticing vapors pulled his gaze to the kitchen, where an imposing individual was stirring an enigmatic concoction on a compact stovetop. They were of indeterminate gender, black clothing draped loosely over their broad shoulders. A thick, tight braid of plum-colored hair swayed as they moved, the ends delicately brushing the center of their back.

Garrett caught a glimpse of their striking facial profile as they reached for an ingredient, awestruck by their chiseled features and deep crimson complexion. Their softly pointed ears dripped with gold rings and tiny delicate chains, which jangled whenever they shook their head.

The humanoid scowled when a NetCom buzzed in the room, revealing a set of sharpened canines as they answered the call.

"Yeah?" the person answered with a sigh.

"Is that all I get?" the annoyed caller scoffed through the speaker. "You've been ignoring me for *three. Days.* And all I get is 'Yeah?'"

"Yeah. Go fuck yourself," the humanoid jeered. "Is that better?"

Their voice honeyed the air with a mystifying clarity, a silvery tone that resonated within their throat.

"Charming. Absolutely charming," the voice on the NetCom muttered. "You're obviously not dead, so do you mind telling me where the hell you have been? I don't appreciate being left to entertain demanding clients while you waste my time."

"I had a bit of trouble on the way." The being gave off another weary sigh.

"Oh, really? How many this time?"

"Six," they replied, absentmindedly itching their scalp.

"Hmph. That's nothing you can't handle. I've heard reports of you taking down an entire platoon."

"Yeah, well, reports also say that I eat orphans for breakfast and drain the blood of hapless souls that cross my path," they snapped.

Garrett stifled a twinge of dread at the remark, questioning his immediate safety as his muscles stiffened.

"Regardless, that has never stopped you from coming to me before," the voice pointed out. "You've finished a contract with a limp on numerous occasions."

"Something came up and I had to deal with it."

"Don't tell me you lost it," the voice hissed.

"For *fuck's* sake, Annon." The person let out an annoyed rumble. "I have it."

"So?" The voice emphasized with an exaggerated hum. "When can I expect to receive it? The client was not happy to hear their delivery was delayed, and it took some thorough persuasion to get them off my channels. I don't want to have to talk to them again unless I *have* to."

"Goddammit, Annon, you can have it tonight." They dropped a fist against the counter.

"Good. Don't keep me waiting."

"Yeah, whatever," they said as they rammed a knuckle against the NetCom, ending the transmission. "The hell you going to do about it if I don't, you whiny freak?"

Garrett's heart jumped into his throat as the silence resumed, the salted ire in their voice elevating his nervousness. He let off an involuntary twitch as he forced his body still, hoping they hadn't noticed him awaken.

"So, you're awake," they said as they walked back to the stove, their back turned toward him.

"Uh, yeah." He let out a nervous breath of air as he opened his eyes.

"Hungry?"

"I, uh, sure?" The notion had not crossed his mind, the uncertainty of his personal safety toying with his awareness.

The humanoid turned around and approached, imparting a daunting perspective of their size as they towered over him. He was mesmerized by their almost majestic presence, their severe, icy gaze piercing through his soul.

"Hasn't your nanny taught you not to gape at outsiders, Upworlder?" They snapped him out of his daze, handing him a plate.

Embarrassed by his ignorance, Garrett timidly sat up to take the offering, avoiding their eyes as they walked to the nearby dining table.

"Sorry, that was extremely rude of me," Garrett apologized as he looked down at the plate.

The unfamiliar sweetly spiced aroma emanated from the disorderly pile of thick white noodles, dotted with bits of oddly colored vegetables and chunks of what he assumed was meat. The tangled chaos was covered in a generous coating of a congealed, dark teal-hued gravy. Though presentation was lacking, the dish was not dissimilar to what he might find in the streets of the market districts.

He cautiously picked up the utensil on the plate and took an experimental bite, finding the unsettling appearance serving no justice to the taste. A savory, almost nutty flavor danced across his tongue, the vegetation fresh and crunchy, offering a delightful sour contrast to the heavy sauce. Garrett restrained himself, resisting the urge to inhale the entirety of the meal as he remembered his manners as a guest.

"I, uh, thank you. For saving me back there. I know I was probably the least of your concerns." Garrett cleared the anxiety from his throat. "Why did you help me, by the way? I mean, if I may ask."

"I don't know." They shrugged, busying themselves by dismantling a pistol on the table.

"Okay," he replied, a nervous smile twitched across his face. The awkward silence clawed at his ears, and he tried a less engaging subject. "This is very delicious. Um, what is it?"

"Edible," the person stated, tightening a screw. Garrett poked at the plate, uncomfortable with their lack of willful communication.

"My name is Garrett, by the way." He paused, looking at them expectantly. When they made no indication of acknowledgement, he pressed further. "What's yours?"

"I am called Nara," they replied flatly.

"That's unique. Does it mean anything significant?" he asked.

"It means 'Nothing.'" Their expression hardened. "Now it is my turn for questions, Upworlder."

"Wait, how do you know I'm—"

"Your 'walk around aimlessly in dangerous places because I am invincible' aura radiating a mile around you," they remarked. "That's how."

Garrett opened his mouth to reply, then immediately clamped it shut, realizing the futility of any argument he could offer. He jumped in his seat as Nara stood up from the table, walking toward the front door. They extracted a shiny object from their coat, shooting him a curdled glare that made him shrink in his seat.

"Where did you get this?" Nara demanded, thrusting the medallion in front of his face.

"I'd ask you the same question," he stammered, instinctively slapping the front of his pants. "It was in my pocket the last time I checked."

"Do *not* toy with my patience, human." Their hostile tone chilled his skin, accelerating his heart with each syllable. "Where. Did. You. Get. This?"

"I got it from the market on Verner Row," Garrett managed, trying to contain his fear.

They narrowed her eyes at him, standing unnaturally motionless as they waited for him to correct himself, maintaining their accusatory gaze. Knots kinked his throat as Nara's mental invasion permeated his thoughts with itching paranoia, slowing time to an uneasy crawl. The deafening silence reverberated across his ears, plucking synapses across his brain.

"Okay, I got it from a friend," he finally cracked. Nara tilted their head, glaring at him expectantly. "Who got it from another guy in exchange for his tab, and I don't know where that guy got it from. That's all I know."

Nara turned back to the table and pocketed the medallion, still visibly displeased as they slipped into their seat.

"So, what is it?" Garrett inquired, drinking in a deep breath as the ethereal vise released his lungs.

"It's mine, that's what it is," they snapped.

Valuing his personal safety, Garrett left the issue alone. The abundant supply of armaments littering the walls convinced him that Nara was not a forthcoming individual, and any further discussion would garner unfavorable results. He couldn't help but feel a hint of indignation toward them, upset that the chance to research an unusual relic was stolen from him.

He raised his wrist to check his NetCom, curious about the time of day.

>> *42 unread messages from: Baran, Chief Security Officer, G Estate.*

Oh, SHIT, Garrett panicked, *The regalia's this evening. Oh, fuck, I need to get out of here.*

"Shit, how far are we from Crystal Point?" he asked Nara, hurriedly typing out a response to his keeper.

"About an hour by foot," they impassively reported as Garrett let out a breath of relief.

As he scrolled through the history of incensed panicked messages, an idea percolated through his mind. It was obvious that Nara could move around the Undercity with ease and was more than capable of fending off any assailant. They could prove an invaluable ally for his excursions, and possibly put Baran slightly at ease.

But they were obviously disinterested in social interaction, so befriending them was an impossible solution. Money was always a motivator in Under, however, and he had learned long ago that everything down here had a price.

His conspiring abruptly halted when his eyes went back into focus, meeting Nara's offended stare as they paused their cleaning routine.

"I don't suppose we could continue this conversation about my gratitude later, could we?" He smiled nervously. "I think I'm okay to go home now. I feel really good, actually."

"Just wait for the drugs to wear off." They clicked their tongue.

"How bad was it?" Garrett glanced down at the bandage uneasily.

"Small energy round, nothing vital." They shrugged. "You're still gonna feel it in the morning."

"I guess that's a good thing?" he commented. "I need to leave, quite urgently. But I have a proposition for you."

"Oh?" their disinterested expression tested Garrett's confidence.

"It has become increasingly, ehm, *complicated,* for me to get down here recently, and I think it would make it easier to move about if I had an escort to guide me around." Garrett fished for words to clarify his proposal. "I mean a bodyguard, a hired gun."

"I'm not a full-time babysitter," Nara scoffed.

"I'll make it worth your while," he added hopefully.

"My while is worth quite a lot."

"I will fully fund your equipment and resource needs. Weapons, ammo, armor, whatever else." Garrett projected his most charming businesslike grin.

The panels along the wall shuddered as Nara erupted into raucous laughter, throaty bellows that caused the hanging blades to vibrate within their holsters. The room settled as she suddenly clamped her mouth shut, hurling a condescending side-eye in his direction.

The hell is this kid playing at? Nara thought.

"In addition, I can help you out with your work," Garrett continued, placing his last card on the table.

He would not be able to set foot in Under without dancing around the home security system, much to Baran's annoyance. While his technical skills did not stretch beyond academic level, his ingenuity and keen pattern recognition ability had often unveiled access points that would have hindered the most stalwart network intruder.

"Let me get this straight. You, an Upworlder, are offering to be my remote Hawk?" Nara snorted, waving the tool in their hand dismissively. "Considering how you ended up here, you would be nothing but a colossal nuisance."

"You can't judge my computer skills based on my combat ability," Garrett refuted.

Nara leaned back and considered the proposal, letting Garrett stew in uneasiness with the prolonged silence.

Joy. Another Upworlder who thinks he can catch bounties for a living, Nara mused. *This will be the shortest contract I've taken up in a long time. All I have to do is wait for him to flee, then I get some extra materials out of the deal.*

Despite the nature of her work, Nara had grown bored with routine run-and-gun jobs, each day blurring into the next as she effortlessly navigated the monotonous political web surrounding Arcadia. The city used to offer her a challenge, a taste of mortality as she haphazardly accepted increasingly risky contracts, only to be buried in paychecks that fester in her amassing bank accounts.

The kid offered her something different, a unique handicap that had the potential to rekindle the fire in her calloused soul. And more importantly, a noisy enough distraction against the infuriating projections her sadistic mind subjected her to during her vain attempts to relax.

But how they'd met concerned her greatly. While the human boasted of caution, his intrusion on the Galavantier goons nearly cost him his life. He was lucky, and if there was one force in the universe she never interfered with, it was of Luck. The medallion he carried was an omen, and she was uncertain of its allegiance to good or evil. Either way, it had ended up in her hands, and the salient coincidence left her riddled with apprehension.

She searched his expression for any doubts, but she felt in him a sincerity she had rarely seen within humans. Not a single shred of malice was hidden in that salesman-like face, only blind desperation and a need to flee from an unknown force.

"Well," Nara started, doubting her sanity as the word passed her lips. "My armor has needed an upgrade for some time. I suppose I can work for you—for a little while. Part-time. Extremely part-time."

"Really?!" Garrett blurted in disbelief. He quickly cleared his throat to regain composure, fishing out a device from his pocket. "I understand completely. Here, I have a spare NetCom. You can reach me there whenever it is convenient for you."

"Mmmhmm, sure." She reached over and took the device, resolving to have it checked for suspicious software before connecting with it. "Isn't your tea ready or something? Shouldn't you be leaving right about now?"

"Well, not alone, I should hope. Can't really go far without my bodyguard, right?" He grinned widely.

Didn't take long to regret my words, Nara thought, narrowing her eyes.

"Okay, don't get too . . . comfortable with this arrangement," she rebuked, moving toward a gun cabinet. "I'll drop you off at Iron Grove. I have other business to attend to in another direction."

"Fair enough." Garrett attempted to stand from the sofa, teetering slightly as his legs protested against the sudden demand to function. He managed to keep himself upright after a series of semi-calculated steps forward, the vertigo waning as he reclaimed his equilibrium.

"Managing?" Nara wryly questioned as she slipped on her coat.

"Yeah, I'll be all right," he replied, only half convinced. He followed behind Nara as she headed out the door, moving as fast as his disoriented body would allow him.

After an uncomfortable climb through an obstacle course of jagged holes and crumbling stairs, they left the decrepit apartment complex. The Undercity air greeted them as they emerged, illuminated by the dim smolder of archaic electric lights, tall pillars of rusted metal stretching their glowing orbs to the sky.

"So, uh, Nara, was it? Any family name?" Garrett quietly asked, hoping for some semblance of small talk.

"No," she answered coldly.

"Oh. I see." His mind raced for another subject to force into the conversation.

"And your family name?" she inquired.

"I don't think I should disclose that," Garrett remarked, her question taking him by surprise.

"That may impede this relationship."

"Or benefit it," he countered. "You don't know me, I don't know you. No questions asked."

"If your heritage endangers me in any way," Nara warned, "I will do more than sever my connections with you."

"While your point is painfully clear," Garrett began, "I keep my affiliations secret from any and all business relations. It protects everyone in the long run and makes it even easier to cut ties if the situation requires. No association, no mess."

"I see." His argument pattered against her suspicions.

"So, I'm sorry for asking this, but are you—" Garrett stopped himself, trying to articulate a potentially volatile question. "I mean, how should I refer to you? Like, in the third person?"

Nara sighed wearily. "Though grossly inaccurate, I generally go by human feminine pronouns to keep their heads from exploding."

He frowned. "I'm not sure I understand."

"She." Nara shook her head. "Just call me 'she.'"

"Noted. Sorry."

"Whatever."

"So, tell me," Garrett started, his nervousness powering his mouth, "how did you end up in Under?"

The air churned as Nara abruptly whirled around, a venomous glare contorting her frightening face.

"I am never going to discuss that with you, and you will never ask," she rumbled through a muted growl.

"Whoa." He recoiled with a shaky step. "Okay."

Nara slowly ground her heels into the pavement as she turned around, wordlessly accepting his acknowledgement as she resumed her course. Garrett released an uneasy breath as he waited for his heart to normalize speed, swallowing hard as he followed after her.

Garrett throttled his curiosity as they continued the journey in silence, stifling a throng of unyielding questions that tormented him as the reality of his new relationship overloaded him with possibility. Baran would inevitably express concern over the situation once he brought it up, doubting the trustworthiness of his new hire. Since he didn't have answers for the impending interrogation, Garrett hoped his evasive confidence would assuage the guarded man.

The half thoughts and conversation starters fled from his head as Nara halted, pointing to the makeshift forest of Iron Grove.

Wiry tree constructs jabbed their rusted branches toward the sky, artfully crafted using found junk littered about Under. The park served as a memorial to the foliage that had once inhabited the planet. A shameful quiet weighed over the misty corroded sculptures, a testament to the mark humanity had left on the earth.

"This is as far as I am taking you," Nara announced.

"Thank you again. I'll try my best to make it up to you if you give me the chance. Talk to you later." Garrett waved as he wandered into the shadows.

Nara breathed out a loud sigh, watching the foolish human disappear in the street.

"What the fuck am I doing?" she muttered as she headed toward her next destination.

CHAPTER 2

##2.0##

Garrett fussed with his collar in the reflection of the glass, thankful for the change of clothing stashed inside the chamber. He inhaled several cleansing breaths in an attempt to steady his nerves, steeling himself for the questioning.

When the elevator slid to a stop, he ran one last hand through his disheveled hair, then crept through the tunnel that led to the kitchens of his estate. He feigned nonchalance as he ventured into the foyer, where Baran was waiting with arms crossed, blocking the path upstairs.

The impeccably groomed red-headed man glowered at him with vibrant blue eyes. His pale skin was flushed with displeasure, emphasizing the sharp lines of his gaunt face. Though considerably shorter than Garrett, he exuded an aura far beyond his physical presence.

At one point, Garrett thought a man of his frail appearance was an unusual choice for a chief of security at a multitrillion-credit corporation, until he had witnessed him devastate several kidnappers single-handedly. On multiple occasions. Since then, he had gained a fearful respect for the man.

Garrett projected his warmest smile, but before he had the opportunity to open his mouth, the tempestuous man intercepted him.

"Where the *hell* have you been?" Baran fumed. "I've been contacting you for days."

"I'm sorry," Garrett replied. "I didn't see my notifications and I lost track of time."

"That is a hell of a lot of time to lose track of." The man's scowl deepened. "What the hell were you doing?"

"Sorry. You know how I get when I am on a trail. I get so focused I—"

"And this trail led you where, exactly?"

"Nowhere, unfortunately." Garrett let out a disappointed sigh. "The trail went cold before I could find anything."

"You could have *called.*" Baran shot him a stern look, refolding his arms over his chest.

"I know, I know. I'm sorry."

"Sorry isn't going to save you from a bullet to the head," the officer snapped.

"Nothing happened, *seriously*. I'm fine," Garrett muttered irritably. "I know the regalia is this evening, and I am here right on time."

"What is that on your face?" Baran interjected, his eyes trained on a faint yellow splotch barely visible on Garret's forehead.

"Huh?" Garrett brushed a hand over his temple, stifling a noise of discomfort with the gentle pressure. Though he had repeatedly inspected his appearance in the elevator, his scrutiny was no match for Baran's acute observation. "I'm not sure. I must've slept funny on my face or something."

"You are neglecting your promise to me," Baran added.

"I—" Garrett ground his jaw at the guilty stab, irritated by the man's awareness of his psychological weakness. "I'm sorry. I will be more communicative next time."

"Yes, and on that subject, your father is expecting you on the private channel. I suggest you don't make him wait too long," Baran warned.

"If it makes you feel any better," Garrett began, testing the waters. "I think I have a plan that would alleviate your spirits, at least a little."

"Hardly likely. I have the responsibility of watching over the legacy and heir of the largest corporation on Arcadia," Baran scoffed.

"I've hired a bodyguard in the underground."

"I—" Baran sputtered incohesive syllables as he processed the declaration. "Oh, have you, now? I can't even begin to . . . where did you find him? How much did you have to pay? What do you know about his reputation?"

"I promise you, this one is absolutely trustworthy." Garrett smiled sincerely. "My instinct tells me so."

"But your common sense should be exercised instead!" Baran exclaimed. "What the hell has gotten into you?"

"Baran, listen to me, please," Garrett implored. "I have the utmost confidence that this is the right person to keep an eye on me."

Garrett winced as Baran simmered in silence, sensing the gears grinding in the man's brain as he contemplated the scenario. He was foolish for bringing the matter up so soon, but he knew if he waited, Baran's uncanny attention to detail would make it increasingly difficult to explain. His best tactic against the doubting man was the element of surprise.

"You'd better pay him enough to keep him on your side," the man uneasily declared.

"I have. Don't worry," Garrett stated. "Everything will be just fine."

"That statement makes me incredibly uncomfortable. And if you get me axed . . ." Baran warned.

"Relax, it shouldn't come to that," Garrett assured, skirting around the man to head for the stairs. "Now I've got to go answer that call. We'll talk about it in more detail later. Thanks for the spare clothes. 'Bye!"

Garrett raced off to his bedroom before Baran could pursue him.

##2.1##

ANNON KEPT his office dimly lit, illuminated by the soft smolder of a substandard desk lamp. His taste in decor reflected his personality, tracing uniform patterns in sleek, precise lines. The furniture glistened with shiny black surfaces, and not a single mote of dust infected the sterile environment.

The man himself was the epitome of order. His suit was of the latest fashion and immaculately pressed. His pale pointed face was hairless, projecting an expression of chronic unease. A perfectly straight part divided his sleek, long white-blonde hair, all flyaways forcibly restrained by a softly perfumed product.

"Finally!" the slender man perked up when he saw Nara at the door.

Nara sat down in the cushioned recliner and propped her feet on his desk. She made an obnoxious show of cracking her knuckles, waiting for the inevitable noises of disgust from Annon as she situated herself.

"Client been driving you mad?" Nara inquired, feigning interest.

"More than you could imagine." Annon fidgeted, his gaze fixated on her boots.

"Nothing too severe, I hope?"

"Oh, you know these collector types. They always want what's not for sale but don't want to get their hands dirty to obtain it." The agent shook his head irritably.

Nara sighed at the man's inane prattling as she dug the ring out of her pocket, tossing it on his desk.

"That's it? No case or anything?" Annon tsked in disapproval. "The client's not going to be happy about that."

Nara released her annoyance as she shifted in her seat. "Found it on some asshole's finger. It didn't come with a case."

"Huh. Cheeky bastard." He delicately picked up the ring and inspected the stone. "And please don't give me any details. I know the way you work, and I don't want to know if the finger was still attached when you 'found' it. Or if he could walk after you relieved him of it."

"I wasn't about to bore you with details." She shrugged.

"I'm docking this garment out of your cut." Annon scowled as he pulled a handkerchief out of his desk, carefully wrapping the ring inside. "You're lucky I like you."

"You like me? I always thought you kept me around because I actually came back after a job," she scoffed, re-crossing her legs.

"Yes, well, you're too damned good to let go, so I try to keep you somewhat appeased—or at least not pissed off enough to scatter my brains across town," Annon declared. Nara smirked at the observation. "Speaking of, why do you go to other employers anyway? You know I charge you the lowest commission rate."

"Because other employers are nicer to me, and they don't hassle me when I can't fulfill the contract to the precise minute of the deadline, or bitch about the condition of stolen goods and handkerchiefs. Do I need to go further? Besides, you don't always give me a job, and I am not exclusive."

"That's because I don't want to waste your talent on petty errands." He leaned over his NetCom and began sifting through menus.

"And this job was more than a 'petty errand?'" Nara retorted, raising a questioning hand.

"Well, I figured you were bored, that's all. No one has wanted any intel gathering or someone 'taken care of' in quite some time." Annon sighed, tracing his finger over the projected screen. "Almost makes you wonder if world peace was finally declared, and everyone stopped trying to kick the shit out of each other."

"Beats me, though I'd hate to have to look for another line of work." She reclined in her chair, balancing it on two legs.

"Hmm. Food for thought." Annon shook his head and reached into his desk to remove a file. "In any case, I have another contract for you, if you're interested. Or bored, I suppose."

CHAPTER 3

##3.0##

Garrett flinched as he reached the meeting point, flailing an arm out to catch a fluttering projectile. He gave Nara a questioning look as he shook the wadded mess open, unfolding a black cloth face mask.

"Put that on," she ordered him.

He blinked. "Why?"

"Because, as an Upper, I don't know how recognizable you are, and since you will not tell me your family name, you will conceal your features," she declared. "You will not put me under any further unnecessary risk."

"The hood isn't good enough?" he asked as he tied the article over his face.

"No."

The fear on the Galavantier thug's face troubled her, the kid's identity nagging at the back of her mind. She hoped to be rid of him quickly and drain him of any resource she could while the contract lasted.

"I don't carry dead weight, so while you are down here, you will learn to use this," Nara ordered, handing over a small pistol. "That one is designed for the inept, so you should have no trouble operating it. You will use this piece only, and you will never aim it at me."

Garrett took offense at her demeaning attitude, despite a level of accuracy to the assumptions. His book knowledge of small arms function was somewhat advanced, thanks to Baran's insistence on simulation training. His real-world experience, however, was limited to lecture and demonstration of the security officer's personal collection, never having fired them himself. Much to Baran's discomfort, he did not possess a weapon of his own, having nowhere to conceal it in Upper and no permanent basecamp in Under.

"I've handled a—"

"*Handled* is worlds different from *used*. And even then, your experience is questionable. If you haven't evaluated the weight of someone else's life in your conscience, you've never handled a gun."

"I . . . you have a point." He frowned at her grim words. He gingerly slipped the armament into his pocket, hastily changing the uncomfortable subject. "So, where are we headed?"

"Market," she declared, heading off in the opposite direction.

"What are we getting there?" He was growing slightly irritated conversing with her back.

"As I said before, my armor needs an upgrade," she replied. "And I assume you have never been a Hawk before, so you will need personal surveillance equipment."

"Ah, I see." He tried to maintain the dialogue, but the conversation stagnated as he struggled to keep up with Nara's broad stride.

He was relieved when the marketplace made itself known, the murmuring commotion of the traders a welcome contrast to the dreary streets. He took in a hearty breath of air as the amalgamation of scents wafted toward them, spicy smoky odors of the food vendors competing with the heady exhaust of caravan vehicles and the distinctive perfume of organic life.

The market grounds were teeming with people from all manner of profession and species. Hawkers shouted their specials from all directions, drowning out the raucous buyers zealously haggling over merchandise. Creatures of every identifiable animal genus, and some not so identifiable, cried in distress from their constrictive cages.

Brightly colored digital displays projected looping videos of vendor offerings, flickering obnoxiously to distract the milling consumers. Items from weapons to priceless artifacts and religious icons could be found here, and intergalactic visitors could find the comforts of home only a stall away.

Nara merged into the bustle, her imposing stature parting the sea of indifferent bodies. Garrett contained his curiosity as he ducked into the gap she formed, prying his eyes away from the statues and jewelry.

She stopped in front of a modest weapon kiosk, her attention drawn to an array of small circular badges radiating a faint electronic glow of every color in the visible spectrum. She delicately brushed her hand over the pieces, selecting a bright blue device for further inspection. She raised the object to the meager spotlight hovering above the stand and scrutinized the indentations, feeling the serial number engraved on the back. She then glanced expectantly at the bored merchant, who gave her an approving nod.

Garrett watched in fascination as Nara rolled up her sleeve, tracing his eyes over the unusual characteristics of her exposed forearm. A thick, chitinous plating spanned the front of her arm, emerging from the soft flesh like a natural vambrace. The curious armor was a deeper hue in comparison to her skin, and emblazoned with an even more remarkable display of body art.

A venomous serpent coiled around her forearm, the pattern of ornate scales seamlessly blending the contrasting textures. The soft flesh was inked with a deep red that matched the shade of the armor, transitioning into glimmering furrows of a rosy golden metal that glinted in the tenuous lighting of the market. The creature's head rested on her wrist, its malicious expression emanating from two cerulean blue gems set into the eye sockets.

Ignoring his ogling, Nara pressed a sequence of buttons on the badge. The device snapped to her arm, forming a thin bracelet around her wrist, the blue lights intensifying as it calibrated. Shining metallic plates burst from the adornment, hungrily consuming her forearm with its silvery carapace. She flicked a nail over the material, humming a noise of approval.

The merchant stepped in and drew a dagger from their belt,

offering the handle to her for examination. Nara accepted the blade, flexing the point against the countertop to test its durability. Before Garrett could question the exchange, she rammed the dagger into her arm, the edge screeching in protest with a burst of sparks. The silver barrier deflected the blow, sending the blade darting off its sleek surface, leaving behind a superficial scratch marring the texture.

The metal reacted with the damage, the gashed area shifting into a viscous liquid. The healing material flowed over the wound, restoring the surface of the armor. With the repairs completed, the device hardened to its protective state.

"*How much?*" she addressed the vendor, satisfied with the results of her test.

"*Twenty,*" the merchant replied.

"*Would you take fifteen?*" she haggled, tilting her head inquisitively.

Garrett watched the conversation, picking out the few nuances he understood of Darktrade, the common tongue of the Undercity. He knew enough to conduct his own business, but sometimes, he was lucky enough to find someone who was willing to speak Hightrade, the accepted official dialect of Arcadia.

Darktrade was developed to keep secrets from the Upworlders, used as a tactic against the rich for personal gain, such as conning additional fees in a transaction or intentionally misinterpreting the rules to a gambling match. The evasive verbal cues and elaborate code of gestures took advantage of a victim's sense of chronic discomfort in foreign situations.

"*Not for the Nexuz series, I'm afraid.*" The vendor brought his hand to his chin. "*But I can part with it for eighteen and a half.*"

"*Acceptable.*" Nara nodded in approval, waving Garrett back to reality. "Time for you to make good on your part. Give the merchant eighteen and a half."

"Hundred?" Garrett furrowed his eyebrows.

"Thousand," she corrected.

The exorbitant cost jabbed at Garrett's ears, causing a slight whimper to eject from his throat. He promptly composed himself after meeting Nara's expectant glare and produced a thumb-sized tab of translucent plastic from his pocket. He slid the currency slice into his

NetCom, making a withdrawal from his account before handing it to the vendor, who graciously accepted the offering.

"*A pleasure doing business with you,*" the merchant purred, stashing the slice up their sleeve with the wave of their fingers.

Nara politely bowed her head and walked away with her prize, leaving a simmering Garrett trailing behind.

"You know, I could easily have bought a condo down here for that much," he remarked.

"I already have several, but thanks for the offer." Nara regarded him with a smirk. "You said you were willing to fund this expedition."

"You could have at least given me some forewarning," Garrett grumbled.

"You never asked about my prices, and I am afraid that is quite a hefty mistake on your part," she added flatly. "You have the misfortune of conducting business with one of the highest-profile mercenaries in the underground. Congratulations."

"Fantastic."

"Do you have any idea what I actually *do* for a living?" Nara challenged. "And how much it costs?"

"Wait a minute. You're being completely sincere, aren't you?" Garrett looked up in disbelief. "You're not just trying to con more money off me."

"Consider this a down payment." Nara turned around, bearing down on him with unsympathetic eyes. "And I assure you, this is a negligible fee compared to what my time is worth in the common market."

"I see." A disapproving frown distorted his face. "So, what now, Captain High-Profile?"

"Lunch," Nara stated as she sharply turned, heading into the food district.

Alluring savory scents wafted through the air, circulating in harmonious blends of the myriad cuisines represented along the alley of makeshift grills. Chefs sequentially flipped rows of sizzling meats, while their machine-like crews tended to cauldrons of bubbling broths simmering over open flames. Mounds of vividly colored spices provided a fragrant mask over the scent of the more pungent produce imported from neighboring solar systems. Lively drones floated through the air, poking at the tanks of live seafood as they performed their shopping duties for their masters.

Nara approached a stall specializing in soups and stews, browsing through the pictorial menus flickering on a small electronic display. After placing an order, she claimed an empty space on a makeshift standing table hastily constructed from precariously stacked cargo crates. Moments later, a service drone flitted over to them, brandishing a tray with two steaming plastic bowls.

The savory, earthy aroma flooded through Garrett's senses as he took his share, his appetite awakened by the inviting contents. He delicately plucked though the arrangement of roots and vegetables, revealing curly yellow strands bathed in a clear blood-red broth. Pieces of salt-cured proteins floated to the surface, dotted with the anisey scent of an odd blue herb.

"You know, for someone who boasts about an incredible income," Garrett remarked, "I find it odd that you would be eating common street food."

"Street food is fucking delicious. Don't you dare insult it," she countered, slurping up a noodle. "Now shut up and eat, highborn."

As delectable as the meal smelled, his curiosity was a greater force than his stomach, and he found himself distractedly swirling the contents of his bowl to keep his thoughts contained.

"Why are you squirming, human?" Nara startled him with the question.

"I, uh, well," Garrett started, "If I am being completely honest, I am extraordinarily curious about my new hire, but I also don't want to offend them. Therefore, I'm trying to suppress my inquisitive tendencies while I try to interact like a normal person."

"Go ahead and ask." She let off an irritated sigh.

"You sure?"

"If it will keep you from fidgeting, yes."

"So, um, what are your people called, anyway?" he timidly looked up from his food.

Nara extruded a groan from her throat, grumbling several indistinct words into her soup.

Garrett tried to save himself. "I mean, you don't have to answer—"

"They are referred to as the Ara'yulthr," she finally replied.

"Oh, does that mean anything?" He replayed the word in his mind, hesitant to ask her to repeat the pronunciation.

"Does 'Human' mean anything?"

"I, uh, I suppose not," he admitted, feeling his cheeks flush with embarrassment. "What do you mean 'they'?"

"Don't go there." She glared at him coldly.

"Sorry." He brought his eyes down to his soup.

Garrett busied himself with the tangle of noodles, trying not to let the tension sour the taste of the food. He began to doubt the integrity of the relationship, hearing Baran's overbearing voice jabbing at the back of his mind. His first impression on the intimidating mercenary was not his best, and he hoped he could live long enough to correct himself. But his accursed inquisitive mind and his desire to leave this wretched place would fight with him at every step.

Paying for someone to be around him was not an unusual experience. He was accustomed to forced social interactions, surrounded by people with predatory motivation toward personal gain. Still, it would be nice to have someone he could consider a friend, even if the feeling was not mutual.

They continued their meals in silence, letting the din of the lively environment drown out the swell of uneasiness between them.

##3.1##

THE BUILDING before them appeared more of a bunker than a business front, its reinforced blackened steel walls spanning the gap between the feet of two adjacent Uppercity skyscrapers. No signs or markings gave the travelers indication of the contents inside, amplifying the imposing presence of the establishment.

Garrett hung back as Nara pressed an intercom control jutting out of the wall, tracing his eyes over the huge riveted girders that bordered the massive airlock door.

"Ouch! –Oof, yeah?" a voice squeaked through the box.

"It's Nara. Got something I need."

"Oh, hi! Come on in."

After a series of cluttered crashes, screeching metal, and intermittent distressed yelps from the intercom, the door buzzed open. Nara heaved the vault open, waving a hesitant Garrett inside the dark corridor.

With a heavy, echoing clunk, the cavern burst with light, revealing a techno geek's wildest fantasy. Wires and computer parts were haphazardly strewn all over the floors and the walls, emulating a nest of an enormous gadget-obsessed vermin. Half-built robotics and cybernetic body parts stood vigilant amid the labyrinth of cluttered workbenches overflowing with tools and broken electronic boards. Glinting LEDs flashed sporadic, garbled messages, illuminating the path with a rainbow of jarring beacons.

Making their way gingerly through the shiny perilous mess, the duo entered a clearing in the madness occupied by a desk and a few chairs, also piled with half-finished projects. A scrawny young man emerged from the chaos, bits of shredded circuitry slung around his neck. Upon noticing the visitors, he hastily removed the wiry adornments, placing them on top of a teetering pile.

"Hiya, Nara. What can I do for you?" he asked cheerfully, wiping his hands clean on his jumpsuit.

"This is Art," she said to Garrett, gesturing toward the technophile. "Art, this is an annoying little sod who keeps following me around."

"My name is Garrett, actually." He offered his hand to Art, who energetically shook it. "I hired Nara as a bodyguard."

"An Upworlder, eh? Well, you certainly have an eye for quality." The quirky man scratched his nose, leaving a black streak of grease on his tawny beige skin. "How can I be of assistance?"

"Need a Hawk kit for the armor." Nara tossed over the newly purchased badge.

The glinting projectile landed squarely on Art's chest, causing him to perform an impromptu flailing dance as he fought with his limited coordination. As the device rolled town his trunk, he snatched it between his knees, beaming the visitors a victorious grin as he reclaimed his balance. He then plucked out the device and raised it to his face, scrutinizing the serial number on the back of the case.

"Whoa, nice! It's one of those new Nexuz models," Art marveled, the enthusiasm radiating across the room.

"It does what I need it to. I don't care who made it," Nara stated. "You're the one who obsesses over shiny new tech."

"All right, all right, take it easy," Art said. He leaned over to Garrett, nudging him with an elbow. "Give her a bigger, shiny new gun, and I'd bet she'd obsess over it."

"There's no need to be an ass," she retorted.

"You know, I could probably tweak its performance a little," he offered, her remark falling on deaf ears as he mentally tore apart the device. "Make it a bit sturdier, if you know what I mean."

"You break it, you buy it at double cost," Nara warned.

"That's not fair. You know me well enough." Art jabbed a defensive finger into the air.

"Exactly. I *do* know you well enough." She sighed with a defeated wave. "Eugh, do what you want. It isn't on my tab."

"Really? Awesome! You will be totally psyched with what I can do with this thing." Art's eyes lit up with glee. He then met Garrett's worried expression and restrained his excitement with a cough. "Don't worry, it won't cost much. I should be able to get what you need in a few minutes. Just let me do this one thing and . . ."

Art summoned a flurry of tools and components from his collection of pockets, his surprisingly nimble fingers dismantling the badge in a flash. Wire and electronic chips flew from the device, along with the mutterings of calculations transpiring from Art.

Anticipating a lengthy visit, Nara plopped herself down on the only clean spot on the floor, shoving sharp bits and pieces away to make more room. She reclined in the tight constraints, tilting her head to the ceiling as she disappeared into another plane of consciousness, her gaze traveling beyond the concrete.

Her unnatural stillness disturbed Garrett, and the clash of tools banging and ratcheting behind him made him self-aware of the space he took up. He anxiously stuffed his hands in his pockets as he glanced around the room, searching for another unoccupied area to settle amid the chaos. After a fruitless effort, he moved in closer to observe the machinations of the odd little man.

Art began pacing back and forth between a squadron of workbenches, stopping at one only to forget what he needed, then darting to another with a snap of his fingers. His face shifted through a spectrum of pensive stares as he mingled in circuitry, pulling up schematics and digital sketches from a display on his NetCom.

The madness continued as the hours crawled, the entranced technomancer neglecting his guests as his mind surged with tweaks and possibilities. Art's meditative noises began to wane as the symphony of sparks steadily decreased, devolving into flustered grunts as he shoved the internal organs back into the device. Plates clicked back into place as he reconstructed the badge, restoring the piece to a functional state.

"Yeah! That should do it!" Art announced with one final twist of a screw. He raised the device to the ceiling, admiring his handiwork. "Here, try it out."

Nara shot him a suspicious glare as she pulled herself up from the floor. "It's not going to explode on me this time?"

"I am ninety-two point seven percent certain I have everything put back in its place." Art rubbed the back of his neck. "And, uh, sorry about that last time."

"That's a low-ball estimate for you." Her scowl deepened as she gingerly accepted the device.

"It'll be fine, no worries!" the man assured her with a smile.

Nara let off a begrudging sigh as she shed her coat, placing the badge on the center of her collarbone. She pressed the buttons on the face, bracing herself as the blue lights intensified. Upon her commands, two silvery threads curled out from the device, winding around her throat. Liquid metal creeped from the eerie torq, the material slithering over her chest and arms.

Garrett held his breath, an empathic sense of claustrophobia tickling his lungs as he watched her morph into a steel mechanical ghoul. His skin crawled as the silvery-black liquid consumed her body, enveloping her face and legs in a viscous shroud.

The glow of the badge faded as the material hardened, segmenting her limbs across a carapace of sleek plate armor. A featureless void on the face of the helmet scanned the room, analyzing its surroundings with an unsettling gaze.

"So, how does it feel?" Garrett inquired, intimidated by the chilling display.

"Like there's nothing on," Nara commented, rolling her shoulders experimentally.

"May I?" Art produced a small pistol from one of the desk drawers, presenting it to Nara for approval.

"By all means," she agreed, turning her chest toward the machinist.

Art hesitated as he raised the weapon, running threads of equations through his head as he took aim. His hands wavered as he closed one eye, chewing the side of his cheek as he glanced down the barrel.

"Any day now," Nara goaded.

A modest burst ejected from the gun, teleporting across the room with a tiny flash, uttering a soft 'tink' as it vaporized over her shoulder. Reacting to the assault, the area warped and shifted as the quicksilver material rapidly soothed the damage.

"Nice one, Art," she praised, watching the metal return to its reinforced state. Art beamed as he rocked back on his heels, pleased with the results of the experiment.

"Whoa. That was awesome." Garrett gaped in astonishment. "What makes the metal react like that? How does it work?"

"Well . . ." Art inhaled an enthusiastic breath, thrilled to explain his craft to an interested participant. "Basically, the metal produced from within the badge is programmable. The wearer can tell it to create whatever shape desired. In this instance, a full body suit. Once the metal successfully executes the shape to completion, another command tells the metal to harden."

Art paused, waiting expectantly for potential questions. He shifted his glance between the two visitors, who replied with opposing degrees of silence. Taking in another draught of air, he continued his energetic spiel.

"The armor constantly seeks to maintain the configured shape, and when the armor is damaged, the device quickly responds to return to its previous state. What I did was adjust the speed of the process, reducing the reaction time by sacrificing a few energy efficiency points." He pulled off his cap to scratch an itch on his scalp. "At this rate, Nara can take quite a beating, provided there aren't too many holes in the metal at once."

"That's incredible," Garrett enthused.

The mechanic's grin widened. "Oh yeah, that thing can do lots of neat little tricks."

"Wow." Garrett reached out to poke Nara's imposing, metal-encased figure, but upon meeting her disconcerting faceless glower, he swiftly retracted his hand. "So how does the Hawk kit work?"

"Here." Art handed him a key-sized input device. "Take this piece over to her console, plug it in, and the program will run itself. You should have control over the optics just by moving the screen."

"Neat," Garrett said as he inspected the device in his hand.

"Try it out if you like," Art offered as he passed over a handheld computer.

The tablet murmured a cycle of processing drones as Garrett inserted the object into the device, creating a projection which hovered above the unit. The display broadcast a view of the cluttered workshop from directly in front of Nara, defaulting to her visual perspective. The scene shifted as Garrett dragged his finger over the screen, showcasing the perimeter of the room.

"Impressive," Garrett breathed as he continued to prod the technology. "And is there a communication line?"

"There's a nerve amplifier in the helmet portion of the armor," Art explained. "She will be able to communicate to you through thought, but your console will need to have audio hardware to talk back to her. Or you can type a message out, and she'll see it in her helmet.

"*Use your voice. I don't need you flooding my vision with your babbling,*" Nara printed over Garrett's screen. She then turned to Art and vocalized her praise. "Nice work."

"Aw, it was nothin', really." The mechanic toed the floor sheepishly.

"It's a fascinating piece of tech. Um, how much do I owe you?" Garrett inquired uneasily.

"Nahh, it's on the house. I don't often get to play with the latest," Art declared. "All that usually turns up here are obsolete hand-me-downs."

"Are you sure? That's awfully generous," Garret said, another currency slice in hand.

"Nara's a good customer. She always brings me nice things," Art said with a dismissive wave. "Oh! I almost forgot. That badge is locked to your bio signature, so you don't have to worry about anyone else 'accidentally' exposing you with a nicely timed poke."

"Thanks, Art. I owe you one." Nara disengaged the armor, sending pools of mercury shrinking into the badge. She gave the mechanic a nod before cautiously stepping toward the entryway, leading Garrett through the treacherous footing. "See you around."

"Come back anytime to visit me," Art called out to his departed guests. "I'm always here."

##3.2##

NARA STEPPED inside her apartment and dropped her coat on the couch, Garrett slipping behind before she had the chance to slam the door on him.

"If you're going to stick around, make yourself useful and calibrate that device," she grumbled. She peeled off her over-shirt, yanking down a sleeveless tank over her waist as she freed herself from the constraints.

"Sure," Garrett replied.

A shadow of inadequacy loomed over him as he observed her movements, the fitted garment emphasizing her imposing physical form. He traced his eyes over her arms, following the winding path of the serpent's body up to her shoulder. Beveled lines edged the border of hardened plating on her upper arms, accentuating the definition of her muscles. With her crimson skin tone, she resembled a skinless anatomy model in a biology textbook, without the unsettling open-eyed expression.

As his eyes passed slowly across her broad shoulders, a curious irregularity seized his attention. The point of a gnarled furrow was carved into her skin, the path of the jagged chasm leading into the armhole of her shirt. Neighboring flesh contorted around the disfigurement, highlighting the darkened skin inside the creases.

"That must've been an interesting battle," he commented, attempting to appeal to her gruff persona with an invitation to recount a war story.

"What?" Nara's body froze in place, and her eyes narrowed at the human, demanding clarification.

"That scar, on your should—" Her inhumanly fast movement cleaved the remainder of his sentence, the terrifying gaze of the incensed giant gripping his soul.

"You don't. Mention. The scar. Ever," she growled as the vertical pupils of her cold eyes twitched with ferocity.

"I didn't mean to. I . . . sorry," he stammered, dropping his gaze to the floor.

She turned away and stormed into the kitchen, leaving Garrett to struggle on his shaking legs.

"Where—" Garrett cleared the apprehension from his wavering voice. "Where is your computer?"

After extracting a beverage from the compact fridge, Nara wordlessly returned to the living room, pointing to a desk in the corner as she flopped down on her couch.

Garrett timidly slid into the chair, powering up the device and installing the piece of hardware Art had given him. It took him a moment to acclimate to the utilitarian operating system she employed, picking out similarities to the more user-friendly programs he was accustomed to.

As he wove through menus and directories, an intriguing file container labeled "Books" captured his curiosity.

"Oh, you like to read?" Garrett turned his chair toward her, hopeful that he had unearthed some common ground with the stoic merc.

"Kid, for fuck's sake." Nara groaned, rubbing her forehead in irritation.

"Sorry." He dejectedly slumped in his seat.

"Eugh." She exhaled a defeated sigh, the disappointment in the human's voice grating her nerves. "That is all I have left of my home world's archives. Leave it alone."

"Archives? You mean like libraries?" An eager fire illuminated his eyes. "Can you tell me about . . . I mean, uh, I like to read too."

Nara scowled as she took a heavy draught of the bottle in her hand.

"I mean, you don't have to answer," he quickly added. "Or maybe share what you like to read about instead?"

Nara stared wearily at the human irritant, lamenting the terms of the informal contract. Though she should have expected this level of ignorance from an Upworlder, she preferred the peace of frightened gawking and hushed whispers human strangers cast in her direction.

His constant fidgeting and blunt questioning would drain her limited patience dry. Watching him squirm in discomfort as he tried to contain his vehement curiosity was an exhausting furor to witness, and she wondered how long it would take for him to burst.

"There's not a lot of fiction in there," she finally revealed. "Mostly historical documentation."

"Oh, nice! I like to read a lot about history too. But my absolute favorite subject to read is anything about ancient galactic civilizations. It's fun following the theory, constantly changing as new finds are unearthed. It's so hard to keep up with the latest. There's so much out there. You can even find artifacts in the markets around here sometimes," he prattled on, poking at the computer to keep it awake. "Definitely have to scour them over before buying. But you wouldn't believe the stuff I have seen."

"I see," she said, focusing on finishing her bottle. *Oh, gods save me, I just opened the floodgates.*

"Mythology is my addiction. I love reading about how other people interpreted the universe. It can put a lot into perspective," he mused, absentmindedly pivoting in his seat. "Then you realize, you're just as lost as they were. Aimlessly wandering life, trying to figure out where you fit in."

Where the fuck did that come from? Nara shot him a blank stare, waylaid by his spontaneous existentialism.

"Well, anyway . . ." He hummed, nervously glancing at his wrist.

"Ah, crap, I should probably head out. I hope to see you again soon. And maybe continue this discussion later."

"Wonderful," she replied flatly, watching the strange human walk to the front door.

Garrett rested a hand on the knob. "Before I go, can I ask you another question?"

"Just one?" she jeered, clearly exhausted by the conversation.

"This time, yes." He projected a witty smile. "How come you trust me to do something like this? Watch your back, for lack of a more appropriate term."

She didn't have a straight answer for him, uncertain of the reason herself. While the challenge of an inexperienced Hawk had a certain appeal to her, she was not convinced this was the entire reason behind her motives. But the true answer required a deeper level of introspection that she was not willing to subject herself to, at least not sober.

"Humans have a tendency to protect their investments with tooth and claw," she said blankly. "The higher the price, the harder the fight."

"I suppose there's a ring of truth to that," Garrett replied.

"Mmm," she hummed in agreement, leaning back to examine his expression. He was quite possibly the easiest book she had ever read, genuinely curious, courteous, and well-intended. However, his intent alone was cause for concern, a detriment that could inflict unintentional harm to those around him. This coupled with his magnitude of complaisance caused her to question the sharpness of her senses.

"Oh, before I forget, here. I have to leave this with you," Garrett said, placing his gun on the table. "I hope you don't mind, but I have nowhere to keep it Upworld."

Nara raised an eyebrow as Garrett dashed out the door without another mind-numbing word.

CHAPTER 4

##4.0##

Garrett lounged on the windowsill of his room, sipping a glass of champagne. He amused himself by tracing patterns across the glass as he anxiously awaited her call, vacantly staring at the world outside. It had been several days since he'd last traversed through the Underground, but it felt like an eternity.

He watched the trams speed across the laser rails that guided them, tracing a vibrant aurora across the night sky. Floating advertisements and glowing displays electrified the scenery, politely inviting consumers to procure their product, their cinematics flourishing with pop culture references.

The overcast clouds enveloping the sky did not permit the stars to decorate the scenery this evening, so the weather projectors were deployed to take their place. Their optics delicately framed the skyscrapers in a glittering lace of light, adding to the city's energetic facsimile of nature.

Fathoms below his glittering fortress, citizens ambled about the shopping districts, immersed in their own miniscule world of decadence and pleasure. The crowd was a façade of diversity as they wore their genetics as a fashion statement, exhibiting only minor variations of one prefabricated, mass-produced entity. Individuality was a buzz word used to push cosmetic alterations to the masses, phasing in and out of trends as the weeks flitted by.

Garrett found life here to be nothing more than a one-dimensional illusion, filled with a loathsome, naïve populace content with floundering through its own ignorance. The corporations that puppeteered the world made sure the lives of the citizens were filled with the utmost luxury, keeping them quiet with frivolous, shiny entertainments while they fabricated a cutthroat agenda of personal gain. Fear of ostracization kept independent thought in check and the market flowing with the superficial needs of the discontented. Be yourself, the adverts would say, but not *that* way.

Garrett sighed and leaned his head against the window, the senselessness of society fueling a weighty despair.

This wasn't reality. Undercity was a reality that mercilessly threw people into mortal choices Upper cretins could not even begin to comprehend. Though life in Under was far from ideal, people were *human.* They could feel without the shiny billboards telling them how.

"May I intrude?" A stern voice disrupted his discordant thought cycle. He turned to meet Baran's severe gaze from his bedroom doorway, his smoldering expression implying the request was a rhetorical question.

"Sure." Garrett masked the bitterness in his voice. "So, how was the hostile takeover?"

"The company merger, I assume you mean." Baran made his way to a velvet armchair on the opposite side of the room. "It went as it was expected to."

"Hmm." Garrett mustered a noise of engagement, fighting with the apprehension cinching his throat.

"There is one issue I have been meaning to discuss with you." Baran folded his arms across his chest. "But I have not had the chance since I had departed."

"Oh?" The vise squeezed tighter as his brain flipped through the possibilities of the man's displeasure.

"I couldn't help but notice the state of the clothing you left in the elevator the other day," the guardian commented. "Though I must say, it was hard not to."

Shit. Garrett panicked as his heart jumpstarted into a frenzy. He had intended to collect his belongings after the regalia, but when he returned, they were already gone. In his rushed urgency to return to Under, he had forgotten about the tears and bloodstains, the consequences a galaxy away from his mind.

"Yeah?" He pushed the word through his quivering lips, his nervousness biting down on his skin.

"Mmmhmm. I had them disposed of. You are *very* lucky I found them first." Baran leaned forward in his chair and rested his arms on his knees, focusing intently on the floor. "I don't want to know what happened. The less I know, the easier it will be to protect you. But I want you to know that I am very, *very* displeased."

"Yeah," Garrett breathed, keeping his focus on the glass as he chewed the inside of his mouth.

"I am thankful you have returned safely, however. I don't know what I—" Baran stopped himself, quickly clearing his throat. "What would have happened if you did not come back. Please consider how your actions affect this world when you move about down there."

"Yes, Baran."

"I am willing to consider it an accident. Getting caught in crossfire happens all the time, so there might not have been anything you could have done to avoid it," Baran declared. "I'm going to keep telling myself this in order to make myself feel better."

"I–I'm sorry," Garrett said meekly. It wasn't Baran's anger that terrified him. It was his disappointment. The man had reached a level of grim acceptance that made him feel even worse about his carelessness.

"May I see the damage?" Baran shook his head in dismissal. "You obviously received some form of aid down there. I would like to see how it healed up."

"Sure." Garrett turned around and stretched the neck of his shirt over the wound, revealing a small scabbed circular gash, pale ocher bruises mottling the area with a sickly contour. He restrained a cringe as Baran approached, anticipating the man's berating reprimand.

"All right, now I'm confused." Baran scrutinized the injury, delicately brushing over healing tissue. "There was an ungodly amount of blood caked on that shirt. How did it heal so quickly?"

"Yeah. It feels all right now," Garrett replied flatly, shrugging his collar back into place. "Had some help on the way."

"Did you go to a street doc?" Panic saturated the man's tone, his eyes widened in alarm.

"No." Garrett shook his head firmly. "I promise, I didn't go to a street doc."

"Good. There's no telling what you would be missing after a visit with one." He breathed a sigh of relief as he sank onto the edge of Garrett's bed. "So is this scratch your new 'friend's' doing?"

"Heh, no. I was just . . ." Garrett shook his head vigorously, formulating a response to derail the man's suspicion. "At the wrong place at the wrong time."

"So it would seem." Baran narrowed his gaze. "And what do you know about him?"

"Well." Garrett thought about correcting him about Nara, but the additional wall of ambiguity protected everyone involved in the story. The more Garrett could contain information, the better. "Not a whole lot. Just a mercenary doing odd jobs in the underworld."

"What?" Baran snapped up to meet his eyes, the astonishment wrinkling his face. "That's all you have on this person?"

"As far as I know." He hated lying to Baran, but it was easier than hurting him with the repercussions of his careless antics.

"So why the hell do you think he is trustworthy, if you know so little about him?" Baran demanded. "And why did he pull you out of whatever mess you stumbled in?"

"I think I distracted somebody enough for him to make a better move," Garrett replied, uncertain of the answer himself.

"You *think* you did?" Baran folded his arms, scowling in disapproval.

"Well, I didn't see everything." Garrett combed a nervous hand through his scalp. *Good gods, keep it together.*

Baran glowered. "And dare I ask what you were doing to distract that somebody?"

"Like I said, I was at the wrong place at the wrong time," Garrett evaded.

Baran snapped up from his seat, obsessively running fingers through his hair. He began to pace around the room as he processed the fragmented information, the muscles in his jaw pulsing in agitation.

Garrett endured the spectacle with an apologetic frown, internally cursing his recklessness. He hated to see the man in this state, holding the weight of nine worlds on his shoulders to protect him. But the madness of this fortress constantly ate away at his sanity, the temptation of freedom too great for him to ignore.

"There is no question that you have the favor of luck on your side," Baran finally said, his distant gaze focused on the floor. "Luck is the only thing that ensures survival down there. But luck is a limited resource, and we all run out of it eventually."

"I don't think—" Garrett started, but he was cut off by Baran's swift about-face turn, his hardened stare piercing through him.

"It is that paranoia that keeps me awake at night, Garrett. Wondering when your luck will run out." His stoic voice wavered with the declaration. "And wondering when I will find your guts smeared across an alleyway."

"I . . ." Garrett trailed off, the man's profession tearing at his conscience.

"I can't be everywhere at once, and yet, I can't keep you here. You won't be contained. We both know this." Baran rubbed his temples in meditation. "All I can do is ask that you not make it difficult here. You are well aware of your station, and I hope you would take at least some responsibility for it."

"I know, Baran." Garrett hefted an exhausted sigh. "I know all too well. But I don't have to like it."

"More than understood." Baran shook his head and turned his gaze toward the window. "You have faith in this individual?"

"Absolutely," Garrett replied, meeting his eyes with unequivocal sincerity.

"I see," Baran murmured, pausing to study his face. "Either you have found a rare gift from the gods or a demon in disguise."

"I don't believe in either." Garrett couldn't help but smirk at the movement.

"Rule one, there will be no personal questions asked on a job. No exceptions." She paused to latch the rifle onto her back, her armor consuming the weapon under its silvery skin. "Rule two, there will be no excessive conversation. Just report what you need to, then shut the hell up."

"Underst—"

"Rule three, when I ask you to do something, do it immediately and don't question why. I assume you understand how this type of relationship can be more dangerous than helpful." She reached for a utility belt draped over a chair, checking the contents of each uniformly-sized box before securing it to her waist. With another hand motion, she commanded the armor to slither over the accessory.

"I do." He nodded, mesmerized by the morphing material.

"Good. Do you have any questions now?" she asked, rolling her neck around. "Preferably about how the programs run."

"Nothing for the moment. Ask me again when you are on the job." Garrett flashed a dry smile.

"Keep it up, kid. You'll wind up in a ditch with talk like that," she warned as she walked out the door, the half-hearted threat tugging at Garrett's spirits.

He watched over her shoulder as Nara clambered down the wrecked floors of the complex, calibrating his perspective on the touch panels. She approached a formidably sized pile of scrap metal, reaching a hand inside a hollow guarded by rusty jagged protrusions. After a careful prod, the hole responded with a yielding click.

Nara pulled her arm back and rolled the face of the scrap mountain away, revealing a vacant chasm inside. As she entered the refuge, her armor peeled apart over one of her belt compartments, granting access to its contents. She extracted a control device from inside, pointing it at the air as she pressed the button.

A bright blue beam streaked across the room, light curling around the laser as a swirling bubble materialized, taking up half the span of the shelter. The light darted back and forth, disintegrating the illusion inside the shed as it unveiled a sleek, state-of-the-art motorbike silently awaiting her orders.

"Whoa," Garrett said through her helmet. "Nice bike."

"Thanks?" she thought as a translucent sheet of material slipped over her face.

She mounted the vehicle and pressed the ignition sequence, bringing it to life with a gentle purr. Steering the inaudible machine out of the shed, she reached over and slid the door closed. After coordinating her navigation with the vehicle's computer, she darted into the city, morphing Garrett's view to a streaky blur.

##4.2##

"How is it looking down there?" Nara inquired. She was clinging to the face of a sleek black tower, the palms of her armored hand scaled with scads of tiny adherent teeth. She pulled herself next to a human-sized seam, tracing a finger along a control panel adjacent to the outline.

Garrett swirled his view to monitor the guards below, watching two security personnel casually stroll along their patrol path, blissfully unaware of the intruder slithering stories above them.

These units belonged to a special class of citizen colloquially known in Darktrade as "Salaried Mercs." Far from an endearing term, these hired thugs walked with a discordant aura beneath their pristine black padded armor. Their aesthetic clashed with their disheveled hairstyles, slack postures, and mannerisms that would make any Upper citizen blush with secondhand embarrassment.

While their armaments and behavior provided a slew of public relations liabilities, they were often hired by corporations that ran covert research projects in Under bordering on the grey scale of ethical practice according to the Galactic Peace Federation, who regulated industry standards in select locations of the solar system.

"It's quiet down there," Garrett reported, watching the pattern of spotlights shift across the grounds. "Keeping an eye out though."

"Fantastic," Nara flatly replied, popping open the panel to reveal its interface. The translucent peridot display welcomed her with a choice:

>>*EMERGENCY OPEN*

>>*SYSTEM ADMIN*

Not wanting to attract the attention of the entire city, Nara tapped the System Admin Option and was prompted with another inquiry:

>>*USER ID*

>>*PASSWORD*

She extracted a thin metal stylus from her belt, bringing it to a round copper contact point on the control panel. With the click of a switch at the end of the tool, the nib burst apart into four vicious prongs. As she led the tool closer, the teeth hungrily latched onto the panel, sending the display jittering in befuddlement.

Tiny colored lights along the barrel of the tool twinkled a contemplative status report as it tore through the barriers of the login screen.

>>*PROCESSING…*

>>…

>>…

Nara drummed her fingers along the wall, skimming the grounds behind her as she waited for the invasion to overtake the hapless system barriers.

>>*ACCESS GRANTED. WELCOME, FIRE COMMANDER SCHLATZ*

Fire Commander Schlatz? Garrett snorted loudly, then quickly slapped his hands over his nose.

"Problem?"

"Sorry." Garrett nervously shuffled through the menu displays on his screen.

The data extraction from the devious device had granted her a new series of commands:

>>*ALARM TEST*

>>*DOOR MAINTENANCE*

>>*LOG FILES*

>>*SIGN OFF*

A gentle murmur trickled through the air as Nara selected the "Door Maintenance" command, the locks on the fire hatch pattering with a cycle of soft clicks. She glanced around the compound one last time as she plucked her tool from the panel, sending a status report into her helmet:

>>*LOG FILE DELETED. CREDENTIALS ADDED TO DATABASE.*

She reached out and dug her fingers into the crack of the smooth wall, splitting it open with a gentle pull. As she adjusted her grip, she crawled up and leaned her face over the crack, analyzing the environment beyond the barrier.

She peered into the start of a shadowy corridor, light from the intersecting hallway barely reaching its limits. Stacks of hastily piled metal crates and cardboard boxes were clustered near the door, leaving just enough empty space for someone to squeeze through during an emergency.

Dust puffed through the air as Nara split the door open, setting off the respiratory filters inside her helmet. She created boot-shaped patches of clean flooring as she slipped inside, disrupting the carpet of grime with her footsteps. After a quick brushing with her hands to remove her tracks, she slid the door closed behind her, shaking her head admonishingly at the negligence.

her belt.

She delicately placed a flat segmented metal bug the size of a grape on the floor in front of her, tapping it to life with a gentle prod. A circular extrusion popped out of her index finger, and she pinched her thumb over the disc control, swiveling the miniature device around between her fingers. The bug darted around in fluid circles on its dozens of tiny legs as she rotated the control, energetically moving across the floor with her commands.

As the critter headed for the hallway, it conjured a secondary interface in her view, presenting to her, and Garrett, what could be seen through its eyes. Nara coaxed it around the intersection, sending it crawling up the walls toward a set of double doors further down the corridor. Tiny bobs disrupted the camera view as it crawled across a steel placard, passing over the words *Processing Unit 05* embossed on the surface.

"That thing is disturbingly adorable," Garrett commented.

"Mmmhmm," she agreed, a coy smirk hidden beneath her helmet.

With a click of the control, the critter squatted down against the wall, flattening itself to squeeze inside the thin seam beneath the door hinges.

As it entered the chamber, the millipede's eyes revealed the center of the tower, a rusted industrial playground spanning all ten floors of the facility. Tattered conveyor belts and metal conduits coated in oxidation stretched across the center of the shaft in an iron web, while similarly textured steel mesh catwalks traced each floor, bordered with scant railings made from precariously thin metal piping.

The production lines were still, rows of robotic worker appendages sleeping until the next day's shift. Enormous claws of transport automatons gently swayed in place on their rail tracks, clutching clear acrylic pods containing syrupy pools of organic matter.

Nara tweaked with her audio channels, calibrating one ear to listen to her immediate environment, and the other through the bug's mic. An eerie quiet coated the mechanized abyss, amplifying the tiny clicks of the scuttling critter with faint echoes across the chasm. Gentle clacks of chains and rocking machinery muttered in agreement, conferring with a hollow swell coursing through the air.

The rhythmic thunder of clanking footsteps shattered the creepy peace, violently resounding through the chasm as a patrolman entered. They whistled out a jarring tune, amused by the sound of the echoes as they traversed across a metal walkway.

"All right. I'm heading for this elevator." Nara panned the map to the hallway directly across the central tower, flashing the icon in Garrett's view. *"If there's anything you can do to keep them away from me while I do that, that would be great."*

"Uhh, sure." Garrett nervously cleared his throat as he prodded the network once again.

Nara crept out of her hiding place, watching over her shoulder as she slinked down the corridor. From across the wall, she ushered the bug around the border of the chamber, watching the interior of the shaft as the critter scuttled through the industrial arena.

Garrett dove through the streams of file paths and access routes, gently nudging his way into the maintenance controls. After paddling several laps around the transportation system, he politely requested the elevator to be brought up to floor four.

A nerve-wrenching mechanical groan invaded Nara's left ear as the chasm stirred. She watched through the eyes of the bug as the line of claws shuddered, swinging their empty cargo precariously over the abyss. The chamber resonated with an energetic rumble as the engines of the machinery awakened.

"Oh, shit, not what I—" Garrett blurted, frantically tearing over the console. "*Fuck!* Turn it off!"

The system had misunderstood him, perceiving his request meant to elevate conveyor belt four. Garrett scrambled to retranslate, stopping the belt before it began its obedient journey across the pit. The chamber wound down with a purr of acknowledgement as the drifting equipment jerked to a halt.

"The fuck was that?" The patrolling guard's throaty voice pierced through the chamber. They pressed a hand to their ear, calling after their comrades on a radio channel. "Hey, get over here and come take a look at this. Is someone fucking with the console up there again?"

"That works, I suppose." Nara quickened her pace, summoning the critter back to her as she turned a corner. The creature emerged from a

crack under the door to the processing room, obediently pattering to her feet. It let out a disappointed chuff as she picked it up, powering down as it was placed back into her belt.

Garrett let out a flustered cough. "Uh, the elevator should be there now."

"Wonderful," she remarked as she slipped into the welcoming silver chamber.

As the doors closed behind her, she glanced down at a translucent grey box beneath the columns of floor buttons, shielding a shiny red switch underneath. A number pad rested next to the casing, the glowing numbers taunting her with their devious smolder.

The view inside her helmet hazed with a soft white light as a concentrated beam passed over the touch screen. A status message popped in the corner of her vision, announcing its thought process to her:

>>*ANALYZING ORGANIC RESIDUE*

The number pad zoomed into her view, and squares of blue light flashed over the numbers as the helmet ruminated over the amount of wear on each key, spitting out percentages of fingerprint oils smeared over their surfaces. After momentary deliberation, the status message changed, offering her three eight-digit number combinations accompanied by percentages of probability.

Nara reached for the keypad, entering the code with the highest-reported chance of success. With a beep of approval, the case popped open, offering her access to the candy-like control. The chamber grumbled as she flipped the switch, gravity sinking under her feet as the elevator began to descend.

"That was a close one," Garrett breathed.

"Mmmhmm." She pressed herself into the corner of the chamber and scrolled through the map in her view, scanning over the schematics of the basement level.

"I, uh, sorry."

"Apologies don't mean much when you're bleeding out," Nara remarked.

"Point taken." Garrett grimaced at the metaphor.

The walls of the chamber rumbled in protest as it groaned to a halt. A chilling silence greeted her as the doors glided apart, revealing inky blackness dotted with an array of glittering lights beyond the brushed chrome room.

Nara's vision glowed with pale cyan as she leaned into the darkness, revealing the details of the research chamber. Idle supercomputers quietly meditated as they chanted calculations and measurements, their screens softly radiating as the machines ran through their routine checks and functions.

To the far side of the room, rows of glass cryogenic tubes oversaw the operations, wires and piping feeding into the ceiling. Sheets of prototype organic flesh floated inside the chambers, suspended in a syrupy vital fluid.

A line of smaller vessels slumbered next to their macabre counterparts, cradling identical copies of a synthetic human heart. The organs were composed of a silvery metallic substance that simulated living flesh, each pulsing in an unsettling divergent rhythm inside their confines. Artificial veins and arteries branched out in a chaotic web, the glowing green sinew radiating an unnatural aura over each product.

Nara crept through the synthetic spawn fields toward the back of the room, focusing her attention on a massive console spanning the back wall. She knelt in front of the machine, shifting her glance around the room as she brushed a finger along the seams of the paneling.

Garrett panned his camera view around her shoulder, disturbed by the stillness and lack of security in the room. He was entranced by the pulsing viscera, and a sense of curious revulsion crawled over the back of his neck as he witnessed the disjointed choreography.

As he tore himself away from the spectacle, a solid gunmetal canister in the corner of the room caught his attention. The bizarre column was roughly waist-high, capped with a ring of knife-like projections jutting toward the center of the unit. Tiny red blinking lights randomly dotted the surface, highlighting indented seams tracing geometric patterns around the body.

Nara dug her nails into the crack of a side panel, popping it open with a sharp yank. She buried her hands into the guts of the computer, pawing through wires and circuitry until she unearthed a flat card jutting from a port. Freeing an arm from the tangle, she reached down and extracted a thin-bladed pick from her belt, rotating it between her fingertips before diving back into the machinery.

She plucked at one of the cables attached to the card, separating it from the rest of the chaos. With a few quick flicks of the blade, she shaved off a section of the insulation, exposing hundreds of metal threads underneath. After pocketing the blade, she took out a locket-sized computer that sprouted with tendrils of bare wire, stirring it awake with the press of a button.

She coiled one of the wires around the wounded cable, squishing it over the joint to ensure the metals contacted. As she retracted her arms from the mechanical cavity, the tiny device burbled with excitement, broadcasting a new message into her view:

>>*LAUNCHING GARBAGE*

Nara sorted through her tools as the odd little box barraged the console with nonsensical calculations. Her vision teemed with status reports as the distraction software ran through its conning protocols.

Garrett watched the invasion in fascination, trying to interpret the meaning behind the reports. He lost himself in the flood of scrolling text until an itching sensation compelled him to look around the room. He panned his camera back to the corner, discovering a void where the devious canister once was.

"Uh . . ." he started, unsure of how to formulate his observation.

"What?" Nara froze in place.

"I think—"

"This task requires my undivided attention, otherwise something will break and alarms will go off," she snapped impatiently. *"Now what do you want?"*

"Nothing, sorry." He trailed off in bewilderment, scanning the room for the elusive object.

He boosted the volume in his audio feeds, straining to listen for movement as he searched for the strange canister. The view from Nara's kneeling body stunted his perspective, her back obstructed by the cluster of computers surrounding her. Flustered by the limitations, he shifted the camera to the top of her head, where he was met with a glinting predatory grin leering down on him from the top of the console.

An alarmingly silent gunmetal creature was perched on the monitor of the computer Nara worked at, seething red lights across its body glowering with a menacing smolder. Its skeletal physique was accentuated with lance-like extrusions projecting from its limbs, while bands of pliable synthetic muscles stretched between its joints. The head analog was nothing more than a dagger-filled mandible, with two ocular sensors craning around the upper jaw like a mechanized crustacean.

"Nara, *DROID*!" Garrett shouted at the screen, panic lashing over him as the predator raised a bladed arm.

"Where? Ah, FUCK—" She snapped up, hurling a forearm above her head.

A rending shriek burst into the air as Nara met the creature's strike, her arm shuddering as she strained against the force of the bladed arm grinding against her armor. She glanced up at the status window of the invasion program, slinging curses in her head as she watched the progress bar crawl across the screen.

With a furious snarl, Nara shoved the creature away, springing up to her feet as she recovered from the blow. Flashing blades arced across her vision as she withdrew, the droid lunging after her with a fervent onslaught. A jolting impact sent a shudder up her calf as her heel smacked against a computer tower, halting her retreat from the flailing automaton. As the creature lashed another strike, she wrenched her body around, catching an oncoming blade with her wrist.

The creature unleashed a distorted, staticky hiss as it violently tore away from her guard, the bladed appendage interrupting its outcry with a grinding screech as it slashed past the protective coating of her armor. Nerves ignited across her arm as the strike lacerated through the flesh beneath, blaring pangs rippling across her skin as the jagged seams of the armor curled into the gash.

Nara clamped her jaw shut, silencing a pained growl as the metal fervently warped over the exposed flesh. Red droplets slid off the metal in branching trails as the armor melded back together, concealing the injury from the environment.

>>SUPERFICIAL DAMAGE DETECTED. ADMINISTERING COAGULANTS.

"Fucking piece of shit!" Nara barked as a cooling sensation flooded over her arm, the first aid systems inside the suit reacting to the damage.

Garrett clutched the edge of the desk in silent horror, fascinated by the lithe movements of the pointy creature as it bounced in place on the balls of its taloned feet. His eyes widened as the automaton snapped to a crouch, slashing the air behind it with a ferocious beat of its arms.

"It's gonna jump!" Garrett blurted, watching the sentient torpedo take aim on its target with a dip of its shoulders.

"Not. Helpful."

The beast sprang into the air, showering the ground with sparks as it brushed the tips of its bladed fingers along the ceiling. Nara stole the initiative as she charged forward, diving to the ground as she cut beneath the droid's flight path. Gravity aided her evasion as she slid across the floor, rolling onto her back with a pivot of her hip. As the creature glided over her, she snatched its foot analog and yanked it downward, sending it crashing to the floor with a startled electronic bleat. She tightened her grip as she dodged its thrashing limbs, struggling with its mechanical force as it attempted to wriggle free.

Tongues of electricity flared out from her fingertips, sending the creature flailing in an agonized whirlwind of blades as the energy overloaded its electronic neurons. The droid expelled a blood-curdling screech before submitting to the assault, twitching out one final slash across the concrete flooring before it dropped limp in her grasp.

"Sharp piece of shit," Nara muttered as she released the beast.

"Is . . . is it dead?" Garrett asked softly, his eyes glued to the screen.

*"It's a **robot.**"* She threw her hands up, shaking her head incredulously at his question.

Agitated grumbles resonated across her throat as she recovered from the bout. Augments, droids, and synthetic humans were the bane of her existence, their flagrant simulation of vital force a challenge for her senses.

Life is supposed to be noisy, messy, clumsy, and disgusting, scattering traces of its presence over their environment. Artificially fabricated sentience was far too perfect, too refined for her perception, and a blind spot in her capability.

"Where the hell did it come from?" Nara demanded, chagrin salting her tone.

"From the north corner of the room, I think. It came from a can, or something." He shook his head in bewilderment, still reeling from the incident. "Didn't you see it?"

"I was a little busy," she muttered, skirting around the subject.

"Are you all right?" He released a breath of air, slowing his heart to a manageable pace. "I couldn't see the damage."

"I'll live," she said flatly as she walked back to the console.

After busting through the remainder of the computer's defenses, she flitted through operations until she homed in on her target. The system yielded to her assault, presenting her with a selection of actions on the glowing display:

>>*WELCOME, DR. HARRISBURG*

>>*LOG FILES*

>>*PROGRESS*

>>*DATA ANALYSIS*

She produced a data collection unit from her arsenal, inserting it into an open port on the tower. Streams of calculations, temperatures, and measurements sped through the screen as her swift fingers maneuvered through information, the view shifting into an intricate tapestry of charts and diagrams. The machinery clicked in compliance as she extracted the target data from the system, obediently downloading it to her storage device.

When she collected everything she needed, and then some, she plucked out the data unit and knelt on the floor. She dove back into the chaos inside the tower, tugging at the wire connected to her compact computer. With a quick flick of a knife, she severed the material, leaving the coil wrapped around the exposed cable. She then withdrew from the tangled mess, tucking curls of wiring over the evidence before sliding the metal panel back over the tower face.

"Right, now that was the easy part," Nara declared as she stood up, dusting grime off her knees.

"Go out a back door?" Garrett suggested, scrolling through the map.

"A back door?" she stammered, planting her fingertips against her forehead. *"I am in a basement. Underground. The* ***actual*** *ground."*

"Ahh. Yes, that is a rather solid challenge to overcome."

Nara let off a weary sigh as she glanced down at the stationary android, the remnants of her blood encrusting the edge of the creature's arm. She extracted a tiny vial of syrupy metallic liquid from her belt and poured a dollop into her hands, sprinkling droplets over the blades and spatters around the floor. The liquid swirled to life as it consumed the traces of blood, the shiny fluid beads shrinking into themselves as their sustenance steadily depleted.

"Whoa." Garrett marveled as he watched the puddles evaporate, leaving behind clean, dry surfaces.

"Mechanical virus." Nara scowled. *"Not cheap."*

"I can imagine." He shifted in his seat uncomfortably, feeling partly responsible for her need to use it. "You sure you're okay?"

"Just peachy," she muttered as she returned to the elevator.

Garrett resumed poking at the network, hoping to find an easy means of departure to make up for the incident. But as his requests became more persistent, the system began to deny him passage. Eventually, the holes he sifted through disappeared, blocked by the will of the unknown entities piloting the signal.

"Ahh." He cringed, sucking in air through his teeth. "Shit."

"Problem?" Nara inquired, pressing a floor button on the panel.

>>*SECURITY ALERT LEVEL ELEVATED. ALL UNITS ADVISE CAUTION UNTIL FURTHER NOTICE.*

"They, uh, locked the gate."

##4.3##

A HEAVY STILLNESS billowed into the chamber as the elevator doors slid open, the light from the hallway scorching the floor and walls.

"And what does that mean, exactly?" Nara pressed.

"It means I really shouldn't be touching things anymore," Garrett clarified with an anxious cough.

"It's not a problem until it becomes a problem." She shrugged, digging into her belt.

She extracted a tiny mechanical spider from a pocket, turning it on its back to reveal a switch on its abdomen. With a gentle push, the critter twitched to life, flailing its tiny needle-like limbs excitedly as she set it on the ground.

The critter darted over the floor, racing up to the ceiling with an eager tempest of pointy feet. Consumed by its hunting instinct, the creature accelerated toward its hapless victim, stalking a vigilant surveillance unit monitoring the corridor. The predator encircled the base of the camera, rearing back on its hind legs as it sized up its foe. Having uncovered the device's weak point, it lunged onto its prey, ramming two of its wiry projections into the base of the camera. After a moment, it let off a victorious chirp, alerting Nara of a successful connection.

Proud of its achievements, the critter summoned a display into Nara's screen, showing off the perspective of the conquered camera. As she zoomed in on the screen, she reached her hand out past the elevator door, watching her fingers disappear in a hazy mist of warping light as the bug worked its illusory magic.

"I have had it up to here with these useless interruptions!" a muffled voice grated against the wall of a nearby office.

As Nara hastily withdrew her arm, a scrawny, white-coated human burst through the door, storming down the corridor with an agitated pace.

"They have no idea what I am capable of." The ruffled creature sharply turned about-face, slinging their ravings in her direction. "Howling like lunatics while I'm trapped here doing real work!"

Nara pressed her back against the wall of the elevator, holding her breath as the irritated human zipped into the closing doors. She caught a flash of his augmented glasses as he whizzed by, his distracted gaze burning a hole in the wall as he pivoted around.

"Uh . . ." Garrett squirmed in his seat as he watched the oblivious man reach for the buttons.

"I'm going up there to give the Captain a piece of my mind—" The man's frothing abruptly ceased with a breathy squeak as he slowly craned his neck around, staring up at the metallic giant towering over him.

Nara lashed out and seized the dazed man by the collar, yanking him into her clutches. Her victim squeezed out a startled yelp as he collided with her hardened trunk, trailing into questioning bleats as she twirled him about with a disorienting shove. She coiled an arm around his throat, stifling an outcry as she sealed his mouth with her hand. Ignoring the delicate nails feebly clawing at her wrist, she slid her other palm against the base of his neck, tightening her hold as his desperate thrashing intensified.

His struggle abruptly ceased with a violent twitch as Nara injected a tiny spark from her hand, his knees crumpling underneath him. She let the man slump to the ground as she summoned a menu in her helmet display, her eyes speeding through a slideshow of facial profiles.

"He's not dead, is he?" Garrett softly asked, his brain struggling to catch up with the speed of her assault.

*"Not. **Now.**"* Nara growled.

"S–sorry."

The flickering screen halted, displaying a photo of the face matching the body at her feet. Vital statistics scrolled underneath the avatar, projecting a full name, research department, and security classification.

"Kid, I need you to confirm the office of a Dr. H. Nevrit. Now," she barked, scooping up the scientist in her arms.

"Where he came from. Third door on the right," Garrett obediently reported, still shaken by the encounter.

Nara panned the spider's perspective over, pointing it on the empty corridor away from the office door. With a disgruntled growl, she slammed the elevator button to open the doors, marching into the hall with her dispatched cargo over her shoulder.

She snatched the badge dangling from the man's pants, swiping it against the panel above the steel handle. After a rapid-fire beep and thunk from the lock mechanism, she wrenched the door open and dove into the quiet studio. Distorted curses rumbled through her mask as she headed for the desk at the center of the room, shifting into an irritated sigh as she messily dropped the man into the swiveling chair.

Garrett fidgeted with the cluster of menus on his screen, occupying his racing mind with a menial task. He panned his view around the office, scanning the diagrams and calculations tacked against the wall. A void of blank space at the far end of the room caught his attention, and he zoomed in to reveal a neat seam in the wall. He traced a finger along the two rectangular shapes engraved on the surface, highlighting one large, human-sized outline and a small, palm-sized square waist-height from the floor.

"Hey, Nara, what's that?" he inquired as he passed his camera view to her helmet.

"Hmm." She walked over and ran a finger over the outlines. *"I wondered why this office was so small."*

"So, it's a door, right?" He scrolled through the wireframe on his screen, finding nothing but blank space. "There's nothing behind it, according to the map."

"One way to find out." Nara hefted the doctor up from his cozy position, tossing him back onto her shoulders.

As she pressed the man's hand onto the paneling, a stream of light zipped up and down the frame. With a quiet chirp, a section of the wall evaporated, revealing a metal staircase inside a narrow concrete hallway.

"Huh," Garrett expressed, snapping a few shots of the scenery for later use.

"Indeed." Nara adjusted the scientist over her shoulder before creeping up the stairs, the wall rematerializing behind her.

The flight of steps ended at an unguarded doorway, opening into a utilitarian living space occupied by a modest bed, a shower unit, and a portable fridge. There were no windows in this cramped abode, containing just enough amenities to keep a human functional after long hours of grinding clerical work.

"Good place to hunker down for a bit," Garrett commented.

"Yep." Nara plopped the body onto the rickety cot, haphazardly tossing a cover on top of him. A twinge ran through her skin as the wound on her arm protested the abrupt actions. She flexed the fingers on her injured arm, rotating her wrist in discomfort as she surveyed the area.

Another doorway across the room opened into a closet-sized extension, a dim glow illuminating the modest space. Deciding this job hadn't caused her enough trouble, Nara stepped inside, hoping to scrape up bonus material to trade off. She turned toward the light to find an additional workstation, as well as a rather unsettling project suspended on the wall.

A small aquatic tank hung above the desk, barely large enough for the subject imprisoned inside, a silvery blue fish creature from a species not native to Arcadia. Its iridescent scales scintillated against the illumination of the life support system, and its shimmery fan-shaped fins listlessly fluttered inside the soft bubbling liquid. Its sleek, tapered body was viscerally bound by a diverse arsenal of tubes, hooks, and needles, its vacant expression stretched out by machinery.

The creature's long white whiskers twitched in frenzy as it sensed Nara's approach, and it violently lashed out against its restraints. Pieces of its flesh ripped from its tormented body as it struggled, tainting the water with a purple hue. After several desperate gasps from its gills, the creature drooped to the bottom of the tank, unable to endure the agony.

Within moments, the injuries it inflicted on itself quickly vanished, its glistening skin sealing up before her eyes. The water in the tank clarified as the purification system filtered away every trace of residual flesh and blood, transporting it across a network of plastic tubing. A row of sample vials rested inside a plastic case attached to the wall, slowly filling with the gruesome specimens.

"What the *fuck*," Garrett breathed in horror.

Nara appeared unmoved by the display, breaking into the personal computer sitting on the desk. Walls of text assaulted her cameras as she uncovered study journals and documents summarizing research on the regeneration properties of the creature in the tank. Strategies and hypotheses outlined potential uses for its healing powers in human medical applications. Frequent experiments involved dismemberment, abdominal vivisections, and other forms of near-fatal damage to the victim.

"That's horrific," Garrett breathed, nausea seeping into his stomach as the photos of the procedures flitted past his screen.

"Human biotechs are a wonderful breed," Nara commented, pocketing a data unit that she used to extract every scrap of information she found. She logged off the computer and made her way out the door, glancing through her map for an exit strategy.

"H–hey, Nara?" he softly prodded, his eyes glued to the pitiful creature. "Are you just going to leave it like that?"

"I'm not going to jeopardize my position for a fish." She started toward the stairs. *"And they'll just go get another one and start the whole experiment all over again."*

"How would you feel if you were in its place?" he pressed, biting his lip.

His words halted her step, each syllable stabbing at her brain as an icy twinge tore at her throat. She clenched a fist as the ephemeral fragments of her early memories gently brushed against her conscience.

"Nara?" A swell of bewildered concern saturated Garrett's tone.

Fucking hell, Nara thought as she whirled around, heading back into the gruesome closet. She regarded the black beady eyes of the pathetic creature, watching the fight extinguish from their tormented expression.

"You are going to be the death of me," she addressed Garrett as she gently plucked the restraints off the creature's skin.

The creature was still as Nara lifted it out of the tank, the wounds created from its extraction swiftly fading. It seemed to not want to be a nuisance to her as she laid it on the desk, stifling its gasping breath as it suffocated in the open air. Nara shook her head dejectedly as she produced a dagger from underneath her armor, raising the blade above the victim.

Garrett cringed as she drove the knife into the creature's brain, watching in revulsion as it violently thrashed in Nara's grasp. Nausea surged up his throat as the gruesome squelching noises violated his ears, while discomfort sent barbs across his spine. He abruptly turned his chair away from the screen, unable to watch her finish the job.

With one last twist of the blade, the creature drooped over the desk, the light drained from the pitiful creature's eyes. Nara retrieved the knife from the hollow skull cavity, losing herself in the vacant expression of the lifeless creature.

A strange feeling overcame her, inexplicable, and unsettling, corroding her tongue with a bitter resentment. She was accustomed to mercy kills, it was one of the many hazards in her line of work. But for some reason, this barely sentient creature tore a hole into her conscience.

"You okay?" Garrett asked. Her motionless posture disturbed him as she stared through the empty tank, the still-dripping knife in her hand.

"Fuck off, kid," she wearily beseeched as she wiped the blade clean. With a torrent of curses, she turned around to head for the door.

"H–hey," Garrett started uncomfortably, fixated on the bloody mass on the desk.

"What now?" she groaned.

"It, uh, seems kind of a sacrilege to just leave it there like that," he prodded. "Don't you think?"

"Don't even go there," she warned, walking down the stairs and heading back into the office.

Nara dropped a millipede camera and shooed it under the door, sending it on a scouting quest across the hall. She watched the screen as the critter zoomed down the corridor, taking it back to the escape hatch at the far end of the building. A resentful grumble escaped her mask as the critter turned the corner, revealing three security guards loitering in front of the door.

"Of course," she muttered.

Garrett's itchy fingers began to poke at the networks again, testing the waters in the open public streams. The building was teeming with nonessential functions, a cluttered web of engineering requests and status reports. He edged closer to some of the routine commands, pressing through maintenance channels to survey his options.

"Might have a solution," he offered, wading around security protocols, keeping his distance from the rocky shores.

"I thought you weren't supposed to be touching the system anymore,' Nara probed, her irritation radiating through her thoughts.

"I might have a workaround in progress," he explained, his confidence waning as he flitted through screens. "Keyword is 'might'."

An unknown entity was swimming after him, trying to discern his location in the waves. He diverted his route to avoid the shark, diving further into the murky net. A bright shining beacon emerged, drifting toward him with a tantalizing song.

This will either be a perfect distraction, he thought, hovering his hand over the screen, *or a very huge mistake.*

Reality warped with an ominous crimson smolder, and the bright lights of the hall snapped off with a winding moan. The stillness of the air was violently assaulted by a shrieking siren pulsing through the walls.

"What did you just—"

>> *FIRE HAZARD REPORTED ON LEVELS 7 THROUGH 12. ALL PERSONNEL REPORT TO THE NEAREST EXIT FOR IMMEDIATE EVACUATION.*

From the eyes of the millipede, the fire hatch screen burst open into the night, assaulting the watchful guards with a rush of chilling air. The sentries clamped their hands over their ears, screaming confusion over the strident alarms.

"Are you fucking kidding me?!" Nara exclaimed.

"Anyone can turn on safety protocols, but only high-level security ops can turn it off," Garrett explained. "Seemed logical to me at the time. Uh, run for it?"

*"I **know** that! How 'bout a little warning next time?"* she scolded as she burst through the office door.

"I didn't have time," he evaded, his cheeks flushed with embarrassment. *Or the juggling skills.*

"Of course you didn't." Nara bolted down the hallway, her armor reducing her hastened steps to soft pattering. She kept one eye on the bug as she crept toward the intersection, watching the movements of the guardsmen.

One shook their head furiously, frustrated with the inability to obtain orders on the situation amid the chaos. Flailing an arm to the sky, the guard stormed down the opposite hall, leaving the other two alone in the din.

Seizing her opportunity, Nara skulked toward the fragmented party, targeting the stationary guard watching their comrade depart. With their back facing her, she snatched their shoulder, crumpling their balance with a swift kick to the back of the knee. Before they had the chance to recover, she flung them onto the floor, letting them process the attack on their own time as she charged the fire escape.

The last standing unit raised their rifle at her, screaming a cry for help over the relentless alarms. Sparks burst across her chest as she rushed the door, sending the fidgeting officer withdrawing in a staggered frenzy over the piles of crates obstructing their retreat. She took a bounding step forward, the sudden shift of her movement causing the guard to jump back in fright.

As their heel dipped into the breezy precipice, Nara lunged at the hapless grunt, seizing their arm and tearing them back into the building. After flinging the stunned creature to the ground, she slipped down the open doorway with a scrape of her palms.

Friction warmed her flesh as she glided along the face of the wall, the grating noises sending shivers through Garrett's ears from the audio feed. Adjusting her plunge with a gentle tweak of her fingers, she gradually controlled her descent as she surveyed a suitable landing area on the grounds.

She released a hand from the tower to reach into a pocket, extracting three chalky orbs from inside. Powder dredged the air as she crushed them in her palm, initiating a dusty reaction that engulfed her arm with ash. She lobbed the fragments to the ground, flooding the atmosphere with a billowing cloud of black smoke.

Bullet fire rained down on her as she skated down the second floor of the tower, the recovered security unit leaning out the hatch with blazing armaments. Warnings from her energy systems pinged into her ear as a stray shot plinked over her shoulder, chastising her for the damage.

She curled her knees to her chest, aiming her shoulders at the effervescent smog as the storm of projectiles pelted the air around her. With a puissant shove, she catapulted off the face of the tower, diving head-first into the mist below. She pitched her shoulders forward as she dropped, rolling into the pavement with a spray of gravel.

Momentum snapped her to her feet, sending her charging through the powdery murk toward the city streets. Red streaks crackled across the grey filtered view of her helmet, enabling her vision as the light shifted in jagged outlines over the rubble obstructing her flight path.

Nara wove through the glowing rocks and debris as she navigated the protective cloak of air, darting for her stashed bike at the edge of an alleyway. As she vaulted into the seat, she kicked the getaway vehicle to life. The machine shuddered obediently in her grip, charging into the streets and leaving the looming fortress far behind her.

##4.4##

Nara stormed into the apartment, muttering a caustic brew of obscenities.

"That could have gone better." Garret shrank into his seat.

"You don't say?" Nara replied as the armor melted back into her neck, peeling over her malicious scowl.

His eyes traveled to the exposed laceration across her forearm. Her flesh was caked in a thick layer of ichor, the crust molded in the shape of her bracer. Above the torn soft flesh, the droid had eviscerated the gilded serpent, desecrating the beautiful engravings.

"I—sorry. I've never seen one of those things before," he confessed.

"Well, now you've seen one." She walked to the kitchen sink and turned on the water. Trails of red spiraled into the basin as she washed off the mess, picking out large chunks of clots wedged inside the intricate scales of the carving. Jagged flecks of pink gold glinted in the murky water as the solid matter dissolved, leaving the art underneath a fragmented ruin.

Garrett raised his arms in defense. "I mean, it looked like a garbage can to me."

"It moved. Isn't that somewhat of an important cause for mention?" She shook her arms dry and snatched up a cloth hanging on the faucet.

"Well, why didn't you see it then?" he contested.

Nara hesitated, wiping the discomfort from her face with the towel. She wasn't about to reveal a critical weakness to a human she had just met.

"I was busy trying to keep the whole facility from discovering where I was while breaking open one of their multi-billion-credit machines." She glowered, tossing the rag in agitation. "Which is why you were supposed to be there watching for transmuting garbage cans phasing around the room."

Garrett lowered his gaze at the accusation, the events of the evening pulling on him with an encumbering moral bout. While he frequently heard news reports of the atrocities of corporate technology and the violence surrounding Under, it was an entirely different sensation to witness them firsthand. The quandary tugged at his soul, and he was not certain he was comfortable becoming an active subordinate to a probable killer.

Nara cursed under her breath as she examined her clean wounds, delicately brushing over the swollen, irritated flesh. The technology of her armor had kept the gash from tearing open further, but the added stress from the tumbles and falls had aggravated it considerably.

She reached up to open a cabinet, revealing a brimming apothecary stash neatly tucked inside. Colorful concoctions wobbled inside the variegated glass bottles as she ran her fingers across them, projecting shuddering rainbows of light within the cupboard. Plain white labels veiled the front of each vessel, swirling characters handwritten in a feathery black ink emblazoned over their faces.

Nara selected a jar containing a vibrant cobalt blue salve from the shelf and unscrewed the lid, vigorously rubbing the contents into the damaged carving. She then grabbed a violet potion and bit off the top, holding her arm over the sink as she poured the oily liquid over her flesh.

"Doesn't that hurt?" he asked, his face contorting in discomfort.

"Yes," she replied matter-of-factly as she extracted a threaded needle from the cabinet.

He lost the ability to formulate a more dignified response as she drove the needle into her skin, the demonstration sending shivers across his arm. A repulsed fascination churned his insides as he watched her stitch her flesh together, and he questioned her motivation for utilizing the barbaric practice. Painless medical technology was cheap and widely accessible, even in Under.

Prying his eyes from the homebrew surgery, he traced his view up her other arm, noticing no other scars marring her bare skin, not even a scratch on her face or neck. He was puzzled by the observation and deeply curious about the injury hiding on her back.

"I am going out to turn this job in." Nara cleared her throat, disrupting his scrutiny. "I expect you to be here tomorrow to replace the equipment I have used up."

"Of course." Garrett cringed as she bit down on the thread, severing it with a snap of her wrist.

"The door is unlocked. You may leave at any time," she added, tossing the strings aside.

"I . . . got it." He acquiesced and stood from his seat. "I'll be here tomorrow."

She made no noise of acknowledgement as he slipped out the door, leaving him to stew over his ethical ideology as he retreated to his own world in the sky.

CHAPTER 5

##5.0##

Garrett reached out his fist to the apartment door, recoiling a step as it suddenly snapped open, the rouge giant greeting him with a stoic gaze.

"Good, you showed up. Let's go." Nara glided past him and started for the hallway.

"Where are we going?" He shook his head to steady his nerves, flustered by her impeccable timing.

"Tattoo parlor," she stated, climbing down the rubble-strewn stairwell.

"Oh, I see," he said, hurrying after her. "Wait, your arm is okay to be inked already?"

"Yep." Nara dragged her companion into the more obscure region of the Old District in Uncivilized Space. Every building was coated in sedimentary layers of rot, revealing their age with sickly shades of grime. Even the rubbish piles seemed worse for wear, scraps festering in pools of noxious liquids babbling down artificially constructed creeks over the pavement. The foundations of the towers leading to Upper were riddled with gaping holes of molted concrete, exposing rusting metal cores buried inside.

After stretching a pair of gloves over his hands, he took Nara's arm and delicately placed it on a long velvet pillow. He flicked the switch of his needle gun, filling the room with a jarring monotonous drone as he began redrawing the scales of the serpent. His gentle strokes embossed her skin with a beautiful shade of blood-red ink, the color identical to the bordering illustrations wrapped around her limb.

Garrett was mesmerized by the artist's work, losing himself in the intoxicating atmosphere. Even as he toiled on the intricate work in front of him, Matteus' expression remained soft and comforting. He was curious about the man's origins and wondered how he'd become associated with someone as surly as Nara.

"That is fascinating work. Is it your design?" Garrett asked.

"No, I'm just a restoration enthusiast," Matteus humbly replied.

"They were done ages ago," Nara added. "He's the only one on this rock I trust enough to fix them."

"You flatter me, my dear," Matteus responded as he shut off the needle. He picked up a thin wire hose extending from a steel box the size of a liquor bottle. The coils bounced against the cart as he screwed on a bit to the metal tip. "You are the only one of my clients that I have to take the diamond to. You know this, right?"

"Oh, but I always make it up to you. I trust your supplies are still full?" Nara teased. "Need any more colors? I know of a caravan in possession of some fresh raw pigments that should be heading to this quarter soon."

"Yes, yes. You take real good care of me." Matteus sighed and flicked a switch on the machine, sending it into a vibrating frenzy as it squawked with a high-pitched whir.

He set to work etching out the curves of the snake as the drill bit chewed through the bone-like matter, gently pressing in subtle strokes and meeting the depth of the surrounding design. Layer by layer, the scales were reformed, revitalizing the pattern that had been broken by the droid's assault.

"Doesn't that hurt?" Garrett asked as he wriggled a finger inside his ear, the crunching buzz boring deep into his skull.

"Nope," Nara said.

CHAPTER 5

##5.0##

Garrett reached out his fist to the apartment door, recoiling a step as it suddenly snapped open, the rouge giant greeting him with a stoic gaze.

"Good, you showed up. Let's go." Nara glided past him and started for the hallway.

"Where are we going?" He shook his head to steady his nerves, flustered by her impeccable timing.

"Tattoo parlor," she stated, climbing down the rubble-strewn stairwell.

"Oh, I see," he said, hurrying after her. "Wait, your arm is okay to be inked already?"

"Yep." Nara dragged her companion into the more obscure region of the Old District in Uncivilized Space. Every building was coated in sedimentary layers of rot, revealing their age with sickly shades of grime. Even the rubbish piles seemed worse for wear, scraps festering in pools of noxious liquids babbling down artificially constructed creeks over the pavement. The foundations of the towers leading to Upper were riddled with gaping holes of molted concrete, exposing rusting metal cores buried inside.

Old District was where the most forlorn inhabitants of Under dwelled, scaring off disoriented travelers with shifty looks and provisional weaponry. Barks of canine hybrids polluted the air, barely drowning out the noise of intermittent gunfire. Interspersed between the derelict tenements and smoldering abodes, the occasional shop front could be found, protected by autonomous security forces and reinforced fortifications.

Nara stopped at the door of an out of place stonework building, the quaint domicile sitting in an immaculately clean lot, as if the owner had taken the time to painstakingly remove the garbage that floated by. The rocky walls were adorned with brightly colored murals depicting an arched temple sitting on top of a grassy hill, haloed by a gilded sun casting jovial rays over the landscape.

"This is remarkably out of place," Garrett murmured, trying to mask his uneasiness as he glanced over his shoulder.

"Good place to be left alone," Nara commented as she gently pushed the wooden door open, evoking a delicate chorus of plinks from a silver wind chime.

A dim purple glow welcomed the visitors inside the peculiar haven, accented with a sweet herbal smelling haze tracing lissome patterns around the room. Tapestries of black and gold scrollwork patterns fluttered gently along the walls, and shelves displayed neat arrangements of figurines carved from a rainbow of colored stone, depicting icons and heroes from a distant pantheon. A circle of plush organically shaped cushions sat on top of beautifully intricate woven rugs, enticing visitors with a cozy respite.

The far corner of the room was taken up by an out of place modern countertop of sleek black marble, where the massive otherworldly proprietor stood reading an archaic paper-bound book. His skin was a sky blue, and he radiated a gentle aura that reached beyond the tranquility of the room. The man's attire reflected his free-spirited demeanor, wearing a short-sleeved black button-down shirt that displayed his heavily inked arms. His round face was accented with a well-trimmed goatee, which he pensively stroked while contemplating the questions of the universe.

He studied his tome through thick black-framed glasses, which were cosmetic rather than functional. The most distinguishing feature, however, was the pair of white ram's horns coiled at the sides of his head.

"Oh no, not again. Nara, dear, you should really be more careful," he said as he looked up at the approaching visitors, a frown creasing his soft face. His voice was as gentle as his demeanor. The chastising greeting sounded more like a purr than a scolding.

"You always assume I'm here for work to be done," Nara teased.

"You never visit me for any other reason." The man sighed as he set the book down.

She smiled wryly. "Oh, come now, you know I ruin them on purpose just to have an excuse to see you."

He rolled his eyes, moving around the counter. "Sit down."

"Aw, don't get too excited," Nara said as she took off her coat, settling into one of the cushions. "This is Matteus, the repairman."

"Welcome to my refuge," Matteus called to Garrett as he drew a velvet curtain, revealing a closet brimming with tubes, jarred pigments, and medical supplies. He wheeled a cart over to his guests, picking up a beautifully carved black wooden box.

Garrett stared in fascination at the man's graceful movements as he prepared his workstation, meticulously carrying out each action with ritualistic care. Matteus gingerly unlatched the brass lion clasp of the box, sliding it open to reveal a beautifully ornate set of silver picks and jars, the metal adorned with intricate carvings of feathers.

"Sit down. You're making the room feel stuffy," Nara ordered Garrett.

"Huh? Oh, sorry." Garrett slipped into the seat next to her, watching the ceremony in fascination.

Matteus beckoned with a flutter of his hand. "All right, let me see the damage."

Nara raised her arm and let the artist scrutinize her skin with his fingers, tracing the void of soft skin and blank plating splitting the scaled pattern. The flesh was immaculately smooth, no trace of last night's injury defacing the surface.

"Hardly needs any ink at all, and the etching is very clean too," Matteus remarked as he slipped a mask over his face.

After stretching a pair of gloves over his hands, he took Nara's arm and delicately placed it on a long velvet pillow. He flicked the switch of his needle gun, filling the room with a jarring monotonous drone as he began redrawing the scales of the serpent. His gentle strokes embossed her skin with a beautiful shade of blood-red ink, the color identical to the bordering illustrations wrapped around her limb.

Garrett was mesmerized by the artist's work, losing himself in the intoxicating atmosphere. Even as he toiled on the intricate work in front of him, Matteus' expression remained soft and comforting. He was curious about the man's origins and wondered how he'd become associated with someone as surly as Nara.

"That is fascinating work. Is it your design?" Garrett asked.

"No, I'm just a restoration enthusiast," Matteus humbly replied.

"They were done ages ago," Nara added. "He's the only one on this rock I trust enough to fix them."

"You flatter me, my dear," Matteus responded as he shut off the needle. He picked up a thin wire hose extending from a steel box the size of a liquor bottle. The coils bounced against the cart as he screwed on a bit to the metal tip. "You are the only one of my clients that I have to take the diamond to. You know this, right?"

"Oh, but I always make it up to you. I trust your supplies are still full?" Nara teased. "Need any more colors? I know of a caravan in possession of some fresh raw pigments that should be heading to this quarter soon."

"Yes, yes. You take real good care of me." Matteus sighed and flicked a switch on the machine, sending it into a vibrating frenzy as it squawked with a high-pitched whir.

He set to work etching out the curves of the snake as the drill bit chewed through the bone-like matter, gently pressing in subtle strokes and meeting the depth of the surrounding design. Layer by layer, the scales were reformed, revitalizing the pattern that had been broken by the droid's assault.

"Doesn't that hurt?" Garrett asked as he wriggled a finger inside his ear, the crunching buzz boring deep into his skull.

"Nope," Nara said.

"It's like nails. Only a whole hell of a lot tougher," Matteus added, not looking up from his work.

Nara melted into her seat, silencing her mind as the meditative oscillations soothed her arm. Her eyelids slowly wilted halfway down her pupils as she permitted her guard to lower inside the sanctuary.

Garrett opened his mouth to ask a question, stopping himself when he met her somnolent expression. A curious glint drew his attention to her neck, discovering a familiar gold chain trailing into her shirt. His curiosity was shattered as Matteus switched off the engraving machine, sending a tenacious ring thundering across his hearing.

The artist produced a copper tjanting from his arsenal, a tool commonly used in fabric dying, and stirred it around in a tiny cauldron full of shimmery golden pink liquid. After testing the temperature of the potion, he grabbed a ball of black clay, playing with the material between his hands until it was supple. He tore chunks off the ball and rolled them into thin snakes, draping them over the cart in an orderly row.

One by one, he pressed the strands into the edges of Nara's plating, forming a clay barrier between the etching and her skin. He then extracted the stone-handled tool out of the pot and poured a thin stream of the searing liquid into the fresh etchings.

Garrett tilted his head curiously. "What is that?"

"A blend of rose gold mixed with some chemical binders that allows the metal to melt at a lower temperature. The binders evaporate as the mixture cools, leaving nothing but metal fused to the plating," Matteus explained, hovering the tip of the tool along the etching. "It adds a wonderful contrast to the artwork."

"Whoa." Garrett marveled as he watched the liquid trickle into the cracks.

"Impressive, isn't it?" Matteus smirked as he placed the tool back into the pot, satisfied with the casting. He gently rocked her wrist to each side, evening out the paper-thin coating over the design. Several tenacious air bubbles surfaced on the liquid, and Matteus meticulously burst each malefactor with a tiny pin.

"That is stunning," Garrett proclaimed, captivated by the flowing metal.

"There, all finished. Now all we do is wait," Matteus declared as he removed his mask and gloves, wiping his hands on a cloth hanging from the cart. After reorganizing his tools, he stood up and rolled the cart back into the closet. "So, what have you been up to lately, my dear?"

"Oh, nothing much, really," Nara admitted. "Still wandering the streets and getting into trouble."

"Is You-Know-Who still putting pressure on you?" Matteus asked as he tended to a tea kettle gently brewing on a burner.

She scowled. "Yes, earlier this week. And it's getting on my nerves."

"You-Know-Who?" Garrett raised an eyebrow as he sank deeper into the cushiony seat.

"I didn't agree to discuss politics with you, human," Nara rebuked, eyeing the handiwork glittering on her arm.

"Fair enough." Garrett was struggling to keep conscious in the warm, tranquil room. His head began to dip as he let the smoky ambiance dull his senses, his mind wavering through semi-consciousness. A startling clink snapped him upright as Matteus placed a set of ceramic cups onto an ornate black wood serving tray.

"Apologies." Matteus placed the board down on a table, offering a cup to him and Nara.

"Have you heard anything more about the intergalactic tariffs GaPFed is trying to enforce?" Nara asked Matteus as she sipped the tea.

"Not much. Uppercity is in favor of it, as if they need more money up there," Matteus hummed. "It would mean complication for business down here—more fakes, scarce sources of clean herbs and inks, and worst of all, more Enforcer raids. They love the scent of black market activity."

"Great, that's all we need," Nara muttered through her cup. "May have to start sending a runner to go to Upper and get my supplies."

"Indeed. Or get off this rock and get it yourself," Matteus suggested.

"That requires way too much social interaction and travel knowledge for my taste," she scoffed. "Space exploration isn't exactly on my list of lifetime goals."

"It isn't all that bad. But to each their own." Matteus tipped his cup to her.

They sat together in silence, quietly musing in the dimmed light and warm refreshments. As time passed, Garrett succumbed to sleep's tempting call, his chin buried in his chest as he wheezed out timid snores.

"Oi." Nara smirked and gave him a hearty shove. With a percussive snort, he jolted upright, scanning the room in startled bewilderment as he collected his bearings.

"What? I–how much longer?" Garrett stammered as he recollected himself.

"You should be about ready to go," Matteus announced as he peeled off the clay barrier from Nara's arm, rubbing at the drips of gold that pooled at the edges of her skin.

The artist took a metal file from his pocket and began smoothing out the rough flash, creating a leveled transition between the plating and the flesh. Finally, he polished the edges smooth with a wipe of a buffing cloth, creating a beautiful sheen on the surface of the creation.

"That's so fascinating." Garrett blinked as he watched the last of the glittering dust fall to the floor.

"There, that should do it. Now be careful with this one," Matteus chastised, waggling an admonishing finger at Nara.

"You always say that," she taunted as she stretched out her arms. "Pay the man, Garrett."

"Huh? Oh." He was beginning to expect this type of treatment from her and examine how much he intended to invest in this relationship. "How much do I owe you?"

"Three thousand." Matteus smiled warmly as he leaned on his reception desk.

"Ouch."

"Don't forget the tip," Nara prompted as she shrugged on her coat.

Garrett produced a slice from his pocket, mumbling incoherent noises as he begrudgingly keyed in a withdrawal. He cleared the animosity from his voice as he cooled his manner, handing the artist the payment with a meek smile.

"Thank you, kind sir." Matteus beamed. "Do come back again, and make sure she takes care of that work."

"I can only try," he said.

"Goodbye, Matteus. Until next time." Nara waved and walked out of the building.

"It was nice meeting you." Garrett gave a timid bow and hurried after her.

The rain had started again, showering the pavement with its marginally toxic drops. Nara looked up at the sky and inhaled deeply, pausing for a moment of reflection in the dismal environment.

Nara let out a relieved sigh. "Now that I have a burst of mental clarity, let's go get shitfaced."

"Wait, what? You serious?" Garrett felt slightly ill at the notion. The smoky air and sharp ringing inside the parlor had tormented his senses, sprouting an ache across his eyes.

"Yep. Drinks are on me," she announced, heading deeper into the city.

"Oh, that's very kind of you," he jeered.

##5.1##

NARA BROUGHT him to a quieter corner of Old District, an unlabeled establishment at the center of a cracked pavement lot sparsely occupied by parked ground vehicles. The building was constructed from concrete and steel beams, its sloping metal roof providing meager protection from the elements. There was no bouncer at the gate watching for troublemakers, only a sign that read, *Keep Your Weapons Sheathed at All Times.*

As they stepped through the heavy metal door, their footsteps creaked over the sagging wooden flooring. The bar was made of a similar wood, fitted with brass findings that added a hint of sophistication to the room. Ceiling fans quietly whisked around smoky air, their murmuring motors accompanied by the gentle plink of the rain hitting the metal roof. Foggy orbs illuminated the room with a soft glow, the preference of the discerning patrons who wanted to take their time approaching the state of inebriation.

Nara stifled a scowl as she spotted a deathly pale man sitting in the darkest corner of the room, who met her eyes and bowed his head in acknowledgement. Shoving back a discontented grumble, Nara permitted a formal smile to seep into her features as she approached him.

"Keeping well, are you, Cain?" she asked the man flatly, evoking a silent nod in reply.

The man's bloodless skin almost radiated against the dark clothing he wore, shadows of veins creating dark webs under his skin. Disheveled black hair traced chaotic patterns over his odd eyes, which were another marvel of his face. His left glowed a dazzling cerulean blue, while his right burned with a vehement blood red.

Despite his unsettling appearance, he had a striking face of a man who couldn't be more than thirty. If his complexion were more inconspicuous, he could easily be mistaken for a noble in the Upper city.

"Glad to hear it." Nara maintained a neutral demeanor as she slipped toward an empty table in the opposite corner.

"Who was that?" A chill ran down the back of Garrett's neck as he veered his gaze from the eerie man, apprehension gnawing at his nerves.

"Just another businessman. Name's Vausaureth Cain." She beckoned a server over. "We've worked on the same contracts together from time to time."

"Oh, so you're associates?"

"No. We've worked on the same contracts. At the same time," Nara corrected.

"I don't understand the distinction." He drummed his fingers over the lacquered table.

"Some contractors have a twisted sense of humor. They hate two mercenaries for whatever reason and figure they could get rid of at least one of their problems if they request the same job done by both. A little bloodshed happens, and they get a bit of bonus work done in the process," Nara explained.

"Uh-huh. And I see that both of you are currently alive," Garrett observed.

"Yeah, it turned into a bit of a game. Sometimes, I let him win, and other times, I get the mark." She leaned back in her seat, making room for the server to set their drinks down.

"It looks as if he may have a serious advantage over you," Garrett commented as he pushed his drink away, the acetic chemical vapors driving his sinuses into an aching rage.

"And why do you say that?" She raised an eyebrow, taking a sip from her glass.

"That guy has some tremendous augmentation built in him. I can't imagine what he's capable of," Garrett pointed out.

"Yes, and I would not mention that while he's within earshot," she warned with a cold look.

"Oh? What's wrong?" he asked, rubbing his temples.

"Well for one thing, it's rude." She downed her drink and slid Garrett's rejected glass into her hand. "And for another, it's a touchy subject for him. Let's just say his mods weren't voluntary."

"How do you know that? He doesn't strike me as the expressive type," he questioned, scrunching his eyes in discomfort.

"Perception." She ordered another drink and pushed it to Garrett.

"That's your answer to everything, isn't it?" he jabbed, his face warped into revulsion as the vapors of the musty green bog water plucked his nostrils.

"It will be until you learn where to look to answer your own damn questions." She pointed at the tumbler. "Now drink that. It'll fix your headache."

"Well, how about this? I *perceive* that you still have that necklace. I thought you would have sold it by now," he declared, taking an experimental sip of the elixir. It tasted as horrible as it smelled, but he was well practiced at concealing his distaste for the bitter unpleasantry of Upper society norms, and he choked it down with minimal facial expression.

"I told you, it's mine," she snapped.

"So, what is it then?" Garrett forced down another draught of the ghastly liquid.

"You're not going to let this one go, are you?" she groaned, waving another round over.

"Nope." He cleared his throat as he finished off his remedy, using his teeth to scrape the vile sensation from his tongue. "You stole it from me, so I think the least you could do is tell me what it is."

"It's a combat mastery badge," she begrudgingly informed him, heaving a loud sigh. *Upstart little shit.*

"So that came straight from your home planet?"

"Yes." Nara scowled. "Though how it got here is beyond me."

"Wait a minute," he blurted. The remedy coursed its magic through his brain, bestowing him with an invigorating buzz. "That one is actually *yours*, not somebody else's that just wound up on the black market."

"Yeah." She swallowed hard and hit the glass against the table.

"Are those weapons on the front of it?" He recalled the strange armor blades from the face of the coin.

"Yeah." Nara wearily sighed. "Don't get excited. It's just a hobby. They haven't been used in modern warfare for centuries. And most disciplines are just collecting dust in the archives."

Garrett frowned. "That's unfortunate."

"They're outdated. Push one thing aside to make room for progress." Nara shrugged. "Can't keep everything alive."

"Surely, that's the whole purpose of the archives in the first place." He poked at the traces of sickly liquid hanging from the rim of his glass.

"Only so people don't have to worry about it while stagnating on its own initiative." Nara waved the server over again. "It's when people forget about it completely—that's when the real trouble happens."

"Do you still have your weapons?"

"No." Her scowl intensified.

Garrett cleared his throat, taking the cue to change the subject. "What else have you got planned for the evening?"

"Finding interesting and painful ways to ditch you," she bluntly declared.

"And in the meantime?"

"Got some shit to replenish." She threw her head back to polish off her most recent beverage. "Then probably poke around my contacts and find work, I suppose."

"I see." Garrett pawed at the table anxiously, her refusal to maintain a conversation testing his nerves.

"All right, I think I've got a small buzz going," Nara announced, standing up from her seat. "I think we can leave now."

Four pints of pure hard liquor, and that's only a 'small buzz'? Garrett blinked in astonishment.

Nara walked to the bar and gave the innkeeper a slice, sending an acknowledging nod to Cain still lurking in the corner. The cold man watched the two intently, his odd eyes thoroughly scanning over the Upworlder as they departed.

The rain continued to wash over them as they trekked through an unfamiliar maze of highways, murmuring quietly over their footsteps. Though the more decayed paths of Under were a symbol of hardship, Garrett had acquired a taste for the ruined place. Life was straightforward and the tricksters easy to avoid, unlike the web of blood-dyed wool that spanned across the Uppercity skyline.

In the midst of his internal ruminations, he had not noticed Nara's shifting glance panning over the road, nor did he mind her tense posture and quickened pace.

"Well, I suppose that—"

"*Shh!*" Nara raised a hand in warning.

Alarmed by her sudden caution, Garrett strained to listen to the ambiance, picking up a bizarre chorus of sounds, a repulsive blend of wet snarling dotted with erratic notes of rattling chains.

"What's that?" he whispered.

"Trouble. Big trouble," she breathed as she drew a pistol. "Fuck, the borders must've shifted again. Get behind me, and do not let them touch you."

##5.2##

"THEM?" Garrett watched the street ahead, spying four cackling figures creeping into the flickering lamplight. The abominable band of brigands resembled creatures directly out of a macabre horror flick inspired by the musings of an unhinged genetic doctor.

Overshadowing the party was a golem constructed from a spectrum of flesh haphazardly sewn together in a massive lumbering hulk. It shambled forward in a labored gait, balancing its cumbersome mass between a grotesquely hypermuscled leg and a sickly skeletal twig.

Its clothes were torn to rags, barely clinging on its bulging form. Bits of hair grew in matted chunks out of its mostly bald head. The jaw was too big for the rest of its skull, oily yellow fluids seeping from the crevasses of its gums. Flesh sagged below its jowls in a feeble attempt to fight gravity, flapping side to side with each torturous step. It focused on its quarry with two different eyes, a normal human-sized green and a huge distended brown orb. Surgery scars surrounded the socket, the skull hastily busted and reformed to fit the massive globule inside.

A scrawny, bent-backed figure lurked under the brute's shadow, a metal exoskeleton tracing their spine in jagged bony protrusions. Grey flesh stretched over their frame, their facial features disguised under a half mask of metal riveted to their cheeks. Each finger-like digit of their elongated hands was made of a clear tube filled with glowing colored liquid, the nails extruding into long, menacing needles. Drips of the liquid oozed out of the tips, dropping to the ground with a sizzle.

The third carried an air of leadership about them, concealed by a white overcoat spattered with blood and other unrecognizable fluids. Furrows of wrinkles stretched beyond their surgeon's mask, the jagged grin pushing up their high-pointed cheeks under their heavy dark glasses. Their flesh radiated a sickly ivory yellow of aged bone, and their dark hair was greased back over their veiny scalp. A high-powered rifle was slung casually around their shoulders, a glowing green liquid sloshing inside the ammunition chamber as they struggled to pull back a heavy steel chain.

At the other end of the chain was a disjointed hybrid of a humanoid and a starved rat. Black hair-like spines jutted from its vertebrae, leading up to a horrid bug-like skull. Oil-slicked faceted compound eyes excitedly zipped around its vision as yellow-green mandibles twitched open and shut at the front of its face. Its legs were mechanically augmented, long, slender protrusions coiled with springy synthetic ligaments. The creature yanked against its lead, clicking and snarling as it rubbed its mantis-like appendages menacingly.

"Experimentalists," Nara hissed as she drew an energy-based pistol boasting a massive barrel.

The bug beast reared back and sniffed the air with chunky wet snorts, clicking with delight as it spotted Garrett peering from behind his stalwart red fortress. It tugged and heaved at its cackling master's chain, lunging toward a fresh meal.

"Run!" Nara boomed at Garrett as she released a shot, striking the surgeon in the center of the forehead. A smoking cauterized crater hissed from the void of their face as the creature sank to their knees, gravity tugging the lifeless mass to the ground. Nara unloaded several more rounds into the body, spattering its remains over the concrete.

Garrett barely registered the warning as his legs tore into the streets. An echo of clanging chain shadowed his tracks as the bug beast charged after him, gnashing its oozing pincers as it sped past Nara.

He darted back and forth in the alleyway, leaping over boxes and scrap to gain distance on the speeding creature. Fear latched onto his senses as he glanced behind his shoulder, and his body lashed a shock of reprimand through his nerves as his eyes met the bug's ravenous face.

His panic proved his undoing as his ankle caved, his toes catching on a piece of exposed rebar in the middle of the road. A cry of shock escaped his lungs as he fell face first into the pavement, his chest thumping against a jagged edge of concrete.

The creature launched into the air with raised talon arms, screeching out what could only be translated as a warbled battle cry as it dove for its squishy prey. Its obnoxious shrieking was swiftly cut short as a flash of blue light sparked over its body. With a disgustingly pitiful gurgle, its body crashed to the ground, violently convulsing at Garrett's feet.

He gasped in distress and shoved away from the twitching beast, watching in horror as it feebly dragged its talons across the pavement, the massive hole in its head a considerable obstacle in its pursuit. He glanced back to see Nara pointing a gun in his direction, her attention focused on the remaining two assailants.

Glowing green tears welled up in the flesh giant's sagging eye sockets as it began sobbing, wailing and moaning obnoxiously as the sorrow of his fallen companion visibly overwhelmed him. Nara started to slowly edge away while the beast's simple mind was preoccupied with the loss, but the brute suddenly snapped his accusatory gaze to the abominable demon who'd shot his friend. The beast snorted boisterously, wiping tears and snot from his face as he inhaled a deep well of air.

The alley buildings quaked and trembled as the brute let out a thundering wet roar, swinging his gargantuan arm in an exaggerated arc as he charged after her. His passion and dim wits influenced his actions, broadcasting his lumbering attack with an enraged bellow.

Nara darted around the brute, giving him a wide berth as she fired a pulse of energy into the center of his spine. The shot burned a fist-sized hole into the abscessing wall of flesh, barely penetrating through the layers of sinew protecting him.

The giant swung his shoulders side to side in bewilderment, wondering where the squishy red pest had disappeared to, blissfully ignorant of the gunfire damage smoking in his back.

The instinct of the metal skeleton was much more incisive than their companion, and they flung themself on top of the brute's shoulder, cackling and hissing at Nara as they fluttered their needle hands in a threatening display. As the giant slowly turned toward the commotion, the living syringe vaulted off their perch, slashing and ripping the air as they dove after her.

Nara retreated from the flailing torpedo, hurling a pair of bolts into the sky. Upon impact, the energetic rounds tore through the creature's shoulders, severing the dripping arms with a sickening crackle of lasers.

A muffled scream warbled through the alley as the soaring creature struggled to express its agony through the plate bolted to their mouth. Unable to brace themself, the creature crashed face-first into the ground as the two limbs flopped on top of them in succession with a wet thunk, their corrosive payload oozing onto the pavement.

With a thrash and a twist, the creature wrenched onto their back. A determined war cry jittered through their throat as they reared their legs, launching onto to their feet in a fluid undulation. They whirled around and rushed toward Nara, belting out choking garbles of ire as they ran with an awkward waddling stride.

"The hell do you think you're gonna do?" Nara taunted as she fired again, stopping the creature's charge with a splattering of molten plasma.

Hearing the distress of his comrade, the giant finally turned completely around, his wrath magnified as he witnessed the living needle plop onto the ground. Strings of slobber propelled from his face as belted out another tremendous roar.

Fuck, she thought, *it's too cramped in this alley to face this one.*

She scanned her surroundings while the giant continued his posturing, eyeing the chunks of concrete and metal structures protruding from a decrepit wall. Soft and brittle from years of erosion from the chemical rain, the surface offered her a precarious climb to high ground.

The brute gave her little time to plot her course as he stampeded toward her, gargling out a meaty yell as he threw his weight forward. Nara vaulted up the wall, navigating over crumbling footholds as she fled from the impending strike.

Violent quakes shuddered across the aged masonry as the brute's fist crashed into the wall, sending fragments flying into his face. His enfeebled arm flagellated, slapping dust out of his sensitive eyes. Nara seized the opportunity and unloaded another volley into the creature, turning his bubbling torso to hole-filled rotten cheese.

The beast tore his fist out of the wall, flinging down the debris he clutched in frustration. He glared at the fleeing red pest and began to follow her up, tearing out his own handholds from the decaying brick.

"For fuck's sake, I've put ten rounds into you at least. Fuck off!" Nara exclaimed, speeding up the jagged precipice. The brute's ascent thundered beneath her, sending jitters through her bones as she compensated her movements against the concussive rhythm.

Quickening her stride, she reached the crusted rooftop and hauled herself over the ledge. She sprang to her feet and dug a finger through the release catch of a holstered weapon on her hip. The firearm whirred in obedience as she slammed the switch on its side, expanding with knife-edged metal segments as it shaped an imposing barrel in the air.

Nara leaned over the ledge and unleashed a howl of violent black energy into the giant, exposing his sickly green skull to the air. The electric flak spattered over the bulging eyeball, sending the brute reeling in agony. He whirled an arm around as he smacked his face, inadvertently releasing the brick wall. The gargantuan body dramatically rolled away from the building like a felled tree, sending the beast crashing to the ground with a mushy agonized bellow.

She fired at the giant's pustulating leg, melting ligaments away from bone as the creature flailed his unbalanced limbs like an upturned turtle. The angry warbling devolved into pained sobs as she relentlessly drenched the brute with fire. After the creature dissolved into nothing more than a gooey skeleton, silence returned.

"Fucking finally." Nara slithered down the building to a reasonable height before propelling off the disintegrating surface, stirring up a cloud of dust beneath her boots as she landed on the concrete. She slapped her clothing indignantly, then sauntered over to the shell-shocked Garrett staring out to the void.

"You okay?" She bent over him and offered a hand.

"Yeah," he panted as he let her haul him to his feet, his eyes locked on the fallen titan. "What . . . the . . . *fuck*?!"

She addressed her wrist, ignoring his sputtering. "Declan, got a live one for you."

"Really? Let me have a look," the NetCom requested. The tone shifted as Nara moved her arm over the still-twitching bugbeast. "Goddammit, how many times must we argue over the definition of 'alive'?"

"It's still breathing," she argued. "And I only took out nonessential brain activity."

"The *entire* brain is missing," the voice sighed in annoyance.

"Look, it's still moving, see?" she assured Declan as she pointed at the beast, which crawled in place like a windup toy losing its torque.

"Great, that's just perfect," the voice conceded. "You have any others?"

"Yeah, one construct, one needle, and one leader. The gun's ammo is still intact, and the needles should have some shit left in them," Nara informed her wrist.

"It didn't touch you, did it?" Concern saturated the voice.

"Nah, I'm okay."

"Good. I'll send a containment crew over," the voice announced. "Keep watch for any others out there."

"You got it." Nara looked over to Garrett, disconnecting her call. "We're going to sit tight for a little while."

"Uh, okay." The pallor in his face intensified as he watched the bugbeast wriggle.

"What's wrong with you?" Nara inquired, cocking her head to the side. "Do you mean to tell me you have never had an encounter with Experimentalists?"

"No, but I don't travel far in Uncivilized Space if I can avoid it." He rested his back against a wall, taking in slow, deep breaths as the adrenaline ebbed, leaving behind the throbbing pangs in his chest from the fall.

"Good plan," she remarked as she sheathed her weapons.

"Won't the enforcers come by soon?" Garrett asked, his heart shocked to a start at the thought of another run.

"Nah, killing these guys is like shooting rats. They don't care for them either," she replied, poking a box with her toe. "We're safe."

"Oh. Good." He winced, his bruising skin stretching over his chest with each inhale.

"You sure you're okay?" Nara raised an eyebrow.

"Yeah, just fell on something on the ground. That thing didn't touch me," he reported, relieved to utter the words out loud. "Who was that you called?"

"That was Declan Alsbury. He's a good man," she replied. "He pays mercs to get subjects from the Experimentalists, alive or dead, so he can study them and maybe reverse the effects."

"That sounds like a noble cause, but I can't imagine anyone does something like that for free. Or without other motivation," he pointed out, holding his sides. "Also, he sounds kind of like a hardass."

"The man watched his wife and daughter dissolve into pools of gore in front of him," she said. "Then, he cut off his own arm with an axe. Yeah, he has motivation. And yeah, he's a hardass."

"Well, that answers that then." Garrett cleared his throat in discomfort.

##5.3##

DECLAN STEPPED out of an enormous cargo vehicle, cynicism tainting demeanor as he approached the scene. He possessed the air of an intellectual, sporting antique-styled eyewear that glowed with windows of augmented reality, patterns shifting across the surface as he scanned over the bodies lying on the ground. He brushed his shaggy dark hair back with a sleek silver mechanical arm, nodding in approval at the specimens.

A containment crew piled out of the back of the vehicle, geared up in armor sealed against hazardous materials. They dragged out equipment and checked ammunition while they waited for their leader to update them on the scene.

"That's a nice bit of work you've done here, Nara," Declan said as he squatted over one of the arms of needle man, poking at the hand with a metal instrument. "Good sampling of toxins here. You said there was a leader with a gun?"

"Yeah, over there." She pointed toward the fallen surgeon.

"Never got a shot edgewise, did he?" Declan scoffed, itching the thin shadow of hair tracing over his jaw.

"I wasn't about to take a fuckin' chance with them," she replied.

"I should be able to get something out of this mess. Here, that's the current rate now." Declan reached a slice in her direction.

"You insult me. When have I ever accepted a payment from you?" Nara protested, waving his hand away.

"Fuck, not this again. You take the payment this time or I'll shove it down your throat," the gentleman glowered, shaking his mechanical fist at her. "You sucker punched me last time and that's the only reason you got away."

"And I'd gladly do it again, you massive pain in the ass," she snarled. "These pricks had what was coming to them."

"Take the fuckin' money. I'm not a goddamned charity." Declan edged forward, jabbing the slice at her chest.

"Go fuck yourself." Nara slapped his hand.

"I'm not going to tell you again. Take. The fucking. *Money*," the man growled, standing on his toes to raise himself above her chest level.

"Wait. Wait, wait. Is this argument really happening?" Garrett interjected, his gaze bouncing between the two combatants at locked horns.

"Fuck off, kid. This is about winning, not about money," Nara snapped.

Garrett furrowed his eyebrows. "So . . . who's winning?"

"I am," they chanted synchronously, venom seething through their eyes.

The containment crew in the background collectively shook their heads as they continued their messy cleanup task. A ring bleated through the air, and one of the workers stopped to answer a call on their wrist. They hastily approached Declan, tapping him urgently on the shoulder.

"Not. *Now*." Declan held up a hand.

"Sir, we got to go. Someone's got a specimen up at Dagger's Alley. We're almost finished here," the man reported.

"Dammit," Declan grumbled.

"He's got a live one, and he's not sure how long the restraints will hold," the worker stressed. "And he's in a pretty bad shape himself."

"You will wait right here, and we will finish this later," Declan warned Nara, thrusting a metal finger at the ground.

"Like hell I will." She smirked victoriously.

Declan ground his heels into the pavement as he stormed back to the vehicle, muttering curses as he climbed inside the driver seat. After the containment crew finished loading up the last body, the van raced into the street, disappearing into the shadows.

"So, what was that all about?" Garrett inquired.

"Hmph. Thinks he can pay me for having fun. Bastard." Nara spat.

"And that's a bad thing?" Garrett shook his head in bewilderment. "How much was he paying anyway? Couldn't have been much, considering the operation he's running."

"Probably a good sixty thousand," she replied. "I don't know for sure, but that's his standard rate for good chemical specimens. The bodies would serve as test subjects for effect reversal and might be worth a little extra."

"That much?"

"Declan's well off. He's an Upper doc. He spends most of his resources and time finding cures for the experimentalist mutagens." She kicked at a rock, sending it skittering over the pavement. "I'm sure once he finds the ultimate antidote, he will storm the city, shooting everyone he finds in the street with syringes."

"Where the fuck do these things come from?" Garrett glanced over his shoulder.

"No idea. That's all part of his adventure, not mine." She shrugged. "They spawn like vermin, though, and they're a total nuisance for everyone around."

"And they just travel around spreading their . . . disease?" his voice wavered between horror and disgust.

"They go around finding weak victims to play with, injecting them with shit they concoct just to see what it would do to a body," Nara explained. "They watch them twitch and suffer, and the ones who survive are indoctrinated into their collective."

"That's horrifying." Garrett's mouth contorted in revulsion at the visuals his mind played into his eyes.

"To say the least."

"Can we, maybe, get out of here?" he timidly requested as he nervously scanned the street. "Not to be paranoid, but I don't really want to be here anymore."

"Heh. C'mon, let's go." Nara ushered him back toward Civilized Space.

CHAPTER 6

##6.0##

A wine glass clinked against the near-empty bottle on the table as Garrett forced himself up from his chair. Formal gatherings always required a light fog of inebriation to make the evening tolerable. He couldn't recall the reason behind this party. All he knew was that his attendance was required so his mother could parade him around and pawn off his future.

Black. How appropriate, he thought bitterly as he picked up the suit Baran had laid out for him.

He shrugged on the stifling garments and walked over to the mirror to practice his cheerful mask. Through exhaustive effort, Garrett forced up a handsome smile that radiated over his charming features. He fussed with his soft chestnut hair, combing back the rebellious strands that draped over his short back-and-sides.

After he decided he had exerted the bare minimum of effort, he pivoted his shoulders experimentally, his vibrant green eyes scrutinizing his reflection as he tightened the silk noose over his throat. All the hiking and parkour over the ruins in the Underground had served his physique well, and he took a modest amount of pride in the results.

Gossip whispered through the Upper channels, claiming his face was the envy of the noble crowd. But he could not comprehend their perception. He did not see anything unique about his appearance. He merely existed without the use of genetic enhancement. His mother often pressured him to "remove this," "adjust that," and even "just a little bit here," but he managed to evade her army of cosmetic surgeons, mostly by never being at home.

As he finished fidgeting with his clothing, Baran knocked softly on his door.

"Come in," Garrett beckoned with a halfhearted sigh.

"Your mother is waiting for you downstairs," Baran reported, exhibiting a sullen glance of apology.

"Let's get this over with," he groaned and followed his guardian out of the room.

The ballroom was festively lit in pastel colors, enveloping the crowd of nobles in a picturesque ambience as they gathered at the center of the white marbled floor. The tall windows were swathed in deep burgundy curtains and gold fittings, adorning the elegant silhouette of the city lights. Sounds of the droning bourgeoise burbled throughout the chamber, harmonized by the hired orchestra performing a soft melody on the oak wood stage.

Magritte Galavantier was pacing in agitation, her flowing navy-blue evening gown elegantly twirling with her displeasure. She fiddled with an odd strand of her short-cropped, bright golden hair in agitation, a wine glass in hand. When she spotted Garrett descending the stairs, her face strained against her skin enhancements as she scowled, and her artificially dyed violet eyes radiated in disapproval.

Biologically speaking, she was at the peak of middle age, but with routine procedures of cosmetic technology, she'd forcibly beat back the signs of aging in her appearance. Neither wrinkle nor ashen hair polluted her bitter face.

"It is about time you decided to show up. Where have you been?" She stormed up and took Garrett by the arm, forcibly escorting him through the thicket of haughty laughter.

"I was detained," he said, forcing a stoic expression.

"There are people I need you to meet." She harrumphed and scanned the room.

"Mother, *please.* Not another conquest search again." Garrett stifled a groan through his plea.

"Don't give me that. You are not getting any younger, and you won't be able to keep up this charade of 'natural beauty' you have managed to maintain." She scrutinized him up and down disapprovingly. "You're twenty-five now, Garrett. You only have about a decade or two before your looks start declining, and then you will *have* to do something about it."

"Mother!" he placed his palm to his forehead. "I'm just not interested."

"You will learn eventually that marriage has nothing to do with 'interest'." She whirled around and glared at him coldly. "And you should be very grateful. Your father and I are giving you the chance to choose whom you end up with, from select elite, of course."

"I understand this, but—" His mother cut him off with a sudden jerk as she whisked toward a tall gentleman standing near the bar.

"Mr. Allarin, what a pleasure it is to see you attend. I trust you are keeping well?" his mother welcomed the noble as he took her hand warmly.

"Well, indeed. I am glad to be here," Mr. Allarin said with a hearty smile. The man looked to be about mid-forties, with the authoritative gaze a head of society was expected to wear. His face was a clean canvas, no pocks or marks tainting the surface. Garrett might have been impressed if he hadn't already seen hundreds of other people with similar features passing by.

"Have you met my son, Garrett?" She edged him forward.

"I have not. It is nice to meet you, young sir," Mr. Allarin greeted.

"The pleasure is all mine, sir." Garrett shook his hand, gracefully performing the dance he was expected to.

"My daughter, Veronica, should be around somewhere. You should stop and say hello if you get the chance," Mr. Allarin offered.

"I will be sure to do that, sir."

"We must be off to visit the others. Please enjoy yourself." Magritte nodded to the gentleman.

"I am having a wonderful time already, my dear," Mr. Allarin announced with an emphatic bow.

"Veronica is a lovely girl," his mother whispered to Garrett as she skirted him through the crowd. "Mr. Allarin owns the BioMetal manufacturing syndicate. His partnership would be most beneficial in the Galavantier establishment."

"Mother, I just don't like the girls here." Garrett sighed.

"Well, Mr. Talyn of Talyn Tech has a wonderful son about your age," she offered distractedly as she craned her neck, scanning the depths of the gaiety for another target.

"That's not what I meant, mother," He frowned.

"Oh, *wonderful*! Come with me." She ignored his remark and dragged him onward by the wrist, pointing out a young lady speaking with several owners of high-profile biotech empires. "Her. She's a good one. Her father owns Vaylenuran Systems, specializing in neural netways, optics, and augmented reality. *Very* promising."

Before Garrett was able to vocalize an objection, she sauntered over to the young woman and presented her hand.

"Cordelia! How delightful it is to see you again," Magritte greeted enthusiastically.

"Lady Galavantier, it's always a pleasure." The lady turned and smiled warmly.

"Have you met my son, Garrett? You two have a lot in common," his mother insisted as she proudly patted him on his bruised shoulder, forcing him to swallow hard to stifle a wince.

"I have not. It is nice to meet you, sir." Cordelia curtsied.

"It is nice to meet you," he managed to utter with a forced smile tearing at his objecting lips.

"How is your father doing?" Magritte inquired of the young lady.

"He's been ever so busy with the next generation. It is a shame he was unable to attend. He always hates missing out on a party like this."

"He is greatly missed, but I am glad to hear that he is doing well." She looked over to Garrett, gesturing with a wave of feigned inspiration. "Oh, I have a marvelous idea. Garrett, sweetie, why don't you show Cordelia the observatory upstairs? I'm sure she would love the view on the balcony."

"I—"

"I will leave you two alone. I have some other matters to attend to." Magritte waved, gliding toward the crowd. "Please enjoy yourself, Cordelia, and don't hesitate to ask Garrett if you need anything."

His mother slipped into the gentry before he could excuse himself, leaving him bearing the social obligation to the guest. Holding in a distressed whimper, he looked back at the young lady smiling expectantly at him.

"This way, if you wish." He softly gestured, offering an arm to the woman. The lady graciously accepted, allowing him to usher her out of the ballroom.

The observatory was designed to simulate classical architecture while still maintaining the modern aesthetics of clean lines and contrasting metal inlay. Trees and vines entangled themselves around grey marble columns and shapely statues of both animal and human form. A rock waterfall occupied the heart of the room, cascading into a mosaic-tiled pond with a soothing murmur. The ripples cast into the pool were accented by brightly colored fish drifting aimlessly through the water. Small stone channels led out from the pond, offering mesmerizing pathways for observers to follow and gaze at the luscious foliage.

Garrett escorted his guest up a flight of rustic stone stairs to the balcony, gesturing her to observe the scenery from the railing while he hastily retreated to the cushioned bench behind. Irritated by the entrapment his mother had played on him, he let his posture slump as he sat down, resting his arms on his knees as he distractedly stared at his shiny dress shoes.

"What lovely flora you have here," Cordelia said.

"Mmm, yes," he uttered, halfheartedly searching for the effort to feign interest.

"Since we are alone, I suppose we can dispense with formalities." She smiled and sat down next to him, absentmindedly tracing the lines on the stone with a slender finger. "It's nice to shed the mask and pretend to be human once in a while, isn't it?"

"You don't like playing the political games?" He regarded her oddly. *Huh. Perhaps there is someone else who shares my plight.*

"Oh, they have their moments, certainly. It makes life interesting to play different roles." She twirled a lock of her auburn hair, her smile reaching a cloying level of sweetness. "People are incredibly predictable. It's so easy to mold oneself in order to convince them of anything."

"Ahh. I see." Garrett looked back down at his feet. *Then again, perhaps not.*

"Don't you enjoy the power and influence your family line brings?" Her brazen questioning rubbed him the wrong way.

"Not really, no. The entire system is pointless to me. You are told everyday who you are and what you are supposed to be." He was growing increasingly uncomfortable with her presence, an inner sense of foreboding clawing at him from within.

"You just need to be patient, that's all," she divulged as she toyed with the hem of her dress.

"Oh, really?" He raised a questioning eyebrow.

"Aren't you eager for the day you usurp the throne? Make the previous generation fester in the decaying hell they created." She tilted her head back curiously. "Of course, the next generation will start the cycle all over again."

"And you see nothing wrong with this?" Garrett blinked, barely concealing his shock at the candid narrative.

"No." She shook her head confidently. "It is best to take what you can get and do what is expected of you. Because in due time, you will get your revenge."

"That is a cold outlook on life," he commented, restraining his lips from curling in disgust.

"You can maintain your sanity by taking whatever pleasures your mind and lifestyle will allow you, or what you can hide the best." She suddenly stood up and took his hand, pulling him toward the railing.

"I think that is an oversimplif—"

"I'll be forward, Garrett. I like you. I think a mutual relationship would certainly benefit us both," she declared with a honeyed voice, bringing herself uncomfortably close. "Arcadia needs a new generation to pull it out of the dark. And I think we could make that happen."

"I'm sorry." He firmly rejected, swiftly withdrawing in a wide stride. "But I do not think it is appropriate to make such conjectures on a first encounter."

"So, the rumors were false?" Cordelia tilted her head curiously. "Interesting."

She was referencing his indecorous teenage years, a time in his life he wished he could erase from his memory. Before the gate to Under was open to him, he'd adopted unhealthy habits to fill the void that the mediocrity of noble life plagued upon him, his depression and restlessness only transiently sated with spurs of salacious debauchery. The thrill had quickly waned, and he'd grown a distaste for the hollow affairs.

"I assure you, those days are far behind me." Garrett cleared his throat uncomfortably, trying to suppress the shameful heat that rushed to his cheeks.

"How intriguing. My apologies for the presumption." She winked as she slithered to the stairway. "Good night, Garrett. It was nice meeting you. I will see you again."

He waited for her to depart from the observatory before letting off a shudder, his disoriented revulsion taking a hold of his nerves. The perplexing encounter sent his stomach in knots, and he wondered if the woman's brazen saga of cynicism was her true opinion or a ploy to pick away at his guard. Either way, he wanted her as far away from him as humanly possible.

He sank down to the bench and angrily tore off his constrictive jacket, loosening the knot in his tie with an agitated hand. As he stretched over the lounge seat, he slipped his fingers over a compartment hidden inside the stonework, extracting a half-full bottle of heavy liquor. Taking in a heaving draught, Garrett permitted himself to lower his inhibitions and pass out in the garden, a feeble escape from this pathetic "real" world.

##6.1##

The sea of red-hooded judges loomed over her, perched atop the stretched walls of the council chambers, their cowardly features obscured by mist. She venomously hurled threats at her audience, distorted syllables bursting from her throat as she strained against her shackles.

A human stood on a pedestal in the center of the court, the foreigner robed in swirling black mist, their pale features warped into a blank void. They raised a hand and demanded her silence, only invoking the swell of fire within her. Her roars intensified as vile profane clouds spewed forth from her mouth.

The earth rumbled as black thorny vines sprouted from the soil, clawing their way to the air with a blood-curdling shriek. Pain lashed through her flesh as the tendrils wrapped themselves around her limbs, pinning her body to the steel beams she was chained to. The more she fought, the more she bled.

Cracks burst through the ground as the earth clamored once more. A multitude of voices screamed out in agony as they expelled from the rifts. The souls of the fallen demanded revenge, demanded her flesh.

She could hear whispers pattering beneath the swell, disembodied voices clinching treaties as coin exchanged hands. Murmurs of the pact intensified, but the words were indistinct, leaving the empty realization just out of her reach.

Footsteps echoed behind her, a towering shadow crawling over her restrained vision as a figure approached her exposed back. Unable to turn toward them, she watched helplessly as the hazy human signaled to the being.

Silence was restored as the executioner swiftly carried out their rite, driving their curved swords straight through her shoulders. Her agonized roar reverberated through the dismal chamber as her eyes locked onto the glimmering blades impaling her. Droplets spattered onto the featureless face of the Judge, and he wiped it from his face in disdain, flinging the offensive red liquid to the ground.

The world around her dissolved as the sky opened up, washing over her skin with its taunting barrage. With the task completed, the vines receded back into the earth, dropping her onto the mound of dust. Pools of red trickled around her paralyzed body, feeding the earth with her fleeting life.

Another figure crept into her darkening vision. She watched as they sank to their knees, remorse distorting their cloudy face. As they reached out to her, the blackness seized her mind, removing her from this plane of existence.

##6.2##

NARA AWOKE with a start and snapped a frenzied arm around her back, frantically clawing at her shoulder blade. She released a breath of air as she rubbed her flesh, steadying the adrenaline rush.

"Fucking hell," she grumbled as she crawled out of bed, heading for the shower. "What will it be this time?"

She leaned heavily against the wall, letting the pattering of the water wash away the visions in her head. The fragmented portent sent a disquieting paranoia through her thoughts, her ruinous affliction amplifying its effect.

Dreams were not supposed to visit the Ara'yulthr during sleep. They were only summoned through controlled divination, and always at the will of the host. Meditation was intended to navigate through the subconscious, ruminate over a conflict, or strengthen a bond between loved ones. Infecting the unconscious mind was bizarre and unheard of, according to the medical professionals of homeworld.

Only nightmares violated her brain, communing a terrible omen through a disjointed screenplay of nonsensical symbolism and hyperbole. By the time she was able to decipher their cryptic messages, it was too late.

She burrowed through the demonic vision, struggling to recall the faces of the crowd, but everything was clouded over in her mind's eye. All she knew for certain was that she could look forward to another cycle of restlessness poisoning her judgment. She would eagerly trade psychic blindness over this damnable curse.

Need to take a walk, she thought as she shut off the water and dried. After dressing and arming herself, she headed out into the streets. *Need to clear my head. Maybe pay Sentinel a visit.*

The dream replayed through her mind as she navigated through New Haven, and apprehension crept over the back of her neck. Her brain took the initiative to derail her thoughts using the most sadistic methods, and she found herself thinking about the encounter from last night.

She hated dealing with the Experimentalists. They reminded her of her inevitable fate—a mindless killing machine, her mind rotting away as her body sought to destroy everything around it. While it was the natural path of decline for the elderly, she knew she was destined to succumb early, and everyone else thought the same. She'd had far too many close encounters already, and the Fever would take her if she wasn't careful.

Everyone treated her like she was different, like she was sick, and they were fearful that one day, she would annihilate the entire population in a nuclear fire of rage. She hated them for the way she was brought up in this world, but she hated herself more.

She shivered as the self-loathing settled in her skin, and she wished for someone to confide in. Sentinel was the closest alien she knew that was compassionate enough to lend a sympathetic ear, but there was a ubiquitous side of him that she could not comprehend, and her befuddlement defaulted to mistrust.

The young human suddenly came to her mind. While he couldn't solve her mental puzzles, his inane rambling could give her something else to focus on, like creative ways to get rid of him. The damned juvenile was probably more trouble than he was worth, which might be what the dream was trying to tell her. But then again, she still did not know *who* he was, and he might be more of a danger held at arm's length.

She stopped in an alleyway and prodded at her NetCom, summoning the Upworld cretin.

"Uh, yeah?" A somnolent voice transmitted through her wrist.

Nara managed a scoff. "You all right?"

"Yeah, just, yeah," Garrett said wearily. "Bad day. Headache."

"I'm sorry to hear that," she placated. "I got someone you may want to meet. Come on down here if you are interested."

"I—okay. Be down there in a little while. Give me a chance to clean up a bit," he mumbled as he absentmindedly cut off the communications channel.

"What the fuck am I doing with my life?" Nara groaned as she headed onward.

##6.3##

A DISHEVELED, hastily put-together Garrett ambled toward the meeting point. Strands of knotted hair stuck out of his hood, teasing his exhausted bloodshot eyes.

"You look like hell. You been drinking?" Nara jabbed, arms folded over her chest.

"Yes. Profusely," he muttered, yanking his twisted shirt to the center of his body. "Rather not talk about it."

"You sentient? I don't want to have to drag your ass around."

"Yes, just tired," he griped. "I'll be fine once I walk around."

"If you say so." She turned to walk away. "Headed to a friend's domain. You might like him. He's well-traveled."

"Domain?" His mind was too fogged to comprehend the unorthodox terminology.

"Yeah, he's a mercenary boss, wide influence." She sniffed. "Works from different planets, always moving around. He practically owns an empire."

"I see."

They trekked through a dense mountain range of rusted debris, clambering through treacherous valleys of starship scrap and concrete pillars. A clearing opened up inside the desolate fields of junk, revealing a blackened steel fortress enveloped in sickly green mist. The massive walls surrounding the glossy geometric structure were divided by an even pattern of razor-sharp buttresses arcing along the perimeter. Jagged spires pierced the sky, overlooking the horizon as they brushed the Haze with their reinforced edifices. An alien aura coursed through the architecture, as if the citadel was trapped in stasis, waiting for a galaxy-scale war the planet was destined to create eons from now.

Garrett looked up in amazement at the approaching structure, watching the legion of auto turrets pivot in their direction as they ascended the daunting flight of narrow black stairs. He hovered back a few paces as Nara approached a heavy vault door, intimidated by the scale of the stronghold.

A voice from the intercom acknowledged the visitors. "Hey, Nara, what's up?"

"Is Sentinel in?" she inquired.

"Yeah, he's in. What do you need?"

"Just to talk. Nothing in particular," she stated, digging out grime from under a nail.

"Who's your friend?" the voice asked as the turrets trained their barrels on Garrett.

"Just a guest. He won't bother you much," she assured. Silence assessed the situation, the turrets slowly bobbing up and down as they analyzed the threat.

"All right, come on in."

The multitude of bolts on the hatch emitted a chain of dramatic clunks as they receded from the foot-thick metal walls, sending a groan of protest through the hinges as the door creaked open. Nara heaved the barrier away and stepped inside, waving for Garrett to follow.

Garrett gingerly peered into the hallway, where he saw guns. Lots of guns. Everywhere. Plastered all over the walls, hanging over racks, resting on countertops. Large burly soldiers lounged about as they brandished guns, polished guns, and smoked cigars while they talked about guns. And for every gun he counted, there was also a coordinating number of blades scattered about. The spectacle made Nara's apartment seem as inviting as a convent.

These guys aren't fucking around, Garrett thought as he trailed behind Nara. She headed toward a man hanging out over an oddly out of place reception desk, buried underneath a cache of guns.

"Hark, how are you, my friend?" she greeted as she took the man's hand, slapping a one-armed hug around his back.

"Keepin' strong, Nara," the burly man reported, grinning widely.

"Good to hear. Sentinel around?" she inquired.

"Yup. He's in his office. I told him you were coming."

"Got it." She walked up a set of grated stairs toward another heavily steel-clad door, guarded by two large mercs casually leaning on either side. Nara nodded to the sentries as one reached out to open the door for her.

A man regarded her warmly as she stepped into the low-lit office, standing up from a plush leather executive chair. He was of a deep complexion and had long micro braids ending just below his shoulders, each one glistening with silver beads neatly lined up at the bottom of the plait. His welcoming features were traced by a thin line of facial hair contouring his jawline and lips. He was solidly build and considerably tall, but he still had to look up to meet Nara's eyes. He wore a black leather trench coat over a light grey shirt that emphasized his muscled torso. His black slacks were brimming with pockets, each most likely carrying a reserve of ammunition.

"Greetings, Nara, it is nice to see you again." He had a soft, yet deep soothing voice, radiating a compassionate fatherly overtone.

"It's always nice to see you." She looked over to Garrett. "This is Sentinel, the patron saint of the Underground. Sentinel, this is Garrett, another one of my contacts."

"Nara, my dear, you give me far too much credit." The man projected an embarrassed smile, motioning them to the two other leather chairs in the room. "Please, make yourself comfortable. Garrett, you are welcome here."

"Garrett is a bit of a historian," Nara explained as she sat. "And he likes to collect knowledge on dead intergalactic cultures. I figured you would like to meet him."

"Is that so?" Sentinel perked up. "I'm sure I could indulge his curiosities."

GARRETT WAS INTIMIDATED by the man's regal, otherworldly presence, and his brain was still fogged over from the disquieting drunken nap he had indulged in. He was offered the opportunity to interview a man who had seen the galaxy firsthand, but questions crumbled over his fleeting mental state.

"Please forgive my appearance." Garrett blushed, tucking his argumentative hair into his hood. "I am unsure of what to ask."

"Your friend is quite the polite one. Where did you find him?"

Tiny wrinkles materialized at the corners of Sentinel's mouth as his warm smile widened.

"Covered in blood while I was talking with some 'friends'," Nara explained as she leaned back in her seat, resting an ankle over her knee.

"I see. Well, I am glad to know that you are safe now." Sentinel nodded in approval. "And perhaps I could find something to entertain a historian."

"I would be honored." Garrett beamed, trying to contain his eager fidgeting.

"Could you tell me if you know anything about this?" Sentinel requested as he produced an object from his desk, sliding a hand-sized figurine toward them.

The sculpture was carved from swirling emerald green stone, portraying an elk-like creature in repose. Exquisitely detailed fur was etched along its anatomically correct body, tracing lines in wind-swept curls along its body. The beast stood proud on its golden gilt stand, staring out into the horizon with soulful green-gemmed eyes. A magnificent collection of branches adorned its metal-coated antlers, elegantly dotted with swirls of microscopic sky-blue jewels.

Garrett's eyes widened as the beauty of the artifact seeped into his mind, and he leaned in closer to absorb the shimmering details of the piece. He timidly reached out to confirm its existence within this plane of reality, but his manners internally scolded him and he quickly retracted his hand.

"Go ahead and take a closer look. It's not that fragile," Sentinel offered, humoring the young man's fascination.

"I can't even begin to—" Garrett trailed off as he delicately picked up the object, cradling it in his hands as he marveled at every mark and indentation in the beast's form. "This is . . . this is a remarkable representation of Immureyan gem work. It's carved into an Aatsjyak spirit, which recovered legends say was sent to watch over travelers."

"I see," Sentinel hummed, his amusement radiating across his face.

"I have only seen pictures of fragmented reconstructions, and even those were in terrible condition. I mean no disrespect, but I just cannot fathom how something so old is so well taken care of," he admitted, gently setting the icon on the desk. "This civilization died out several millennia ago, but as far as I can tell, it's . . . it's real, it's not a replica."

"Ahh." Sentinel raised an inquisitive finger. "And therein lies the greatest mystery of all."

Nara observed the conversation, Garrett's gushing words drowning out the disparaging noise inside her head. But Sentinel noticed her distant, preoccupied gaze and turned his attention toward her.

"And what brings you here, my dear?" he softly inquired.

"Just bored," she lied. "Wanted to see if there are any business matters you wanted to speak to me about."

"As a matter of fact, I do have one thing for you, if you are interested to hear about it," Sentinel offered, picking up her subtle language.

"If you got anything else you want to say, do it now." She nodded to Garrett. "Else you're getting kicked out."

"Huh?" Garrett looked at her oddly, the magnificent trinket still glittering in his eyes.

"This is a business matter, and you are not permitted to know of my business matters," she reinforced.

"Oh, okay. I thought—"

"Go and talk to one of the guys. They'll take real good care of you." She gestured to the door.

"Right, uhm." Garrett bowed as he stood up from his seat. "Thank you, sir, for showing me such a wonderful piece."

"It was my pleasure. I am glad I was able to share it with someone who could fully appreciate it. Come back anytime you would like to see more," Sentinel offered.

Garrett bowed again and skirted out of the room, still awestruck by the interaction. The priceless artifact would torment his dreams, and he wondered about the story behind Sentinel's procurement of the piece. The man gave the impression of a very powerful authority, and he was more intimidated by him than the entire army sitting in the atrium.

The raucous laughter of the guards hushed to a wary murmur as he walked into the recreation room. A nervous smile twitched over his face as he scurried to an unoccupied counter, easing himself into a bar stool. He wrung his hands in discomfort as he felt eyes all over the room scrutinizing him.

A sudden hearty pat on his shoulder hurled him from his seat, and he latched onto the countertop with a desperate bracing grip. He looked over to see Hark leering down on him, a toothy grin stretched across his face.

"You a friend of Nara's?" Hark asked as the stools violently scooted aside with a grating honk to make room for the giant man.

"Yes, sir, though I don't think Nara would feel the same," he sputtered out a nervous laugh.

"A friend of hers is a friend of ours. Put 'er there," Hark said as he stuck his hand out. "What's your name, son?"

"Garrett." He winced as he pried free from Hark's vise-like grip.

"Welcome, Garrett. What brings you to these parts?"

"Boredom mostly. I do a lot of exploring just to see what I can find," Garrett explained, massaging the back of his crushed hand. *Oh, gods, please get me out of here now.*

"A scavenger, eh? Dangerous work. You look like the cautious type, especially if you hang around the likes of Nara. A guy can respect that," Hark observed. Garrett smiled politely in response, shoving back every trace of discomfort he could manage. "You play cards at all?"

"A little. I know the rules, but I haven't mastered the bluffing yet," Garrett admitted, sheepishly rubbing the back of his neck.

"Bah, nonsense!" Hark laughed boisterously at the confession. "Come on over to the table and we'll set up a friendly game."

"Oh, I don't know—" Garrett suddenly found himself whisked away to a table where three intently focused men were playing a silent but heated game of poker.

"What did I tell you lot about betting your weapons?!" Hark barked, jabbing at the center of the table.

"Sorry, Boss," one of the soldiers meekly apologized as the rest of the crew sheepishly brushed off guns and ammunition rounds from the playing field.

"Start a new hand. We're gonna play a new game," Hark commanded as he plunked down an empty chair behind Garrett.

As the cards were dealt, Garrett steeled himself for the most uncomfortable and humiliating game in his life.

##6.4##

Nara shifted uncomfortably in her seat as the thoughts began to trickle back into her brain.

"He's a nice kid, a rare breed these days," Sentinel declared with a nod.

She raised an eyebrow. "Really? Nothing strikes you as off about him?"

"No. There's not a single shred of malice in him. The only thing I find odd is that he's an Upworlder that is so open-minded." He stood up from his seat and moved to the other side of the desk, leaning against the edge of the marble.

"I trust your judgment. I seem to be unsure of everything as of late," she admitted, rubbing her temples distractedly.

"You seem troubled."

She shook her head in dismissal. "It's nothing. Been having difficulties sleeping, that's all."

"Oh, no." He gave her a solemn frown of understanding. "Would you like to talk about it?"

"I don't know what it would do. I'm afraid of receding back to my mental state from last time," she confessed. "I just started feeling like myself again."

"You know how to take care of yourself," he reassured, tipping his head toward the door. "And that one will do you no harm. Intentionally, anyway. His influence may be a detriment, but I'm only saying that because I don't know where he comes from."

"Neither do I," she scoffed.

"You are always welcome here should you come into trouble," the man assured.

"I appreciate that. Right now, a distraction sounds lovely," she told him. "What was that business matter you wanted to speak about?"

"Nothing crucial, just a small errand while I wait for the results of other discussions." He folded his arms across his chest.

"Anything you need," she pledged.

"A client has made a request for hired muscle to escort him to a trade." Sentinel leaned back over his desk and picked up a tablet, handing the computer to Nara. "It's nothing taxing. Just stand there and look menacing."

"Sounds fine. How much are they paying?" she asked as she pawed through the screen.

"Thirty thousand."

"The client expecting heavy resistance?" She chewed at a fingernail as she looked back up at him.

"He didn't think so." Sentinel shook his head. "He was the nervous scientist type, pretty paranoid."

"Good enough, I suppose. I'll take it." Nara handed the device back to him.

"I'll let him know to expect you. He will meet you at Crystal Point tomorrow evening. His alias is 'Mr. L'," Sentinel said. His expression suddenly changed to mild amusement as he glanced out his door. "You might want to check up on your friend before the boys get rough with him."

"I suppose you are right." She sighed and stood up from her seat. "Good evening, and thank you."

"You are always welcome."

A heavy tension strangled the atmosphere as Nara headed down the stairs, greeting her with a room shrouded in silence. A crowd had huddled around the center playing table, watching the opponents gauge each other over a pile of empty shell casings. From one side of the table, a soldier smugly chewed on a cigar, toying with their hand as they waited for their turn.

The meek Garrett sat at the opposite end, intently focused on his cards. his leg nervously quaked as he took painstaking care to keep his hand concealed from the discontented crowd.

"I call," Garrett whispered shyly, clearing his throat. On cue, the soldier fanned out their hand dramatically on the table, their smirk crawling up their cheek.

"Four of a kind, nines." The soldier grinned. Quiet murmurs echoed in the room as the surrounding grunts chattered in approval. "Your turn, kid."

Garrett inhaled a deep breath and flipped his cards over, dramatically dropping one over the next in succession. Eyes all around widened with each card he cast, the flits of the paper accompanied by excited gasps.

"Royal flush," Garrett announced, his fearful expression twisting into an evil grin.

"How did you . . . there were five people at this hand!" the soldier blubbered, snatching the bandana from their head.

Garrett shrugged as he attempted to scoop the gargantuan pile of shell casings toward him. Raucous laughter erupted through the overcrowded room as he collected his gains, the rancor oozing out of his opponent.

"Boy, you told me you weren't any good at bluffing." Hark slapped him playfully on the shoulder, launching Garrett into the money pile with a shower of metallic clinks.

"I was bluffing." Garret shrugged. The uproar escalated to rambunctious hoots as Nara pushed her way into the fighting ring.

"All right, fun's over. We've got to get moving," she announced. "Kid, give the grunts back their earnings and let's go."

"Aww, c'mon, Nara, you ol' killjoy," Hark teased.

"I got shit to do. I'm not waiting around," Nara called back as she headed down the atrium.

"I'm coming!" Garrett responded as he stumbled out of his seat, summoning another bout of laughter as he chased after her.

CHAPTER 7

##7.0##

"Mr. L, I presume," Nara greeted as she approached a shifty-eyed man clutching a steel case. Her voice warped into a generic machine-like buzz, the inhuman pitch causing the jumpy man to gasp in fright.

"I, uh, yes!" He offered an unsteady hand to her, visibly intimidated by the giant mechanical figure in front of him. "Agent RD? Your employer spoke very highly of you. I am glad to make your acquaintance, sir."

"Are you ready?" she asked, gesturing for him to lead.

"Yes, quite. Please follow me." The mousy man cleared his throat and stepped forward. "I am meeting someone in a bar to engage in a business matter. I am not exactly sure what to expect, which is why I have hired you to escort me there."

Nara nodded her head in acknowledgement, but she couldn't help but smirk under her helmet. *Greenhorn criminals, gotta love them.*

The fidgety figure led her to one of the most popular bars in the Uncivilized Zone, where high-income proprietors fought a constant battle to reclaim territory from the unruly. The flashy atmosphere was tailored to Upper-flavored vice, prismatic colors skating around a black-painted room, shifting with the heavy monotonous beat of the electronic music blaring over the dance floor.

Scantily-clad performers writhed inside transparent black-lit cages, encouraging the patrons to do the same. The vibrant lighting neglected the borders of the room, overtaken by a shadowy maze of booths that obscured the unseemly business taking place within.

The bar summoned the newcomers with its glaring presence. A translucent countertop of frosted plastic showed off the wares, dotted with bright blue lights that smoldered through curls of frolicking fog inside the casing. Lights radiated through a spectrum of liquor bottles, adding a prismatic sensory experience to the intoxicated.

Mr. L shifted to the bartender, beckoning him forward with an insecure hand. He clumsily leaned to whisper into the man's ear, who recoiled and pointed to the back of the club. Bobbing up to his toes, Mr. L squinted in the direction he was instructed, letting out a relieved yet still nervous chortle. He then scurried off and waved for Nara to follow.

"You hear me?" Nara asked Garrett through the remote channel.

"Yeah, I got you," he confirmed as he tweaked his viewports.

"I am not sure of what to expect," Nara revealed as she glanced around the room. *"I need you to locate every single person who has eyes on us."*

"Got it," Garrett confirmed, scanning over the crowd.

Mr. L led Nara to a darkened corner, stopping in front of a cavernous hollow in the wall. Purple light trickled down on a table, bordered by plush bench seats built inside the miniature shelter. A familiar gold-maned face smiled up at them, his slimy arms coiled around two women dressed in coordinating skintight suits.

Well, hello again, Blondie. Nara scowled. The man's chronic cocky smile and rat face were not easily forgotten after the night he'd ambushed her in the streets. Tempting as it was to jump across the table and punch the smarm out of him, she restrained herself. The effort and fleeting pleasure weren't enough to counteract the mark on her reputation.

"Ahh, Mr. L. Good, on time, I see. Let's talk someplace quieter." The sleaze gestured to a door toward the back of the club.

"Uh, sure, as you wish," Mr. L said as he bumbled behind.

The businessman flicked his golden hair over his shoulder as he nodded at the bouncers standing opposite sides of the entrance. One of the guards obediently opened the door, motioning for the boss to step inside. The other approached Nara and held her arm outward, shaking her head in refusal.

"He comes inside with me or the deal is off," Mr. L insisted with a rush of forced confidence.

The guard glanced at her boss questioningly while Nara seized the opportunity to drop a bug on the floor. With a few subtle flicks of her fingers, she let it crawl onto the wall next to the entrance.

"You got the other viewpoint?" she asked Garrett as she opened a menu on her helmet, calibrating the perspective of the bug.

"It's on split screen now," he reported. "You've got quite a bit of attention. I can see about seven people watching you, not including the two guards and the dealer."

"Got it."

"Fine, let him in." The smarmy man looked Nara up and down before shooting a dismissive wave. "He won't be able to do much here anyway."

Upon the authorization, the guard shifted away from Nara's personal space, permitting her to step inside. The door closed behind them, sealing off everything but the rhythmic beating of bass thundering against the walls. Save for a few hanging lights and additional guards standing around, the room was mostly bare. A table and chair set took up the center of the room, giving the place the feel of an interrogation chamber.

"Please, have a seat," the man requested. He pushed a glass toward the edge of the table, subconsciously ordering a grunt to step in and fill the awaiting vessel.

Mr. L timidly shuffled into his chair, nervously eyeing the observers around the room. Nara shadowed the anxious man, folding her arms to widen her presence.

"You know, I really don't like the looks of that blonde one doing all the talking," Garrett mentioned.

"You're not the only one," she commented.

"And those seven have started moving closer to the door," he pointed out, cycling through his viewports. "Not all at once, but they're trying to look nonchalant."

"The odds aren't great, but I've dealt with worse."

"I assume you have brought what we are looking for," the dealer commented as he idly traced a finger around the rim of his glass.

"Of course, yes." Mr. L fidgeted with the latch of case and revealed three vials, flipping the container around for the man's inspection.

"Excellent," the dealer purred as he plucked out an ampoule, examining the pale liquid contents in the light. "My employer is very glad you could come to his assistance, and he is willing to offer you thirteen for them."

"Each?" Mr. L asked, scrunching his eyebrows.

"Total," the oily dealer declared as delicately sipped his drink.

"That isn't what we negotiated," Mr. L confronted.

"Pay close attention to movement," Nara ordered Garrett, sensing the uneasiness in the room as the guards shifted their stances. *Something's not right.*

"I'm on it," Garrett assured.

"I guarantee you, he is being very generous with this offer," the dealer continued, raising his glass in the air, summoning the nearest grunt to refill it.

"Do you realize what I had to go through to get these to you?" Mr. L clutched the edges of his case. "Then you change your mind and offer me this extremely insufficient fee? I–I'm quite insulted."

"This ass had better watch his mouth or he's going to make me work for my money," Nara grumbled as she watched the outburst.

"That certainly is not my concern. If you prefer, I could always give you another option." He paused to take another dramatic sip. "I'm sure, Mr. Ivek Linureste, that your employer at VyynTech wouldn't like to hear about you stealing company property to sell it to the competition."

"Tha-at's not go-od," Nara proclaimed. With a revealed identity, she knew she was about to be thrown into more trouble than the antsy scientist was willing, or capable, to pay for.

"You are a lot more rotten than you sounded over NetCom," Mr. L spat.

"Why, because I have the upper hand? Of course, I was going to find out who you are before meeting up with you. Now the choice is yours," the dealer said as he presented a slice and laid it on the table in front of him.

Just give him the merch and let's go, dammit, she mentally urged, beseeching the universe that the force of her personality would ram some sense into her naïve client. *Fucking walk away from this.*

"Somebody is moving toward the door," Garrett reported. "Make that two."

*"Fu-**uck**."* She surveyed the empty room, scanning for cracks or openings in the walls, but she was locked up in a room with one exit.

"I don't think much of your attitude, sir," Mr. L said as he began to lower the case.

"No, no, no. No. Stop. Right now. You useless pile of refuse," she growled through the channel, her irritation radiating to Garrett, who chewed his lip in apprehension.

The mercs in the room began to slip their hands to their weapons. The faint snaps of unlatching holsters dotted the air. There was no time left. Her client had made his move, and now it was up to her to clean up the mess. But the temptation to leave "Mr. L" in a puddle of his own blood was weighing heavily on her mind.

"I'm sorry you feel that way. But I see you are more of a 'hard' bargainer, so let me make an offer you *shouldn't* refuse." The dealer took another casual sip as a whirlwind of barrels fixed on Mr. L. "You leave the specimens here, and I let you walk out."

"Nara, more goons are headed your way," Garrett announced.

"Shit."

Your move. Let's leave right now, she implored, grinding her teeth beneath her helmet. But Mr. L could not hear the signals as he continued to push the case down. *What the hell do you think you are doing?*

Movement caught the corner of her eye as one of the henchmen clicked a setting on his charging gun.

Ahh, fuck everything, she grumbled.

She snapped her leg up, kicking over the table, scattering the specimens and spilling the hapless beverage over the dealer's expensive-looking suit. Shoving Mr. L to the far wall, she whipped out a pair of pistols and nailed the two nearest gun-ready assailants in the head, their startled expressions frozen as their bodies slumped to the ground.

"Nara, behind you!" Garrett shouted.

She reacted to the warning, pulling another grunt into her grip. She whirled around as another merc barged in, haphazardly firing into her hostage. After they had paused in realization, she threw the meat shield at the invader, shoving them off balance as she directed her attention to the remainder in the room.

The dealer, recovering in his wine-soaked seat, had finally grasped the severity of the situation and pulled out a weapon of his own. As he raised his gun, the tendons in his hand glowed, tracing vibrant purple lines on the surface of his skin. He squeezed the trigger in subconscious response, and three rapid-succession bullet rounds exploded out of the barrel. The projectiles lanced through Nara's armor, the final round punching into her shoulder.

Nara slowly craned her neck, leering at the offending creature. Letting out an irate growl, she vaulted over the table, reaching out to wrap her hands around the dealer's slimy neck.

With fear of the mechanical giant overloading his nerves, the dealer abruptly wrenched to his feet and tore out the door, shoving the cavalry out of his way as if they were paper dolls.

"Fucker has nerve enhancements. Should have known better," she muttered as she spotted Mr. L cowering where she'd left him, terror exuding from his bulging eyes. She grabbed the shaken man by the jacket and hefted him behind the table. *Goddamn priorities.*

"Stay put," Nara ordered with a jab of an authoritative finger. The scientist could only nod in acknowledgement.

"You got more incoming," Garrett interrupted.

She ducked down and scrunched herself next to her client, considering her strategy as more goons poured into the room. Fragments splintered off the surface of the table as the assailants unloaded their ammunition into the feeble shelter. With another volley of fire, a hole burst through the wood, sending a hammer of force against her spine.

"All right, fuck this," she declared as she sprang to her feet.

She hefted the table and hurled it at the grunts, knocking them over in a disorderly pile of hypermuscled limbs. Without giving them the chance to recover, she charged at the blockage of bodies, lunging after the closest victim and yanking them toward her.

The grunt let off a series of startled squeaks as she lifted them into the air, their shocked cries morphing to pleas for mercy as Nara wielded the poor human as a blunt weapon. With their involuntary assistance, she forced her way back into the club, knocking down her remaining assailants as she cleared a path to exodus.

"Yeah, that seemed to take care of them," Garrett breathed in astonishment as he watched the display unfold.

Nara tossed her terrorized shield down and bolted to where the dazed Mr. L was collecting his remaining specimens. She seized the mousy creature by the shirt collar and dragged him to his feet.

"It's over, let's go," she commanded Mr. L as she shoved him through the rift, utilizing the panicked screaming mass on the dance floor as cover.

Several grunts began to collect themselves, wildly firing shots into the crowd. Nara hunched over and covered her flagellating client in her shadow. As Mr. L tripped over his feet, Nara hefted him up and carried him out of the club.

"Enforcers will be here any minute, so stop fucking around," she growled at her shivering cargo as she ran out into the open streets.

The grunts stopped just beyond the club entryway, giving up the chase as she darted through the alleyways. Hearing the gunfire dwindle behind her, Nara headed for the bustle of a traveling marketplace. With a firm hand, she pressed her client into the mingling crowd, slowing her pace to a casual stroll to allow the terrified man respite.

"Now that *that* is taken care of . . ." She grabbed Mr. L by the collar, forcing him to stand on the tips of his toes. "Either you have got to be one of the most foolish people in existence, or my boss has given you impressions that I don't like fulfilling."

"H–he did say a lot of great things about your capability, yes." He cleared his throat and attempted to pry her hand from his garment.

"And because of this, you thought you would get the better end of that deal?" she growled, folding her arms over her chest.

"We're here, aren't we? And they didn't get the better end, I think." A nervous laugh involuntarily forced its way out of his throat.

"That is a matter of opinion." She glowered as she released her grip. *Fucking newbie criminals.*

"I–um, well. Yes." Mr. L sheepishly rubbed the back of his head, questioning the safety of his kneecaps.

"Which brings me to my next point. Even though your deal went sour, you are still expected to pay my fee to the agent, plus my medical expenses. I assume there won't be any problems in that regard, correct?" She stooped down so that her faceplate was an inch away from his nose. "I would *hate* to have to come to your doorstep and collect."

"No, no, no." Mr. L swallowed hard. "No problems at all."

"Good." She removed herself from his face. "Now where would you like to be dropped off, Mr. L?"

##7.1##

Nara burst through her apartment and slammed the door shut, deactivating her armor and hurling the badge aside. She crashed onto the couch, rubbing her face vigorously as she grumbled indistinct words, the stings in her shoulder magnifying her spite.

"Why are people that fucking reckless?" she bellowed.

"I can't answer that myself," Garrett stated, turning around in his chair. Nara sighed in between aggravated growls. "At least it's over now and you didn't lose much."

"Except the last remaining shreds of my patience," she grumbled through her hands.

"Still a payday in the end." He noticed the open tears in her clothing. "And it looks like you're injured. You're bleeding all over your couch."

"It's black for a reason." She waved him off, but his puppy-eyed gaze of concern sliced through her spirits and she rumbled a defeated sigh. "Ugh, fine. Be useful and get the salve. It's in the center cabinet, the flask with the purple liquid. Some cloth should be sitting there too."

Garrett dutifully walked to the kitchen, but his eagerness to assist dwindled as he stared blankly at the collection of chemicals. Doubt riddled his brain as he brushed a finger over every purple liquid in the center cabinet, uncertain which shade was correct. He turned and raised an inquisitive finger, opening his mouth to speak.

"Second shelf, third from the right. Black cap," Nara called out.

Garrett located a pear-shaped flask containing a thick lavender liquid and took it down, along with a couple of pieces of white cloth sitting on the bottom shelf. He returned to the living room and unscrewed the top, pouring a small amount onto the bandage. With a gentle beckoning wave, he knelt next to the arm of the chair and motioned for her to sit up.

"The hell do you think you're going with that?" she snapped, her cold gaze chilling his blood.

"Your back? You can't possibly reach—"

"Human, I've lived alone for many years." She snatched the cloth from him and twisted her arms behind her. "Don't touch my back. Don't go near it. Don't even look at it."

"Oh-kay," he replied, retreating to the computer desk. *She really does enjoy her space.*

A call on her NetCom interrupted her contortion practice, and she picked up the device from the table to respond.

"Sentinel here. I just received your payment from the client," the voice reported.

"Yes, I may or may not have a bone to pick with you about that," she griped through gritted teeth.

"Really?" the voice's concern radiated through the transmission.

"Yes, what exactly did you tell him about me?" she questioned as she toyed with the medicine bottle, creating tetchy scratchy noises as the glass skidded over the surface.

"Nothing more than 'he would take care of you.' Why?"

"I think he took it way too seriously," Nara grumbled.

“Did you have problems? I’m so sorry," Sentinel said. "He was quite happy about your performance, and he even gave a bonus, but I suppose he was apologizing for the apparent trouble.”

“How much of a bonus?” She raised an eyebrow, leaning over the arm of the couch.

“Seventy-five percent.”

“Well, shit,” Garrett blurted, slapping a hand to his mouth as Nara shot him a chastising glare.

"Huh. Wonder where the fucker got the money," she scoffed at the NetCom. “I figured he was going to ghost.”

“Was that worth the trouble?” Sentinel asked.

“Not one bit.”

“That’s the spirit.” He chuckled. “I’ll let you go now. Come and stop by anytime, and bring your friend along. Hark won’t stop talking about him.”

“No promises,” she responded as she ended the call. She looked over to find Garrett staring at her with unease. “Ah, fuck it. Let's go exploring.”

“Uh, okay.” Garrett shook his head and stood up. “Have anywhere particular in mind?”

“Nope,” Nara announced, grabbing her coat. “Let's see what's new at the market.”

CHAPTER 8

##8.0##

The Prismal Caravan set up camp in the Old District with its convoy of bulletproof vehicles, piloted by a private sector militia of merchants. Business was open on the grounds, their reinforced paneling propped open to reveal a variegated assortment of trinkets. An entourage of motorbikes accompanied the fleet, their cargo trailers exploding into makeshift tables and shelters across the pavement.

Though not nearly as large as most of the traveling markets, the Prismal Caravan boasted the most unique vendors, known exclusively for offering antique art and textiles. Despite this, opportunistic food stands shadowed behind the convoy, reaping the benefits of limited competition as they offered sustenance to hungry dealers and collectors.

Nara made her way over to a sweet-smelling truck deviously wafting spiced fumes into the air. She glanced over the foodstuffs on display, tracing her eyes over the ropes of brilliantly colored, jagged rock crystals that draped over the window. Mounds of biscuits and cakes decorated with glistening iced fruit were stacked neatly into pyramids, tempting her with a sugary vice.

A small wood grill beckoned her over with its smoky-scented

allure, crackling seductively as it softly charred an orderly row of skewers. She obeyed the calling, placing an order to the truck owner in Darktrade.

The owner produced two rectangular trays, plucking four skewers of ivory-colored orbs from the smoldering grill and placing them in the containers. They rotated the delicacies, revealing the fire-kissed golden brown that gently blushed the sides of the dough. The artwork was completed with a drizzle of a translucent, coffee-colored syrup, dressing the treat with a brilliant glossy sheen. The proprietor then grabbed two beers from underneath the counter and passed over the steaming order.

Nara paid and collected her bounty, making her way to a standing table. She pushed one of the trays to the opposite end, not waiting for her shadow to join her before diving in.

Garrett sniffed curiously at the offering, dipping a finger into the sauce and sampling the liquid. A strange yet pleasing combination of salty and sweet baffled his tongue, the flavor simple, yet complex. He attempted to take a small bite from the orb, but its surprisingly springy consistency would not yield to his attack. As he struggled, the treat slid up the skewer, threatening to drop onto the questionably clean table.

With a snap of his neck, he thwarted the orb's evasion and engulfed the entire sphere with a sickening slurp. The subtle sweetness of the orb intensified the sauce, complementing its flavor. He washed it down with the beverage, which tasted more like carbonated herbal tea rather than beer.

"What's Sentinel's story?" he inquired, placing the skewer back on the tray before humiliating himself further. "He seems to be rather hospitable for a mercenary boss."

"You strengthen loyalty with compassion rather than fire," Nara replied.

"You think so?"

"Ask any of the people working for him. He's just like a father to everyone," she said as she plucked another orb.

"Really? What did he do for you?" he asked. He made another attempt at the delicious snack, following her lead and prying the orbs off the stick before eating them whole.

"He gave me a job that fit my skillset," she explained. "I didn't need to learn something new in order to adapt."

"Learning isn't all that bad," Garrett countered, popping another orb into his mouth.

"It's also not exactly a high priority in your head when all you've got left are your own bare hands," she said, gulping down a swig of her beer.

"I guess I don't see your point. Even if I lost everything, I would still have the capability to learn. And maybe I could work on getting it all back, or at least something else of equal value." He looked up to meet Nara's smirk of skepticism. "What?"

"The words speak of integrity now," she remarked through her drink. "But would he say so *after* the fact?"

"I mean, I have no way to answer that." He shrugged.

"All right, enough of that," she announced, dropping her bottle down on the table. "Let's see what other trouble we can get into."

Garrett grabbed his other skewer and followed Nara into the crowd, munching contentedly as he absentmindedly eyed through the displays. A small idol caught Garrett's attention, a golden figurine of a young man sitting on a throne. The subject brandished a spear, reclining with two hounds curled up at his feet.

"Huh, that's a Feyntinet icon," Nara commented, picking up the artifact.

"Yes, a Fifth Era relic, in fact," Garrett said, raising an eye at her.

The shopkeeper butted into the conversation. "No, you'll find that a Third Era."

"What? How do you figure?" Garrett questioned the man.

"Well, look at the coloration. It's inked, not enameled. And it is clearly a depiction of the god Auselros, patron of the hunt," the salesman pointed out. "Also, take a look at the inscriptions. It's missing the RE and UT runes that were used in later periods."

"They have found evidence of RE and UT used all the way back to the First Era." Garrett scrunched his brow indignantly, taking no notice of Nara, who had begun to scrutinize the piece for herself. "The new dig sites on Myrmith have found tablets using the inscriptions."

"Auselros lost his influence at the end of the Fourth Era when his temple was destroyed by the Haalmat empire!" The shopkeeper laughed derisively.

"Which points to a small artisan, and it was probably created for an underground cult that was still worshiping him years after the temple's destruction." Garrett seethed. He had spent far too much time researching the Feyntinet civilization to be demeaned by the pompous vendor.

"You're both wrong," Nara interrupted, the two men turning to her in surprise. "It's a replication. There's a maker's mark from an old Tev'rnan factory. It's small, and severely defaced, but present."

"Huh?" The combatants replied synchronously, blinking at her.

"The ink is also a uniform shade, implying that it was created through machines. Still old though, probably a couple of centuries." Nara pointed out a tiny symbol on the bottom of the figurine for them to analyze.

"I mean . . ." the vendor trailed off.

"And it's not a statue of Auselros. His spear was barbed, and he was never shown seated in art. This is a queen from the Fourth Era, Gemnal of the Earth," she added, delicately placing the idol back on the table. "She was also known for her hunting prowess, so the misinterpretation is easily made."

Garrett stared in disbelief. *How does a mercenary like her know so much? She can just pull out the fine details of a pantheon spanning millennia from the top of her head.*

"Are you taking it with you or not?" Nara probed, not particularly interested in his conclusions.

"Tev'rnan replicas are a niche market." Garrett sighed in disappointment, turning away from the vendor stand.

They left the shopkeeper dissecting the statue in frustration, muttering about using teeth as a method of payment. The two continued to mingle around the caravan, casually browsing for interesting stands as they drifted through the peaceful flow of people.

"Elam!" A voice suddenly pierced through the crowd. Nara froze mid-step as the call reverberated through her ears, ice seizing her throat as she fought a morbid thought from her head.

It couldn't be. She shook her head in disbelief, resuming her path.

"Elam'Mutavreh!" the voice shouted again.

No! Her panicked voice echoed through her brain, evoking a thunder in her chest. *No, no, no, please, no.*

Nara slowly turned around to find a member of the Ara'yulthr race frantically pushing his way through the crowd. Her skin rushed with heat as the approaching invader's face triggered excruciating memories, and her fists balled up into quaking bludgeons. She lashed a violent snarl through bared fangs, sending the warning rippling through the crowd and stopping the man in his tracks.

The individual was considerably shorter than Nara, and his build was drastically different, possessing a modest, lankier physique. His skin was a much brighter crimson hue, mottled with blood-red freckles. A narrow jawline peeked out of his hood, the shadow of a neatly trimmed goatee defining its shape.

"That is *not* my name," Nara boomed.

The figure stood frozen, uncertain how to react to his visibly irate kin. He removed his hood, hoping to be recognized as a friend. His desperate eyes shone a sparkling peridot green, and a mane of long, straight black hair was kept in order by a low-falling ponytail.

"It is I, Bellanar. From the Dru'umalek clan scribes. You must remember," the anxious man stated, speaking a foreign language. *"I am here to ask for your help. Your people need you."*

Nara glowered at the man's statement, her lips curled into a scowl. She advanced on the nervous man, her vehement expression causing him to shrink back toward the crowd.

"They are NOT my people. If you value your life, you will leave my presence immediately," Nara commanded, slashing the air in front of her with an open palm. Her voice resonated through the grounds, her native tongue seething through her gritted teeth. Eyes began to take note of the thickened tension, and a small bubble of space opened around the two giants.

" I–I cannot. Please, you must help us. Loremaster, he has been silent ever since your . . ." Bellanar searched delicately for the right word, fidgeting with his hands. *"Departure."*

"The nerve you have to speak to me about him." She glowered.

Garrett was stunned at the interaction taking place in front of him.

While the strange man appeared to be speaking normally, Nara's incensed tone seemed to reverberate inside his skull, shaking his brain with the jarring echoes emanating from her throat.

"He does nothing but stare out toward the oceans, obsessing over the same book he has been reading for years. It is a pathetic sight," Bellanar recounted with a burdened sigh. *"He has washed his hands clean of all political matters and will not attend the World Council."*

"Pathetic indeed. But I will not help you. His actions are his choice alone." She abruptly pivoted around and stormed away.

"A senseless war is coming. You would let innocent people die in such a wasteful manner?" he sputtered half-accusingly, reaching a pleading arm out to her. " *Without a blink or breath?"*

The fire intensified beneath her skin, and she reeled around. Her eyes scorched the air as she marched toward the fearful man, bringing herself uncomfortably close his face.

"The wheel must turn, Bellanar," she chanted wrathfully. *"The indicted has pierced me, and I shall aid Xannat to cast their own blade."*

Bellanar's eyes widened in horror, devastated by the ancient curse spat in his direction. Every shred of the fickle confidence he had built up was torn from his body, and he was left frozen in the wrath of the forgotten warrior.

The crowd around them murmured in hushed whispers as the bubble widened around them. Uneasy observers watched the scene warily, bringing hands to weapons as they anticipated bloodshed.

"I–how could you?" Bellanar breathed, edging backward in disbelief. *"Millions of lives just vanish into dust for the most banal of reasons! You cannot just simply walk away and ignore that!"*

"It is not my concern. I will not help you." Nara turned her back to him.

The man shook his head in denial, refusing to accept her rejection. Stifling his agitated nerves, Bellanar lunged forward, wrapping his shuddering hands around her wrist.

"Please, Elam. I implore you. You are our only hope, Peacekeeper." His voice trembled as he struggled to force out the last syllables. *"Warlord."*

"Then all hope is lost," she jeered.

Before Bellanar could conjure a reaction, she twisted her arm around, slipping her wrist from his tenuous grip. She snatched his outstretched hand and heaved him in front of her, sending him into the dispersing crowd. Her might overwhelmed him as the force of the attack stole his balance, hurling his flailing form to the concrete.

"Get the fuck out of my sight!" Nara hissed in Trade, marching around the distraught mass.

##8.1##

GARRETT TOOK a moment and leaned against the entrance of a secluded bar in the Old District. Nara's hustled stride provided a challenge to his ineffectual human endurance. When he slowed his panting to a reasonable thunder, he warily stepped inside to find her drinking alone in a corner, listlessly toying with a glass as she drowned in thought.

"You're hard to keep up with when you don't want to be found," Garrett said as he approached, wheezing in discomfort as his body objected the intensive trek.

"Why are you here, human?" Nara pinched her temples in annoyance.

"I just–hang on." He raised a finger as he let out a series of debilitating coughs, his throat rebelling against the words. "Just wanted to see if you were okay."

Nara muzzled a tiny laugh in her throat as she witnessed the pitiful spectacle, her chortle overshadowed by the human's vocal display of exhaustion. She shook her head dismissively as a smirk strained against her will.

"So," Garrett let out a final sputter as he leaned heavily against the table. "I take it you don't want to tell me what that was all about?"

"It was nothing." She downed her drink and ordered another three from the service drone.

Garrett clamped his mouth shut, watching discomfort color her face. There was a reason she didn't want to speak about her past, and the curious man who ambushed them at the market seemed to be a painful reminder to her.

"Hey, let's take the roof roads back to your place. The open air and the climb would do us both good," he offered. "I can also show you the routes I use to get around, open for criticism, of course."

"Interesting proposal," she said impassively.

"Can I—" He belted another cough and pointed at one of the drinks on the table. Nara slid a glass over with a sneer, watching him drain the contents with several hearty gulps. "Thanks. Shall we?"

"Lead on." She gestured as she slid out from her seat.

Garrett consulted his NetCom as they ventured out of the bar, selecting the most treacherous route that he had charted in his navigation programs. He led his reticent companion out of Old District and into the fragmented relics bordering Civilized Space.

A different flavor of silence loomed over the crumbled remains of the suburban shopping quarter, one of solace and a ghostly tranquility. Since the buildings were in no state to be used as shelter, and the contents picked to the bone centuries ago, no one was around to disturb the travelers. The battle-scarred storefronts desperately clung to their toppling living quarters above, the giant brick dominoes collapsing over the streets.

Garrett tunneled through the vertical trail, clambering over perforated rooftops as he guided her to the edge of a downed communications tower. He tried to hide his fatigue as he shimmied across the steel frames, releasing his breath in controlled bouts as his muscles screamed for reprieve.

When they reached the center of the tower, he sat down on one of the beams and raised a hand in surrender. He flopped over on his back and stared up at the swirling Haze, letting his lungs voraciously consume as much polluted air as his body desired.

"I'm sure you've been here before, but I like to come up here and have a think," Garrett revealed. "It's a pretty view, in a macabre sort of way."

"Mmm," Nara quietly agreed, settling down next to him.

From this height, they could see the decayed beauty of Undercity, what wasn't obscured by clouds of smog. Street lamps dotted the horizon with a lingering glow, illuminating the skeletons of buildings with ethereal light. Bright neon beams from the markets and Civilized business districts broke the monotony of the pattern, offering a vibrant focus for meditative thought.

A soft wind curled around them, complimenting the peace with a murmur of adulation. Silence drowned out the bustle of the common grounds and the trepidation lurking in the shadows of the city, surrounding the duo with a comforting chill blanket.

Nara leaned back and soaked in the atmosphere, taking a morbid enjoyment from the stillness. The human's tactful evasion of the heated fray in the market took her by surprise, and a hint of gratitude trickled through her spirits.

Despite the solace and magnificent view, she could not help but replay the encounter in her head. The man's arrival had cast a deep bitterness over her thoughts, and the disturbed nights she had endured had amplified her resentment. Fate was about to drop on her doorstep, and she was uncertain whether she would have enough armaments to beat them back.

"So now what?" Garrett rolled over on his side, his movement breaking through her seething.

"Now, I am going to take a nice break, and I am going to get drunk off my a—" A chirp from her NetCom interrupted. She raised her arm and took one look at the identification, growling in irritation. "What could you possibly want now, Annon?"

"I have a job for you," the NetCom announced, unmoved by her attitude.

"Can't. I'm on vacation," she stated, tossing a chunk of concrete off the tower.

"Oh, no. You aren't getting out of this one," Annon insisted.

"Give it to someone else."

"*You* have to do this one," he persisted.

"And why is that?"

"I can't trust anyone else to get it done right," Annon admitted.

"Well, tough shit. I'm on break. Call me back in a week." Nara brushed off her collar dismissively.

"You owe me," the voice suddenly hissed.

"For *what*?" she snapped. "Making you wait an extra millisecond longer to get a chintzy piece of jewelry?"

"I am sending you the details via Chat." Annon cut the channel off.

"God damn it." She glowered at her wrist, furiously typing out a message on the screen.

>>*Annon, what could possibly be SO IMPORTANT that you can't assign it to someone else?*

>>*Christ, calm yourself. It's far too delicate for anyone else I have on deck.*

>>*Well, out with it.*

>>*The military on the Ourbos colony has invested a hefty amount of money to establish a research base here in Under. But they aren't sure they are running along protocol, possibly doing some unorthodox experimentation on the side against the benefit of the colonies.*

>>*And why are they talking to a merc agency? Don't they usually send their own agents to inspect the facilities?*

>>*They don't want the facility to know it is under suspicion. Break in and take a look around, but you are not to be seen, tamper with, or otherwise disturb the facility's functionality.*

>>*What the hell am I supposed to be looking for? 'Unorthodox procedures' is kind of a broad topic.*

>>*They will give you access to minor details on their current research projects. Anything that deviates from this list should be reported to the employer.*

>>*How much?*

>>*Fifty.*

Annon shared a screenshot displaying the authorized offer.

>>*That's not bad. Not great, but not bad. I think you should press for a bit more, given this 'delicate' situation.*

>>*I'll see what I can do. The less you fuck up, the more leverage I have to negotiate additional compensation. I'll send you the details. Now unless you have any more questions that are not insults or complaints, you should probably go and get ready for the assignment.*

>>*Yes, actually, I do. Genuine inquiry— exactly how far is that stick up your ass?*

>>*USER HAS LEFT THE CHANNEL.*

##8.2##

"Ugh. Nothing here either," Nara lamented. She was huddled behind one of the Ourbos station's massive terminals, digging into the file system through her personal interface. The network on this station required limited persuasion to grant her access, so she sifted through the mountain of data from a comfortable remote position in a secluded office.

Her entry into the complex proved to be swift and effortless, thanks to all the personnel and security reports that were handed to her from the Ourbos directorate.

"I can't be much help if I don't know what I'm looking for," Garrett stated, keeping an eye on the surroundings from her apartment.

"Yeah, whatever." She leaned her head against her helmet and scratched an itch with the interior metal. *"Going to have to get a bit aggressive, I suppose. If they want to hide things, they aren't going to label it nicely for everyone to see."*

"Sounds like fun," Garrett commented as he watched the storm of files and menus zip through the screen.

Nara commanded the torrent to a halt as her trails led to a suspect program beneath the primary administrator account. When she initialized the procedure, a separate operating system booted up, functioning independently on an isolated partition of hardware. She traced the path to the executable, unearthing a secured storage bank on a terminal located in the basement level of the building.

I think I've found what I'm looking for, she mused internally. The reports she was given never mentioned a basement level in this facility.

"Hey, someone's headed for this room," Garrett reported.

As she scrolled through a mess of files, she unearthed illogical scrawlings illustrating a high-priority project, all of which referenced another set of files deeper in the hidden system. She poked her digital feelers through the location, uncovering detailed maps of the unsanctioned basement.

According to the map, the basement was rigged with holding cells and surgical stations filled with commercial-grade testing equipment for organic matter. Further scrutiny uncovered volumes of research reports on a neurochemical experiment: a drug designed to maintain a constant consumer base. Not only was it highly addictive, but it also had the capability to prolong and even worsen an illness's symptoms after a delayed period of nonuse.

The notes described each phase of experimentation in gruesome detail. Subjects were kidnapped from the streets and then force-fed dangerous quantities of not only their product in development, but also other common street drugs for comparison. Recordings of the subjects' feral behavior were excruciatingly documented with cold, unfeeling narration.

"Involuntary human experimentation was definitely not on the approved list," she said as she duplicated the files.

"That someone I mentioned is definitely entering this room," Garrett added, averting his gaze from the horrendous video feeds Nara was playing in her helm.

She swiped the open screens away from her view and compacted her body against the wall, concealing herself behind the terminal. On her Hawk's cue, the office door opened behind her, announcing the arrival of a researcher. The man hurriedly stepped inside the office and headed straight for the console she took shelter in, parking himself on the desk chair.

"Three other desks in the room, and you have to pick this one," she grumbled as she ordered her bug to crawl inside the office, granting Garrett the ability to watch the man work.

After ten minutes of uncomfortable waiting, the scientist had engrossed himself with a project, giving no indication when he would be leaving. As Nara quietly eased herself into a slightly less contorted position, she flipped on a program inside her visor.

A colorful spaceship emerged on the screen, darting around her vision as it anticipated an onslaught. Menacing glowing insects appeared from the top of her view, zooming in on the hero. With her commands, the spaceship charged to intercept the invaders.

One by one, the enemies vanished from the display with tiny explosive bursts. The scrolling numbers at the top of her screen increased exponentially as she progressed, as did the squadrons of enemy creatures spawning from every side of the screen.

"I–okay," Garrett reacted to the antics.

"You are not allowed to do the same," she ordered as she decimated several more wings.

"Can I talk then?" he asked.

"No."

He disregarded her orders. "You've had to do this before then, I take it?"

"Yep."

"What was your longest w—"

"Six hours," she quickly butted in.

"Damn! That must've sucked."

"Yep."

The researcher suddenly shifted in his seat, leaning his elbow on the desk and cradling his chin on his fingers in concentration. Upon hearing the movement, Nara swiped the ships away and watched the man attentively.

"Hey, Setton, you got a sec?" the scientist said to an intercom. Silence replied. "Setton, you hear me?"

Nara had crippled the communications channels, setting all devices to redirect messages to a dummy account that led nowhere, causing every piece of broadcast data to be lost in transit.

"Huh. Weird," the researcher said. He was about to try the intercom again when another scientist entered the room.

"Hey, Wayne, have you been getting any of my calls?" the other asked.

"No, I was actually just calling you," Wayne stated.

"I can't seem to get through to Technical to get them to fix the problem either," Setton added.

Wayne pondered as he rubbed his chin. "Odd."

"Yeah, it is. Hey, come over here and let me show you something I found," Setton beckoned, leading Wayne out of the room.

"And that's my cue to leave." Nara slowly stood up, stretching her limbs to regain blood flow.

She crept out into the hallway, ushering her bug companion forward to scout the area ahead. To her dismay, she spied a perplexing addition to security—two soldiers outfitted in sleek armor suiting.

Instead of mimicking the colors of their environment like hers, their suits were painted a dull charcoal grey. Lines of cerulean lights streaked patterns across the limbs of each soldier, tracing around white identification numbers stamped on their shoulders.

"Huh. They weren't mentioned in the personnel files either," Nara observed.

"That's a bad sign, isn't it?" Garrett piped in.

"Not necessarily. They're not moving in alarm," she replied. *"I just have to make sure I don't set them off."*

She backed up and turned around, quietly slipping away to avoid an encounter. But her retreat was abruptly halted as another armor-suited soldier sharply turned the corner at the opposite end of the hall.

"Ah, shit," she muttered.

The soldier snapped forward in reaction to the intruder, tearing a device from their hip and hurling it in her direction. As Nara instinctively ducked away from the projectile, the device coasted harmlessly past, hovering toward its destination in the hallway behind her. A bright crackling blue ball of light manifested in the corridor, emitting four rapid-fire flashes over the white walls, then evaporated into the ether.

"Ah, ***shit,"*** she repeated as she watched the two other soldiers run to the call of the signal beacon.

As they closed in on her, the blue accents on their armor began to slither down their arms, gathering at the palms of their hands. Their fingers glowed blindingly as they flexed each digit in a slow, calculated rhythm, summoning a crackling spell across their bodies as they crept forward.

Nara dashed toward the lone guard in front, slipping between the technomancers before they encircled her. The soldier intercepted her evasion as she slinked away from the attack pattern, striking out with an open palm. She wrenched her shoulder back and dove underneath the oncoming arm, letting only the very tips of their electrified fingers delicately brush against her wrist.

A blue snake of energy lashed out from the soldier's fingertips, splattering shocking tendrils over her arm. Immense pain pulsated through her bones as the energy bypassed her armor, leaving a feeling of a searing metal rod being driven into the entire length of her limb.

Then nothing.

Her arm refused to respond, leaving a void in her shoulder. She could feel the useless limb swing lifelessly against her hip as she stumbled forward. The dead weight disrupted her balance, and she messily slammed her shoulders into a wall as she recovered her footing.

"Fuck," she muttered as the numbness seeped partway into her chest, stifling her breathing. *They don't want to kill. They want to capture.*

She quickly regained her equilibrium and faced the three soldiers sidling toward her. They maintained their smooth, calculated pace as they fanned around her, silently coordinating their attack as they advanced. Her body pulled her down as fatigue began to set in, her deadened lung refusing to inflate.

"You okay?" Garrett blurted in alarm.

"Busy now. Find me an out or shut up," she snapped. *If I run, I will attract more. If I fight, I can kiss the contract goodbye.*

Shit, shit, shit! Garrett thought from his desk, clutching chunks of his hair as he clawed his brain for tactical insight. *What the hell is she doing? Why doesn't she attack them? I have to do something.*

An odd pattern of thought suddenly whipped through his brain as he poked through the facility's networks, uncovering pin-sized holes in his frantic search. The perforations began to widen as he poked and prodded through software. He began to construct bridges over the voids, making his own connections through the system. With his tenacity, he was granted a helm from the obscure reaches of the netway.

He jumped in his seat as Nara suddenly let out a surprised grunt. Her back had hit the wall as the unit cornered her at a dead end.

Just one more second, Garrett assured himself. *Hold on.*

"Dammit," Nara muttered and drew a pistol from under her armor.

She was given only a small demonstration of the soldier's magic, and she assumed their fighting style would not allow her to get close enough to incapacitate. She had no other choice than to use lethal force. The risk of losing more use of her body was too great.

Nara and the soldiers abruptly froze as whirrs and clicks rumbled inside the ceiling. She glanced up at the disturbance to witness an automated turret drop down and assemble itself. Four barrels glistened in the artificial light, rotating in twitchy circles as it calibrated.

I know I locked those . . . out. She hurled a glare back at the soldiers, who exhibited a more confident stance as they resumed their advance.

The turret stole her reaction time as it powered up, the barrels emitting an angry winding hum as they spun wildly in place. Nara flinched as the turret suddenly dipped down, pressing her back against the wall to evade the oncoming barrage.

Three pulses of blazing blue energy spewed from the gun, and in a blink, the guards jerked rigid, collapsing on the floor at her feet. Nara turned to the red-hot machine above her, which dipped in acknowledgement.

"Good one, kid," she praised.

"You look clear from the other side if you want to run for it," Garrett informed.

"Find me the nearest maintenance access," she directed as she bolted for the next hallway.

"Hard right," Garrett announced as another command ejected from his fingertips.

"Nice." She smirked inside her helmet as she watched the wall slide back, revealing a dark corridor. She dove inside the entryway as the metal crept back into place behind her.

Through the pale aqua light of her night vision, Nara collected information on her new surroundings. Material coating the neglected walls was peeling, flaking with corrosion, which was a direct contrast to the sleek spaceship-shiny metal corridors of the main facility. Pipes dripped caustic fluids from above, the valves that controlled them sealed tight by oxidization.

The system of dilapidated tunnels was not meant for living beings to traverse, but the maintenance drone that drifted by didn't seem to mind the intrusion as it headed for a control panel. The peaceful creature flitted its hands in the air until the digits formed the shape of the tool it desired. Sparks flew around its orb-like body as it poked and prodded the console.

"Now, how the hell did you manage that?" Nara inquired, pushing the wave of panic back.

"No idea. It seemed obvious at the time. I have this weird ability to break things in my favor. Could never repeat it, though. Or explain why," Garrett admitted. "How's your arm?"

"I'll live," she said as she rolled her numb shoulder, taking an experimental breath as the invisible fist began to relinquish its grasp from her lungs. *"I think it's time to go home."*

"Agreed," he said, flipping through the map. "There should be an outdoor access point fifty meters from you, as a matter of fact."

Nara navigated the bends and curves of the tunnels until she arrived at the exit. The metal wall was opened for her once again, and she stepped into the night air.

Huh, she thought, *perhaps this relationship can work out after all.*

##8.3##

NARA ROTATED her still-tingling wrist in discomfort as she sat on the edge of her bed, enduring the mind-melting torment of a video conference hosted by Annon. She glared at the man in irritation as he ignored her, his eyes glued to his screen. He had insisted that she be present for the final negotiations of the contract, leaving her stewing in silence as he rudely carried on his digital conversation with the client.

"Are you going to be done soon?" she demanded, massaging the joints in her knuckles.

"I thought you would want to know right away about this one," Annon replied, his eyes never leaving the screen.

"I fucking just got back. I'm tired and I'm in pain. I really don't care how the job went right this minute," she muttered. He disregarded her protests as he typed on the display, narrowing his eyes in concentration. "Oh, for fuck's sake, really? I can't see what's on the screen, you know. And these negotiations take forever, especially when *you* are conducting them."

"It won't take much longer," he insisted.

"I'm hungry, too. I could have finished three meals before you have concluded this business transaction," she moaned. "So just tell me in the morning."

"Well, they haven't complained to me about any noise," Annon said as he sat back, ignoring her irritability. "And they didn't receive any request for assistance from the facility, so we can assume you did a good enough job."

"Fantastic," she sneered. *They certainly didn't need assistance with that unauthorized security. That whole place was rigged to be a trapping ground.*

"Well, you should receive payment soon if they're satisfied with the work," Annon placated.

"Great," she grumbled. "I'm leaving now."

She slammed the channel off and headed for the living room, where Garrett was prodding at the settings for the surveillance.

"Now, as I was saying before I was so rudely interrupted," Nara announced, tossing her armor badge on the table. "I am going to get smashed. Care to join me?"

"I mean sure, but you're sure you aren't sick of me yet?" Garrett confirmed.

"Yeah, I am," she stated matter-of-factly as she slipped on her coat. "But I figured I owe you a beer or two from that incident back there. And I need a change of environment. C'mon."

"Uh, okay." He shrugged, trailing behind as she headed out of the apartment.

The thick night air accompanied them as they walked in silence through what used to be a public park. Centuries ago, the ground was covered with neatly manicured greenery, but now the cracked, barren earth was nearly indistinguishable from the crumbling paved pathways. The scalloped fountain in the center of the land was busted into jagged concrete shards, its basins filled with stagnant water collected from the rain, murky and vile from air contaminants. Twisted craggy forms of what were once trees lined the paths, clawing at the sky in agony.

Garrett let the swirling sounds of the eerie environment trickle across his ears, the fluttering of desiccated foliage mimicking human whispers. But as he watched Nara's gaze shift through the street, he paid closer attention to the sounds echoing in the decay. The trees, in fact, were not speaking. The noise was definitely human voices, escorted by a refrain of gentle footsteps. And they were drawing near.

He looked at Nara for guidance, slipping his hand to the gun at his belt. But she paid him no mind as she fabricated her strategies and contingencies, focusing in on the dead foliage across the street. Violence was coming, and Garrett was unsure whether he would be ready for the fire.

"Well, look what we have here," a voice from the trees scoffed as a vicious looking woman stepped into the road. Jade green wire-like strands were interlaced through her arms, the luminous veins highlighting her heavy musculature. "Red Death has graced me with their presence."

"Who are you, exactly? My memory seems to have a blind spot for small-timers," Nara taunted with a sneer. "Ah, and it sounds like you've brought a few friends with you as well. Two . . . no, three."

"Well, you are a little hard to handle. Besides, the bounty is large enough to feed a small army. I don't think we'll have too many problems." The hunter flashed a vile grin.

"Someone hasn't done their research." Nara looked up at the sky, raising her voice so the hunter's companions could hear. "And I'm surprised they believed you when you told them you would share. I hope they know what they signed up for."

What the hell is going on? Garrett thought, tightening his grip on the handle of his gun. *She mentioned friends. Should I be on the lookout?*

He scanned the scenery and pinpointed another hunter slithering toward them from behind the desiccated grove. The stalker raised a massive three-barreled gun at them, their finger depressing the trigger.

Fuck! There's no time. I have to do something! Garrett panicked, his concern leaving him blind to Nara's rising hand.

Garrett snapped his pistol out and slid behind her back, sticking his arms up to aim at the creeper. He felt the gentlest pressure nudge his palms as he unloaded the weapon, sending a volley of red toward the intruder. The bolts of energy disregarded his target, scorching the bark of the trees with a puff of ash.

As the air cleared from the barrage, the hunter violently recoiled, their throat torn open by Nara's practiced aim. They collapsed to the parched earth with an unsettling gurgle, spilling sustenance over the soil as they drowned in their blood.

But the gunman had also made his mark, on the wrong target.

Garrett belted out a cry of shock as a wave of agony mauled his torso. Three gargantuan holes bled liberally through his clothes, tracing a visceral bandolier across his chest.

Nara felt his pressure as he staggered back, his unexpected actions slapping her defensive calculations out of her brain. She pushed against him to support his body, but his knees buckled under him and he slid to the ground, painting a trail of fluids down her coat.

You fuckwit. She glanced down at the fallen youth. *We're neck-deep in the Fringe, and you pull this heroic shit.*

"End of discussion," Nara snarled at the bounty hunter before her.

She summoned a rapid storm of clicks from inside her sleeves, raising her arms up as metallic segments materialized from under her wrists. Rhomboid shards slid from her coat in uniform sequence, constructing long, glistening blades beneath her palms.

The veiny woman was given little time to retreat as Nara rushed toward her, the blades ravenous for a taste of flesh. In a desperate reaction, the hunter stepped inside the attack and latched onto the demon's arms.She hefted a grunt of pain as the blades hungrily tore into the skin of her shoulders, the light of her strength augments intensifying as she strained to surpass the alien's brute force.

The wrathful demonstration disintegrated the hunter's confident smile from her face. Her damaged enhancements gradually weakened as the blades tore through sinew and wires. Panic saturated the hunter's features as she wriggled to disengage from the demon's grip.

The hunter's two support members decided to make an appearance from behind the trees, aiming weapons at Nara's back. She was aware of their presence. After the blitz on their leader, they made little effort to hide their fearful noises.

With a vile grin scrawled across her lips, Nara wrapped her leg around the hunter's. Using her embedded blades as a pivot point, she torqued the woman around, the poor soul ejecting tormented screams as the metal tore into her artificial neural pathways.

Blood splattered in a veil of mist as a volley of fire chewed through the hunter's back. The barrage abruptly halted when her comrades collected their wits and realized whom they were shooting. With an agonized grunt, the woman slid up the blades until they left her body, synthetic fluids streaming down her lifeless arms as she pushed away from Nara. She attempted to draw her own weapons as she staggered back, but her desensitized fingers twitched in revolt.

The woman managed to take a single step back as Nara stepped in, hurling a fist across her temple with a sickening crack. She let out a quiet moan as she dropped to the street, the light of her augments flickering out as she succumbed to the assault.

Nara leered at the two stunned minions holding out their shaky weapons. She ground her jaw to calm herself only enough to form a tangible sentence.

"You have two choices: run or fight," she challenged, her chest heaving in drunken fury.

The two mercenaries, not as foolish as their boss, took flight nanoseconds after she finished her threat.

"Smart choice." Nara whipped the liquid from her swords before they collapsed back into their sheaths in a faint purple flash.

Circumstance did not permit her to collect herself as Garrett burst into a fit of coughing, spewing liquid onto the concrete. She sank down next to him and turned his body over, propping him up on her knees.

"Can you still hear me?" she called out, extracting several silver pellets from her pocket. He gave out a weak nod in response. "Good. Don't freak out."

He parted blood-encrusted lips in a feeble attempt to ask her intent, but no sound would pass through his mouth. Another violent eruption of coughing seized his body, and he felt Nara turn his head over. Tiny patterings sent pangs over his flesh as she dropped the pills on top of his wounds. With a few tiny clicks, the capsules sprouted legs, and the critters crawled about in circles over his torso as they tested their new freedom.

He gasped and squirmed as they dove in and burrowed into his injuries, forcing Nara to restrain him as the creatures performed their task. After reaching their visceral goal, they burst inside him, creating metallic barriers and sealing off the damaged tissue. But the agony of the procedure was too much for him to handle, and he promptly dropped unconscious in her arms.

Nara permitted herself a miniscule sigh of relief as she re-evaluated her situation.

"All right," she announced to the air. "We're going to hang tight here a little while until I . . . figure . . . out . . ."

She warily craned her head around, staring out at her surroundings as dread seized her nerves. An eerie yet familiar silence pierced through the trees, a warbling vacuum boring into her ears. Then a soft howling pushed its way into the atmosphere, steadily growing in intensity.

"Oh, *fuck*!" she cursed at the seemingly empty street. "Not now!"

She strained to discern the surge, trying to pinpoint the direction of the noise as she hefted Garrett over her shoulders. There was no time to hide amid the grove of gaunt, barren trees. They were coming for her.

Six cloaked figures emerged from the streets behind, silently hovering toward their prey.

##8.4##

"No, no, no, fuck, fuck, FUCK!" Nara launched to her feet and bolted through the decayed trees, adrenaline coursing through her veins in a maddening rhythm.

Her living cargo bogged down her flight, forcing her to expend crucial energy shifting him around as she navigated the mazeway of streets. She had hoped to outlast them, charging through Uncivilized Space until they lost interest. But the cloaked beings were drawn to her, their supernatural forms shifting effortlessly through the ruin. The farther she ran, the closer they were.

They want me this time. Through the frenzy of her panicked thoughts, her sense of navigation dissolved, and Nara found herself face to face with a massive wall of brick stretching to the sky.

Fuck! She redistributed the weight on her shoulders and frantically clawed up the wall.

Against her better judgment, she risked a glance down at the street, meeting eyes with the empty faces of the eerie figures staring up at her. The scene flicked her spine with a chilling jolt, and she commanded her body to push faster, restraining her shaking limbs as she scaled up the wall.

Her ascent halted mid-stride as an unknown force shoved her into the wall, her forehead slamming into the brick. A startled roar expelled from her throat as the force manifested into searing waves of agony across her chest. Pangs tore through her neck as she glanced at her shoulder, alarm sparking her nerves as a metal gauntleted hand clawed furrows deep into her flesh. Blood leached from the wound as the grip tightened, burrowing down into her clavicle.

The ghastly hand was affixed to a wire mesh rope sprouting from the arm of one of the hooded figures. As she pried at the menacing weapon invading her bones, the specter snapped its arm back, sending a shrieking whir across the alley as the rope obediently retracted.

Gravity snatched her balance as she clawed at the concrete mortar, pulling her away from the wall as she struggled to retain her grip. Her arm lashed out painful shrieks of reprieve through her brain as the frigid metal gauntlet shredded muscle, winding its fingers around the bone underneath. The escalating torment pierced through her screaming nerves, forcing her to release her tenuous hold of the wall.

With her functional arm, she pulled the unconscious Garrett on top of her, bracing herself as she plunged to the ground. The air burst from her lungs as she crashed into the jagged concrete, and a sickening crunch echoed in reply as she felt a chitinous plate on her back crack.

The metallic rope coiled itself around her neck, panic forcing her to release the body as she tore her nails at the constricting restraint. She ferociously thrashed and contorted as the mechanical snake slithered around her, enveloping her inside a synthetic sinewy carapace. Her muscles screamed with thorny reprimand as she fought against the cocoon scraping over her brutalized flesh.

Her struggle was violently cut short as blue vines of lightning coursed through her nerves, sending her convulsing inside the entanglement to the tempo of the relentless flickering tendrils. With a final excruciating bellow, she ceased her defiance, her battered body dropping limp inside the suffocating carapace. Upon her submission, she felt herself slide across the pavement toward the feet of her captors.

So this is how I die, she thought bitterly through the swell inside her skull.

Having subdued the instigator, two of the figures broke formation and glided over to Garrett's body. Their ragged cloaks fluttered as they stood motionless for what seemed like an eternity, scrutinizing the fallen human with apathetic interest. Beams of white light projected from their hoods, delicately sweeping over the scene in labored passes. After an apprehensive eon, the specters slithered back, regarding each other in subliminal conversation.

The wraith that manipulated her leash elevated her from the

ground, dangling her inches off the pavement like a piece of cured meat. She clamped down on her lip as the force shifted her weight onto her wounds, the pain tearing through her thoughts.

Anger welled up inside her mind and the edges of her vision ignited with a spectral fire. Quivering tongues danced across her eyes as they radiated over the smoldering street lights. An anomalous burst of energy coursed through her limbs, the strength to fight charging her spirits as she strained against the metal shell, wrenching her torso around inside the coil.

Another lashing of electricity crackled from the snake, forcing her still as it exploded inside her brain. The coils tightened as the surge drained her deviant second wind, inducing a tempestuous spell of coughs as it squeezed her bruised lungs.

One of the figures ahead glided back to Nara, bringing its featureless form inches away from her face. Even though the specter appeared mechanical, she sensed a diminutive trace of life from within the robes, but its origin was elusive to her perception.

A beam of light snapped out from the void inside the hood, causing her to flinch as the ray assaulted her eyes. The beacon laboriously swept over her features, analyzing every crack and dimple that embellished her face. Her chest accelerated to a frantic tempo as the metal snake bit her cheek with a tiny shock, sending a chilling liquid sensation crawling over her skin. An unearthly force paralyzed her as the scanner passed over her eyes, the beam saturating her vision with the blinding flare as she helplessly stared at the wraith.

With a barely audible electronic plitter, the light shifted to a vibrant emerald green, then vanished from the air. The creature lowered its head, backing away from Nara after it extracted the indiscernible answers it desired.

The fuck? Nara thought. The chill dispersed from her flesh, and she furiously blinked the glaring spots away from her vision.

The figure across from her bowed and draped a sleeve over Garrett's head. Flickers of white light wove across the human's body, evoking a moan of relief. A wave of panic washed over Nara as she witnessed the enigmatic ritual, but weariness clouded her functionality, her nerves refusing to speak to her brain.

A metallic shriek drilled through the air as her captor brusquely uncoiled the bindings encasing her, unceremoniously dropping her to the pavement with a wheezing thud. The claw relinquished its grasp of her shoulder, tearing out a spiteful chunk of flesh as it receded back into its master's cloak. In a blink, the robed figures withdrew, vanishing into the streets, leaving her a trembling pool of sweat and blood.

She forced herself to sit up, shakily bringing a foot around to support herself. Her rebellious ankles seized up as she tried to stand, the throbbing cracks in her plating screaming in agreement as she pitched toward the ground. Her brutalized shoulder seeped fluids down the front of her chest, and she could see bone shining brightly through the grievous furrows hollowed out of her flesh.

I can make it back, she thought. *I have to make it back.*

Thoughts racing everywhere and nowhere clouded her mind, the pain tearing through her cognition. Her strength diminished as she teetered over, violently weaving side to side as she struggled to keep herself upright. Conceding to her body's demands, she raised her NetCom to her face with a trembling arm.

"Serr'Maht," she gasped, her native voice slipping over her tongue. *"I'm in trouble."*

"Where are you? What happened?" Sentinel questioned, concern overriding his calm demeanor.

"I saw—" Her body refused to let her continue as she collapsed onto the pavement.

"Nara!" The voice boomed from her wrist. "Hark! Get a squad over to Pyral Street in the Gorge! Now!"

##8.5##

StayAwakeStayAwakeStayAwake

Footsteps approaching.

"Well, what have we here?" *Voices, faint, yet near. Laughing.* ***Disgusting.***

Fire blurred her vision. Shadowy figures fluttered into view.

"Looks like someone left us a meal ticket."

...Protect...

She felt herself rising. She heard her bones crack as they shifted, settling back into place.

"Whoa, big guy, why don't you make this easy on yourself?"

...Protect...
...Destroy...
...Tear...
...Burn...

Screams. The shadows dissolved.

New figures emerged. Calm, slowly approaching.

...Asylum...

The fire receded. Darkness again.

CHAPTER 9

##9.0##

A howling mist churned through the streets, masticating the faces of the buildings with its corrosive maw. The walls groaned as the structures dissolved. Jagged bricks and chunks of foundation soared into billowing fog, nourishing the swirling storm with a whirlwind of ammunition.

She darted through the maze, watching the buildings morph and curl, their forms stretching out to conceal the sky. Her path twisted into erratic turns, and she felt her flight slacken as the road channeled her through an uncertain destination. The noise bored through her ears as the world continued its perverse evolution, the coiling metal monoliths transmuting into flagellating trees.

Bright light pierced the horizon as a glade appeared in front of her, promising a place of safety. But as she approached, the ash cloud consumed the haven, unleashing a wall of hooded figures to intercept her flight. Behind her, the smog vomited a squadron of apparitions, trapping her between the two unbroken lines of wraiths.

She stopped herself in the center of the trap, watching as the line of eerie soldiers curled around, boxing her inside the forest clearing. A metallic zipping noise ripped the droning atmosphere as a specter unleashed its attack, its claw biting into her flesh. The coterie chimed in with a chorus of systematic whirs as each robed figure consecutively released their talons, ensnaring her body within a spiderweb of snakes.

Pain forced her voice out in shrill bellows as her blood cascaded over each cold, unfeeling hand latched on to her body. The hands burrowed deeper into her flesh as she strained against their voracious hold, her life steadily draining into the earth below. Through her anguish, she stared down each of the empty hooded figures, demanding answers to their reasoning.

Ignoring her venomous ravings, the saturnine beings wordlessly retracted their weapons, tearing out muscle as each malevolent instrument withdrew. She screamed as the sound of her rending flesh echoed inside the barricade of figures, drowning out the cacophony of metallic shrieks from the spectral weaponry. Her eyes beheld the bones of her pitiful skeleton shining back at her, shreds of tissue clinging desperately to her form.

Only one claw remained.

As the creatures sequentially vanished, the last figure lashed its hand back, dragging her to her knees. She eagerly awaited the final strike and the feel of Death's comfort at last. But the creature hesitated, gliding over to her paralyzed form.

She struggled to meet eyes with the figure standing before her. Blackness crawled over her vision as it drew back his hood, revealing a familiar face. Her mind tore her out of reality, disrupting the figure's features as the void claimed her.

##9.1##

A FOGGY HAZE TOYED with her senses as Nara stirred, her eyes unable to process the shadowy creature leaning over her. Lacking mental clarity, her instincts seized control, launching a fist at the intruder. Pressure caressed her knuckles as she planted them against the creature's ribcage.

"Jesus, Nara," the voice of Declan wheezed as he recoiled from the assault. "Watch it!"

"Sorry," she muttered half-earnestly as she forced herself up.

"You're a fucking mess," he panted, supporting himself on the rails of the bed as he clutched his chest.

"I'm fine," she snapped. She scoured her teeth with her tongue, discarding an awful bitterness from her mouth—the metallic, chalky essence characteristic of human blood.

That's not good, she thought uncomfortably. *I don't remember biting anyone last night.*

"Like hell you are. I'm going to check over you and get you cleaned up," the medic chastised as he began to remove a bloodied bandage from her shoulder. "Then you need to get back to sleep."

"I said, I'M. *FINE,*" she snarled as she bashed his hand away. Declan hurled a venomous glare, grinding his teeth at the combative patient.

"You will go down or I will put you down," he fiercely rebuked, clearly having had enough of her obstinacy. "Your recklessness has gotten you—"

Nara snatched him by the collar and pulled him close, flaunting her shining fangs through her open, scowling lips.

"You will leave me in peace or so help me, I will destroy your world and everything around it," her native voice boomed across his ears. *"And when you have witnessed the raging flames, I will tear you limb from limb until the echoes of your screams haunt your loved ones in the afterlife."*

Declan hid the startlement from his eyes, standing unshakably calm within her grasp as he maintained his disapproving composure. It would be a cold day in the deepest level of Hell before he would back down to one of Nara's challenges.

But Sentinel sensed the distress from the hall, and he stepped into the medical ward to intervene before blood was drawn.

"Declan!" Sentinel barked. "Leave her alone."

"All right," The medic conceded, slightly relieved to take the order. "I'll just give you something to calm you down a bit then."

Declan slapped a drug dispensing device onto Nara's wrist, pulling his shirt away as she loosened her grip of him. He walked over to Sentinel, adjusting the tousled fabric indignantly.

"I have no idea what she just said to me, but I think I don't like it," Declan admitted.

"Trust me, my friend, it was not very nice," Sentinel replied with a pat on the shoulder. "Now go take a walk. It's been a stressful night for all of us."

"Yeah." Declan shook his head and left the room, heading off to mend his ribcage.

Sentinel hesitated as he approached, a frown wrinkling his face as he watched Nara stare off into space with a disquieting expression, cradling her head in her hands.

"Are you all right?" he gently prodded.

"I'll be fine," Nara murmured, barely acknowledging him.

"Do you want to talk about it?" he offered.

"I . . ." she forced out a heavy draught of air. "I honestly don't know what happened."

The images from her dream haunted her, the events of the encounter twisting its intent. She was beyond exhausted with her subconscious playing games with her, but she was just as afraid to take a rest.

"It's all right," Sentinel assured. "Take your time. It's over now."

She abruptly changed the subject. "How's the kid?"

"In much better condition than you, I must say," he said. Nara let out a grunt of agreement.

"It started off as a group of hunters," she found herself narrating, shaking her head in defeat. "And that clueless human decided to play heroics on me."

"I see." Sentinel leaned against the wall next to her, listening intently to her words. He waited patiently as she processed the events in her mind, letting her pause in the safe surroundings of his haven.

"We were deep in the Fringe. Enforcers smelled the fight and went to investigate. After that, it's kind of a blur. I have no idea why they let us go." She rubbed her face vigorously. "Did something weird to the kid too."

"Yes, he hasn't stopped smiling since he arrived. It's kind of disturbing the boys," Sentinel reported. Nara raised a questioning eyebrow at the remark. "Declan says he'll be fine. And you're safe now. That's all that matters. You should try and get some sleep."

Nara shook her head firmly. "I'd prefer to stay awake."

"Is there something wrong?"

"I . . . can't sleep. That's all," she evaded, trying not to relive the grisly visuals vexing her mind.

Sentinel nodded in understanding. "Just make sure you take care of yourself. I know that's a tall order for you, but please give yourself permission to relax, at least for a little while."

"Thank you. I will try." She let out a pained sigh as she eased back into the pillow.

"I will leave you now. Shout if you need anything," the kind man offered.

"Alcohol. And lots of it." Nara pointed at the air.

"That's not a healthy way to treat your insomnia," Sentinel gently cautioned.

"I know," she acknowledged as a disappointed frown creased her face.

"I'll see what we have in stores." He smiled as he turned away.

Nara appreciated Sentinel's unflappable patience. Through all of his influence, the vastness of his empire, he somehow managed to find time to talk to her on a personal level. She often felt the need to divulge every detail of her woes, every concern, to his compassionate ears, despite her jumbled emotional cargo stopping her from constructing a cohesive thought.

But tonight had torn a deep scar in her mind, and she needed to voice her illogical ramblings to someone who had the potential to comprehend.

"I have been at war for nearly a century," she confided to the man, switching to her native voice. *"I have cut down waves of scoundrels and singlehandedly decimated armies, facing Death without a blink. Every waking moment, I had always begged for their arrival, for them to finally claim me from my miserable existence. But this was the first time I hesitated, and that disturbs me."*

"Fear meets all of us eventually." Sentinel wisely nodded. *"Everyone's breaking point is different, but they have them all the same."*

"It is an unsettling experience, I will admit." Her eyes softened upon the relief of the narration. *"Thank you, Serr'Maht. For everything."*

He regarded her warmly. *"You know it was nothing. I'm just glad you called."*

"The kid's all right, you know?" she declared, a smirk crawling up a corner of her mouth as her burned-out mind derailed. "Bit dense, but everyone has flaws."

"I think so too," Sentinel affirmed with a smile as he exited the room.

Declan intercepted him in the hallway, concern painted over the man's face as he processed their conversation.

"Are you going to tell her about how she was found?" he questioned Sentinel, his severe tone radiating across the walls. "Covered in blood, injuries everywhere, yet somehow still standing upright."

The warlord raised a hand up. "Not right now."

"She had a guy's throat in her mouth. While he was choking out on the ground," Declan pressed. "The shift in her eyes, the horrid noise echoing for miles. I've told you before, that's not Nara."

"She doesn't need to know," Sentinel affirmed, shooting him a stern glare.

"That's extremely concerning, especially considering her background. That could be the start of a psychological develop—" His objection was cut off by a firm grip on his shoulder.

"And if *you* tell her, I will be forced to do something I will regret," Sentinel warned, his eyes shifting to ice. "And you know I am a man of my word."

##9.2##

GARRETT AWOKE to the familiar surroundings of Nara's apartment. The fantastical vivid imagery his psyche graced upon him burst from his memory as he peeled open his eyes. Ache swirled across his body, but he felt bizarrely relaxed, as if he was run over by a steamroller made of pillows and opiates.

"So, it appears I will be stuck with you for a little while," a voice lamented.

Nara stared at him from across the room, slouched in a chair with her arms folded. Her eyes cast a dimmed glow of exhaustion, and her messy braid stabbed the air in disorderly tufts. A wide patch of black gauze poked out in raised wrinkles underneath the fabric of her shirt, the binding enveloping the span of her chest.

"I hope you don't have any future plans in Upper," she continued. "Because you aren't exactly in presentable condition to be parading around home."

Garrett groaned as he sat up experimentally, heaving a whimper as the gnashing pain hurled him back against the cushions. The effort drained his energy, sending controlled pangs across his skin as he panted for breath. He desperately strained to recall the last events before he'd passed out, but his memory was reduced to an oozy garbled blur.

At least she was able to make it back okay, he thought.

"How long was I out?" he asked, gingerly stretching out his arms. He snapped them back over his shoulders as his chest scorned him with agony.

"Couple of days? A week? Hell, I don't know myself," she said indolently. "The major holes should be sealed up by now, and all that's left is for the flesh to heal over."

"Okay." He nodded, gritting his teeth.

Looking over to the table, he scanned through a massive hoard of empty bottles stacked in disorganized castles. The haphazard structures spanned over the apartment, a miniaturized feudal colony of intemperance. He had never seen what her idea of a bender entailed, but the amount on the table alone was enough to kill at least three hearty humans. While she was always drinking in front of him, it was always a casual descent into inebriation. Steady, but casual.

"You okay?" he asked with a frown of concern.

"I'm fine," she said, avoiding his face. "Things just got a bit . . . complicated, that's all."

"Oh?"

"I'd rather not talk about it right now." She was still deliberating on whether to disclose the encounter to him, but she was still coming to terms with it herself, wondering if it was just another horrendous dream.

"Okay." Garrett suppressed a shrug as he dropped the subject. But the concern was gnawing at him, and he tore through the goo-smeared images glopping inside his skull. "At least now, we can get to know each other better."

"Riveting. That is exactly what I would like to do." She waved an arm over her head. *Even injured, he's still a fuckhead.*

"I mean I—" He stopped as his head heaved him through a torrent, his thoughts sloughing in murky fragments, refusing to pass his throat. The lights of the apartment, as dim as they were, started to sear his vision as his body demanded reprieve. "What was I . . .?"

"Here, drink this." She walked over and handed him a bottle of sickly green liquid.

"This is going to sound weird," he started, taking the offering in his feeble hands. "But could you tell me a story?"

"I—what?" She scrunched her face. "The drugs Declan gave you must still be working."

"I don't have the ability to carry the conversation," he divulged as he fiddled with the bottle. "And I just can't deal with the silence right now."

He drained the concoction, pleasantly surprised by an odd fruity flavor. A bitter, earthy undertone lurked heavily in the aftertaste, sending a prickly cool sensation down his neck. It wasn't the most unpleasant experience he had ever endured, but it could have been gratitude for his continued existence speaking on his behalf.

"The hell do you want me to say?" Nara irritably rubbed the inebriated fog from her mind. "I'm not an interesting wealth of tales."

"I don't know. Your favorite legend? Fairytale?" Garrett wiped the elixir from his mouth. "What are your gods like? Just fill the air. Please."

"Not sure what you expect. Organized religion isn't really a thing.

Not anymore." She shrugged. "What gods they did have were reduced to concepts. Moral codes for some."

"And they are?" He turned his expectant gaze to her.

"Ugh. Really, kid?"

"Please." His face twitched in discomfort, his mind threatening to disconnect from his body. "I can't process right now. I feel . . . off."

"Fine." Nara let out a disheartened sigh, slumping back into her seat at the table. "The first is known as *Xannat,* and they are the concept of fate. They represent everything that cannot be controlled in nature."

"Interesting." He sank into the lounge, absorbing every syllable.

"There are people who are more superstitious than others, and they believe that *Xannat* can be influenced through their actions," she continued, "giving them a sort of karmic characteristic."

"That's a theme I've read about frequently," he observed, fixing his gaze on the ceiling.

"The second concept is *Ötmarr,* and they focus on the individual," she said, scratching a nail across the surface of the table. "They encompass personal judgment, the overarching struggle between following and breaking rules to cause the least amount of collateral damage. Harm none, but don't ignore harm."

"I can see how those two ideals conflict." He let his eyes droop as her voice saturated his brain, grounding him in the dismal room.

"Funny you should say that. When they were deified, their stories were nothing but battles between each other. Horrific and grueling struggles spanning eons." A sigh wisped from her lips as the absurdity of their plight weighed over her own struggles. "But they all end the same way. *Ötmarr* always loses."

"That's really demoralizing," Garrett commented.

"I didn't make it up." Nara shrugged. "Many of the tales are illustrated on the walls of the archive buildings. Murals and reliefs are everywhere, some sort of morbid reminder or some shit, I don't know."

"The archives." His eyes glittered in delight. "What are they like?"

"A network of data and books," she said, trying to quantify the infrastructure in digestible parts. "The capital houses everything recorded since the beginning of written history, plus anything acquired from other races they trade with."

"Oh, my gods," Garrett breathed. "That's sounds . . . *beautiful*."

"There are other libraries with copies of everything scattered about the planet, some known to the public, others kept in secret by the *Loremaster*, who oversees it all," she continued. "In case shit gets fucked. They spent a LOT of time making copies of everything, both in new and old tech."

Garrett could not contain the grin that radiated from his face. A meticulously maintained library guarding information all the way back to the start of history, a concept straight from his wildest dreams. Books about daily life, science, mathematics, and technology. The possibility left him with a rush of spirits. As his imagination soared, he turned over on his side and let out a wistful sigh, longing to gaze upon the limitless expanse of tomes.

"The hell is your problem?" Nara met his gaze and scrunched her face in displeasure.

"Nothing. It's just . . ." He tried in vain to wipe the cheeky smile from his face. "I must say that for a hardened soldier, you are extremely erudite."

"Shut the fuck up," she snapped.

Garrett watched her sink into thought, her eyes burning holes in the table as she plunged into a depressive mental whirlpool. Like clockwork, she threw back her head and drained her bottle of liquor, just to open another and repeat the process. The self-destructive descent made him uncomfortable, a reflection of his own unhealthy escapes.

"What do you miss about your home planet?" He finally broke the silence, his inquiry invoking a snort of disgust. "If anything."

Nara gazed through the barred window, watching the comforting glow of the streetlamps diffuse through the foggy night. She regretted encouraging the conversation, and she dreaded what he would remember the next day.

"The foliage," she quietly disclosed, her eyes focused on the street. "The trees, the leaves. Something that is real, far from this playground of metal and concrete. The air stinks of rot and misery. There is no life here, only processed filth."

"How did you end up in this shithole? Seriously," Garrett asked of her with somber eyes. "It couldn't have been by choice."

She looked at him sullenly, rotating her bottle on the tabletop like a prayer wheel. The soft scraping noise filled the air in a mesmerizing rhythm as she considered his motivation. Her sources told her that he was trustworthy, and his actions, while unintentionally destructive, projected an altruistic character. But there was something stirring in the back of her head, a battered red flag that violently swayed in the winds of her thoughts.

"Tell you what. I will make a deal with you." She paused with a hefty draught of her drink. "If you can successfully catch me off guard, then I will know you have the ability to listen."

Garrett considered the offer, her voice dragging a grave burden. The swirl of chemicals running over his mind fractured his thoughts, and he hoped he had not said anything to cause harm. He scolded himself for pressing the issue, wishing for sobriety and less pain.

"It will be something I will need to practice. I am not sure where to begin," he admitted. "But I accept the challenge."

"Hmm." Nara didn't know how to take his response, and she dreaded the obligation should he succeed. Reliving the painful memories for the sake of his irritating curiosity made her skin itch, but something about the severity of his inquisition made her feel strange, like he was someone she could almost rely on. He had attempted to save her life twice in the past week, even though the most recent chain of events had left her worse for wear.

Garrett disrupted her pensive deliberation with an inebriated smile, the grin coming off more sinister than he had intended.

"What?" she snapped in annoyance.

"Nothing. It's just nice talking," he whispered, his eyelids too heavy for him to prop up. "You always have this rough abrasive front to hold up. But once you get talking, you speak like an intellectual. Like someone who has actually read a book."

"Yeah, whatever, kid." She shook her head, relieved to change topics.

"Hey, how come . . ." he started, voice trailing as the weight of each word grew cumbersome over his tongue.

"Kid."

"Yeah?" He raised his eyebrows, but the eyelids remained glued shut.

"Go the fuck to sleep."

"Okay." He had already obeyed the order.

##9.3##

NARA WASN'T in the apartment when Garrett finally woke up, and neither was the fortress of empty bottles. Even though soreness mauled his muscles, he was feeling restless, and the need to get up and walk around forced his action. He rolled over on his side, waiting for his body to protest as he gingerly placed his feet on the floor. Gathering his mettle, he slowly pulled himself up and stretched his limbs, wincing as his injuries grumbled inside his chest.

The silent ambiance made him jittery, and he searched for a means to occupy himself while she was gone. He eyed the computer sitting in the corner of the room and set out to adjust the settings on the camera for Nara's next assignment. She would probably tear his face off for not staying put, but the throbbing ache in his bones convinced him to carry on.

A voracious stiffness gripped at his flesh as he brought himself to stand, sending him pitching toward the ground. He slapped a hand at the arm of the couch to brace himself, collecting his balance as his senses whirled through his brain. Through the mild disorientation, he felt surprisingly functional, and he risked an advancing step away from the safety of the chair.

The glint of a shiny gun cabinet caught his eye as he crossed the room with improving coordination, and a devious giggle burst from his nose.

Aw, hell, I'm already in trouble, he thought. *Might as well go all the way.*

Keeping his eyes fixed on the front door, he slid open the top drawer of the cabinet. The lush, gooey fabric inside tempted his digits with a promise of sensory delight. He pressed a finger on the surface, grinning madly as it yielded with the pressure. His finger sank deeper, the strange gel-like material enveloping his knuckles with a cool therapeutic sensation. He fluttered his fingers inside the lining, molding patterns around the malleable putty trapped beneath the cloth.

Well, that was satisfying, he thought, the material oozing back to its default state as he rolled the drawer shut. *I'd better stop fucking around before I get caught.*

He rubbed the crud out of his eyes as he settled in the computer chair, stirring the machine to life with the flick of a wrist. The icon labeled *Books* tempted him on the screen, a glittering file of mysterious knowledge. He recalled Nara's tale of the archives on her planet, and the thought of getting a sample of what they concealed tempted him with tenacious prods. He knew she would gut him for invading her space, but his curiosity overwhelmed him as he opened the storage folder.

A menu answered his summons, spewing a list of words over the display, words in languages he couldn't comprehend. He swiped his finger across the screen, scrolling through filenames until he reached a list of antiquated human titles, finding mostly historical pieces about galactic politics and battle charts, both planetary and interstellar. Ancient classical works passed over his fingers, most prominently *The Art of War* by Sun Tzu and Machiavelli's *The Prince.*

Another folder obediently revealed its contents, exhibiting an array of combat manuals from a plethora of disciplines. Training texts of long-dead melee weaponry were collected here, categorized by era and completeness of the document. War diaries and strategy notes from major generals in history of both winning and losing sides were included in this section as well.

"Wow," he breathed as he sifted through the mass of knowledge. *No wonder she sounds so educated. It's all obsessively sorted by era and location.*

He migrated back to the origin path, deviating toward a peculiar unlabeled folder isolated from the rest. Upon opening the structure, he was presented with a complete collection of cookbooks from a famous chef in Upper.

That's oddly uncharacteristic, he mused.

A chill ran up his spine as an inexplicable sense of doom tore his face from the screen. He jumped from his seat as Nara entered the apartment, sending his heart fleeing from his body. A sinking sensation swelled in his aching chest upon meeting her eyes, as if the hand of Death had reached into his soul and given it an impish pinch.

She eyed him suspiciously. "The hell are you doing over there?"

"I uh, well," he sputtered. "I figured I would recalibrate the cameras for next time."

"Uh-huh." She leaned over to the console screen. "You were all over my books. Why?"

"I . . . was bored," he sheepishly admitted.

"Ugh, whatever." Nara scowled, tossing a device on the desk. "I have something for you. I was getting checked out by Declan and made a detour on the way back."

Garrett examined the gift curiously. "A neural link?"

The earpiece was an experimental form of covert communications used in the Underground. It channeled thought to another recipient wearing a second device, performing similarly to wireless data signals. Some devices, if not calibrated properly, were known to spout off thoughts that were never intended to be received by the sender, thus a considerable amount of reliance and discretion between two users was essential.

Corporations had briefly worked on the development of a link that could allow multiple users on one frequency, but most experiments had led to unfavorable results. Test subjects had been recorded experiencing irreparable side effects, including identity distortion and memory erasure, and the individuals in question were transferred to permanent assisted care. There had also been recorded anomalies where images and video, often of a gruesome nature, had been implanted into subjects from an unknown influence, shattering the sanity of the users.

"Yeah. I figured that incident in the Gorge could have been

avoided if we'd had some form of communication," Nara said as she flopped down on the couch.

"I . . . thank you," he whispered, dumbfounded by the new level of trust she'd bestowed on him.

"Yeah, sure." She ran a dismissive hand through her hair.

"How's your injuries?" he inquired as he poked at the settings on the device.

"I'll manage." Nara shrugged. "And you?"

"Nothing I can't deal with," he said with an uneasy laugh.

"Let me take a look," she said as she walked over to him.

Garrett timidly complied with the request, removing his shirt with cautious, measured movements. He winced when Nara knelt in front of him, stifling a whimper as she slowly peeled off the bandages, the tacked surface abrading his skin with tiny stings. Cool air trickled over his fresh flesh, tracing over three sickly yellow and red patches, each blemish surrounded by a purple nebula of bruised skin.

"That hurt?" Nara asked as she gently brushed her fingers over one of the wounds.

"Not too much," he lied through gritted teeth.

"Uh-huh." She smirked as she moved around to his back. "You should be okay to go back Upworld, provided you don't do anything too exciting."

"All right." He scrunched his eyes tight, trying not to flinch at the pressure of her examination.

Nara traced a finger across the speckled galaxy of bruises spanning the width of his shoulders. With an admonishing shake of her head, she stood up and walked to the kitchen, grabbing a jar of salve from her stores.

She handed him the open jar. "Here, put that on the wounds. I'll get your back."

The vessel popped out of his grasp as her lightest touch sent twinges of pain through his muscles. He clenched his breath to stifle a cry, grinding his molars to endure the assault. In a delicate choreography of anguish, he warily leaned over to pick up the fallen jar from the floor, bracing himself as he scraped a dollop of the grease into his hands.

The self-inflicted agony drilled through him as he wiped the medicine over his chest, the barely scabbed over wounds throbbing with the softest touch. He tried to push through the pain until a sudden wave of dizziness swirled through his head and he braced himself against the arm of his chair.

God damn, he groaned. *How the fuck does she manage to maintain her composure? Her shoulder's completely mangled, but she's acting like it's just a hangnail.*

"You all right?" Nara asked, removing her hand.

"Yeah." He cringed, trying in vain to preserve his departed dignity.

"That should toughen up by tomorrow," she claimed with a smirk. "You can scream if you need to."

"Won't be necessary," he assured as he continued to paint the herbal grease over his wounds.

"Suit yourself."

The jar bolted out of Garrett's hand again as his NetCom blared from the end table.

"Shit!" he exclaimed as he scrambled to pick it up, a horrified expression emblazoned over his face.

Castigating pain caught up with him, sending him crashing into the couch, panting from the exertion. In a feeble attempt to compose himself, he took several deep breaths before scrolling through his messages, ignoring Nara's amused grin from across the room.

>> *136 unread messages from: Baran, Chief Security Officer, G Estate:*

>> *Where the hell have you been?!?!*

Garrett could hear Baran's voice boom through the text.

>>*I was tracking a piece through the markets.*

>>*Not convincing. Your father has been demanding your presence. Get back up here. Now.*

>>*I'll be there later this evening.*

>>*You better.*

>>*USER HAS LEFT THE CHANNEL*

"Fuck," Garrett breathed, running a shaky hand through his hair.

"In deep shit?" Nara inquired.

"Yeah." He groaned as he flopped over on his back. "Any chance you have some painkiller you could spare? It would be easier to hide this mess if I wasn't flinching every three seconds."

"Yeah, here." She tossed him a tiny vial of black liquid. "That is some serious shit. Only drink half of it at a time, else you aren't going to have to worry about your future anymore."

"Tempting, really." Garrett let out a disgruntled sigh. "I guess I need to leave."

"Guess so."

"Hey . . ." he began, casting her a serious look.

"What is it now?" she moaned as she shrugged on her coat.

"Thanks. For everything."

Yeah, he's all right. Nara grunted in acknowledgment. "Let's go."

CHAPTER 10

##10.0##

Baran was waiting in Garrett's room, seated on the edge of his bed with a look of rancor etched into his features.

"Where the *hell* have you been?" the guardian demanded.

"I was out. I couldn't have any form of audio disturbances," Garrett explained, keeping his gaze to the floor.

"Don't evade me." Baran glowered. "Have you any idea what your father has put me through?"

"I'm sorry," Garrett murmured.

"Explain yourself." The man's seething expression burned a hole into his soul.

Garrett tried to slip toward the closet, but Baran bolted up to intercept him, raising a hand to his chest. Pain surged through his body with barbed lashings as he slammed into the man, his eyes welling up with tears as he sank to the ground, clutching his throbbing muscles.

"God *DAMN* it!" Garrett's voice ejected from his throat.

Baran recoiled with horror as he witnessed the reaction of the panting youth, snapping his hand back. He watched Garrett slowly compose himself, looking up at him in desperation. Paranoia flowed through his veins as the severity of the situation shadowed his nerves.

"Remove your shirt," Baran ordered.

"I'm fine, really," Garrett breathed, standing up on shaking legs.

"Do. Not. *Test* me." His eye twitched violently as he uttered the warning.

Garrett was fearful of the man's hostility, sending his body trembling as he complied. He slipped off the garment and revealed the sickly, grotesque remnants of his injuries.

Baran stared at him aghast, circling him in agitated steps as he soaked in the severity of the damage. Words refused to form inside his throat as he turned his back to Garrett. In a traumatized daze, the man walked to the wall, leaning his head against his wrist.

"I . . . don't know what to say," Baran quietly admitted.

"I'm fine, honest," Garrett responded, almost pleading.

"What in nine hells happened down there?" the guardian managed, his gaze never leaving the wall.

"Bar fight," he lied, clearing his throat to project a more convincing tone.

"Bar fight?" Baran echoed in distress.

"Yes. I was caught in crossfire. My friend bailed me out and patched me up," he explained, trying to calm the exasperated man. "I'm fine. Honestly. Please."

After a few unnerving seconds of silence, Baran mustered an emphatic sigh, which Garrett couldn't interpret between relief or vexation.

"Your . . . father. He wants to speak with you when you have cleaned up," Baran managed to speak. "I . . . I don't even . . ."

"I'm sorry," Garrett apologized again, but Baran only shook his head.

Garrett cursed his lack of cautious foresight. His reckless initiative turned out to be one of the most selfish stunts he had ever acted upon. He nearly got Nara killed, and Antonin must have severely chewed Baran out, threatening his job again.

"I told him you were out with friends. Nothing more," Baran murmured remorsefully.

"Understood."

Garrett popped the cork off the bottle Nara had given him and downed half of the contents, the taste stabbing him with nettles as it trickled down his throat. He managed to choke it down as he slipped the bottle back into his pocket. He then donned more appropriate attire, avoiding eye contact with Baran, still silent against the wall.

"Words cannot describe how sorry—" Garrett began, but Baran raised a hand at him.

"Just . . . hide it. Swallow your tongue if you have to. Hide it," he implored.

"I will. I promise."

"I have somewhere I need to go," the guardian announced. "I'd say remain here until I come back, but I don't expect much from you."

"I will st—" Garrett began, but Baran had already left him to reflect on his actions.

Guilt overwhelmed him as he ambled to the common room, sending his thoughts racing. He brushed off his clothing in agitation as he summoned the elevator to the office level, waiting impatiently for his judgment.

Why do I keep doing this? he thought morosely as he stepped inside the chamber. The Underground was a place of escape from his miserable reality, but his privilege to leap between worlds at will made him feel selfish for enjoying himself. He didn't want the opulence of Upper life, but he wasn't sure if he could commit to living in the warzone of the opposing world.

He was lonely. That was the extent of his plight. Apart from Baran, he had nothing in common with the people of Upper. People didn't make friends here. They made contacts, business alliances, and treaties. It was a tiresome game of war that he wanted no part in.

Then he met Nara, and for the first time, he felt a connection. She was someone he could be himself around, and while she may be irritated with his antics, he didn't feel the need to mask himself to have a simple conversation. He didn't know much about her, and the thought of giving up hanging out with her filled him with despair.

But he also could not ignore how much of a potential danger he was. Even if she wasn't risking her life to save his sorry ass, if his father ever got wind of her identity, there's no telling what would happen to either of them.

He pushed the emotional beasts back into their cage and steeled himself for the interrogation, stiffening his gait as he marched to the lair of the master. With one final cleansing breath, he raised his knuckle to the door, giving a gentle tap.

"Enter," a voice beckoned.

Garrett slowly creaked open the door and slipped inside the realm of Old-World décor. The flooring was custom made from lab-grown cherry wood, each slat grooved with unique grain lines, unlike the mass-produced lumber offered to the mainstream. Matching wooden bookshelves lined the wall, displaying a variety of gadgets, taxidermy trophies, and other gilded decorative pieces.

A magnificent artisan-carved work desk encompassed the center of the room, its surface made of a deep red-stained wood. The legs were composed of immaculately polished brass castings, each depicting a female figurine dressed in classical Hellenistic style.

"You missed the unveiling last night," Antonin scolded from the expansive window, his back facing Garrett.

"Yes, sir." Garrett kept his response short, his form rigid.

"Where were you?" the man demanded.

Garrett could never tell what expression Antonin felt through his condescending tone of voice. The patriarch was well practiced in repressing all emotion in order to save face, and he had no qualms about berating him using as little effort as possible.

"Out at the sims with a few friends," Garrett reported.

"Don't you think there is a more productive use of your time?" the man insinuated.

"Yes, sir."

"I don't know how to get this through to you." Antonin turned around, eyes narrowed at the young man. "But your role in this company is much more important than you can imagine. And while you may think you have all the time in the world to indulge yourself in meaningless hedonism, I assure you that the time for that is quickly running out."

"Yes, sir." Garrett possessed a will of stone when it came to

Antonin's insults, using the old man's tricks against him as he stood calmly with an apathetic mask.

"How are your studies, by the way?" Antonin inquired.

"Proceeding well. Here are my marks, if you would like to look them over." Garrett passed a file from his NetCom over. He kept his gaze on the screen as Antonin wiped a finger over the text.

"Good," the man muttered, half-impressed as he examined each figure. "I suppose you're at least capable of retaining information, even if your sense of responsibility is left wanting."

Garrett bit his tongue, letting the comment slide over his back as he swallowed his ire. The drugs Nara gave him provided an additional shield of resilience. It was hard for him to care about being slighted by the malignant words while under its influence.

The man assumed he was a worthless wreck cavorting about Upper, incapable of comprehending his enigmatic business plans. It didn't bother him. The less the man thought of his capability, the easier it would be to surpass him.

"Yes, sir," he replied.

"I expect you to be at the next gathering promptly," Antonin ordered. "You may leave."

"Yes, sir," Garrett said and sharply pivoted to escape the miserable room.

"One more thing," Antonin called out. "I know you have disabled the cameras again. I am permitting them to remain that way. For now. But don't think I couldn't have them reactivated in an instant. You're not as clever as you think you are."

Garrett gritted his teeth, restraining a scowl at the biting taunt as he slid the door quietly shut behind him. He ran a hand through his hair, digging out the bottle of painkiller in his pocket. The tantalizing liquid danced as he twirled it between his fingers, the slick, oily swirls promising sweet relief.

"Won't need to worry about the future, huh? Tempting indeed," he addressed the air.

Shaking his head in futility, he put the bottle back in its place. He needed to get away from here, even though he had only just returned.

The air was stifling, and the stench of lies and deceit enameling the walls overwhelmed him with nausea.

Fuck this. I'm going back down until I feel human again. Sorry, Baran.

##10.1##

THE FEW DAYS' retreat at Darius's inn provided an uneasy quiet. While Garrett's body was permitted to recuperate, the time off had also strengthened the mental burdens surrounding his existence. Guilt was an oppressive force that afflicted his judgment.

He was able to pacify Baran's antagonizing despair through distant communication, but he wasn't ready to face the man in person just yet. The issue with Nara was still a troubling uncertainty, and without knowing the details surrounding the incident, he could not deliberate on the impact of his presence.

Since she would not tell him directly, he ventured out to find the one person who might be willing to ask on her behalf. After minor protests from his stiffened argumentative muscles, he climbed through the heaps of junk toward the magnificent fortress of Sentinel's clan.

He barely made it onto one step of the entrance before the turrets zoomed in on him.

The voice of Hark shouted through the intercom just as Garrett reached for the buzzer. "Hey, kid! You're all right! Nice to see you in one piece!"

"You heard about what happened?" Garrett asked in bewilderment.

"Heard about it? I was the one who hauled your asses back to safety," Hark proclaimed. "Me 'n a few of the crew here, that is."

Hauled us back? Garrett thought. *What the hell happened?*

"C'mon in, kid!" Hark welcomed him as the locks of the fortress door hissed open.

With a straining grunt, Garrett heaved the massive door open and stepped inside, where he was greeted by a grinning Hark bombarding his personal space.

"Hey, kid! You look great! You fancy a game?" Hark gave him a jovial nudge.

"Not this time, Hark. Is Sentinel in?" he inquired.

"Yeah, sure, he's in his office. I'll go tell him you're here," Hark said as he walked upstairs to the ominous black door, hurling a set of obnoxious bangs against the metal. "Hey, Boss! I got the kid here, wants to talk to ya!"

"Send him in," a voice responded from the call box.

Hark sent Garrett through the door with a hearty amicable slap to the back, propelling him into the warm ambiance of Sentinel's office.

"And what can I do for you?" The man greeted as Garrett halted his momentum with a calculated stomp.

"I apologize for the intrusion and for my forward request. But something has been troubling me, and I wonder if you would be able to help," Garrett requested, easing into the chair in front of the desk.

"Enlighten me. Please," Sentinel permitted.

"I'm not sure where to begin, if I am being perfectly honest." He let out a sigh, searching the floor for his thoughts.

The man smiled. "Take your time."

"A few nights ago, Nara was ambushed by bounty hunters. I was caught in the crossfire, and I didn't see the rest of the fight." Garrett paused, trying to piece together the fragments of his memory. "When I awoke in her apartment, something was off. She was extremely troubled. I think something else happened that night, but she isn't telling me."

"I see," Sentinel hummed, folding his hands under his chin.

"If you happen to have the chance to talk to her, could you find out for me? And please don't tell her I was here," Garrett implored. "The subject seems to cause her discomfort."

Sentinel paused and leaned back in his chair, taking in a long, pensive breath. His hesitation left Garrett uneasy, leaving the young human shifting uncomfortably as he awaited his reply.

"I am trusting you to keep this within the strictest of confidence," Sentinel informed, a shadow of severity veiling his face. "While you were out, she had a run-in with the Enforcers."

"Christ," Garrett breathed. His heart crawled up to his throat as the man's words seeped into his brain. He leaned his elbow on the arm of his chair, holding his head in his hand as a feverish nausea overwhelmed him.

"I am sorry to trouble you with this," Sentinel sympathized, watching Garrett's reaction curiously.

"But she was able to get away from them, I see," Garrett mentioned, trying to find positive light in the situation.

"She was caught," Sentinel explained, "trying to carry you."

I fucked up. The words reverberated through Garrett's brain as his expression degenerated into pale horror. "How did—"

"She didn't tell me much else, unfortunately." Sentinel shook his head.

"I . . . *shit*." Garrett's astonishment glued his eyes to the floor.

Sentinel pivoted his chair meditatively, examining the young man's earnest features, hiding a tiny approving smile behind his folded hands.

"I . . . thank you. For dragging us back," Garrett said, remembering his manners as he picked up the pieces of his composure.

"It was nothing."

He unintentionally voiced his thoughts out loud. "Now I'm left wondering why she didn't just leave me there."

"You might not be able to tell, but she does have quite a bit of respect for you." Sentinel tapped his cheek with a finger. "She's just not good at showing it. Or she's really great at hiding it, however you want to look at it."

"I didn't mean to—wait, really?" Garrett perked up.

"Certainly," Sentinel replied. "She may not have said it in words, but there are many ways to communicate without your voice."

"I wish I knew the languages better. I appear to be terrible at reading signs." Garrett let out a quiet scoff. "She tells me I am not perceptive."

"I can teach you," Sentinel offered. "It is a skill that takes a considerable amount of practice, but it's not impossible to learn."

"You can?" Garrett blinked. "All right, what's the catch? I'm not much of a fighter, and I don't relish the idea of killing someone on your behalf."

"My, my, what presumptions we have." The man let out a soft chortle. "Let me put it to you this way. Friends are an invaluable resource, and if we have a means to keep our friends from harm, don't we have an obligation to protect them?"

"Sure." Garrett raised an eyebrow, uncertain of the strange man's morality.

"I assure you, my intent is not of malice," he explained with a smile. "Would you like to begin?"

"What, now? You're not busy?"

"Unless you aren't feeling up to it," Sentinel offered as he stood up from his desk. "Follow me."

The ethereal man escorted Garrett out of the den and down a series of rivet-riddled stairwells. The clandestine tunnels of the bunker eventually opened into a massive arena the size of a starship cargo deck. Grunts of exertion echoed through the empty chamber as troops flung each other into the cushiony embrace of safety mats, their plays highlighted by the bright spotlights cascading from above. A forest of rods, staves, weights, blades, and other more intricate implements of destruction lined the walls in a neat row of racks, offering an array of options for the discerning warrior.

"The training room," Sentinel declared with a wave of his hand. "One of several in this facility."

"Impressive," Garrett marveled, staring up at the high vaulted ceiling. *This fortress is huge. How deep down does it go?*

"Break time, everyone," Sentinel called out to the ruffians as he glided up a staircase to an observation deck overhanging the arena. He made himself comfortable in front of a console, stirring the machine alive with a prod.

As the mercs released their hold of each other, the featureless arena warped into an urban obstacle course. Ruined buildings stretched from the floor, assembling a toothy concrete maze spanning half of the room. A glittering night sky engulfed the gunmetal grey of the ceiling, adding an immersive atmosphere to the environment.

"All right, everyone, situation ID-9: formation Alpha, if you please," Sentinel addressed the soldiers.

"Yes, sir!" Synchronous shouts echoed through the makeshift

street, accompanied by footsteps and noises of shifting within the maze. The subdued starry glow was violently disrupted as a shining orb materialized into the air, piercing the simulated street with a column of light.

Sentinel leaned over the balcony to address Garrett. "Let's see what you can do. Please proceed to the target beacon without alerting my units."

"Uh . . ." Garrett hesitated as he approached one of the structures, poking at it experimentally. He was surprised to find the building solid, the rough concrete surface abrading his finger.

"They'll give you a head start before patrolling. Go ahead," Sentinel assured as he opened up a camera view from his watch, displaying a birds-eye perspective of the training room.

With a submissive shrug, Garrett crept into the artificial street. He took advantage of the simulated decay of the wall next to him and clambered up the face, taking slow, calculated strides to suppress the sounds of his presence. After protests from his creaking joints, he hauled himself over the parapet, taking shelter against the other side of the barrier. He slithered to the north side of the building, peeking over the brick to scan the horizon.

The world Sentinel had created was far from barren, giving him a playground of busted concrete, overturned ground vehicles, and heaping trash piles. Without the perimeter of the training room shattering the illusion, Garrett would have almost believed he was inside a street of Under.

The beacon taunted him from his vantage point, twinkling irritatingly from only a short distance away. It deviously hovered in the center of a six-lane intersection, taking shelter far from the reaches of Garrett's rooftop trail.

What the hell would Nara do? he thought bitterly. Pushing back a sigh, he turned his attention to the patrols on the ground level.

The soldiers took break time seriously, lounging on top of piles of concrete and engaging in idle chatter through puffs of cigarette smoke. A few units took up simplistic patrol patterns, walking in slow labored paths around the simulated street.

The synchronized performance of each mobile merc played out

like a well-choreographed dance. Each guard moved in a square path through the alleys, turning and pausing at the same time as their fellow patrolmen. Garrett traced his eyes over the display of precision, counting off seconds as the patrol loops stopped and started at the same time across the arena.

Confident that he had imprinted the routes to memory, he crept along the roof and headed toward his target. He imitated a ground-dwelling mammal as he advanced through the pathway of fallen structures, bobbing his head up to check his surroundings before leaping across the gaps of the neighboring buildings. When he reached the end of the sky road, he peeked over the ledge to gain insight on the surrounding mercs.

Two guards played an uncharacteristically peaceful game of cards below him, using a set of cargo crates as furniture. One additional unit on either side of the gambling duo strolled through the street in uniform circles, both seemingly disinterested in the world around them.

Four on the street, he thought as he watched their movements. *Easy enough to keep track of.*

When the patrols turned away from him, Garrett skulked to the opposite side of the roof. After peering over the edge for activity, he gently made his way down the face of the wall.

As his feet touched the pavement, a cough rippled through the air, sending a spasm across his chest.

Shit! he cursed and dove into the busted window of the ground floor. As he rolled into a crouch, he watched the afflicted merc pass him by, releasing his viselike grip on his lungs to steady his nerves.

When the pattering of footsteps faded in the distance, he skulked to the back of the building, where he emerged into a storeroom covered in a chaotic layer of busted tiles and overturned shelving racks. He navigated through the treacherous maze, gently stepping through obstacles as he made his way to a workbench.

The crunch and crackle of his footsteps sent chills up his legs as he advanced, causing him to restrain a whimper as paranoia turned his head around. Silence assured him as he hesitated, the swirling air murmuring through the cracks in the masonry. He progressed to the back wall, hefting himself on top of a steel workbench to reach the narrow ventilator windows

The rays from the beacon taunted him from the corner of his vision, obscuring his view of the gambling grunts with its mischievous radiation. Nervous sweat began to percolate over his skin as his anxiety rose, his eyes obsessively shifting over the street.

Between the innumerable rumors and ungodly creatures he had encountered during his years scouting the Undercity, standing on the ground level made him excruciatingly uncomfortable. His nerves began to mutiny across his arms as he strained against the light, hampering his concentration as he scanned for the patrols.

How the hell does Nara do this every day? Garrett thought. *My hands won't stop shaking.*

Pushing back the edginess crackling over his brain, he stepped down to the floor and headed for the back door. He peered through the tiny square window, watching the patrol mosey past the gambling units. But as he continued his search, an unsettling feeling sadistically brushed the hairs on back of his neck.

Three on the street. Where's number four?

"Hi!" A bubbly voice cleaved through the silence, sending a jolt across Garrett's spine.

"Hi." He frowned as he turned around, meeting eyes with a cheerful merc excitedly waving at him.

With an electric crackle, the building melted to the ground, the dissolving cityscape announcing the game over. Garrett's shoulders slumped as the decrepit tiling vanished from under his feet.

"That was a good first run," Sentinel praised as he approached. "Good work, everyone. As you were."

"Yes, sir!" the mercs barked and resumed their training rituals.

"I honestly had no idea where she had disappeared to," Garrett said disappointedly.

"Perception is not just about sight," Sentinel explained. "You must learn to use your other senses. Listen to what the environment tells you. Feel patterns in the air, smell the force of life itself as it crosses your path."

"I see." Garret mulled over the experience.

"It comes with quite a bit of time and practice," the man added. "We can also try some sensory deprivation training to help with the process."

"Ah," Garrett murmured, uneasy about the concept.

"Would you like another run?" Sentinel offered.

"Absolutely," Garrett eagerly replied. "Provided I do not overstay my welcome."

"You are always welcome here." Sentinel smiled, amused by Garrett's determined expression.

##10.2##

GARRETT RELAXED at the Arcade Café with a cup of soothing tea, watching the colors shift in the laser trails with each passing car. Though exhausted from the night of training, a warm, contented feeling lifted his spirits. It was a quaint peacefulness amid the world of progressive technology and simple inhabitants.

But his enjoyment was cut short as a chill crawled over him, intensifying as a familiar apparition closed in on his position.

"Hello again, Garrett. Fancy seeing you here," Cordelia greeted with a wily smile. Her politeness was just as simulated as when he'd first met her, as well as her sickeningly sweet demeanor.

Oh, fuck, he thought, *not again.*

This woman terrified him more than Nara's indignation and Baran's disappointment combined. She took far too much pleasure in deceiving others, and her worldview absolutely disgusted him. Her visit could not have been coincidental, having cornered him in a public place.

"Hello," Garrett greeted, swallowing the lump in his throat.

"I've been meaning to get a hold of you since our first encounter," she said a she slipped into the stool next to him.

"Oh?" he replied. *I bet you have.*

"Yes, you're ever so slippery. Every time I ring your estate, you seem to be elsewhere."

"I have been busy with studies as of late," he evaded, downing his beverage. "My concentration requires an isolated environment in order to function."

"Ahh, secrets." She winked. "How fascinating. Where in the vastness of Upper can you find such a place?"

"If I disclosed that, it would no longer be a secret, now would it?" He forced up a smile of his own to match her guile.

"I usually see you by the GaPFed starports. Lost interest in them?" Cordelia inquired.

"Work has been piling up recently." He hid the apprehension in his voice. *What does she mean by 'usually?'*

"I understand completely." Her predatory smile brightened. "It's hard to keep your eyes on everything in an empire."

"Was there something you needed? Or are you just here for a social call?" The skin of his arms began to itch with an oily revulsion.

"Oh, the Midwinter's Ball is this weekend. I was wondering if you would do me the honor of escorting me." She folded her hands in front of her, a façade of an innocent plea.

"Under normal circumstances, I would accept. However—"

"Oh, that's wonderful!" she interrupted, clapping her hands together with delight.

"Please forgive me. I have another engagement on that night. I must apologize, but it is most inconvenient," he persisted, evading the social entrapment.

Panic began to overwhelm him, her obvious hunt for information triggering his defenses. Due to his social standing, he had to take care of his words and how he formulated rejection, and she wholeheartedly took advantage of his plight.

"Oh. I understand." Cordelia sighed dejectedly. "Perhaps next time."

"Indeed," he said as he drained the last drops of his tea, hiding his distress behind the porcelain cup.

"Well, I'd best be off. I will see you again soon, Garrett," she promised with a most unsettling smile.

"Good evening." He bowed his head. His eyes locked on her as she walked away, making sure she left the bar. *Dear gods, she is tenacious.*

He wiped the sweat from the back of his neck as he recollected himself. The dreadful woman had to know that he wasn't interested in her company, but she didn't seem to mind using his trepidation as a weapon. She was a skillful pretender and opportunistic, two qualities he loathed in any character.

Just what I needed, another reason to hate coming home. He shook his head and headed out before any more trouble decided to appear.

##10.3##

THE COMPULSION TO run overwhelmed her as the hunters bellowed behind, the mysterious assailants pursuing her through the shadowy woodland. She thought she knew this forest well, but the trees appeared to shun her, bending their branches away to deny her shelter.

The clamor began to dwindle as she ran, but the ground she had gained was not great enough for her comfort. She looked down at her hands, watching cracks in her skin open, oozing sickly dark fluid. Webs of gashes wrapped over her flesh as the fractures multiplied, slithering up her arms.

The predators smelled the blood, speeding toward her as she began to succumb to her injuries, pain drilling through her nerves with every step. She commanded her battered form to persist, refusing to submit to their wants.

The ground beneath her quaked as steel walls plowed their way out of the earth, their shadows looming over her as they rose into the sky. They directed her flight, blocking her path to the trees as they closed in on her sides. She tried to outrun the constricting trap, but the barriers materialized faster than her viscous movements.

The gnashing pack of beasts stole her vision, a cunning distraction as another wall spawned directly in front of her. Her body violently collided into the devious obstruction, and ichor splattered over the surface, causing the wall to weep tears of red. She peeled herself away from the barrier, gazing in horror at the patterns painted over the metal. The sanguine liquid traced a hauntingly familiar person, their eyes smoldering with blinding ethereal light.

As the specter raised an arm, fleshy silver irises split open on the metal walls, raining down scintillating daggers over her. The assault continued for an eternity, shredding the remnants of her flesh in an unyielding barrage.

With a crack of thunder, the storm subsided, sending her to her knees. The blood-spawned wraith stepped out of the wall, their liquid form dripping as they approached. Her heart knew who they were, but her mind refused to vocalize her suspicions, hurling her thoughts between fear and hate.

They stood over her, watching, silent. The soil grew saturated with her blood, the red pools surrounding her broken body morphing into black obsidian. Vines sprouted from the hardened earth, delighted to be nourished by the vital liquid. The tendrils crept toward her, but she was too weary to attempt escape.

The vines slowly enveloped her as she succumbed to her fate, her mind acclimated to the pain. Darkness swallowed her vision as the rocky coils began to crawl over her face. She gave up the fight. *No more.*

But just as her spirit began to diminish, someone, or something, outside her confines slashed though the vines. A burst of blinding light invaded her sight as her prison split open into a sunlit sky.

##10.4##

"WHAT THE FUCK?" Nara snarled as she jarred awake.

Her mind was tormenting her again. The indistinct face flashed through her eyes, the blurry images teasing her with a fleeting significance.

Does everyone dream like this, she thought bitterly, a*nd simply ignore it? Is my mind just too weak to cope with this shit?*

She tore the covers off and angrily stormed out of bed, scrubbing her face in agitation. Even though she was barely an adolescent by her people's standards, she felt too old to be riding this mental roller-coaster. Emotional grunge coated her skin with grime, and she headed to the kitchen to wash the filth from her face.

"What the fuck am I supposed to do? Work obsessively until my body expires?" she demanded from the basin. "And after that? Do I just ignore my brain telling me that the world is fucking on fire?"

She glanced at the bed morosely, contemplating her old sleep habits from when she was a soldier. Even though it devoured her sanity, she'd enjoyed the peaceful rests that visited when she first came to this shithole of a planet. While they lasted.

Her eyes moved to a glass bottle of tantalizing red liquor on top of her fridge.

"Fuck it, let it burn," she muttered as she snatched the flask.

She flopped on the couch and popped off the seal of the drink, grumbling obscenities as she steeled herself for her descent into mental fog. The burning bitterness grounded her as the liquid crawled down her throat, half the contents of the bottle disappearing with one heavy draught.

The silence of the apartment was fertile ground for her incessant thoughts, which began to trickle in before the chemical influence had the ability to block their path. All she ever wanted was a moment of stillness, to be allowed to relax without the universe demanding her flesh. She had endured a lifetime of misery and deceit, and she wondered when the other side of the coin would begin to show itself.

Bellanar was a herald of misfortune, and while she knew it wasn't fair to inflict her anger on him, she wondered why he'd thought she would willingly help. She was no longer a citizen, and what influence she'd carried had dissolved with her exile.

The thought of subjecting herself to their punctilious bureaucratic methodology sent a twitch across her arm, and the glass vessel sobbed a grating crackle as it snapped inside her grip.

Fuck, she muttered as she dropped the shards on the table. *When does it—*

Her musing was interrupted by a disturbance in the hallway, the cautious footsteps of a solitary human ascending the ruin of her apartment.

"Aw, hell, what is it now?" she vocalized as she stood, scouring the furniture for a covering. Giving up the search with an irritated grumble, she slipped her coat on and wrenched open the front door, revealing a startled Garrett at the step.

"Yes?" she sighed wearily as she leaned against the doorframe.

"I know you didn't call," Garrett apologized, clearing the reaction to her disheveled state from his throat. "But I was in the area and I wanted to drop by to see how you were doing."

"Mmpfh," she mumbled as she walked back into the living room, permitting him to step inside.

"I got something for you," he informed, producing a piece of hardware from his pocket. "I was over at Art's place to see if he had any new Hawking software, and I also let him take a look at my NetCom."

"That's a brave course of action," Nara remarked as she dropped onto the couch.

"Yeah, I was there for quite some time." He rubbed the back of his head and handed the device over. "I got something a little extra for your armor."

"Oh?" she accepted the gift and looked it over curiously.

"I thought you might want something other than the Chameleon mod to color the suit. It seemed kind of ineffective, so Art scrounged up a Mirror overlay.

She raised an eyebrow. "That's not a cheap piece of hardware."

"Eh, not really, but I had some contracts come in and had some spare cash."

"Contracts?" Nara tilted her head.

"Yeah, I trade relics across the galactic markets." Garrett shrugged impassively. "Side business, really."

"I see." She regarded the shiny object in the palm of her hand, taken aback by the consideration. "That was thoughtful of you."

"Nah, it was nothing." He figured that was the closest thing to gratitude he was going to get. "I don't think I've had the chance to apologize for all the grief I caused."

"Don't mention it."

"Yeah, but—"

"No, really." She met his eyes severely. "Don't mention it."

"Ahh." He glanced over to the table, where the remnants of the liquor bottle lay. "Got it."

The swirl of inebriation began to wash over Nara's thoughts, and her mind skipped as she pondered the motivation behind the gift. With only having a narrow scope of friendly allegiances in her network, she found humans' bizarre relationship rituals unsettling. She was acquainted with their quid-pro-quo ideology, but the concept of generosity just for the sake of it was perplexing. A curious sensation came over her, a strange inexplicable elation over the human's gesture.

Her whimsy was shattered by the obnoxious bleating of her Netcom. The smirk sprouting over her lips matured into a virulent scowl upon reading the identification of the caller.

"Fffffffff," she hissed as she answered the call.

"Oh my, um, hello?" The voice of Annon poked through the device. "Is this wor—"

"What. Do you want. This time?" Nara grumbled, grinding her eyes with the palms of her hands.

"I have another job for you, and it's—"

"Nghhh," she bellowed. "Give it to someone else, for fuck's *sake*."

"I can't. The client specifically requested you by name."

"And you told them I don't work for you, right?" She narrowed her eyes at the device.

"Not after they told me their budget."

"I hate you. So much," Nara growled. "I hope you know this."

"Meet me in my office. You'll want to hear this in person," Annon ordered and cut the channel.

"Fff-*uck*!" she barked and peeled herself from the couch. With a haggard stride, she shambled her way into the bedroom to root around for her clothes.

"I've got another errand to run myself," Garrett announced, heading for the door. "I'll see you back here whenever you get that job."

"Hey." She leaned over the doorway, stopping him as he reached for the knob. "Thanks."

"Sure." He smiled warmly and turned to head for the city.

CHAPTER 11

##11.0##

The meticulous calculations dancing around Annon's brainwaves hurtled out of his ears as Nara knocked on the doorframe of his office, the noise of the intrusion causing him to sharply blaspheme. His reactionary scowl relaxed into a semi-approachable smile when his eyes met with his prized moneymaker.

"Ahh, come in," he said and motioned her inside. His smile flattened as he witnessed the bedraggled merc shuffle toward him, the heels of her boots squeaking against the marble floor.

"Is everything all right?"

"Yeah, just drunk," Nara confided as she flopped down on the empty seat, air whooshing from under her as it escaped the cushion.

"I'm sorry to hear that, but I am glad you came by as soon as you did, if that means anything at all to you," he sympathized. "But I'm afraid you will need a good chunk of your wits for this one."

"Oh?" She leaned her elbow against the arm of the chair, resting her head in her hand as she broadcast a mild look of annoyance.

"Well, a great bit of caution, anyway. I'm sure you won't have too many qualms about being messy in this situation."

"Quit skirting around and just give me the damn details," she grumbled.

"Fine, fine." He paused to throw her a sour glance. "It appears that an Upworlder has had a rather nasty exchange with some Experimentalists and wants a bit of revenge."

"Really, now? I can't imagine what an Upworlder would be doing that deep in Undercity to be within reach of the Fringe," she retorted.

"Apparently, it was his daughter who had suffered the ordeal, and he understandably wants some excessive bloodshed. He has tracked down a stronghold in the uncivilized zone and requested that it be depleted of all its life." Annon's face wrinkled with disgust. "Or the closest thing that can be considered life when it comes to the likes of them."

Nara folded her arms gruffly. "That's not the easiest thing to pull off alone."

The agent artfully plotted his words. "While I am not questioning your ability, nor am I giving you suggestion on how you should do your work, the client has hired several other, ahem, *lesser* mercenaries with barely flowering reputations to put on a frontal assault. This would give you more than a decent opportunity to sneak around and take out the remainder of the crowd inside."

"If it's deep enough in the Fringe, I can just nuke the place and be done with it." Her head dipped as she muttered the words, sleep threatening her attentiveness.

"The client has specifically ordered against that course of action." Annon pondered as the absurdity of her suggestion dawned on him. "Do you actually possess enough explosive power to demolish a building of reasonable size?"

"Yes," she stated matter-of-factly.

"I see then." A hint of worry colored his cheeks. "I will remember to increase the reinforcement budget for my office."

"Any idea of the numbers?" Her jaw stretched into a debilitating yawn, her enlarged canines giving her the appearance of a sunbathing feline.

"It is uncertain, but the stronghold in question can't accommodate more than fifty living humans. Though who knows how many . . . things . . . they can shove inside."

She scowled. "Great."

"So, I suppose some heavy artillery is in order. That's always a bonus," Annon suggested, pointing a finger of encouragement at her.

"Fun." Her scowl deepened.

"The group will meet you in three days' time and await your orders. Your call sign for this mission is 'Generalissimo'."

"Is that some kind of joke?" she growled.

"I fail to see the humor." Annon raised an eyebrow. "The client defined it, not me. Is there a problem?"

"I don't have leadership experience." She glared at him coldly. "I work alone."

"Really?" His face sharpened into surprise.

"The hell are you getting at?" Nara challenged.

"Nothing, it's just that I find that rather shocking, actually. You have this aura of authority about you." He gestured into the air.

"No, I just don't give a fuck."

"Right, my mistake." Annon cleared his throat uncomfortably as he slid a file in front of her. "Anyway, here are the details."

##11.1##

"You okay?" Garrett asked through the apartment channel.

"I really don't want to be here," Nara confided as she approached a squad of ten mercenaries hanging out in the alley. She couldn't shake the feeling that someone was making fun of her.

"Is this everyone?" she asked out loud with a deepened, disguised voice.

"And you are?" one of them sneered.

"The Generalissimo." Nara sighed at the absurdity of her title. "A problem?"

"Not yet," the merc rebuked.

"Good." She rolled a slight snarl over her lips. "I said, is this everyone?"

"As far as we can tell," another responded.

"Fine. Who here has dealt with this type of threat before?" she asked the gathering, counting the raised hands. "Good. Then you can enlighten your comrades of the severity of the situation. To minimize splash damage, only energy weapons will be permitted on this mission. You are not allowed to be touched by the enemy or any of its byproducts. Casualties will be shot on sight. Is that understood?"

"The hell do you think you are?" another merc heckled.

Nara walked over to the insubordinate member, casting a towering shadow over their shrinking figure.

"I can assure you a bullet to the head is much more pleasant than the screaming agony of transformation." She paused to let their imagination warm up. "Should you survive the initial attack, which may boil parts of your flesh as your body tries to fight off the paralysis, you will be dragged inside that warehouse where pieces of you will be added to their collection of meat. Afterward, you will no longer have a sense of humanity within you, no matter where they decide to stick your brain, with or without your skull."

The merc hesitated, but before they gained the courage to muster a response, one of their comrades grabbed them by the shoulder, shaking a head in warning.

"He's right. These guys aren't worth fucking around with," another chipped in.

"So why are we here, if it's so dangerous?" the loudmouthed merc asked.

"If you want to leave, then by all means, go for it. I'm not paying your tab," Nara scoffed as she fidgeted with her NetCom. "Or you can stay here and live to tell about it if you do exactly as I say. And I suppose, more importantly, cash out on a rather lucrative contract."

Nobody moved.

"Are. We. All. *Here* then?" she growled impatiently as the mercs stared down at their feet. "Good."

"You're the boss," the dissident one shrugged in submission.

"Whatever. I've cased the joint a bit before meeting you. Snipers, anyone?" Four mercs raised their hands as she pulled up a screen from her wrist, projecting a map of the area. "I want two of you up on each of these towers here. Understood?"

"Yes, sir," they murmured in semi-unison, about as synched as a bunch of disgruntled roughnecks can get.

Nara pointed at an energetic bouncing individual, wearing belts and bandoliers all over her body, each holstering rows of canisters. She was stout and barely reached Nara's waist. An exaggerated cartoonish smile stretched across her face, which was emphasized by thick, tightly braided blonde sideburns that outlined her jawline.

"You, the smiley one. What's your specialty?" Nara asked her.

The excitable lady yanked one of the canisters off a belt and lobbed it on the ground. In a puff of cobalt smoke, a small metal droid popped up with its bug-like legs, dancing playfully in circles and waving tiny gun protrusions at its master's command.

"Machinist. Technician," the lady chirped proudly as the critter climbed up her bare, heavily tattooed arms. The creature stood in attention on her shoulder, then saluted Nara with a wiry pointed leg.

"Wonderful," Nara said flatly. "When everything is finished, you will be sent inside to disable whatever electronics they have before these things come crawling out of test chambers."

"Yes, Sir!" The gadgeteer saluted enthusiastically, clicking her heels together.

"You, the quiet one in the corner. What's your specialty?" Nara pointed to a merc skulking in the back.

He was a wiry built individual, possessing an acerbic aura. All sorts of straps and cases were symmetrically fastened to his legs and chest. A metal pack resembling an exoskeleton rested over his shoulders, with two rifles held securely in specialized quick-release holsters. His attire was form-fitting and simple, accessorized with a pair of goggles and a sleek black mask that concealed the majority of his face. Tufts of charcoal-colored hair poked out of his head coverings and flowed loosely to his shoulders. The only flesh he exposed was his fingertips. Each olive-toned digit poked out from a pair of cutoff gloves.

"Recon," he stated tersely, arms folded across his chest.

"Name?" Nara asked.

"Alpha."

"Good," she commented, appreciating the succinct answers. "You are coming inside with me."

"Acknowledged."

"The rest of you are general gunners, I presume?" She passed a hand over the screen, zooming in on the forward entry. "Focus your attention on the main entryway. Any questions?"

The boorish merc scowled. "Yeah, you really think we can get out of this mess alive?"

"If you have a better plan, I'd love to hear it," Nara challenged, checking the charges of her pistol. The merc looked to his comrades for an answer. "I thought not. Now shut the fuck up and don't do anything reckless. Anything else, or can we get on with it?"

"No, sir," some of the group mumbled.

"Good. Alpha and I will make our way up the roof," Nara continued. "Keep aware of your surroundings, and don't be surprised if your cover dissolves at your feet. If you have to retreat, do so. And keep that machinist alive. Is that all understood?"

"Yes, sir," a slightly more coordinated chorus replied.

"Good. Let's go," she said as she walked off, signaling for Alpha to follow.

"Hey, Nara," Garrett called out through the communication line.

"What do you want, human?"

"Have you done this before?"

"Fuck. Off." She growled.

"It was just a question," Garrett stated, taken aback by her biting reaction.

##11.2##

NARA WALKED along the length of the rooftop, relieved to have a quiet approach. She made one final check to her weapons, listening for irregularities to the disgusting noises squelching below. Confident that the creatures were unsuspecting of the assault, she knelt next to the access hatch and rallied her troops.

"Snipers at your posts?" she called out on the team's frequency.

"North side locked and loaded," the first sniper team responded.

"South side ready."

"Good. Gunmen status?" Nara asked.

"All set here."

"You may fire when ready," Nara authorized.

Sizzling metal erupted through the streets as the machinist unleashed two of her minions to burn the warehouse door open. The racket was shortly cut off by a percussive thud as the massive metal gate crashed onto the concrete. Inhuman screeching and gunfire soon followed, stealing any possibility for silence to re-enter the area.

Nara waited for the distraction to fully deploy, then she signaled for Alpha to move in. On her orders, he flipped open the unlocked hatch and headed down into the fortress of flesh and fluids. When he was clear, Nara opened her own access point and followed suit.

As she descended the ladder, her helmet switched to thermal vision, allowing her to examine the entrails of the dark room. Practically every tangible surface was warm, enveloped in pulsating globules of yellow and orange.

From the sparse scattering of cool shapes in her surroundings, she discerned an array of mechanic tools and cutting implements, undoubtedly maintained by an Experimentalist butcher. Tables and racks lined each wall, covered with piles of dirty saws and vises saturated with sticky fluids and rust.

The vents of Nara's helmet intuitively sealed as the sensors detected unsafe matter. She caught a whiff of rotting meat before being fed sterile air from the armor's life support system.

She paused on the bottom rung of the ladder to search the floor, scanning for a patch of bare metal grating amidst the visceral filth. After some angling, she sprang from the ladder, correcting her flight with miniscule adjustments before delicately landing on mostly clean foundation. She crept forward in wide, oscillating strides from one bare space to another, cautiously advancing toward the main passage to survey the interior battlefield.

Though its initial purpose was unknown, the warehouse had been modified, or more accurately, evolved to adapt to the requirements of the Experimentalists' grisly lifestyle. She was on the second level, which overlooked the expansive ground floor with a steel-grated walkway bordering the perimeter. The metal path gave access to the additional store rooms, offices, and stairways that were originally built into the complex.

But now, the place resembled a brutally tortured biological test subject. A twisted network of transparent pipes carried unknown fluids of every hue, the liquids flowing upward from giant tanks on the ground, as if providing the chambers above with sustenance.

The only semblance of organization within the entire facility was provided by the systematic rows of tanks positioned along the bottom floor of the warehouse, each containing a semi-living creature. The further back in the ranks, the more grotesque the inhabitants appeared.

Parts of the walls were infested with strange pulsating growths, teeming with nasty barbed black metal talons. The sentient flesh barriers appeared to serve no allegiance, lashing out at any creature that dared to run too close.

Nara glanced at the wall next to her, placing a steadying hand on it after confirming the safety of the surface. She leaned forward into the chaos to examine the ceiling directly above her, finding the structures mostly devoid of infestation.

Let's see if Art calibrated this correctly, she mused as she initialized her new Mirror overlay.

A faint electronic purring droned into her ear from inside the armor as a force field enveloped her in invisible energy. As she waved a hand in front of her face, she grew mildly concerned that she could see her own appendages, having to trust that outside observers could not.

Garrett also took the opportunity to paw through the new settings accessible to him. Numbers and blips scrolled across his various screens, feeding him a feast of information on the armor's status. He pushed and poked at menus, placing useful reports in a logical arrangement in front of his face.

"Any movement?" Nara asked.

"Nothing I can see. I think everyone's focusing their attention on the fight outside," he reported, quickly glancing at the camera ports before returning to the tantalizing data streams.

"Gunners, how are you holding up?"

"Good so far, but I think they're still recovering over the initial surprise. Give us a minute or two before we start screaming."

"Alpha, get up to the beams and try to aim for the Surgeons first," Nara ordered. "They have the codes to bring out reinforcements. Just look for the ones that look mostly human."

"Affirmative," Alpha confirmed.

Using the noise of gunfire and abysmal screeching as cover, Nara scaled up a support column that was miraculously standing upright, despite the corrosive decay coating the surface. She ascended to a crossbeam spanning the ceiling and tested its integrity with a tap of a boot. Satisfied, she pulled herself onto the structure and crouched, creeping out of range from the flying fluids and organs.

As she slipped a rifle into her hands, she made a mental headcount of the creatures inside. There was enough to overwhelm the squad flat-footed, but she had every intention of evening the odds.

She fired several rounds into the chaos, transforming questionably alive things to certainly dead things. Limbs, tendrils, and other unmentionable appendages whipped around in a confused frenzy as the frontal assault slowed, giving the gunners below a chance to reload.

She spotted Alpha in the corner of her eye jumping from beam to beam, hurling grappling tools around like throwing knives. He was never in the same spot for more than a few seconds, just long enough to aim at and execute his targets on the floor.

Furious at the acrobatic show, one of the larger beasts suddenly tore a chunk of metal plating off its own skin, causing sickly green goo to squirt out of the pulsating muscle underneath. It then let out a throaty, moist bellow as it flung the mass at the soaring nuisance.

A crack of whipping wire pierced the air as the shrapnel severed Alpha's grappling line mid-flight.

But the techno-trapeze artist appeared unmoved by the disruption, flicking his wrist by instinct to sprout another cable from his arm. As the wire wrapped around the nearest beam, momentum jerked him to one side. He deftly flipped over the support, hurling his weight around to execute a delicate landing on his toes, just as the wire snapped back into his arm with a furious zipping sound. Barely pausing to recover, he reloaded his gun as he leapt off the beam again, continuing his flight pattern.

"Looks like they've seen us up here," Nara commented as she shot at the giant before it decided to assault them with more self-mutilation.

"Hey, Boss," one of the gunners piped in. "We lost our cover fire from the other end. It's getting kinda hairy out here."

"South side, what's your status?" Nara queried.

"We're a little busy over here. Buggers started crawling from out of the windows and climbing up to say 'Hi.' Ahh, shit!"

"Snipers, report!"

"Too many up here. We got nowhere to run, and we'll be cornered in a few moments."

"If you can get into the building, hide there. I'll be out there in a minute to cover," Nara ordered as she began to slink across her aerial road to the end of the building.

"A minute's a long time to wait, Boss."

"Mechanist, you got any friends you can throw their way?" Nara asked.

"Negative, every'un's occupied. These guys are right pissed off." The machinist let off a sharp whistle into the communication line.

"All right, I'll be there in just a—WOAH!"

Nara suddenly snapped her torso back, dodging a ball of green slime that whizzed past. Another soon followed, plopping on the beam she was kneeling on with a wet smack, the impact shaking her footing violently.

An annoyed growl belted from her throat as the erratic vibrations stole her balance, and she snapped an arm out to snatch a bar in the support beam before she fell into the fray. She let momentum swing her forward while she concocted an escape from the predicament.

"Nara, below you!" Garrett yelled into her helm.

She glanced at her feet and discovered the source of the noxious sputum. Swimming in a massive open-air tank and gurgling angry shrieks at her was a being that resembled something found in a sub-par ocean-themed monster film.

It was a giant creature composed of a green brain-like orb that sat on top of a short stalk of vertebrae. The mass of wrinkly orange flesh that served as its torso sprouted numerous tentacles that lashed around viciously in the purple murk it bathed in. It squawked once more through a giant mangled, cracked beak and glowered at her with enormous human-like eyes. Eyes that glowed with heavy cybernetic augmentations and certainly possessed the capability to see through her armor's disguise.

As the creature whipped a tentacle back to hurl another gob, Nara jutted her hand out in front of her. The armor on her forearm split open with a rapid series of sharp metallic clicks, ejecting a pistol toward her palm. She caught the weapon as the armor reformed itself and fired off several pulses of cerulean energy into the giant brain mass.

Its shrieks reverberated throughout the walls, drowning out the sizzle of flesh as the green matter began to dissolve. Its tentacles flailed furiously, splashing liquid over the sides of its containment tank.

Nara changed her target to try and contain collateral damage, focusing her attacks on the flailing tentacles, preventing even more hazardous waste from spilling over onto the floor below.

"Watch my back," she ordered Garrett as she rained another barrage.

"Right," Garrett acknowledged, diving into the sea of menus.

According to the new sensors in the interface, Nara was not even holding onto the beam. The grips in the armor were. Calculations spewed off to inform her of how much force was being spent to combat the recoil of her weapon, keeping her body exactly where she wanted it to be.

A rain of tentacle chunks splooshed into the vat as Nara continued her assault. But the remnants of the creature showed no signs of perishing. The stumpy, pathetic mass only became angrier, chaotically flailing its multitude of cartilaginous stumps in its own broth.

Nara then moved on to the only other vital object it exposed—its synthetic eyes. She squeezed off two shots, one for each eerily glowing ball. Electric sparks crackled across the reflection of the water as the plasma hit the centers of the silvery orbs.

The creature let out an ear-splicing shriek, the noise reverberating through the walls of the warehouse. Its irises violently flickered, then fizzled out as Nara followed up with another blast. Having reached its limits, the amalgamated lifeform finally quieted, letting out a series of defeated gurgles as its weakened body descended into the bubbling liquid.

The commotion yanked Garrett away from his watch, violating his ears as he observed the carnage in repulsed fascination.

As the death throes finally silenced, Nara sheathed her weapon and permitted herself the chance to recalculate her strategy.

But a corrosive sizzling adjacent to her announced that her troubles were far from over. She glanced up at the beam she held on to and witnessed the metal nearby slowly dissolving with a vehement hiss. Shiny silvery droplets plummeted toward the murky pool below as the remnants of the creature's sputum ate away at her only means of support.

"Ahh, fuck," Nara growled as she flung herself forward, gripping another bar ahead of her. Hand over hand, she propelled herself, swinging her way along the beam as swiftly as a jungle creature would navigate treetops.

The corrosive bilge did not allow for mistakes as it ate away at the beam with an increasingly voracious appetite. She could feel the metal construction began to bow from her weight, creaking and groaning as she pressed on.

Suddenly, the welding of the support pillar gave off a final squawk of protest, and the beam violently jerked toward the purple mire.

"Shit!" she cried out as gravity interrupted her mid-stride, hurling her downward. She lost her momentum as she clawed at the air, the solid bar that she was aiming for deviously slipping away from her grasp. As she maintained her grip on the bar behind her with her opposite hand, she clenched her core muscles to regain control of her wildly flailing legs.

"Nara, the goo's getting closer," Garrett warned as he frantically clawed through the armor's UI for an answer. *Art, did you put anything else useful in here? Defense systems, cleaning, little robots, anything at all?*

Fuck, fuck, FUCK, Nara chanted in her head as she hoisted herself up with her only anchored arm. She kicked her legs out to propel herself forward, quickening her pace to outrun the ravenous corrosion behind her. But with her hastened motions, the support beam began to curl downward, straining to shake off the annoyance of her weight in rhythmic bobs.

Through his cameras, Garrett scoured the area beneath her feet for any escape possibilities. The caustic vat below burped up vile pockets of air, murmuring the promise of a painful demise. He caught a glimpse of the catwalk on the other side of the room but dismissed it as too far from her reach. Defeated, he decided some unenthused words of encouragement might help her.

"Just a few more paces and you should reach—" Garrett began, but she had already flung herself away from the crumbling support. His breath was stolen from him as he forced his eyes shut, unable to witness the result of her descent.

Nara ignored the sinking feel of gravity as she fell, focusing on positioning herself toward her target. The arc of her descent felt right to her, but the creaks of rending metal behind her did not give her an alternative.

"Gunners, heads up!" she barked at the group channel as the beam let out a crunching wail.

With an onslaught of grinding shrieks, the remnants of the support structure tore itself away from the ceiling. It plummeted into the viscous bubbling vat below, dissolving away with incensed frothing and spurts.

Nara continued her flight and watched the railing of the catwalk zip past her vision, the barrier nearly scraping against the face of her helmet. She felt her fingertips brush solid material and instinctively clamped her hand tight. A pained grunt expelled from her lungs as the muscles in her arm strained to stop the fall, her weight yanking her toward the pit below.

She steadied her movement and then pulled herself up, resting her hips on the railing to give her arm relief from the tension. But her chance for respite quickly vanished when she was confronted with yet another obstacle—the spiny, pinkish growth that infected the wall in front of her.

The lifeform gurgled and burped fluids out of random pockets and sores, and the shiny spikes that studded the mass pulsated with a slow, almost breath-like rhythm. Yellowish-green fluids seeped from the base of each protrusion, trickling venom down the length of each spine.

The entity had noticed her, and it quivered in offense at the sudden intrusion, retracting several of the obsidian spears in preparation to strike.

"Ahh, FUCK," Nara cursed as she flung herself backward, gripping the railing with both hands.

As soon as the fleshy mass lashed out, a flash of emerald light darted past her face, and the spiny torpedo was launched across the room. She glanced over to see Alpha lurking in the opposite corner of the building, smoking rifle in hand. He gave Nara a salute before directing his attention to more creatures crawling up the walls.

"Nice one, Alpha," she said as she glided along the railing, shimmying past the limits of the growth before hauling herself over the railing once more. "Heading to you now, South Side."

Now I know how Baran feels, Garrett thought as he released the air in his lungs.

##11.3##

THE SNIPER's perch was overrun with grotesque fleshy ivy composed of a horde of creatures scaling the face of the tower. The building's walls were etched with furrows of black char that the mass excreted behind them as they ascended.

"Hold your fire," Nara ordered as she popped a device out of her belt. She tapped the buttons on the object, then hurled it at the snipers. After its trajectory ran out, two tiny jets snapped out from its sides, continuing to coast toward its destination.

The tiny ship paused in front of the snipers and then burst apart, transforming into an orb covered in electrically charged spikes. The arcs of energy intensified, and it hurled out an aura of pale blue energy that enveloped the mercs.

That should take care of the splash, she thought as she extracted a larger gun from the arsenal in her back, one she rarely had the opportunity to play with, or the ammunition.

"Hold on to something. Going to shake the place up a bit," she ordered the snipers as she took aim. She braced herself as she pulled the trigger, and the weapon aggressively jolted into her shoulder in response.

A screaming arrow of blinding luminosity zoomed out from the barrel, eager to reach its target. Fractions of a moment later, a thunderous crack split the air, then a line of bright green light snapped out, tracing the width of the tower.

The snipers looked over the edge of the roof to watch a radiating web of green sprout from the face of the tower, humming excitedly with energy. They stared inquisitively through their protective bubble as it crackled. The glow of the curious weapon intensified with each second, and swirling noises surged around the mercs as it charged itself for its next move.

The noise climaxed into a tremendous boom, and the tower quaked with its ferocious roar. Caught off guard by its sudden clamor, the snipers crumpled to the ground as their balance was snatched from under them.

The sheet of sparks plunged toward the ground. A swirling cone of wind trailed behind it with an unnerving wail. As the scintillating net encountered the fleshy blockade, the glaring light intensified, radiating the street with an eerie luminescence.

Amid a resonance of steam and sizzles, the weapon swiftly burned a clean path for itself through the organic obstacle. A multitude of agonized cries echoed over the vibrating energy as the relentless death net devoured its way through the horde, mincing each unfortunate creature into miniscule fleshy giblets.

The creatures, cursed with a hive-mind mentality, possessed a limited sense of self-preservation. Despite being rained on by bits of their companions, the ones below continued their ascent in ignorant bliss, awaiting their gruesome demise.

As the net swiftly cut through the remainder of the horde, the collective agonized wails began to dispel from the air. The weapon's light abruptly vanished with one final burst as it collided with the road, scorching its mark into the concrete. Steam and wet bubbling noises rose from the puddle of fused flesh, announcing the termination of the hazard.

Well, those won't be very useful to Declan, Nara thought as she looked down at the smoking mass.

Garrett stared wide-eyed at the screen in disbelief, uncertain if he had actually witnessed destruction of this magnitude or if his mind was just toying with him. Once the initial shock of the spectacle wore down, he slowly peered over his shoulder, eyeing the numerous gun-filled cabinets garnishing the apartment. As his imagination took the best of him, he grew steadily uncomfortable about the notion of sitting in the center of a potentially volatile weapon containment area.

"I only had *one* of those, so if you get into trouble again, abandon your post and run," Nara announced to the snipers after they had regained their balance. "For now, take care of the stragglers."

"Boss, we got troubles on the ground here," the squad of gunners reported.

"Alpha, cover the gunners from the entrance until I get there," Nara ordered.

"Affirmative."

"All our cover's disintegrated. Been dodging loogies left 'n' right," the gunner added.

"Keep your distance! Retreat into the open street if you have to. Don't let them corner you. I'll be down in a minute," she barked as she ran across the roof to meet the wave of flesh, brandishing a less devastating weapon.

As she fired into the wave of horrors, images of her past duty back on her home world flickered through her mind. She recalled painfully familiar tactics, running up and down forest-covered battlegrounds, providing cover fire to multiple distressed squads. Her sprinting had become a honed skill through self-imposed, arduous training, and yet it was not an achievement she was proud of.

This lucid sensation was uncomfortably crawling through her brain. She could almost smell the humid green air invading her nostrils. The creeping nostalgia began to irritate her as it slowly trickled deeper into her mind.

She concentrated on the kick of her rifle to shake the chill out of her nerves. The weapon nudged her shoulder obediently, gently assuring her with each squeeze of the trigger. It was a comforting pressure, a sense of control which she was severely lacking in her life.

"Things are crawling up the roof behind you, Nara," Garrett reported, dissipating the noise in her head completely.

She turned to face the disorderly amalgamation of meat that staggered their way toward her.

Four creatures had managed to flop over the parapet and shamble toward her. They appeared to be newly created and had not completely acclimated to the hive network integration that controlled the mass. They appeared to be composed of only a single complete humanoid organism. Nothing had been spliced onto their bodies to amplify their combat abilities. Shreds of clothing that might have revealed their pasts clung to their discolored, seeping skin.

It also did not take much effort for Nara to dispatch them, their knees slowly sinking to the ground as she carved out black, cauterized holes into their forms with her insatiable armament.

"Gunners, how's it looking down there?" Nara inquired as she fired more rounds into the bodies, taking thorough precautions to ensure their demise.

"Think they're starting to run out of squishy, Boss."

"The leaders all dead?" she pressed.

"Alpha's been making quick work of them from above."

"All right, last push. Let's clean them out."

##11.4##

"Two on your side, and again on your six," Garrett reported. The ones on her side were more of the same, and Nara took care of them just as quickly, but the one creeping behind her possessed more diabolical characteristics.

The gaunt, silver-skinned humanoid outstretched its arms toward the sky, rotating its neck side to side with a series of brittle cracks. Its slender fingers moved over its face, tracing fluttery patterns across its skin. It brought its digits down its neck, then over its chest, finally focusing its attention in the center of its sternum, caressing with swirling gestures.

With a sickening cackle, it dug is dingy claws into its flesh, then it began to pull its chest apart, filling the air with wet bone-breaking pops and tearing sinew. Another ribcage revealed itself within the gory spectacle, divided evenly at the center of the creature's chest cavity. Lung-like apparatuses pulsed as the being continued its ritual of self-replication, moving up its neck to free an additional spine.

It then dug a finger inside each of its eyes and anchored the palms of its hands onto its temples. Cracks and crunches saturated the air as it laboriously pulled apart its skull. A hollow formed as bone separated, creating two additional sockets, devoid of eyeballs. The jaw severed in half, shared between the two forming creatures.

And then the two ghastly heads were finally free, testing out their new mandibles with rapid clicks of teeth. With a gurgling grunt, it heaved its leg apart, completing the separation of the two organisms. Having completed their gruesome ceremony, they stood at attention in front of Nara.

"Oh, that is so gross." Garrett winced as he watched the display. Nara appeared unmoved, having been given ample opportunity to recharge her weapons.

Peering straight ahead, the devilish duo began to approach in synchronous steps, cackling in a harmonic echo. Upon being drenched in Nara's explosive fire, the creatures revealed an irritating characteristic. Skin was merely a wrapper for the beings, peeling off in flapping chunks with each hit from her energy blasts, uncovering their armored metallic bones. They continued to advance in the same rhythmic momentum, unimpressed by the flaying of their membranes.

All right then, change of plan, Nara thought as she withdrew, flicking a switch on her rifle.

A surge of scintillating needles sprayed out of the barrel, illuminating the gaps between their ribcages with minuscule bursts. But despite all of their leaks, the creatures stayed their course.

She moved her aim down, tearing through the flexible ligaments of their legs. After the volley of masticating energy bit through enough fleshy material, the creatures dropped to the ground in a pile of undulating limbs. They stretched out their arms and crawled toward her, their cackles unchanged by their apparent disadvantage.

With an annoyed grumble, she continued her shredding rain of destruction on the unyielding creatures, draining an entire charge into the sculling bodies. As they continued their labored advance, she matched their speed with impatient, measured steps back, letting let out a perturbed sigh as she reset the ammunition in her gun.

Their cackles began to soften as another volley invaded their vitals, their grotesque, synthetic life force draining onto the roof. A final whispering burble declared their defeat, their advance ceased at the relentlessness of Nara's onslaught.

"Fucking finally," she muttered as she emptied another charge into the bodies, decimating every portion of mush inside the carapaces.

Garrett stifled an uncomfortable whimper as he witnessed the display, lowering the volume of his audio feed. He tried to watch the energy meters of the armor's interface bob up and down, but his eyes were distracted with the labored death dance.

Nara let out an irritated sigh as she reloaded, taking in the fragment of peace in the skirmish.

"Gah, where are they all coming from?" a familiar, blustering voice split the calm.

"Probably a few burrows in the facility that go underground," another gunner answered.

"The fuck?!?"

"Chin up, love, they're pulling from reserves now," the machinist encouraged cheerfully. "Look! Don't even have a full set of limbs among them!"

"A 'full set?!' That's like twenty with these things!"

"There would be less if you stopped yappin' and kept shootin'."

"Do I need to come down there and break you up?" Nara bellowed.

"No, Sir!"

##11.5##

AFTER ONE LAST clamorous discharge of weaponry, the air inside the complex was finally still.

"Status report," Nara requested as she collected her weaponry from the ground.

"All quiet, sir," the gunners announced.

"Dead here . . . again . . . or whatever," a sniper commented.

"All right, gunners scout out the area to the nearest console before the machinist enters," Nara ordered as she headed back down into the building. "While she's doing her magic, sweep the upper floors for any other movement."

"On it."

"Mechanist, if you got a few spare friends you can add to the effort, this will make the job a hell of a lot quicker," Nara added as she began dissolving the bodies and bits left on the ground, firing at heads and limbs.

Others began to follow suit as the machinist made her way to the main console, a cheerful pink energy field surrounding her and evaporating the caustic liquids on the floor with simmering hisses.

"Hey, Boss!" one of them called out to Nara from the upper floor. "You might want to see this."

"Bet you I won't," Nara remarked under her breath as she made her way to where the two mercs were staring in stupefied awe.

Inside the storage hall resided the wailing laments of mostly completed humans. Some were attached to the wall with only metal chains, while others were coated in an oozing chrysalis sprouting from the ceiling. Their bodies were emaciated and drained of recognizable life and fluid, but artificially forced to stay alive for another deranged purpose.

"Holy shit!" Garrett exclaimed to Nara in her helm, covering his agape mouth as he held back a wave of nausea.

"Survivors," one of the mercs whispered, a look of quiet disappointment on his face.

Feeble groans pushed their way through a few of the victim's mouths, a plausible reaction to the presence of the mercs outside the room. A delicate clacking of metal amplified the unsettling ambiance as one of the tormented souls struggled to reach out to them, a faint spark glinting in their listless eyes.

Garrett let out a breath of relief at the glimmer of life in the desiccated forms. He was glad to see that the team would be able to rescue at least a few souls from this nightmare.

"What's the problem?" Nara asked flatly.

"Well, what should we do with them? It looks like—" The merc's thought was sharply cut off by Nara's abrupt movement as a pistol leapt into her hand.

"Nara," Garrett breathed, "what are you going to do?"

She snapped an arm up and aimed, firing one round and splitting the head of one of the enfeebled subjects.

Two. Three. Four. Five. Six. Seven. Eight. Each shot in rapid succession, like a machine executing a routine function. She continued her benevolent assault until only limp bodies and skull fragments remained.

Garrett, as well as one of the soldiers in the room, stared slack-jawed at the execution in horror, while the other merc had his back turned away from the scene, silently nodding in approval.

"Now you know," Nara said as her weapon popped back into her armor. Sensing the bugged-out eyes of the merc next to her, Nara forced out a lukewarm effort to assure him. "You may have been able to salvage the bodies, but the minds are tainted. There is no return from this."

"But . . ." the merc managed to eject. "S–some of those were children!"

"And those would have been the worst off," she said flatly, tilting her head toward his partner. "If you encounter any more, have your friend here erase them. I don't need you getting cold feet. Some of them will try and attack you while you're vulnerable."

Garrett remained silent at his desk, swallowing a bitter taste from his mouth. While he knew she was not human, he had just been delivered a prime example of just how alien she could be, and he was unable to comprehend how anyone could act so unfeeling.

As his thoughts fluttered, he dreaded the possibility that the rest of her race held similar ethical values, and he feared whatever future encounters he might have with them. It was disappointing, thinking about an entire race composed entirely of apathetic beings. A society could not progress in a healthy direction without care for others. He shook the thought away from his mind, hoping that her jaded past was responsible for her callous actions.

Nara left the two mercs to continue their sweep, not having patience for those burdened with an oversensitive moral compass. She made her way over to the machinist, who seemed to be having the time of her life playing with the pretty lights of the console, pressing buttons and gyrating like an orchestral conductor preparing for the final movement of an epic concerto.

"How long we got?" she asked the excitable tinkerer.

"I'm done!" She beamed as she pulled out a small chip from the console, raising it in the air victoriously.

"All right, you heard her! Let's pack up and go home," Nara announced. "Watch your backs for any stragglers as we retreat."

The mercs were all too relieved to leave the damned place.

##11.6##

"That went well," Garrett said from the desk as Nara entered the apartment, still shaken over the events in the warehouse.

"Just want to get paid for this crap." She made her way to the fridge and grabbed a drink, then began disarming herself, scattering her weaponry over the table.

Garrett sat in awkward silence, hoping she would initiate conversation despite her oddly foul mood. To his relief, her NetCom interrupted his discomfort.

"It's Annon. I have your reward," the voice said.

"Fan-fucking-tastic." Nara took a mighty swig from her drink.

"Indeed. Additionally, the client had left a rather odd message to accompany it," Annon mentioned.

"Oh?" she raised an eyebrow at her bottle.

"Yes, it read, to quote, 'HA! I'll have a field day with all these specimens you brought up. Oh, and here's the 60k from the street incident too. Thanks for bringing my guys back in one piece. And for training the greens. You saved me a LOT of trouble," Annon read in a bemused tone. "Any idea what that means?"

The cogs painfully ground together with a horrid wrenching noise inside in her head. All of a sudden, her eyes flickered with malice, causing Garrett to slowly roll backward in his chair.

"Son of a *fucker*!" She growled and slammed her drink down on the table.

"Pardon?" Annon asked.

"You give that money back *this instant*," she demanded.

"Okay, now I am utterly mystified," Annon proclaimed. "And I can't. It was done in an anonymous, one-way transaction. Even if I could, I wouldn't know whom to give it to."

"God damn it, Declan! If I ever see his face again . . ." she started.

"Right, well, then." Annon cleared his throat. "If there isn't anything else, I'll be going now. Enjoy your payment."

"Yeah, eat me," she grumbled, turning her heat to Garrett, sitting uncomfortably quiet and staring at his feet in deep contemplation. "The hell's eating you?"

"Huh? I . . . nothing." He stared back into the flooring. He had no idea how to introduce the subject, but he felt he couldn't look at Nara the same if his fears weren't addressed. "Did those people have to die?"

"Oh, for *fuck's* sake." She covered her face with the palm of her hand and released an emphatic sigh at the naiveté's concern. "Look, even Declan, with all his funds and resources, doesn't have the technology to reverse the effects. Cleanly. He can revert some of the physical damage, but the mind is totally shattered. And he's even tried memory erasure. These things scar deep."

"I see," he acknowledged, but his discomfort wasn't assuaged.

"Look, you should know by now that down here is not for the pious, and you have seen firsthand the evil that takes place." She swallowed a heavy draught of her drink. "You will see pretty fucked up shit. And you wanted to shadow a mercenary anyway."

"I know, I just . . . maybe if you weren't so eager, or if you maybe looked as if you thought about it for a minute before acting . . ." He trailed off. *Or showed a little compassion.*

"It's something you get used to." She shrugged. "I've had to put down quite a few vets in my time who couldn't recognize their own squads, started killing them left and right. There is no time to think when that happens."

"I suppose," Garrett admitted.

"Would it have been better if it were a human who'd pulled the trigger?" she said coldly as she stared into the bottom of her bottle.

He hadn't thought about it, and was slightly ashamed to think her actions were the result of a cultural predisposition.

"I . . ." He contemplated the question as it struck something dark in his mind. "I'm not sure. I haven't actually seen a human do something like that firsthand."

"Then you're looking in the wrong places, kid," she scoffed. "At least I had the decency to shoot them in the face."

CHAPTER 12

##12.0##

Garrett emerged into the next room of the training arena, apprehension tainting his confidence. He had come to accept the discomfort of the sensory deprivation drills in his months of study, but Sentinel had warned that this particular exercise would test his limits.

He was placed in a chain of simulated rooms, and the objective was to move to the next with little to no contact with the patrols inside. Each room had given him one disability to overcome, starting with blindness, then audio impairment.

He took one step forward, and his vision went black.

All right, I can deal with this again, he thought. *I got a good look at everything before the lights went out.*

But a powerful sense of foreboding crawled up his spine as he drew in a deep breath and was served a startling reminder that his hearing had also not returned.

His eyes widened as a vacuum swelled inside his head. He clamped his hands over his ears to try and drown out the dysphoric sensation, the blood surging under his skin. The air was pushed out of his lungs by an invisible force as panic drowned his senses. He stumbled back into the wall, slamming his head against the cold metal surface. His hands started shaking as he gasped for air, his lungs heaving in a desperate attempt to convince himself that he was breathing.

A horrid sense of vertigo overwhelmed him as he sank to his knees, panting in silence. He wrapped his hands around his throat as the flesh began to close in on itself. His heart thundered in his chest, sending aching shockwaves twitching throughout his body in a maddening rhythm. The darkness filled his brain as his thoughts raced, terrified by what could be hiding in the shadows.

His body was torn in every direction by the scattering need to flee, but his brain conveyed that there was nowhere to go. Dizziness swirled his sense of direction, and he felt liquid drain from his head, steadily approaching the verge of unconsciousness. A sickly green cloud crawled over his eyes, causing him to obsessively blink it away.

He didn't know if he could survive much longer.

"Do you want out?" a voice suddenly split into his ears, causing him to exclaim in shock, though no sound passed through his lips.

Comforted by the minute presence, Garrett forcibly restrained his breathing, exacerbating the storm in his head.

He couldn't quit now or he would never learn.

"I . . ." he vocalized, unsure if he could communicate.

"It's all right. I can still hear you even though you can't hear yourself," the voice assured.

"I'm okay." He was uncertain who exactly he was trying to convince, the voice or himself.

"Just take a minute and calm yourself. Slow breathing. The room is exactly the same as it was when you entered."

"O—kay," Garrett meekly replied, ordering the cannons in his chest to cease fire.

He slid his back up the wall to bring himself to his feet, but his swirling head tried to heave him back to the ground. As his torso abruptly lurched forward, the nerves in his legs instinctively kept him upright with a maladroit stomp.

"Easy there. You're doing fine," the voice promised. "This room is small. If you would like to continue, try to get across and we can take it from there."

Garrett forced his eyes shut, convincing his mind that he was voluntarily subjecting himself to the darkness, a false sense of control that he desperately needed.

He reached a shaky hand outward and advanced toward one of the pillar structures his memory allowed him to recall. A sense of relief washed away a shred of anxiety as his sweaty palms grasped the cold, stone-like structure.

Good, I was right about that, he thought. *Are there patrols here? Can they see me? How the fuck am I supposed to hide from them?*

As his breathing began to slow to a sustainable pace, he became aware of a curious sensation prickling the palm of his hand. Uncertain whether his mind was toying with him, he tried to tune out the pounding in his head so he could concentrate.

The pillar cast soft but constant vibrations down his fingers, soothing the nerves under his skin. He slipped his hand higher up the column, discovering a cool draft swirling the air above. He paused and let the current trickle around his hand, taking an odd comfort in the drastic temperature difference.

He followed the air flow with his other arm, tracing the borders of a wall of cold air next to him. The swirling air currents dissolved his tension as they danced around his fingers, manifesting into a battle of thermodynamics.

He pulled his hand back, letting the bumps on his skin recede from the warmth around him. He then took a cautious step forward, leaving the security of the pillar. A shiver raced up his spine as he stepped through the chilling barrier, the cool air now shifting to a mild, wintery scale.

In slow, undulating motions, he stuck his arms out and waved his awkward, fleshy antennae to collect data from the air around him. He leaned to one side, stretching his arm out, sensing warmth again across the way. Steeling himself, he ordered his legs forward, leaving the bubble of cold air.

Three steps later, he discovered another bubble the same size, warm this time. Puzzled with the significance, he returned to the chill behind him. He tried moving in other directions and found other warm bubbles spaced approximately the same distance apart. An image played through in his imagination—he was standing inside a room plotted with a grid of air currents.

The room had been designed to give the subject a sense of environmental control, and if the bubbles were consistently placed, he could map out the general size of the area. While he had to trust his navigational instinct and memory to keep him from getting hopelessly lost, he had a starting point to paint a mental picture inside his brain.

He crept forward, continuing to draw the images to memory. After mindful calculation, he predicted the location of the structural pillars set around the room, which were also uniformly placed in a grid pattern. He let out a long breath of air, and the stiffness in his muscles began to uncoil as he grounded himself with his new-found knowledge.

Just as his heart calmed to a delicate thunder, one of the bubbles of cold air adjacent to him violently churned, tearing the surface apart.

"Oh, shit," he cursed silently in the open air. Someone else was in the room, right next to him.

Sparks discharged across the surface of his skin as a hand clamped onto his shoulder. In a fit of panic, he grabbed the offender's wrist and pried if off himself.

Shit. He panicked as he maintained his hold on the attacker's arm. *I can't tell where they are.*

The scraps of his fighting knowledge began to trickle in his nerves as he whirled around, yanking the attacker toward him. As the body slammed against his chest, a rasp of balmy air danced across his neck, a breath of exertion from the assailant.

Much better, Garrett thought.

The close-quarters combat felt unnatural to him without his senses. Since he could not see his combatant, he resorted to experimental tugs and pushes, trying to get a sense of where the offender's joints were located.

But the attacker was reacting with his movement, squirming around to rescue their trapped limb, causing Garrett to squeeze their wrist tighter. After a few seconds of this graceless dance, Garrett attempted a guess at the individual's approximate height.

As the offender began to pull away from him, Garrett slipped a leg behind their knee. Hurling his weight forward, he lunged after what he assumed was the general area of the person's neck. As he latched onto the person's throat, the palm of his hand met with a protruding lump in the center. It pulsed as the attacker gasped. He heaved his shoulder forward, flipping the attacker over his leg. As the offender slipped out of his grasp, Garrett felt the ground shudder as they landed hard on the simulation's floor.

Garrett didn't wait to see if they were injured, or to even to confirm whether they would get up and chase after him.

He bolted away from the assailant, using the bubbles of cold air to guide him forward, chanting in his head and counting.

Cold. Hot. Cold. Hot. He suddenly skirted to one side, evading a pillar obstacle that split the air drafts apart.

Hot, cold, hot, he continued in his head. *Shit, how many did I start from?*

His question was soon answered as he slammed face first into a solid metal wall. He pinched the bridge of his nose tightly as stabbing pains cavorted over his sinuses, and his body doubled over in a useless attempt to reduce the sensation.

"Fuck!" he silently shouted as he blinked away tears. He stood up straight and composed himself, grumbling obscenities of embarrassment at the situation. *Shit, what now? Where the fuck is the door, left or right?*

Panic iced his nerves as he considered his pursuer lurking in the shadows. He took off in one direction, sliding his hands around the wall as he ran. As his hand brushed toward the ceiling, he noticed another stream of air churning above him, and it was flowing in the opposite direction.

Shit, he grumbled as he abruptly turned around. *Wrong way . . . I think?*

Both of his hands frantically scoured the surface of the wall, capturing the sensation of the air above him. The currents pushed harder against his skin as he moved forward, and the icy streams gradually numbed his digits.

A shock ran up his arm as the nail of his finger suddenly bent upward. His fingertips had collided with a protruding metal box jutting out of the wall. He frantically ran his hands over the familiar shape as a crazed chortle rippled out of his lungs, the air spreading his lips into a maddened grin.

Sweet merciful gods, he thought as he slammed the door control.

He felt the air next to him rush apart and conflict with the pressure of the room inside. He burst through the room, his throat letting out a small whine as he waited for the door to shut behind him. His knees refused to go any further, hurling him back against the wall in protest. He consumed the new air in voracious gasps, a pattern that did not permit him to relax.

To his relief, his senses began to re-enter his brain as the tension of the encounter peaked. He rolled the rest of his body onto the floor once he could see where it was.

"That was very entertaining to watch," Garrett heard the voice say to him. "I think you have learned something today."

"No more, please," he beseeched the air, unsure of where the voice was coming from.

"I can oblige that request."

##12.1##

GARRETT ORDERED A COLD, soothing tea from the service drone to calm his still shuddering nerves. The humiliating experience still rattled his senses. He had selected another venue far outside his realm in Upper to calm himself, not wanting another chance encounter with Cordelia, the creature of impeccable timing.

He let the buzz of the city distract him, watching the people pass around the observation bubble of the bar. Taking an interest in the noises immediately nearby, he found himself eavesdropping on a discussion between a few of the locals sitting at the next table over.

"Thanks so much for answering my call. I just couldn't wait to see you," a bubbly young woman cheered at her partner.

"My pleasure." The man she was speaking with smiled so widely that Garrett was certain he strained something in his face.

"The weather is lovely, is it not?"

Though Garrett couldn't explain why, the overwhelming banality of the conversation suddenly irked him. He shook an impulsive cringe from his shoulder as he absorbed the prepackaged introductions and pleasantries. The people engaged each other as if they had computer screens for faces, displaying a limited number of responses selected with a tap of a finger. It could barely be considered interaction at all.

"Why, yes, it is. Xircon created a lovely ambiance this evening," the man replied.Even their body language was constructed through a program, rigid and formal. They projected the same monotony their vocal organs synthesized.

It's too simple to read, Garrett thought. *I bet I could convince these people to buy insurance off the trash droids.*

"Did you see—"

"The borealis this morning? It was quite good," Garrett quipped condescendingly into his teacup.

"I'm sorry, sir?" The man turned around questioningly at the interruption.

Whoops, Garrett thought. *All right, get out of this one. It shouldn't be too hard.*

"Huh?" Garrett answered in an annoyed tone with a finger over his ear. "Oh, nothing, I was just on a call."

The man instinctively apologized with a bewildered scrunch of his eyebrows. "Ah. Excuse me."

Well, that was not very smooth, Garrett thought as he cleared his throat. He skirted away in discomfort, abandoning the remainder of his tea.

Are people really this simple? he mused as he briskly walked through the streets, heading toward home. Upworld was depressingly boring and offered no resource for varied human interaction. In a city so populated, it was hard to imagine loneliness thriving. He desperately wanted peers, or even a single confidant that he could entrust his feelings with.

The night had left Garrett exhausted, and he wanted nothing more than to melt into his own bed. But when he opened the door to his room, a disquieting surprise was eagerly awaiting him.

"Hello, Garrett!" Cordelia waved vigorously.

I really should be careful with what I wish for, Garrett thought as he felt the blood drain from his face.

She was wearing a short-cropped dress, the bright blue fabric immediately informed him that she intended to drag him away from his home.

"Cordelia." He inhaled, instinctively disguising the exasperation from his voice. "What are you doing here . . . in my bedroom?"

"Oh, your mother sent me up here when she realized you were out. She said you wouldn't mind," she reported cheerfully.

"Did she, now? How . . . hospitable of her." He breathed through clenched teeth. "How long have you been waiting?"

"Only a couple of hours, but never you mind." She stood up and walked toward him, causing his instincts to take over and back away from the predator.

"And what can I do for you?" He cleared his throat and fidgeted with his clothing, trying to hide the look of terror from his face. *I need to get her out of here.*

"Oh, don't be so formal. You know me well enough." She patted him derisively on the shoulder.

"I apologize. I just didn't expect guests . . . in my room," he emphasized. "So, what do you need?"

"Well, a new club opened up on Emerald Circle, and I was wondering if you would like to come with me." She scanned him up and down and chortled. "It looks like you need a night off."

God damn it all, he thought bitterly. *You know you're being fake. You know **I** know you're being fake. And you also know I can't just tell you to fuck off.*

"Honestly, I have a bit of a headache, and the bright club scene would aggravate it dearly." He held his head in discomfort, a convincing gesture considering the pounding in his skull.

"Oh, that's okay. We can have a nice quiet evening at Feldar's Coffee House." She took his arm and started to lead him away.

"That isn't what I had in mind," he said as he elegantly rolled himself out of her grasp, utilizing one of the evasion maneuvers Sentinel had taught him. He ran through strategies in his mind to get her out of his house, but exhaustion clouded his judgment. The only thing that came to mind was the direct, forceful approach.

He took her hand and ushered her into the doorway as politely, yet firmly, as possible. The puzzled expression she gave him as she allowed his guidance made him feel uneasy. He was uncertain whether her countenance was honest, but he refused to take any chances with someone who enjoyed deceiving so much.

"While I do not have any intentions whatsoever to be rude," he started with a charming smile, "I have had a rather tiresome evening, and I am in severe need of sleep. I would not be pleasant company this night, so perhaps another time. Thank you for stopping by, though."

"I see." She gave him a dejected look. "Well, I will be in touch with you soon."

"Of that I am most certain." He smiled gracefully as he shut his bedroom door quickly, not allowing her to respond.

He knew she was going to linger before leaving the premises, so he sat down in the middle of his floor, scanning the room for anything amiss. Ignoring his aching muscles, he waited anxiously on the solid surface for a safe length of time to call out to Baran.

"Baran. I need you. Now," he bade.

"What's the matter?"

"I can't talk here. Got a place to go?"

"Yes, the chair appears to be reupholstered," Baran informed, letting Garrett know their usual spot should be accessible, utilizing jargon they hadn't needed for years.

Garrett let him know how long it would take him to travel. "Something to do with the northern constellations."

##12.2##

GARRETT MADE sure to take an indirect path to their meeting place, one of the few quiet and discreet bars in the Uppercity.

The establishment manufactured nostalgia as it pumped the air full of mellow jazz. The archaic noise bounced around eggshell painted walls, which were bordered with black floral silhouettes. The furniture was made from elegantly fabricated faux cherry wood, sculpted into dramatic arches and trimmed with brass filigree.

The ambience glowed in soft yellow light projecting from the sconces that mimicked tree branches climbing up the walls. Even the staff maintained the atmosphere by dressing up in sharp suits styled from something out of a Film Noir simulation.

Baran was waiting for him at the bar, drinking scotch from a tulip-shaped glass.

"Thanks," Garrett managed to breathe, still processing the severity of the situation.

"What's troubling you?" Baran asked again.

"It's Cordelia. I can't seem to get her away from me." He tried to hide the tone of panic from his voice, but his heart wouldn't stop fluttering, diverting his focus in several foreboding directions.

"I can take care of it, but you look like hell. What's the matter? It's not like you haven't had stalkers before." Baran smirked as he polished off his drink.

"This one's . . . different. Sociopathic." He stared blankly at the wood of the bar, grabbing at any appropriate words to describe someone so vile.

"Again, that pretty much describes all stalkers of various degrees." Baran gestured with the empty glass before setting it down on the bar.

"Hyper-intelligent. She isn't stalking me for my relationship status. She's a shark, a snake, a wolf." He could no longer hide the shaking from his voice as desperation set in. "And she somehow always knows where I am."

"Well, those are a bit rarer, but still not uncommon." Baran shook his head, but his attitude immediately shifted when he met the look of terror in Garrett's disturbed eyes. "All right, what would you like me to do?"

"I need you to check for bugs." He paused to consider the worst. "Especially in the elevator. I have a feeling she knows about my field trips."

"Sure, I will check that out. Hopefully, it's nothing," Baran reassured.

"I have a . . . feeling. I can't describe it, but that one is tenacious. Mother let her into my room today, and she sat there waiting until I got back, well into the night. Who the hell knows what she pawed through."

"I see." Baran furrowed his brow in concern. "I can't do much about your mother's actions. She's very keen on merging you with another family. But I can keep an eye out for tampering. You're right, someone like that is probably after information."

Garrett breathed a sigh of relief. "Thank you."

"Want a drink?"

"I . . . sure." Garrett shook his head back into reality. "I can't keep her away from me without being rude. You know how well that's received up here."

"Yep, word travels fast," Baran said as he waved the bartender over, who refilled his glass with a hospitable smile. "Like I said, I can only do so much, despite being a damn good gatekeeper. I can't be everywhere at once."

"Understood."

"Relax," Baran firmly ordered. "You got somewhere to go for tonight? I don't know how long it will take me to scour through everything, and you aren't needed up here for a while."

"Yeah, I do." Garrett nodded wearily. "You sure you're okay with me hiding out?"

"I'll be fine, if that's what you mean." Baran threw his head back as he finished his second drink. "Use the elevators in Tenshinn jurisdiction for now. They're smaller and no one uses them. I'll call you when I've looked through everything."

"Thanks for looking out for me," Garrett said.

"It's my job. Don't make it difficult for me," Baran warned.

"I try not to." Garrett played with a thought in his mind. "But you're the kind of person who can get out of trouble no matter what."

"You have no idea, kid." Baran shook his head. "You have no. Idea."

##12.3##

Three system trackers and two cameras, Baran thought as he walked toward Antonin's office. *All infecting Garrett's personal devices. Someone who was looking for a quick deal in trade secrets would have just brute-forced their way into the master rooms. But she is after something long-term beneficial, a permanent relationship with the company. Garrett was right. She is dangerous.*

Baran shook the implications from his head as he stepped through the door, greeted by the stone-faced Galavantier sitting at his desk, examining figures and trade statements from the evening.

"Ah, good, I've been waiting for your report," Antonin addressed him, not looking up from the documents scrolling through his screen.

"The assault on the Gladius Clan was successful," Baran reported. "All members, as well as affiliations, have been tracked down and eliminated. There is no one left to trouble the facilities again."

"And the project data?"

"Retrieved before duplicates could be transmitted," Baran assured.

"Excellent. That will be all," Antonin dismissed, eyes tracing along the lines of numbers.

Baran hesitated, shifting weight on his feet as he carefully formulated words regarding the pressing matter.

"Sir, about Ms. Vaylenuran," Baran started, hoping to catch more of his attention.

"A charming girl, isn't she?" One corner of the executive's mouth slyly ascended.

"I suppose." Baran cleared his throat. "But I have some concerns regarding having her on the premises."

"Oh, do you?" Antonin broke away from his figures and looked up at Baran, an eyebrow raised in disapproval.

"Yes. I have uncovered several surveillance tags on the complex. All have been taken care of."

"Very interesting." Antonin drummed his fingers on the desk as he considered the news.

"Yes, sir," Baran confirmed as he steeled himself for Antonin's impending reaction. “And I would advise keeping her away from this compound."

"Clever girl." Antonin’s grin infected the opposite corner of his mouth. He paused and tilted his head, folding his hands under his chin. Noises of contemplation quietly emitted from his throat as he considered the new intelligence.

Baran gritted his teeth in apprehension. Nothing made him more uncomfortable than the boss’s knowing smile. And Antonin knew it, taking advantage of his uneasiness at every opportunity.

Antonin broke the grinding silence. “No, actually, I intend to bring her closer."

“Sir?" Baran furrowed his eyebrows. *What is he planning?*

"She is an ideal person to have control over an establishment this large, but she has a lot more to learn. If she wants to gain favor with me, she will have to get beneath your watchful radar, now won't she?" Antonin’s smile widened. "But rest assured, I have more than enough faith in your capabilities. You would not be standing here otherwise."

"I'm not sure I understand, sir." Baran swallowed a lump in his throat. But he understood completely. As if he wasn’t under enough pressure, another weight was casually tossed onto his shoulders by Antonin’s twisted humor.

"Let her play her games, and we’ll see how far we can get ahead of her," Antonin announced.

"I don't think it's advisable to play with fire like that,” Baran pressed, trying to keep his voice calm. “And, to my knowledge, Garrett has no intention of passing his affection to her.”

"Soon, he will have no choice in the matter.” Antonin glared at Baran coldly. “He had better come to a decision quickly, or it will be made for him. To make his transition smoother, you should assure him that it is in his best interest to be with Ms. Vaylenuran, using whatever means you deem necessary."

"That was *not* part of the arrangement." Baran’s jaw clamped shut after he uttered the last syllable, his blood boiling underneath his skin.

"Remember your place, Baran." Antonin narrowed his eyes. "Where is he, by the way?"

"He's out to the market at the starports," Baran replied, exhaling venom through his nose.

"Remind me again, what exactly does he do there?" Antonin pressed a finger over his lips, broadcasting his impatience.

"Shopping, I would assume." Baran shrugged as he slowed his heart. "He likes to talk to the merchants from other worlds. He often sits at the stations to watch the trade ships take off and land. I think he has plans to travel someday."

"I have frequently ordered you to dispel those starry-eyed ideals," Antonin commanded, stamping a finger on his desk. "His place is here, on this planet."

"I have, as much as possible," Baran continued. "But I can only do so much while minding matters Underground, in addition to the security compounds up here."

"That is not good enough. It has been made irrefutably clear that grooming him was to be your utmost priority in our business relationship," Antonin scolded.

"Yes, and I—" But the overlord refused to hear his case.

"You do not want me pulling out of this deal," Antonin warned. "I assure you that I have nothing to lose in doing so. You, on the other hand, I can promise a very dark future."

Baran could only hold his gaze at the floor as the threat lashed at him.

"I am not satisfied with his progress," Antonin declared. "He may be capable at managing money, but you know the extent of skills this position requires. And if he is not ready for it, he will be united with someone who is."

"Yes, sir," Baran replied, straining to maintain his expressionless gaze.

"And Baran, he had better start learning soon. His time of airheaded disregard for responsibility is ending. You will make this clear to him," he commanded.

"Yes, sir." Baran bowed, excusing himself out of the room. As he walked down the hallway, he hastily typed an encrypted message to Garrett.

You were right. I took care of it. I need you to stay away for a while longer. I'll call for you when I have finished up here.

CHAPTER 13

##13.0##

Garrett looked back down at his NetCom as he walked alongside Nara, reading the text over and over in his head. Even though it didn't explicitly say, Baran's cryptic message told him that a catastrophic storm awaited him Upworld. Possibilities swirled around in his brain, leaving him dreading his return home.

I could always just move down here in Under, Garrett contemplated, *or even better, I could hire a ship and just leave the planet altogether. But Baran . . .*

"Problem?" Nara inquired, peering inside the bottle of the beverage she'd procured from the food vendors.

"Huh?" he snapped out of his getaway plans. "Oh, no. Just coordinating my schedule with someone."

Nara uttered a noncommittal noise as she tossed her head back to finish her drink, then chucked the bottle at an unmarked receptacle.

Garrett eased out a breath of air as he let the droning of the marketplace distract him from his fretting. He tried to implant the notion in his brain that whatever issue was pressing him at home, he would not let it ruin his outing down here. Skimming over the crowd, he let his eyes wander through the sea of shoppers as he tried to suppress the apprehension deviously poking at him.

As he perused the stalls for interesting stops, a ghostly sensation prickled the back of his neck. He turned toward what he perceived as the source of the discomfort and spotted a peculiar entity off in the distance.

A humanoid figure concealed by a heavy, ratty brown cloak peered at them from the edges of the crowd. Garrett squinted to discern their features through the void inside the hood, but only a glint of light where eyes should be flickered back at him.

The compulsion to blink overtook his eyelids, and the figure vanished from the streets. Garrett scanned the perimeter of the marketplace, searching for the peculiar individual, absorbing details of the faces in the crowd one by one. But the voyeuristic presence had eluded him, leaving no trace of its presence, apart from the unnerving feeling crawling over his skin.

"You know, I have the distinct impression that we are being followed," Garrett announced as he uncomfortably scratched his arm.

"Because we are." Nara looked at him oddly. "Though I am surprised you noticed."

"You must be rubbing off on me." He smiled nervously.

"I see." She hummed and raised an eyebrow.

"The brown-cloaked figures, right?"

"They've been tailing you since you got shot. The *first* time," she emphasized.

"Who are they?" Garrett asked, anxiously glancing over his shoulder.

"Shadows. They won't bother us. In fact, we're safe so long as they're here," she explained. "Start worrying when they leave for good."

"Then whoever hired them has found what they needed?" He had heard whispers of the ubiquitous guild of information dealers through the shadier realms of Under. The Shadows were a surreptitious band of mercenaries who held an unyielding neutral alignment, taking no part in the wars encompassing Arcadia. If you needed secrets and intelligence to gain advantage over an adversary, you didn't find them—they found you.

"Yep." She glared at him questioningly. "You wouldn't happen to know why they're here, would you? Or perhaps who hired them?"

"I haven't the slightest," he said earnestly. "No one I know has connections down here."

Garrett's face scrunched up pensively as he considered her interrogation. He didn't have much in the way of contacts, or enemies. He had no friends, and a very limited family circle, provided a dysfunctional group of individuals who sometimes inhabited the same household as him could be considered a family.

Antonin would also never risk tainting his good name by associating with the likes of the criminals down here. But the man also never actually taught him much about how the business was run. As large as the media claims the Galavantier estate to be, an underground operation wouldn't be out of the realm of possibility.

Baran was never any help whenever he asked about matters either. He would just desperately plead to stop assaulting him with so many questions. It would not surprise Garrett if he was purposefully covering up unpleasant details, but he also couldn't see Baran taking pleasure in denying him information either.

Garrett found himself reflecting on his unconventional relationship with the hybrid chief of security. To him, it resembled a bizarre domestic tug-of-war, with Baran being used as the rope as he played conciliator between him and his patriarch. While he appreciated not having to engage with Antonin directly, it left him wondering what exactly it was that constantly tore Baran apart.

The thought suddenly made Garrett question the man's loyalties, and his brain started speeding to conclusions about conceivable abhorrent acts he was potentially concealing from him. Memories of Nara's infiltration exploits flooded into his mind, and he involuntarily recalled the gruesome displays megacorporations were capable of inflicting on living beings. Pieces of organs pulsating in chambers, the tortured fish openly displayed as casual office décor, the Experimentalist test subjects . . . they all looped through his mind in macabre detail.

A shudder twitched down his spine as his imagination assaulted his brain, letting suspicions overtake him as he considered both his own and Nara's safety.

The intrusion of the cloaked figure amplified his anxiety, leaving him feeling inexplicably violated. He clenched his jaw as he tried to ground himself, but the sense of paranoia pushed him to an unbearable edge. He impulsively looked over his shoulder again, only slightly relieved that the visitor had not reappeared.

"Hey," he softly voiced to Nara. "Can we go back to your place? I need to take a rest for a bit."

"Yeah, all right," Nara replied and promptly changed direction, giving no indication that she acknowledged his mental state.

They left the murmur of the crowded marketplace, back into the comfort of the familiar silent streets. Garrett took a few deep breaths from the cool night air, collecting himself from the chaos in his brain.

He appreciated her discretion, but Garrett was convinced she suspected something was off. Instead of pestering her with conversation, he saved the subject for later and distracted himself with the ambience of the Underground—the gentle energetic hum of the lights, the soft echoes of their footsteps, and the delicate breeze carrying debris across the hollow ruined buildings. There was much less to pay attention to, allowing him to sort through the mess of half-thoughts infecting his brain.

Whatever happens, he told himself, *I need to develop some contingency plans.*

He considered broaching the subject with Nara. While it would be easier to move around with someone who had contacts, he also didn't want her to get involved in any likely political conflict. She would also inevitably ask questions he wasn't comfortable answering.

He pondered indirect topics to test conversational waters. A guise of expanding his network to find good suppliers might work, or on the extreme level, people who were quick at moving living cargo around the Undercity. The concept of being shoved in a metal box for a month or two sounded worlds more appealing to him than a lifetime of whatever hell was destined for him Upworld.

Maybe I should ask Baran what to do. Garrett scoffed at his absurd internal statement. *He's fantastic at dealing with this sort of balancing act.*

He mulled over his predicament as they climbed up the busted stairs of Nara's flat. Her opinion would be invaluable to him, and he felt that he owed her an explanation for his strange behavior. After carefully choosing his phrasing, he opened his mouth to initiate his conversation.

He was about to speak when her arm sharply snapped up to her side, whisking the words out of his lips. He froze as he watched her look straight ahead, not where she was aiming.

A pitiful yelp cried out from the darkness as she fired a shot into the hallway. Her wrist made a miniscule movement as she recharged her weapon for a second shot.

Garrett took a quiet step back as he analyzed her tense posture. Confused by her show of anger, he peered into the shadows to see a familiar man approach, arms raised in surrender.

"Do you have a death wish, Bellanar?" Nara slowly turned her head toward the crimson prowler, her eyes radiating a vicious glare. *"Or are you just that naive?"*

"Well," the intruder started, swallowing back his fear, *"I had hoped that you might have calmed down from our initial encounter."*

"Is your curiosity satisfied?" she challenged, aiming her pistol higher.

"Please understand." The man took a deep breath. *"I have no one else to talk to. No one else who will listen."*

*"And you think **I** would?"* She edged forward. *"You actually feel safe crawling into my hole in the universe after all that has been done?"*

"I . . ." He hesitated, knowing he only had the chance to speak a few words before she would either chase him away or kill him outright.

"I'm. Waiting." Nara spoke in Trade.

"It . . ." he attempted, willfully choosing the topic that would get the most rise out of her. *"It's Warlord Abberon."*

He barely had time to wince as Nara lunged at him, grabbing him by the jacket and slamming his back against the nearest wall. A pained wheeze burst from his chest as the air forced out of his lungs.

"You DARE breathe that name in my presence?" she bellowed with an unearthly voice, shuddering the crumbling walls of the complex.

"My . . . my apologies, Warlord." He bit his lip in apprehension, averting his gaze.

"Do not refer to me in such a manner. I am not your Warlord, or your liberator." Her tone shifted from anger to weariness, almost pity. She then released her grasp and shoved the man away from her.

The trespasser steadied himself from the momentum and turned to face her. He was about to open his mouth again when she stabbed the air behind her with a finger of warning.

"Get out of my sight, pestilence."

Startled by the wavering of her voice, the man hastily backed away, withdrawing into the darkness of the ruins.

A percussive roar rumbled from Nara's throat, drowning out the footsteps of the retreating visitor. As her frustration came to a head, she raised a fist and struck the wall in front of her. The concrete groaned as it split into jagged fissures around her knuckles, the wall quaking with the force of the blow.

Stunned by the emotional encounter, Garrett maintained his distance and considered vacating the premises as well. But his body froze as Nara abruptly turned, heading toward the apartment entrance.

"Get in, and don't drag your heels," she barked as she slammed the control to her door.

He pried his feet off the ground and followed her in, softly shutting the door behind him. He then slipped around her quietly as she began disarming herself and headed to the safety of the computer desk.

He watched Nara from his seat as she moved about the room, taking an uneasy note of her body language. Instead of her usual weary stagger, her posture was tightened up in discomfort, or possibly frustration. Both responses looked similar to him. She appeared to be suppressing something, rolling her shoulders around and straightening her back, controlling her breathing to a quiet rhythm.

In his observation, Garrett accidently caught her eyes, and he quickly looked down at his feet. He knew she wouldn't want him asking questions, and he hoped she wouldn't interrogate him about his fits of paranoia in the market either.

Neither of them was in the mood for conversing, so they sat in the apartment in apprehensive silence.

Until a blaring NetCom alert shattered the tension.

She stood up and glanced at the caller's number, letting out an irritated growl.

"Oh, fantastic, exactly who I wanted to talk to today," she muttered as she answered the machine.

"I have a job for you," Annon reported through the channel.

"I would never have guessed," she spat. "Usually, you call to inquire about my wellbeing. Or invite me out to a meal at one of your exclusive dining locations."

"Just come to my office, if you please." The agent barely had time to let out a sigh as Nara cut the channel.

"Do what you want," she muttered to Garrett as she slipped her coat back on. "I'll be back . . . sometime. Maybe."

##13.1##

Nara was still seething from Bellanar's intrusion, and the annoyance of Annon's call wasn't enough to obstruct her compulsive pondering. Something cataclysmic was about to occur on her home world, and hope must be scarce if the man was willing to risk his life and endure her anger. Unfortunately for his people, they'd made their choice when they passed final judgment on her.

She told herself long ago that she didn't care about their fate, but she was wondering why it bothered her now.

Abberon. Bellanar's strident voice resonated through her brain.

Acid began to crawl its way up her throat as she continued forward. She angrily kicked a rock at the office building, focusing on its echoes as it hopped across the ground. Her blood suddenly froze to ice, and she halted her step as the sounds danced over an irregularity in the street.

She had taken this route to Annon's office enough to learn the patterns of soundwaves as they ricocheted from buildings and rubble heaps. But this time, something else was nearby, disrupting ripples of vibration within the street.

She kicked another piece of scrap in front of her, listening closely as the anomaly moved, the echoes rebounding off the new obstacle.

Someone was watching her from above.

Slipping a pistol into her hand, she observed the reverberations trickling around her as she glanced up at the crumbling rooftops, sensing a humanoid presence above. It was familiar, but faint. Definitely not a Shadow, but barely human, a fragment of a sign of life.

She scanned the crooked skyline for the intruder, but the deeper she searched, the more the fleeting sensation weakened. A moment longer, and it was gone.

She tightened her grip on her gun as she walked into the agency, glancing over her shoulder as she stepped inside.

Annon was pacing back and forth when she entered, fervently breathing in a cigarette with distasteful, but effective, ingredients. He jumped back when he noticed her in the reflection of his office window, then nervously dusted himself off to regain his composure.

"Ahh, you're here. Good. Sit down." Annon put out his cigarette in an ashtray, then turned around and clutched the back of his chair, avoiding Nara's initial gaze.

"You got something for me?" she impassively asked as she seated herself.

"Yes. Yes, I do. Something quite lucrative, as a matter of fact." He waited to see her reaction, but the stone-faced soldier merely looked at him with arms folded, waiting for him to continue. "A client wants you to recover something called 'Project Samson.' They don't know what it is. All they know is that they want it."

"Oh, that sounds promising," she scoffed.

"I, well, yes." He fidgeted, drumming his fingers over the chair. "Anyway. They know exactly where it is, through their intel, but they haven't been able to get insider information on it. They only know that it is a huge breakthrough in the biomechanical market."

Nara raised an eyebrow. "And where is this 'Project Samson'?"

Annon folded his hands nervously and pressed his index fingers into the corners of his lips. Little meditative humming noises babbled from the inside of his closed mouth, as if having a conversation with someone else, ignoring Nara in the room.

"Why are you hesitating, Annon?" she grumbled. "You're going to have to tell me sometime if you want me to do this damn job."

"Project Samson . . ." He cringed as the words trickled off his tongue. "Is located at one of Galavantier's research and development facilities."

"Ahh, fffff-*uck*." She hissed and pinched the bridge of her nose.

"They are paying seven million," he quickly added.

"Fuck!" She bit her lip as the dilemma slapped her over the head.

Money was never a motivator for her. It was the challenge of high-risk contracts. A job paying such a ludicrous amount was guaranteed to stack the odds against her capabilities. The adrenaline from recklessly treading on Death's coattails balanced out her brain chemicals with an almost opioid effect, allowing her to forget about the demons that wracked her consciousness.

It had been a long time since she'd toyed around in Galavantier's underground factories, and she even promised a few individuals that she would never do it again. But the night's events left her in a reckless mood, and tempting *Xannat* was a very appealing distraction.

"Fine," she finally mumbled. "Give me the details."

"Oh, excellent!" The agent clapped through a breath of relief. "I'm so glad that you are—"

"Shove it directly up your plasticky ass."

"Right." He pawed through his information feed to find the job listing and handed the data to her. "Here you are."

"Fantastic," she seethed as she stood up and snatched the document. "If you don't hear from me in two weeks, I'm probably dead. Good luck finding someone else to do this job though."

She disappeared from the office before he could babble out a response.

Her eyes fervently scanned the horizon as she stepped into the streets, searching for the unwelcome spectator who'd visited. She wasn't in the mood for a fight, especially with a synthetic lifeform. But the still air told her nothing, and the miniscule trace of life was nowhere to be found. Whoever was watching her had either left the area, or masked themselves from her completely.

Giving up on the search, she let her shoulders relax and continued her trek home. Everything around her felt off—the job and its lack of detail and Bellanar's unwelcome visit. Even the human was acting peculiar.

Perhaps he was taking her words to heart, learning through actual experience instead of seeking the fastest route to knowledge. But his ambiguous motivation still troubled her. No one has that kind of drive without seeking blood in return. Especially humans.

As she stepped into her apartment, she was welcomed by Garrett's uneasy smile.

Warmth, concern, and a heavy shadow of weariness, she thought as she scrutinized the human's expression. *Not a single shred of malice, as Sentinel put it.*

Wordlessly, she headed over to the far end of the room, then knelt on the floor to unlock the bottom drawer of one of her cabinets.

"I've got my job details," she explained to Garrett over her shoulder as she extracted a device from the drawer. "And this one is very, *very* dangerous. I require your unwavering attention."

The strange box resembled an electronic cat-o-nine-tails, with each wire sprouting from a small plastic tab and ending with a sharp needle-like barb. She then pulled out her armor badge from her coat pocket and plugged it into a spare port. The sinister peripheral snapped awake as she calibrated the device to the armor. With a sizzle and a jolt, the barbs explosively snapped out, expanding into tiny, multi-pronged arrowheads.

Garrett stared at the device with repulsed curiosity. The purpose of the contraption baffled him, and his imagination told him that it was unwise to ask.

"Do not take this sentence lightly." Her voice resonated through his ears. "I am putting my *trust* in you."

A lump formed in his throat, imprisoning his response inside his lungs. He slowly nodded in compliance, daunted by the severity of the arbitrary task she was shouldering him with.

"Good. I'm glad you understand," she said as she stood up. "Get logged in. We're doing this tonight."

##13.2##

Tiny dots of illumination glittered through her vision as she walked through the maintenance corridor. She brushed a hand along the metal and wires until she uncovered the beveled seams of an access hatch. With a few swipes of a prying tool, she popped the panel open and clambered out of the safety of the compartment, entering a void of blackness.

Her helmet clicked through cycles of visual settings as she advanced through the dark, while a status alarm chirped a noise of warning into her ear. She glanced over at the interface feed and watched the environmental system trigger, supplying her with breathable air as it reported cautions regarding the uninhabitable vacuum outside the armor.

While her suit was working for her in harmony to keep her safe, the hellish contraption she'd augmented it with was also performing its visceral task. At Nara's command, it happily bore itself into her flesh, injecting wires across her limbs, spine, and neck.

She turned around to rest her back against the wall, panting for breath as an intrusive weight expanded inside her chest. She winced as she turned her neck to one side, the needles of the inhibiting device jabbing deeper into her skin.

A weak laugh escaped her lips as she pondered over her predicament. She knew better than to attempt a job before acclimating to the inhibitor, but the chain of jittery, sleepless nights was an unappealing symptom to endure, as was the whirlwind of overthinking brought about by the mission's ambiguous objectives. She knew she wouldn't be able to rest until the task was completed.

She could hear Declan's chastising voice inside her head. After all, she gave him her word that she wouldn't do anything this irresponsible anymore. But then again, he'd also agreed to build the mechanism in the first place, so he shared a part of the blame. At least, that's how she justified it back then.

She tweaked a setting in her sights as she cast aside her self-depreciating thoughts, tailoring a visual filter that combined night vision with energy emission patterns.

"Are you doing okay?" Garrett asked, concerned about the amount of time she took to configure her HUD.

"Yeah, just . . ." her brain fogged up as she formed a complete sentence. *"Just give me a minute."*

She tried to fill her chest with air, but the insidious hardware constricted her circulatory system, shrinking her lung capacity in half. She watched her vital signs pitifully throb across her display as the machinery took control, throttling her internal systems to a precarious rhythm. Everything inside her operated to imitate a human life sign, from her breathing and body temperature to the jarring percussion of a human pulse.

She resorted to taking half-breaths, re-training herself how to inhale and exhale as sweat began to crawl over her body. Dizziness and nausea toyed with her cognitive function as the artificially induced fever lashed across her skin.

"Why are you doing this to yourself?" Garrett's concern deepened as he saw the display start to sway.

"Explain . . . later," she managed. *"Keep talking, you may . . . get demo . . . dem—"*

"I understand. I will ask later," Garrett interrupted.

She peeled herself from the wall and continued forward. Her muscles resisted with each stride, as if the air around her was made of a syrupy liquid tugging against her limbs. She swallowed hard as she continued, forcing down the sickly feeling clutching onto her skin.

A crackle of pink light flashed across her vision, and she halted her advance with a weighted step. She waved a hand at the invisible obstacle in front of her, feeling a warm resistance across her palm.

"This. Off." She pointed at the force field.

"On it," Garrett confirmed as he began to break into the network. As his fingers flailed madly across the digital console, a curious familiarity dawned on him. Though his experience was limited, he had broken into enough systems to find parallels in each network he encountered. However, the one in this facility had exponentially more patterns he recognized from the security protocols at his home in Upper.

He wasn't knowledgeable in the art of writing structures. He depended on code-generating AI to fill in the gaps where needed, but it struck him odd that a high-profile corporation like this one would use a universal backbone in something as crucial as security. Perhaps every company coincidentally hired the same coder through freelance, but outsourcing something this vital sounded illogical to him.

He directed his attention to a map he extracted from the system, sharing the viewpoint with Nara as he worked on gaining access to the scintillating obstacles in front of her.

The room she traversed was a giant open square, divided by a grid of automated force fields. The map's key represented the walls of the grid in two distinct colors, purple lines symbolizing harmless physical obstructions and red dashes denoting lethal electrical traps.

Seconds after Garrett had imprinted the maze into his memory, the walls vanished. With a blink, they reappeared in a completely new pattern, randomly generated by the network's algorithms. Tiny blue dots of movement stole his concentration as they traveled in synchronous paths along the simulated hallways. He watched the blips react as the grid morphed again, passing his eyes over the status updates they broadcast to the network.

As the transition took place, the dots paused, informing the system that they awaited the next pattern to manifest. When the grid reactivated, they murmured course corrections to the system's main database as they adapted their flight to the newly created environment. The transition completed its cycle in a matter of seconds.

Garrett entered a series of commands, then tapped the force field in front of Nara, temporarily disabling it.

"It's off now," he reported as he kept his eyes glued to the feed.

"Thanks." She hated to admit it, but she was relieved that the human was watching in the background. He was quickly picking up the armor's controls and learning to adjust to rapid environmental changes.

She continued forward through the maze, watching the walls and the bots on her map as she progressed.

Garrett observed intently as one of the blue blips began to move toward the wall he'd interfered with. He tapped the dot, sprouting a new screen that provided him with details of its spontaneous course change. It was responding to the unscheduled environment shift, investigating the status of the altered force field. As he watched the interactions on his screen, fragments of thoughts clicked together in Garrett's head.

The shifting walls. No light, no air, he mused as he considered the components inside the facility. *There are no living guards here. At all.*

While Nara moved on through the phantom labyrinth, Garrett studied the adaptive behaviors of the curious machines. With a few experimental taps, he influenced their flight path, ushering them away from her position. His proactive meddling made Nara effectively invisible, keeping her from encountering any drone.

"They'll catch on," she warned a she watched their shared screen.

His hand snapped away from the monitor as he contemplated the consequences of his actions. Modifying his strategy, he resorted to making more subtle variations, switching the walls from solid to electric instead of outright deactivating them. He was confident that he could provide a safe passage for her, and he could not comprehend why she needed to throttle her life signs.

"Got an entry point yet?" Nara asked.

Garrett scrolled across the map, spotting a square of energy that opened to a column of empty space stretching down to the lower levels.

"That should be it over there," he stated as he highlighted the outline on the screen for Nara.

She made her way to the opening, examining the swirling screen. A series of perforations outlined the perimeter of the energy gate. At one corner, a featureless lock protruded from the ground, protected by a glass casing. Inside the glass, a coin-sized indentation sat in the center of the metal plate, indicating where a user should place their fingertip.

She knelt and flipped open the case, then extracted a clear packet filled with an opalescent briny liquid from her belt. She placed it on top of the lock and waited for the security device to accept the offering. A tiny snap of plastic initiated a series of sickly squelching noises bubbling from underneath the sac. The packet deflated as an automated syringe popped up from the lock, extracting a sample of the fluid.

Known in the Underground as a "Body Bag," the liquid-filled sachet was composed of synthetic blank cells designed to simulate human blood, a tool used to overload biometric locks. Each artificially engineered cell inside the bag was composed of a random series of gene fragments suspended in a protein solution.

As a sample is extracted from the bag, the cells inside bombard security devices with an infinite number of genetic combinations. Once the cells uncovered a sequence of DNA the lock accepted, cells with a similar configuration influence the other cells around it to mimic the genetic structure.

Breaking the lock, however, was not a quick process.

The device hummed with confusion, rapidly clicking in distress as it deliberated on what to do with the foreign goop. While the lock crunched through calculations, a bot from the back of the room broke away from its flight pattern, heading straight for Nara's position.

"Uhh, Nara?" Garrett poked at the bot's symbol on the map, generating a flash in her visor.

>>*UNSCHEDULED VISIT REPORTED. INVESTIGATING ANOMALY. GRID PATTERN OMEGA ENGAGED,* the bot broadcast to the network.

"Time to move," Nara announced as she rolled onto her backside just as the holes around the gate ignited with red-hot beams. She glanced up and scoffed at the electric spikes scorching the metal panels of the high-volume ceiling.

"I can't seem to find anything on my end to disable the override," Garrett informed. "Access to it must be partitioned off somewhere else. I'm looking, though. I'm looking."

The speeding bot burbled another series of commands as it

continued to its destination. The walls acknowledged its orders, and the grid lines spontaneously burst with crimson light, sealing Nara inside a viciously sparking cage.

A friendly beep chirped behind her, informing Nara that the lock on the security gate had been released. She let out a growl as she glared at the gaping maw of the access hatch taunting her from the other side of the lethal fence.

The bot floated into Nara's square from the darkness, red electricity gently stroking its shiny chrome chassis as it moved through the wall. The droid moved with a slight bob as its levitation motor propelled it, emitting a constant electronic purr as it glided around the room.

Fins of segmented metal jutted out from its sides, delicately waving in the air as it advanced. The only recognizable facial feature on the device was a giant eye-like lens, which shifted side to side, producing soft, rapid zipping noises as it adjusted its focus.

Nara froze as she watched the flight of the looming scouter bot. Cornered within the confines of the deadly walls, she tried to formulate an escape option in her head. Testing the physical sensors of the robotic annoyance, she slowly rotated her knee away from the scout, preparing for a retreat. In slow, zen-like motions, she leaned her shoulder with her leg, shifting her weight for a calculated step.

But just as she lifted her heel off the ground, the bot snapped around to face her.

Fuck, she internalized as her muscles seized up.

>>*MOVEMENT DETECTED. SCANNING.*

A ray of green light burst from the bot's eye, feeling around for the disturbance in front of it.

Nara lurched back to evade the beam, but her body was refusing to move as fast as she wanted it to go. The beating in her chest shuddered as her organs strained against the inhibitor, her nerves pushing her muscles to move faster. As she managed a quick side step, the droid's scrutinizing light brushed over her leg.

>>*LEVEL ONE ENTITY DETECTED. BASE LEVEL HUMANOID.*

Base level humanoid? Garrett thought from behind his screen. *The hell does that mean?*

Blue blips across the map swarmed toward Nara's position, moving to join their leader at the center of the grid. Their babbles of acknowledgement flooded the data streams as they advanced, calling out flight patterns and tactics to their squad mates.

Garrett continued his furious search through the network for access to the bot's commands, but the system refused to respond to his orders. The droids, the walls, and even the environmental controls slipped out of his grasp as the system began repairing the holes he took advantage of.

As the squadron of droids made their entrance through the crackling barriers, the leader's fins burst apart, elongating into razor-sharp spines. Three narrow barrels popped out from underneath its eye, sparking with furious energy.

Holy fuck! Garrett stared wide-eyed as each bot followed the leader, filling his ears with a flurry of clicking and snapping. He watched in horror as they closed in around her, buzzing excitedly as tendrils of electricity voraciously licked their barrels.

"Red. Button." Nara tersely barked.

"What?" The corner of Garrett's screen pulsed as a large circle labeled FORCE RESTART struck his eyeballs.

"I say GO. Twenty seconds. Then button," she uttered digestible fragments of orders as she pulled a long pin-like object from a compartment in her forearm. *"NO. MORE."*

"Wait, what?" Garrett repeated, hoping for a more cohesive explanation.

The drones moved into their final flight positions around Nara.

>>*WEAPONS ARMED. ENGAGING.*

"GO!" She rammed the pin into her wrist, sparks spraying the air as she penetrated the flesh beneath her armor.

"Wait! I don't—" Garrett jumped in his seat as his objection was cut short by warning sirens ravaging his screen, flooding the apartment with strobing light. His eyes involuntarily bounced, tracking the lines of her vitals as they chaotically spiked and plunged across graphs on display. He stared in stupefaction as her armor screamed at him, demanding that he fix the grave situation.

An sense of foreboding pulled his attention toward the center of the screen, just as his viewport lurched downward. The camera violently bobbed up and down as it kept up with the erratic shift in Nara's breathing.

"Nara?!" he cried as he bolted up from his chair. He swiped his viewpoint around her body, witnessing her sink to one knee in the middle of the warzone.

The reset button centered itself on his screen, a pulsating beacon amid the chaos surrounding them.

Fuck, start counting, he severely reprimanded as he forced himself to sit back down.

1…2…3…

Fire radiated across Nara's wrist, carving a path up through her ribs. Her organs wrestled with the technology, fiercely thrashing around inside her as the devilish device choked out her systems. Slower and slower it pulled her down, each pulse a lance of pain as her body struggled to regain control. The air was sapped from her chest as scorching agony assailed her skull with merciless onslaught.

…4…5…6…

>>*ANALYZING . . .*

The bots terminated their attack, disoriented by the sudden break in their detection signal. Three of the drones circled the immediate area around Nara, swiping at the air with glowing beams of sensory light.

…7…8…

The room spiraled as Nara struggled to keep upright, the needles of the inhibitor flaying every nerve. The fire in her chest consumed the muscles of her throat, leaving her choking for air as her trachea pinched shut. Her vision flooded with billowing clouds as the tempo inside her skull amplified to maddening rhythms, threatening to set off bone-cracking explosions inside her brain.

...9...10...

Garrett struggled to control his twitching fingers over the button, his heart hammering uncontrollably as he strained against the time. His eyes neurotically paced between the network feeds and the reset, watching the droids vocalize their alerted state.

...11...12...

Darkness enveloped her as Nara succumbed to the inhibitor's will. The room around her began to dissolve, and the only sound she could hear was the rush of blood swirling through her ears. The pervasive pain began to dull as her senses numbed and a soothing chill creeped over her body.

A moment later, then nothing at all.

...13...14

Garrett's view plunged to the tiled floor as Nara collapsed.

"Nara!" His fingers flinched over the reset, his hand narrowly grazing the button on the screen.

The armor status shrieked at him from the console, and vital lines flattened across the graphs on display. His eyes fixated on the camera view as her body remained alarmingly still on the ground.

This is supposed to happen, he assured himself. *This was part of the plan, right? She's not dead. She's okay. She's okay. W–what the fuck?!*

....15......16

The drones broke from their circle, feverishly sweeping their scanners across all corners of the enclosed space. Several bots zipped beyond the enclosure, sniffing for a trail in the adjacent quadrants.

They had lost the scent but were not convinced that their quarry had left the area.

.......17

The bots continued scouring, warbling idle chat along the network as they reported each crucial detail of their search.

Garrett clenched his teeth as he watched the spectacle, ignoring his throbbing veins pulsing over his temples. His knuckles whitened over his balled fists as he deliberated over the situation, not wanting to revive her while the drones still fluttered about.

..........18

"C'mon, get the fuck out of there!" Garrett screamed at his screen.

She gave him explicit orders to follow, and time was slipping away from him.

..............19

The barrels of each drone ceased sparking, retracting back into their shells.

>>THREAT NEUTRALIZED. RESUMING FLIGHT PATTERN 01859. THIRTY SECONDS UNTIL STATUS RESET.

And just like that, the drones retreated, prattling to each other as if nothing had ever happened. The walls continued their shifting patterns, and the lasers guarding the gate to the floors below evaporated.

....20

Garrett's hand reacted before his brain told it to, focusing all of his energy into the screen as he slammed the button down.

What happens now? He glared at the ground in his viewport impatiently. *The sirens are still blaring. Why isn't this working?*

##13.3##

JUST AS HE was about to implode from the stress, the line on the vital graphs soared upward, then immediately crashed again. With another hefty thump, the pulse tempered itself, picking up pace until it steadied to a stabilized measure. Silence returned to the room as the sirens quieted, satisfied with the status of the monitors.

Tendrils of searing white light tore through Nara's vision, and a knifelike pain shredded through her flesh as her chest opened up. Burns of electricity lashed over her nerves as she jolted back into existence. The armor forced her brutalized lungs to inflate, and she exploded in a violent fit of coughing. She savagely drank in the synthetic air as she wearily rolled over, waiting for the whirling room to cease. The fog of her vision gradually restored as the percussion in her head subsided to a dull tempo.

Yep, she thought as she tore the metal bar out of her arm, *hurts about the same as it did back then.*

She stabilized her panting and hoisted herself up on shaky legs, waiting for her natural systems to relax. Her bones creaked as she uncurled her back, supporting her upright as she regained her sense of equilibrium with a few experimental stretches. She rolled her neck side to side, taking a moment of respite before allowing the inhibitor to reduce her functions again.

"You . . . okay?" He blinked, the cringing inflection in his voice raised to meet his concern. *What just happened?*

"Yep." She let out a trio of pitiful coughs. "Just gonna walk it off."

"Oh. All right."

Nara walked over to the access hatch, still open and waiting for her after the encounter. She peered over the ledge into a narrow shaft illuminated by a hazy green light. Satisfied by the featureless tunnel, she sat down on the rim of the gate and slid inside, grabbing the ladder nearby. Clicks from her steps echoed through the passageway as she descended into the abyss below. Her aching muscles nagged at her with each shifting stride, forcing her to slow her pace.

"You couldn't have maybe, I don't know, warned me about this maneuver beforehand?" Garrett voiced, a hint of salt encrusting his tone.

"Didn't know you cared," she taunted as she continued her descent.

"I–what the f—" His cheeks glowed in anger, flustered by the absurdity of her reply. Sputtering a series of frustration-laced croaks, he shook the jittering from his nerves, still rattled by what she'd forced him to do.

The last rungs of the ladder extended past the access shaft, and Nara emerged into a vast cavernous chamber. She stepped onto the metal grated floor and surveyed her surroundings, taking mental notes of the structures around her.

The chasm was infested with artfully geometric nets of blackened metal pipes and steel beams. The conjoined web stretched across the center of the room, enveloping a giant support pillar that spanned from floor to ceiling.

The pipes hissed at the air as they brought their liquid cargo from one section of the cavern to the other, fueling whatever machinations were taking place below. Windows dotting the length of the pipes revealed gently palpitating cyan radiation, casting a cold gloomy aura around the central pillar.

The ominous green light that saturated the room radiated from transparent chambers lining the walls. Each vessel contained glowing coolant that kept the area at a frigid temperature comfortable to electronics. To assist with environmental controls, machines churned out soft clouds of thermal fog. The vapor continuously billowed over the floor, curling down to the ground level, where the products of the research facility were contained.

Three circles of diamond-textured metal flooring were suspended at different intervals of the main support pillar, surrounded by waist-high railings to protect the safety of the engrossed researcher. Catwalks at each cardinal direction split out from the central floors as stairs threaded along the walls of the cavern, providing ease of access to each level. Each floor was outfitted with numerous computer consoles that monitored pressures, temperatures, and statuses of various projects with blinding whirrs of numbers and processor clicks.

Garrett retrieved the map of the second floor from the system, capturing additional images and storing them on his computer for later reference, and profit. Puzzled by the lack of obvious security measures in the area, he delved deeper into the floor plans, examining areas between walls, the pipes, and even the flooring for any surprise traps. Apart from the extensive environmental controls, there appeared to be no obvious obstacle in Nara's way.

A small division of maintenance droids navigated the clusters of pipes, checking seals and production qualities. Their small, bug-like appearance gave them a whimsical demeanor as they clambered over the central netting, prattling off soft beeps and whistles as they critiqued the efficiency of the pipeline.

Garrett pulled up a file list inside one of their systems and spied a precarious set of commands that enabled them to act as security should certain alarms trigger.

"You should be okay to just walk around," Garrett reported. "Just don't poke around too much on the ground level."

As Nara quietly made her way down the spiral stairs, an odd, yet familiar sensation crept over her. She switched her visual settings, watching flashes of red outlines zip through the thermal fog of the ground level, tracing over large containment chambers and machinery in front of her.

"The target coordinates are right here, I think," Garrett informed, pointing a blip out in their map. "A small cryogenic chest of some form."

"Any activity?" Nara asked as she skulked along the first floor, stopping midway across the bridge above the waypoint.

"Nothing that I can see so far . . ." His voice trailed off as he scrutinized the chest with uncertainty, spotting a faint distortion on the camera feed.

"Give me a minute to think of a plan of attack," Nara requested as she leaned over the railing.

Wait, ***is*** *that something?* Garrett thought as he zoomed the camera in.

The mist below was toying with his ability to distinguish shapes, despite the helmet's visual augmentations. As he observed the area around the target, a crystalline blur passed over the cryo chest, warping light in a jagged mosaic. The movement mimicked video static, but Nara's cameras were not reporting any errors in the feed.

"Wait a minute." He vocalized his concern, remembering the first time he'd hesitated.

"What?" Nara stopped her scan of the area.

"I see some sort of distortion on the scanners. I can't get a reading on it whatsoever," he reported, trying to lock on the movement with the helmet's interface. "It's like this hazy glitchy thing."

"Where?"

"Down on the floor, near the tank." He pointed out the area on the map with a marker on the screen.

Nara glared at the cryo chest, tracing her eyes around the shape of the light sorcery, discerning a vaguely humanoid form.

"The fuck is he doing here?" she snarled into the feed, the eerie sensation now a meddlesome itch. *That presence.*

"What's wrong? What's going on?" Garrett probed, trying to piece together what Nara had seen.

Nara watched the intruder crack open the seal of the container. Trails of white gasses spilled onto the floor as the lid rose. The bright sterile light inside the box distorted around the hazy figure, making the prowler identifiable.

Shit, she thought, *I'm in serious trouble.*

The hazy perpetrator was not going to let her pass without a fight, and she was intimately aware of the mercenary's combat proficiency. But the stakes were too high for her to walk away. She needed that specimen, and more importantly, she needed fewer distractions surrounding her.

As she slid a rifle into her hands, she summoned a menu to her screen.

>>*CONFIRM DISCONNECT?* The blue outline asked.

"Wait, what are you doing?" Garrett questioned uneasily.

>>*YES*, the button flashed.

And with a blink of light, the menus and charts of the cluttered interface disintegrated, leaving Garrett staring at the computer's featureless home screen in shock.

"Nara, can you hear me!?" he exclaimed, tapping at buttons in a hysterical flurry.

But the console did not respond to his inquiry.

##13.4##

He knows I'm here, Nara scowled, raising her rifle. *Let's see how determined he is to avoid me.*

She gently squeezed the trigger, ejecting a soft pulse of energy from the barrel of her gun. The bolt splattered over the visual disruption, delicately nudging the trespasser's shoulder forward. The intruder's cloaking effect flickered and broke apart in spidery cracks, revealing a black metallic shell of armor underneath.

Before Nara could cycle the charge, the camouflage healed itself, shrouding the man's armor back under its illusory blanket. Undaunted by the warning shot, the thief resumed their objective, extracting a shiny glass vial from inside the cryo container.

Oh, fuck this shit, Nara fumed a she watched the vial levitate through the intruder's cloak. *Fuck the alarms, fuck security. No more time. He needs to leave.*

With a snap of her wrist, she commanded the needles of the inhibitor to disengage from her body. Pangs shot across her limbs as the device complied, the barbs tearing away from her muscles as they retracted back into her armor.

Her chest burst open as it expanded to its natural capacity, enabling her freedom of movement as she savagely devoured heaping swallows of air. The swirling around her head began to subside as her first aid system took over, numbing the flesh wounds created by the malevolent device. Mental clarity returned to her with a rush of chemical stimulants, and she raised her rifle again, flicking the switch to a more lethal setting.

"Forgive me, comrade. I can't let you do that," she apologized under her breath. She purged the remainder of her sickly fatigue through a restorative exhale and fired once more.

Molten red exploded from her weapon as a vicious missile sliced through the air with a howling war cry. The noise ceased with a crackling splash as the charge hit its mark, engulfing the pixelated haze below her with synthetic fire.

The force of the impact threw the intruder forward, and his faceplate smashed into the lip of the container with a shattering crunch. As the thief unconsciously thrust an arm out to brace himself, the glass vial launched from his grasp, disappearing into the murky atmosphere.

The man's armor fizzled in angry sparks as the surge of energy tore through the synthetic illusion, unmasking the gruesome damage Nara had inflicted. A jagged chasm split apart the protective shell across his shoulders, revealing corpse-pale flesh dripping with sickly black organic fluid. Silvery liquid metal crawled over the humanoid's back as the armor reacted to the injury, meshing and hardening to its normal blackened state in a fraction of an instant.

Unhindered by severe physical trauma, the figure snapped back upright, clawing at the table as if possessed by a demonic spirit. The man bolted after the lost vial, disinterested in the adversary with the smoking rifle behind him.

You fucking asshole, Nara growled as she vaulted over the railing, infuriated by the resilience of her rival.

Thermal smoke whooshed away from her form as she landed on the ground floor, only to immediately swallow her up with its misty veil. Just as she lifted a foot to pursue her quarry, the green lights illuminating the chamber above clacked off, replaced by a bloody crimson smolder.

Its slumber disrupted by the rowdy quarrel, the facility's security system bellowed a warning inside the chamber:

>>*SECURITY BREACH. SECTOR F9. SUBJECT 552984729 HAS BEEN COMPROMISED.*

Transmissions flitted across the network channels, commanding the maintenance drones in the vicinity to break from their routine tasks and engage the intruders.

>>*INTERNAL BIOSCAN INITIATED.*

The chamber detonated in a flare of white light, causing Nara to recoil as her visual sensors overloaded. While her cameras scrambled to recover, a streak of the red outlined humanoid blazed past her peripherals.

The hell do you think you're going? Nara challenged as she chased after the figure.

>>*SCAN COMPLETE. LEVEL FIVE ENTITY DETECTED. ANOMALY 0975 RECOGNIZED. COMPENSATING ATTACK PATTERN.*

Really? 0975? she grumbled as she slid under a table, waiting for the inevitable reinforcements to appear. *They couldn't have bothered to put my name in their system? Now I'm insulted.*

Echoes of mechanical fluttering droned inside the chamber as the maintenance bots swarmed at the central pillar. Their multitude of limbs extended from underneath their square frames, briskly accelerating them to their destination.

Nara ignored the spectacle above as she spotted her rival dashing to the corner of the room. She patiently watched him as he feverishly scoured the floor for the precious object, letting him hunt for the vial in her stead.

Ignoring his observer, the man frenziedly twisted around, diving to his knees as he frisked the ground in front of him.

Nara burst out of her cover, sprinting to catch up to the thief. She slid into the man and planted a truculent knee to his ribcage, cutting off his search as she knocked him over onto his side.

Reacting with the grace of a street dancer, the man pivoted around on a hip and swept a leg behind her knee, pulling her down to the floor with him. With his attacker distracted, he scrambled to snatch the devious vial rolling away.

Nara growled as she recovered her balance, latching onto the man by the calf. As her opponent's fingers brushed the base of the glass vial, she injected a debilitating shock from the palm of her hand.

The man choked out a stifled cry as the surge coursed through his body. A violent spasm thwarted his command over his muscles, and with a sharp clink of glass, he involuntarily slapped the vial deeper into the mist. Wrenching his leg from Nara's grasp with a retaliating kick, the man scrambled to his feet and chased after the accursed object.

Nara dashed after him, only to be interrupted by a message on the security broadcast.

>>*CONVERSION COMPLETE. TARGET ACQUIRED. FIRING.*

She glanced over her shoulder to find a giant metal cephalopod scuttling along the walls of the chamber. A bundle of glassy spires jutted out from the center of the saucer-like torso of the mechanical beast, each casting a shifting rainbow of colors as the golem approached the intruders.

"Ahh, shit!" Nara exclaimed as she darted behind a set of cooling tanks. A thin streak of cobalt pierced the ground next to her, instantly vaporizing as it hit the flooring.

>>*TARGET OBSTRUCTED BY PRIORITY A SPECIMEN. CALCULATING NEW COORDINATES.*

As the bot pondered over its next destination, Nara pinpointed the man sprinting through the haze. She fled from her cover and barreled after him, intercepting his flight path. Pitching her weight forward, she slammed her shoulder into the fleeing perpetrator, knocking him underneath a catwalk.

The man took several rebounding steps to the side as he was propelled from his target, whirling his arms in controlled arcs to counteract the force.

>>*TARGET CLEAR. HEADING TO NEW COORDINATES.*

Well, this will be just a wonderful fight, Nara grumbled as she tuned in to the clunking of the security bot's gait.

She lunged to grab at the man's shoulder, but her arm seized up as a blur of motion cut off her strike. A gasp stole the air from her lungs as an impact sliced through her abdomen, the sensation shadowed by a searing pain gnawing through her flesh. She unconsciously stepped back while her brain pieced together the attack in her memory. Confidence in her combat ability waned with a sinking feeling in her gut as a glimmer of the offending weapon caught her eye.

A silvery streak of metal protruded from the man's armor in a honed edge, tracing a lethal border around his forearm. His fingers merged into a single knifepoint, slick with a fresh coat of her blood.

Having stunned his opponent, the man whirled around and charged into the mist. The savage blade liquefied as he retreated, relinquishing control of his fingers as it receded into the armor.

Fuck, he is no longer playing nice, she griped as her first aid system reacted to the injury. Vital reports chastised her actions as she snapped a pistol into her hand. The pharmaceuticals pumping into her veins steadied her nerves as she took aim at the fleeing figure. She slung curses in his direction as she ran after him, releasing a flurry of shots at the intruder's legs.

Nara caught up to the man as he staggered forward, his armor struggling to absorb the onslaught. She sprang onto her quarry, wrenching him toward her as she slithered an arm around his neck.

As the thief thrashed in her grasp, she stamped a foot behind his knee, bashing him off balance and shoving him to the ground. She let out another shock from her armor's defense system, paralyzing her victim with a volley of numbing lashes.

Seizing control of his twitching muscles, he conjured another blade from his armor. He jerked his chest forward, pulling Nara down on his back as she clamped onto his throat. Feeling her leg shift behind him, he whipped his arm around and slammed the dagger into her shin.

A metal shriek pierced the air as the man drove the edge deeper, tearing through her suit with minimal resistance. Her organic carapace diverted the impact of the weapon, but the blade continued to gnaw at the chitinous matter underneath. Each grating scratch sent shivers up her spine as her attacker persisted with a second blow.

With a sickening crunch, he cracked through her plating, burrowing the point into her soft flesh until it met with bone.

Nara hurled a vehement roar into the chamber, causing the delicate machinery around the combatants to shudder with the agonized vocal resonance.

Her first aid system screeched warnings in her ear, administering emergency medical fillers around the invasive metal. The cold liquid scorched across her nerves as it set to its task, patching the tissue around the embedded dagger.

>>*TARGET ACQUIRED. FIRING.*

"*FUCKING* . . ." she thundered as she redistributed her weight onto her functional leg.

With the knife still buried in her muscle, she violently wrenched her quarry up by the neck, hauling him behind a holding chamber. Through clenched teeth, she sharply pivoted her shoulder, flinging both of their bodies out of the security bot's aim. As her quarry strained against her grip, another bolt blazed past them, letting off a taunting piff as it harmlessly evaporated on the ground.

>>*TARGET OBSTRUCTED. RECALCULATING.*

Shards of pain forced Nara to release the man as he savagely twisted around, yanking his blade out of her leg with a spray of blood and medical fluid. Refusing to give her a chance to recover, he smashed the back of his helmet into hers, propelling her backward as she wrestled to keep herself balanced on her injury. As she braced her footing, he coiled around her and released a quick-bladed jab underneath her ribs before fleeing from her grapple.

I need to get that vial away from him, Nara muttered internally as she doubled over. *He'll destroy me if I fight him outright.*

She limped out of the droid's vision as her systems sealed the voids in her flesh with synthetic braces.

Fuck, I've got to get back in there. Garrett's mind raced as he retried the connection to Nara's armor.

"No-no-no-no," he repeated under his breath as the severity of the situation washed over him, the unresponsive machine taunting him with its featureless screen. "Fuck!"

He bolted to the couch behind him and tore through his overnight bag, extracting a shiny black handheld computer.

Fuck, of course that's the only one I brought with me, he cursed as he feverishly sifted through the rest of the contents. *I hope it will do.*

He jolted the device awake with a swipe of a finger and began to key in the address of the facility's network location from his memory.

>>*DESTINATION CONFIRMED*, the device reported to him, *ESTI-*

MATED 3.47 MINUTES UNTIL TRACER ATTACK. SIGNAL WILL DESTRUCT IN 2.5 MINUTES.

"Wonderful," Garrett griped as he set to work uncovering the system's vulnerabilities.

THOSE DRUGS NEED to work faster. Nara gritted her teeth as she tore a dagger from her own arsenal.

As the simulated adrenaline coursed through her, she edgily waited for the man to circle around before tearing after him. Thrusting a palm in front of her, she intersected his retreat and slammed him against a containment vessel.

The man wrestled to break from her assault, pressing his palms against the barrier to stabilize his footing. But she cut his effort short and rammed her knee into his back, forcing his chest against the cool metal wall. Denying him the ability to counter, she brutally drove her knife into his shoulder, gouging the tip of the blade into the socket.

Through a pained gasp, he thrashed his other arm at her in a feeble attempt to wrench himself out of her clutches.

Forcing the dagger through artificial flesh and circuitry, Nara wrapped her free arm around his unruly limb. She gave him no quarter as she jabbed her boot into his calf, pulling his shoulders close with her blade-wielding hand. A sickening pop emitted from his confined elbow as she strengthened her grip, bending his back in a precarious arc.

But as she maintained her advantaged position, she felt the man redistribute his weight as he took a labored step back, leaning heavily against her for support. Ceasing his attack, the man strained to steady himself with his dissident limbs. Nara shifted to brace the sudden extrinsic burden, releasing the man's arms as she propped him upright.

The armor dissolved around her opponent's head, revealing the familiar pale face of Cain, drenched in black ichor.

"I . . . yield." His piercing odd eyes stared at her pleadingly as he restrained his erratic panting.

"You usually have more fight in you than this," she growled. "What the hell has gotten into you?"

"There was . . . no time . . . before you arrived . . . destroy." He gripped onto her shoulder with a quaking hand.

"The hell are you talking about?" she demanded.

"Had . . . to stop you." His vocalization deteriorated as he concentrated on his balance. "Severe injury . . . need recover . . . please shoot me . . . before—"

"And then what, just leave you in here?!" she snarled.

"I—" The man's rebuttal was abruptly cut short as his eyes rolled to the back of his head, a glassy film dimming their ethereal glow.

Nara caught him as he collapsed, pulling him over her knee. She fought to keep him steady as he lost control of motor skills, shivering uncontrollably in her grasp.

"Too damaged. Please . . . now." Inhuman whispers pitifully traversed his lips. "Find it. Destroy . . ."

You selfish fucker, making me do this again, she spat.

Through raging waves of internal conflict bedeviling her brain, she obediently drew a pistol, placing the end of the barrel to his forehead. With a merciful squeeze of the trigger, the tremoring man jolted one final time, then dropped lifeless in her arms.

>>*TARGET ACQUIRED. FIRING.*

"Fucking, fuck!" She fumed at the interfering droid, pleading for a breath to recover from her onerous action.

>>*2.15 MINUTES REMAINING UNTIL SIGNAL TERMINATION.*

Fuck, Garrett cursed as he dug into the network. *I don't have time to get into the security cameras. I'm going to have to do this blind.*

He summoned a command interface to the screen, hurling a volley of symbols as he waded through the system. He scoured through functions and properties to find a landmark he recognized, but the surrounding areas had warped into storms of fragmented textual garbage. Metaphorical walls were lined with thicker barriers, and the holes he previously took advantage of had shrunk to a pinpoint.

He traveled along the maze of files and operations until he uncovered the system status reports, sifting through torrents of data gurgling info on the reinforced security.

"Level five entity detected. . . Security protocol Omega initialized," he read out loud, scrolling through a list of triggered systems. "Shit, what the hell did she trip? Droid combat mode at the highest alert, laser grid on first floor set to 'all active'."

He followed a trail of procedures that led him to a visual map of the security functions. Pulling the diagram closer to his face, he traced patterns over the flashing red lines and icons emblazoned across the two floors.

"Lower level bio scanners active. Oh, hell. That's bad. That's very bad." His finger stopped on the diagram as a realization struck him. "Shit! Is her body still suppressed?"

>>*1.45 MINUTES UNTIL SYSTEM TERMINATION.*

"Ahh, fuck!" He fervently swiped through the map, eyeing the blazing red grid blocking all exits on the upper floor. *These walls need to come down now.*

He flew through the network, trying to scrape up any vulnerability in the ironclad barriers that would yield to his brute force prodding. But the security held steadfast against his advances.

>>*1 MINUTE UNTIL SYSTEM TERMINATION.*

All right, this isn't working, he thought. *Time for a more unconventional approach.*

Abandoning the security channels, he dug his way into the maintenance upkeep, where he found reports on the energy flow of the first-floor security walls. Finding little resistance to his pokes and prods, he unearthed several tantalizing controls within his reach.

An orderly series of brightly glowing bars lined up across his screen, each filled with a gradient of colors, a radioactive green at one end and an infernal red on the other. Each bar was incremented in hash marks of accumulative numbers, the unit of measurement a mystery to Garrett.

Underneath the meters was a trio of candy-bright dials with more enigmatic numbers, its glittery display a tantalizing beacon to the user. The indicators of each control were set at a precise degree around the circular interface, leaving the marker on the graduated graphs above hovering at a comfortable yellow-green level.

Exactly what I needed. He smirked as he passed his finger over a dial, rotating the control harshly to one extreme. Having no idea what he had just accomplished, Garrett watched the screen intently as the pointers on the temperature meters rose, dancing playfully up the critical orange bars.

>>*WARNING. RISK OF SYSTEM OVERLOAD IF BARRIER OUTPUT EXCEEDS 200%. FAILSAFE MUST BE DISABLED BEFORE PERFORMING EFFICIENCY TESTING.*

"Yeah, about that? Not part of the plan, really," he taunted as he slid his finger across another dial. A rush of glee tickled his hands as he watched the lines on the output graph spike. The pointers crawled their way up to the vermillion levels, delicately kissing the deeper reds at his oblivious command.

>>*ENERGY OUTPUT AT CRITICAL LEVELS. UNSTABLE TEMPERATURE FLUCTUATIONS AT GENERATOR 3-12. INITIATING EMERGENCY SHUTDOWN.*

With the satisfying noise of panicked electronic alarms, the vibrant crimson walls on his map blinked off, relaying the success of his meddling actions.

>>*PRIORITY ONE REPAIR BEACON TO ALL MAINTENANCE DRONES. CIRCUIT REPLACEMENTS REQUIRED IN SECTORS A, D, AND F.*

That did it, I hope. Garrett sighed as he glanced at the shutdown timer bleeding away. *Now on to the flying bots upstairs.*

He pulled up the first-floor schematics on his screen, watching the blue blips interact inside the open arena. As he tried to count their number on the display, their behavior radically changed.

The drones dotted the perimeter of the floor as they zipped along the map in symmetrical pairs, one half mimicking the movements of their counterparts across the room. At matched speed, they raced toward each other until they occupied the same square on the grid. Bleeping acknowledgments through the network feed, they initiated a curious dance, swirling around each other in trancelike circles, orbiting their soulmates like binary stars.

The spectacle reached a dramatic climax as the bots smashed into each other and the blips merged into their partners, leaving a single-file line of drones dotting the center of the floor.

"Wait, what?" His eyes widened as he searched for the missing bots. "There were sixteen on the floor, and now there's only eight?"

He scrutinized the status feed for answers, but the network fed him useless orders to standby. His eyebrows furrowed in bewilderment as the curious drones performed another circular dance, searching the room for new partners.

The remaining set of blips performed another bizarre ritualistic dance across the screen, then once again, half the drones disappeared from the map.

"Wait. What the fuck is going on?"

But just as he was about to search for an answer, the screen exploded in a streak of white light. A series of fizzles and squeaks announced the demise of the device he was using, and a heady odor of burnt electronics whisped out of its external ports, tracing ghostly patterns over the inanimate black glass.

"No! FUCK!" he exclaimed, slamming his hands onto the desk.

He stared at the lifeless machine remorsefully.

Shit, I hope that was enough to help.

Nara dropped to her knees and crawled under an instrument console, dragging the body of Cain with her as the bot let off another charge.

"I fucking. Hate. Everything," she growled at the corpse. "Especially you."

A thunderous rumble dramatically interrupted her bitter strife with security, vigorously quaking the arena as the noise coursed through the walls. The trigger-happy crawler stopped in its tracks as the red lighting fizzled off, draping the combatants with darkness.

>>EMERGENCY. CRITICAL DAMAGE ON SECTOR A-F. ALL MAINTENANCE UNITS REPORT FOR EMERGENCY REPAIR.

Obediently, the mechanical nautilus burst apart into its insectoid counterparts, melting into a fountain of slithering droplets. The bug modules swarmed upstairs, burrowing into crevasses inside the walls of the chamber.

"Leaving so soon?" she grumbled as she rotated around.

She kicked her leg out, whacking a leg of the table with her boot. The jolt was accompanied by a dainty scraping noise scuttling over the concrete floor. She glanced over her shoulder, discovering the pestilent vial impishly rolling toward her, spiraling around itself in playful circles. With a scowl, she snatched the devious vessel, angrily pocketing it as she seethed at the absurdity of her situation.

She skulked from under her shelter and hoisted the body over her shoulder, muttering expletives as she formulated her departure. As she made her way up the stairs encircling the chamber, she scanned her maps for another exit. To her annoyance, the only way out was the same way she'd entered.

She bitterly stared up at the ladder to the upper floor, gruffly adjusting her morbid cargo as she stepped onto the bottom rung. A disconcerted feeling edged toward her as she pulled herself up, leaving her suspicious of her surroundings as she began her ascent. The echoes of her footsteps resonated through the unnerving silence of the tunnel as she vigilantly progressed, amplifying her sense of dread.

"Where are the drones upstairs?" she warily asked the air as she sifted through the disturbingly featureless map.

>>*AUGMENTATION COMPLETE. ENGAGING HOSTILES,* the security broadcast answered.

"Wait, what? Aw, hell."

She barely had enough time to shrink back down the ladder before an unnatural force lunged at her from the exit hatch above. A colossal skeletal claw flexed its digits with mechanical squeaks as it rapidly plunged toward her, blocking her exit.

As she shifted away from the menacing device, the metal talons latched onto the body on her shoulder. Seemingly pleased by its newfound discovery, the insidious machine pulled the man off her, eagerly retreating into the darkness above with its prize.

"No you fucking don't! That's my deadbeat, not yours!" she snarled as she leapt from the ladder, snatching the corpse at the torso.

Unburdened by the surplus weight, the malevolent machine yanked its quarry out into the barren arena, revealing itself to the intruders.

Two spindly arms jutted out from each side of the beast, ending at four flat, jointed protrusions that appeared more like tools rather than fingers. Fin-like metal plates perfectly tessellated along the structures, encasing its artificial musculature and wiring in a metal exoskeleton.

Conjoined to the arms was a structured amalgamation of the gliding drones that once occupied the room. Its trunk was a shadowy form composed of a multitude of lenses, each tasked with overseeing a division of its full-circle perspective. The lenses were attached to a rail system along a latticework cylindrical frame, which was divided into hexagonal cells that spiraled around the internal structure.

The motors of its counterparts had migrated to the bottom of the machination, lining up in a ring formation around the central frame. The jets worked cohesively to propel the automaton, hovering the golem elegantly over the ground. It hummed quietly in the eerie atmosphere, the energy it exuded barely processed on Nara's visual sensors with a dull aqua smolder.

"Oh, I wondered why the ceilings were so damn high," Nara muttered as she dangled in the open air.

Nara shamelessly clambered over the body to pull herself up to the droid's hand, making a diminutive effort to restrain her flippant kicks at the victim as she gained leverage. Gripping the droid's wrist with both hands, she zapped the metal appendage with her armor's defenses.

Nara clutched the robot arm as the fingers drooped, winding both of her arms around its wrist as the arm sharply dipped. The body slipped out of its snare as the surge disrupted its grip, sending it crashing to the floor with a sickening thud.

In a unified squeak, every single lens scattered over the beast's body snapped to her direction, rotating menacingly as they focused on the armored parasite latched to its appendage.

>>*TARGET ACQUIRED. ENGAGING.*

"Shit."

While the shock impaired the droid's arm circuits, the charge did not reach far enough to impact its shoulder servos. Using this to its advantage, the beast hurled its body sharply around, flinging its weakened limb in an arc around the arena.

She fought with her armor's grip controls, clawing at the beast's scale plates to maintain her balance. But as inertia overwhelmed her, she slid off the mechanical limb, hurtling toward the wall with a spine-chilling screech of grinding metal. Shredding agony entwined around her nerves as the impact tore at her lacerated torso, sending searing twinges across her skin.

Letting out an exasperated whimper, she slowly eased down the smooth metal wall, letting her body curl onto the floor as her first aid sirens chastised her with berating alarms. As she lay prone waiting for the medical system to catch up, she briefly questioned her life choices in between pangs of suturing muscle.

"Ow," she grumbled as she picked herself off the ground, rolling a shoulder back into place. "I am so done with this shit."

>>*DEPLOYING PRIMARY WEAPONS.*

The beast retracted its arm as it straightened its posture, while its insides churned and murmured as it performed a new set of functions. Amid a chorus of flicks and clacks, silvery pipes burst out of the torso, situating themselves in between the lenses. Splotches of blue flames dotted around the droid inside Nara's visor, gradually intensifying as the weapons charged up.

She tore her rifle from her back and fired haphazardly at the beast. After releasing her barrage, she compacted to a ball on the floor, resorting to shrinking herself from the beast's weapons in a room devoid of cover.

>>*FIRE…*

Three eyes of the creature shattered as the lenses disintegrated from her volley, their fragments clattering over their neighbors below as they trickled to the floor.

>>*PRIORITY. VISUAL SENSOR DAMAGE IN THIRD QUADRANT. COMPENSATING.*

In a cycle of whirs and clicks, the damaged lenses flipped over their railing, tucking themselves neatly inside the wirework frame. Neighboring lenses zipped down the cells, filling in the vacancies while spacing themselves out equidistantly around the frame. After a synchronized shudder, the lenses announced their comfort in their new positions with a confirming clack.

"Yeah, I should've expected that," Nara grumbled, taking the opportunity to distance herself from the beast.

>>*MODIFICATION COMPLETE. VISUAL ARRAY AT 100%. RESUMING ATTACK.*

The droid started to glow once more, illuminating the room with its malicious energy. As the barrels crackled with its sizzling ammunition, the automaton burst with scintillating spears of light, lancing the walls with a honeycomb pattern.

Nara ratcheted around, squeezing her body into a gap of the laser barrage. When the wave subsided, she jolted back up to her feet, firing at the creature once more.

"Six eyes down. Seven. Eight," she proclaimed as glass rained down on the ground. "Ah, fuck it, good enough."

>>*PRIORITY. VISUAL SENSOR DAMAGE IN SECOND AND FOURTH QUADRANT. COMPENSATING.*

Seizing the opportunity, Nara slid across the floor to where Cain was resting. She chucked him over her shoulder and sprang for the maintenance entryway as the beast finished its repairs.

>>*VISUALS NORMALIZED. PURSUING TARGET.*

She pushed her agonized legs forward, struggling to keep her path straight as she charged through the corridor.

The hallway shuddered as the droid slammed against the wall, shoving its arm into the vent after her. Hindered by its massive stature, it thrashed blindly after its quarry, quaking the floor and ceiling behind her as it violently smashed its hand against each surface.

Fire crawled into the edges of her vision, the bright lights of her HUD beginning to fade.

I'm almost out of here. Just need to hang on a bit longer, she assured herself as she shook the fatigue out of her head.

Her medical systems blared in her ear, informing her they had gone into critical overdrive. A sting pierced her neck, followed by a cool rush flowing through her veins. The fire across her eyes began to subside as a force of energy pushed her faster.

She stared up at the street exit ahead of her, frowning at the four red-warm blots circling the open hatch above. The cavalry had arrived, and she had no patience to deal with them courteously.

She halted her flight and lobbed a device into the opening,

watching the warm blips on her vision back away in panic as it hovered above the city streets.

The device ruptured in jagged chunks of metal, and the vibrating core inside whistled out a ring of force that cleaved the air with a sonic howl, launching the welcoming party away from the access hatch.

As the patrol scrambled to recover, Nara pulled herself out of the hole, carrying her inanimate payload onto the concrete with her. She bolted back to her feet, dropping a smokescreen as she made a break for her vehicle.

More militia arrived at the scene, barking out orders in the commotion. Shots rained down on her from behind the smoke, and several lucky pellets battered against her armor as she fled. The suit pleaded at her with intermittent buzzes of warning, informing her of its depleting energy stores and imploring her to seek shelter.

"Ahh, fuck it, his armor's better than mine anyway," she growled as she shifted the body over her back, making the corpse endure the brunt of the assault.

She hunted for the beacon of her motorcycle on her display, the gleaming dot of hope that would ferry her away from this disaster of a mission. With a quick remote command, she initialized the bike's engine, warming the vehicle up for her escape.

Swarms of laser blasts careened beside her, forcing her to zigzag across the street as she traversed. The body jolted against her back as she heard shots ping against his armor, and she forced her muscles to quicken her pace with the advancing onslaught.

Spotting the vehicle in its hiding place, she siphoned the rest of her strength and poured it into her legs as she galloped toward exodus. Engaging the cloaking shield, she leapt into the seat and furiously shoved the body into the passenger section. With an irate kick of the clutch, she zipped off into the streets. Battered, but still alive.

CHAPTER 14

##14.0##

Nara burst into her apartment with the lifeless body slung over her shoulder.

"What the—who is . . .?" Garrett stammered as he ejected from his seat, but the armored figure paid no attention to him as she stormed to the bedroom.

A string of incoherent obscenities rumbled from Nara's throat as she laid the fallen mercenary on her bed. Her cursing intensified as she fought with her agitated hands, punching the button of her armor at her chest. The hard plates obediently shifted into their liquid state, sliding back into its original compact form.

Catching the badge in her hand, she heaved out an angry snarl and flung the object across the room. She clutched her scalp as she stood at the bedside, ignoring the cracked, caked blood and injuries that littered her body.

Garrett gingerly crept toward the doorway, about to offer his assistance when he witnessed the grisly spectacle in the room.

He recognized the ghostly features of the man Nara had introduced to him as Vausaureth Cain, despite the sickly black ichor obscuring the features of his face. He winced when his eyes passed over the gaping hole in the man's skull, turning his head away in revulsion before his brain could imprint the morbid sight to memory. His curiosity had never been satisfied so quickly in his entire life.

Nara sat down on the edge of the bed and leaned over the body to examine the head wound. The black liquid had stopped flowing, forming a thick visceral patch over exposed flesh, a much more effective scab than natural human blood. The synthetic bone material of his skull merged with the fluid and began stitching up the cavity, slowly sealing the bullet hole she'd inflicted.

"Fucking synthetics," she grumbled in her native voice. "Bet you just strolled right in with no trouble at all."

She felt the clasp of the armor around his neck, but as soon as her fingers brushed the top of the button, his biometric lock triggered, slapping her hand away with sparks of electricity.

"Oww, FUCK!" she howled indignantly as she snatched her hand back. She furiously shook the sensation away and rested her head in her hands, internalizing a storm of speculative quandaries as she stared out the barred bedroom window.

Garrett softly stepped inside when he heard the room quiet down. He stopped a safe distance away from Nara, feeling the tension radiate off her with an unsettling warmth.

"Hey, you okay?" he delicately asked.

"No." She exhaled deeply and combed her restless fingers through her hair. "No, I am not."

"What happened?"

"I don't know what the fuck just happened." Her voice raised as she directed her response to the wall in front of her. "I nearly lost seven million credits. All because of this corpse on my bed, which, technically speaking, is not dead."

Garrett raised a perplexed eyebrow, braving a quick glance at the body on the mattress.

"I just couldn't leave him there. He's way too fucking valuable to leave in unknown hands. But I don't want this body here. In my house." She paused and muttered incoherently, shaking her head furiously. "And I am only about 65% sure I wasn't followed as I ran back here. I wasn't really paying attention."

She massaged her temples and began chanting streams of words in a foreign tongue, struggling to block out reality around her.

Garrett cautiously approached as he noticed her blood-soaked clothing clinging onto her frame. He surveyed the extent of the damage from arm's length, spotting several bullet wounds and cuts. He leaned over to examine her front side, letting out an empathetic wheeze of air as he discovered the massive gash across her torso.

"You're badly injured," he pointed out, but she ignored his statement with a wave of indifference.

He walked over to the kitchen and pulled several jars he recognized from Nara's medicine stash, hoping at least one of them would be appropriate to use on deep wounds. He then filled a bowl with warm water and dug out several cloth bandages neatly folded in a drawer underneath the cupboard. He made his way back into the bedroom and knelt in front of her. Wetting a cloth, he began washing the blood off her minor injuries while he deliberated on how to take care of the severe ones.

Nara imitated a statue as he worked, giving him no indication whether he was helping or causing her pain.

As he swiped a thin layer of floral scented salve onto a gash, Nara suddenly barked a sharp curse at the air. In his startlement, his finger accidently slipped deeper into the wound, causing it to reopen.

"Relax," he hushed as he wiped away the blood.

"I will relax once Death himself wrests my thorny soul from my defiant, brawling carcass," she growled, glaring at him with her cold eyes.

"Whoa, okay, you are not speaking Trade. I didn't understand a word of that." Garrett leaned away from her, anticipating another outburst.

Nara sighed in frustration and flopped back, her head thumping against the body on the bed.

"Here, let me clean you up a bit more. You are safe now, and you can think about the situation later," Garrett assured. "Right now, you need to calm down and sleep."

She wearily mumbled in his general direction. Since her tone was altogether not aggressive, Garrett interpreted the words as permission to continue.

He leaned over to examine the slash across her torso. While the damage was not deep enough to warrant emergency surgery, her abdominal plating would prove a challenge to his novice stitching skills.

As he went back to the kitchen to hunt for a needle and thread, he was overcome with appreciation for the disturbingly graphic first aid sims Baran had made him watch before he was permitted to travel into the Underground.

"I'm trying my best, and this will probably hurt a lot more than it has to," he preemptively apologized as he sat down next to her. "Please don't move? Maybe?"

Uncertain how to start, he gently wiped away layers of blood to reveal the skin underneath. He then picked out shreds of fabric from her shirt that had bonded to the incision. Not wanting to move her around too much, he tore the slash in her garment wider, tucking the excess fabric underneath her to give him unhindered access to the wound.

After the area was clean enough for him, he applied a heavy dose of the healing salve to each segment of the lesion, hoping there was some form of numbing agent infused into the potion. With threaded needle in hand, he held his breath as he began to suture the wound. When he made the first puncture, he hesitated, anticipating a violent flinch. But to his surprise and relief, she did not stir, giving him the confidence to resume his stitching. Prick by prick, he continued, moving down the cut at a more comfortable pace as he observed Nara out of the corner of his eye.

She lay disturbingly still in front of him, her distant gaze accusing the ceiling of an indiscriminate transgression. Nothing appeared to shake her out of her distressing reverie, much less the steady pattern of jabbing and prodding Garrett inflicted on her.

He didn't know whether to be thankful or concerned by her lack of reaction, but he was reassured by the uniform rhythm of her breathing, taking it as a probable sign that she was not in immediate danger.

A few stiches further and he was finally at the other end of the wound. Content with his effort, he tied the thread in an overhand knot, then snapped the excess off. To finish, he applied more salve on top of the seam, then patted a small section of clean cloth on top. He wiped the excess potion onto his pants as he considered what to do next.

Nara had drifted off into a mild snooze, or at least he thought she did since her eyes were still half-open. It bothered him that he couldn't pick up her massive form and move her into a more comfortable position, but he quickly reminded himself that the situation was ultimately better for his own personal safety.

He didn't want to leave her in this state, but he also didn't know what else he could to do to help. The stab wound in her shin was out of his realm of knowledge, so he smeared more of the healing salve on top of the flesh and left it as is. He then retreated to clean the blood off himself and tidy up the apartment from the chaos of the evening.

##14.1##

HOURS PASSED when Nara's shallow sleep was broken by a tiny twitch underneath her head. She sat up and turned around just as the body on her bed sprang upright with an anguished gasp.

The man fervently scanned the room, steadying his panting as he analyzed the status of his safety. He blinked away grime from his eyes as he acclimated to his surroundings, his search abruptly halting as he met the Nara's seething glare.

"You, good sir, have some serious explaining to do," Nara threatened through bared teeth.

Cain eased out a few experimental breaths before scooting his back against the wall, wincing in pain as he made contact with the solid surface. When he finished readjusting, he gave her a noncommittal shrug.

"What the hell were you doing there? You usually stay away from biotech companies that large," she questioned him with disdain. "And I had assumed you had a pretty damn good reason to."

Her inquiries were met with a cold, avoidant stare.

Trying a different approach to her interrogation, she leaned over and picked up her belt from the floor. She pawed around at the contents of one of the pockets and fished out the shiny glass vial she collected from their violent altercation.

"What *is* this?" she demanded as she thrust the object in front of his face.

"That is . . ." his voice quivered as his eyes lit up with hope. "That is the complete genetic work of a new life form."

"And why should you care?" Nara pressed, trying to squeeze context out of him.

"That is the DNA of a humanoid that would be used for the purposes of law enforcement, once they have finished . . ." His eyes fell out of focus. "Conditioning it. It is still in developmental stage."

Nara could already guess where the story would end up. She shook her head and looked back at the window, mulling over the impending ethical burden she would be forced to take part in.

"I was already trying to stop one company from producing it. I couldn't allow you to let another have this product." Cain shivered as he searched for his words. "You forced me to act before it was too late."

Physically drained from hefting a mental weight from his mind, Cain rolled over on his side, his back facing her as he scrunched his knees into his chest.

That face . . . Nara thought as she let out an exhausted sigh, weaving the vial between her fingers. *It always gave me so much grief.*

"I . . . I'm not sure what to do with it," Nara confessed.

"Please destroy it," Cain beseeched.

Nara shook her head in disbelief, internally pleading for someone else to be in her place at this moment. She held at least seven million credits in her hand, exponentially more to the right sources. But it wasn't just the money that complicated the situation. She already had one company pining for her skin, and she wondered how much backlash she would endure if she were to piss off another.

And what if she destroyed this one specimen? The company would reproduce it again. The only damage done was a minor setback of a few months.

What the hell would someone from home world do? she thought bitterly. *They relish in these grave moral decisions.*

"God damn it," she growled as she crushed the tube in her hands, shards of glass embedding into her skin.

She absentmindedly watched the blood trickle out of the cuts, the glistening liquid distracting her from the predicament. She'd never had to admit failure to a mission of this importance, and she did not want to start now.

She walked over to the kitchen and flung the sanguine glass mixture into the sink, making a call through her NetCom with her other hand.

"Annon, it's me. I have news."

"Good news, I hope." The agent perked up.

"No."

"No? Well, what on seven earths do you mean?"

"It wasn't there," she mendaciously reported.

"It wasn't *there*?"

"Did I fucking stutter?" she snarled.

"This better be a joke, sick as it may be," Annon scolded through the channel.

"Yes, because I love to joke about wasting my time, especially when I am trapped inside high-security compounds with optimized enforcement droids. It's my absolute favorite activity."

"What the . . . how . . . what the hell happened?!"

"Not sure." She shrugged. "I got all the way up to the target, opened the holding tank, and was welcomed with an empty box. So, it was either being used at the time, or your client had the wrong coordinates. Either way, I'm not going back there again, fuck that. I'm in enough trouble already."

"You have no idea," Annon hissed. "What the hell am I supposed to tell them?"

"Well isn't that your job? Sitting in the cushy chair, raking in the cash while jackasses like me do the actual work? Fuck, charge 'em an inconvenience fee for wasting my time if you're feeling ballsy. Figure out something."

"Well yes, but—"

"End of discussion," she interjected.

"You will re—" Nara cut off the channel before Annon finished his threat.

She walked back to her room and flopped on the foot of the bed, resting her head in her hands. She drew a deep breath and slowly released it through pursed lips, waiting for the severity of the situation to pummel her full-force.

"The hell did I just do to myself?" she muttered aloud. She looked over her shoulder to find Cain regarding her uncomfortably. He made an awkward attempt to sit forward, reaching out to her with a shaky hand.

"What?" Nara questioned as an eyebrow curled up in bemusement.

"I . . ." He retracted his hand, struggling with his aching mind to search for the proper words. "I am in your debt. Severely."

She turned away from him, cringing internally as she listened to him choke on each syllable. This night was a train wreck of the most magnificent scale, and she was not in the mindset to deal with additional emotional cargo.

Radio silence for twenty years, she thought as she glared at the floor, *and now this. Goddamned conscience.*

"I am going out to have a drink. Or twelve," Nara announced as she stood up from the bed. "I will be out for quite some time. You are welcome to stay if you need to."

But you'll probably just disappear again, she muttered internally as she walked out of the room, grabbing her coat as she headed out the door.

##14.2##

"Fucking life-draining fuckers," Nara grumbled into the night air. "Just one thing after another, isn't it?"

She stewed over the night's events, bitterness poisoning her expression as she aimlessly ventured through the streets in search of a distraction. Her mind bounced sporadically through each incident, refusing to focus on one single event, leaving her thoughts a murky cloud of exhaustion and disdain.

Seeing Cain in her home conjured memories too uncomfortable to relive, fragments of better days that took weighted effort to push behind her. It was a long, bitter length of time before she could make peace with the abrupt dissolution.

But in the end, she knew two broken machines cannot merge to make one functional device. Both inevitably lose themselves in the reconstruction process.

The storm of fragmented recollections was almost enough for her to forget about Bellanar's intrusion, but the foreigner's pleading eyes flashed at her from a neglected part of her soul. Her brain initiated a one-sided argument, assuring her that she was unsympathetic toward whatever turmoil that transpired back on home world. But her ingrained sense of duty howled at her with a tenacious, grating voice.

She shrugged in discomfort as her scarred shoulder suddenly itched under her coat, the reminder sending shivers down her neck.

"FUCK!" she blurted, jolting the sensation away. Her bellow echoed at her through the empty buildings, a cold useless response to her angst.

Pain lanced through her lungs, reprimanding her for the outburst. It spread across her chest like wildfire as what little energy she had remaining rapidly escaped from her body. The tearing injuries nagging at her flesh demanded immediate reprieve after the taxing effects of the inhibitor.

She doubled over in the street, slowing her breath as she struggled to keep herself standing. Whatever the human did to patch her up, it was quickly wearing off. She groaned as she eased upright, then began to hobble toward the one place in the underground that could offer her a shred of comfort.

After a sequence of haggard stumbles and annoyed grunts, she pitifully conquered the stairs up to the shop of her trusted galactic apothecary. Familiar herbal scents swirled into her sinuses as she wearily slid the front door open.

Upon the arrival of the spectacle, the gentle blue giant standing behind the counter looked up from his battered analog book. Both of his eyebrows reached up above his horn-rimmed glasses in concern.

"My humble friend," Nara proclaimed as she leaned heavily on the doorframe. "I'm afraid I will require the full-service treatment."

"Oh, no. What happened to you, my dear?" Matteus hastily approached, ushering her inside and shutting the door behind her.

"A long, tiring series of events," she sighed. "I have an excess of funds at your disposal, and I will steal for you whatever priceless artifact you may require if you make me leave this planet for the next few hours. Three artifacts if you make me forget days."

"You know exactly my opinion on that issue," he scolded as he led her to the counter.

"Yes, yes." She waved him off, bracing herself on the furniture. "Only if I can also go back in time and return it to the rightful owner, I know."

"Well, you are one of the few clients who are capable of respecting my wishes in that regard," he said with a smirk as he approached a massive black wooden door at the back of the room.

A hearty clunk resonated through the shop as he flipped the latch of an antique wrought iron mechanical lock. With both hands, he grasped an aged metal ring set in the jaws of a carved stone gargoyle and heaved the door aside. He then collected his guest from the counter and escorted her inside.

A comforting aura radiated from inside celestial blue painted walls. The clandestine sanctuary was a perfect blend of mystical Old-World aesthetic and modern technology. Every detail, including the position of the furniture, was arranged in a harmonious composition. Soothing energy assured the newcomers with a hospitable, ethereal glow.

The domed ceiling above was formed by stained glass panes of deep blues and purples. Their swirling patterns were sporadically broken by orbs of contrasting sheens representing celestial bodies and glimmering constellations from a faraway galaxy. A glow of soft light shone behind each panel, the resulting reflections dotting the room with a rainbow of diffused glints and sparkles.

Nature-carved stones of varying heights bordered the perimeter, each possessing a collection of white candles and curious golden icons of ancient deities from long-forgotten traditions. A sweet, smoky scent permeated the air as incense gently smoldered, tracing a haze of relaxation through the atmosphere. A miniaturized waterfall constructed of neatly piled rocks filled the chamber with its gentle chattering, inviting listeners to enjoy its soothing narrative. A small stream trickled its way toward a pond on the opposite side of the room, where aquatic plants and rainbow scaled fish peacefully swayed inside its crystal waters.

Nara stepped inside the spiritual haven and groaned painfully as she shed her coat, which Matteus obligingly assisted with and carried off. Every part of her ached, and the hazy air actively obstructed her mental functions.

She let Matteus guide her to a carved stone seat in front of the simulated waterfall. Much to the delight of her tender muscles, the throne was heated to an inviting temperature. She sank into the oddly comfortable chair and let her back absorb the warmth, fighting off the immediate urge to fall asleep.

Matteus set a small copper cauldron next to her that contained a bundle of dried herbs. He took out a lighter and ignited the bouquet, then softly blew the flames out. He fanned at the smoldering pot to encourage the herbs to release their inebriating smoke.

"Well, you're still breathing," he assured as he helped her remove her shirt. "So now, you have another notch in the armor to tell others about."

"This notch has been here for quite some time," she commented, wincing at the slightest movements.

"Even the largest chinks can be repaired. But you are right, some of them may never be perfectly clean," he sympathized as he examined the injuries on her torso.

"I don't . . ." She trailed off, incapable of processing his metaphors.

"Did you do this stitch work?" he inquired, tracing a finger near the gash across her abdomen.

"Why, is something wrong?" she asked in a brief snap of sobriety.

"No, it's executed properly," he assured as he continued his examination. "It just doesn't look like your work."

"Hmm." She murmured unintelligibly as she eased back into a state of semi-consciousness.

Matteus continued his inspection along the back of her neck. He softly tsked as he encountered the grisly series of wounds created by the inhibitor.

"Ahh, I see *that* man has been harassing you again," he commented.

"Close. Took a job that was a little much to handle." She grunted as she leaned over to attempt to undo the clasps of her boots.

"I see," he said as he shooed her hands away, removing the shoes himself. He slid open a stone panel underneath her feet, revealing a bubbling whirlpool of effervescent water.

Nara released a whimper from her throat as she lowered her toes into the churning liquid, the warm fizzing soaking through her flesh. She absentmindedly watched Matteus trace a finger over her arms, his gentle motions mesmerizing to her lowered cognitive performance.

He continued removing her clothes, wincing empathetically as he delicately peeled her torn pant leg out of the dagger wound in her shin. He then continued to examine her arms and legs for the extent of the damage, sighing softly in disapproval.

He gingerly opened the palm of her hand, his eyebrow raised as he uncovered the curious superficial cuts dotting the surface of her skin. As he rotated her hand experimentally, the dim ambient light caught glimmers of glass from inside the still-seeping gashes. He looked up at Nara questioningly, but the merc averted her gaze, unwilling to respond to subliminal interrogation.

He gently laid her hand down and produced a tray of clean, warm towels, along with a basin of water delicately scented with sweet flowers. He then began cleaning off the night's grime from Nara's skin, gently scrubbing away the frustration and gloominess. With the help of the sparkling waterfall behind them, Matteus rinsed off the final shreds of her discontent.

He walked over to a glass bowl of simmering water perched on top of a stone pillar and extracted several black pots of salves from inside. He carried them back over to his client and brought out an assortment of wooden tools and gauze wrappings from his storage. He gently unscrewed the lid off one of the jars and stirred the waxy balm loose, then started to spread the warmed remedy over Nara's injuries.

Inebriated by the fumes Matteus had smudged into the air, Nara watched the motion of the apothecary as her mind melted into a warmer place. The salves stung slightly as they seeped through her cuts and holes, but her chemically dulled senses provided an ample diversion from the tenderness.

Matteus finished wrapping the last of her open wounds, then he assisted her up from the stone throne. Slinging his shoulder under her arm, he half-carried her over to a cushioned table at the center of the room, laying her down on her back.

He dotted the lip of the table with a line of incense cones, meticulously placing them in a symmetrical pattern. He circled the table a second time, lighting each cone in order of placement.

He reached up to the ceiling and poked at a floating mechanical mobile composed of translucent rough-cut crystals, brass bells, and metal filigree symbols. The device awoke to his command and turned in slow, rhythmic rotations, reciting a gentle saga with delicate metallic clinks.

From a drawer underneath the table, Matteus extracted a large marble mortar and pestle, along with an assortment of ingredients—a vibrant range of oils, herbs, both fresh and dried, and other strange dusts from far distant worlds.

Glass clinked and clicked as he began his ritual, methodically combining elements into the stone basin. Powders painted the air in colorful tufts as he carefully measured out his concoction. Fragrances melded into a softly scented waltz as each new component was introduced into the enigmatic formula.

With the initial mound of ingredients to his liking, he began to grind the mixture down, imbuing the air with soft scraping sounds at each turn of his wrist. As he continued churning away at the oil-soaked powder, he coaxed the healing elements out of the materials and began to form a homogeneous blend. When the remedy began to structure itself, Matteus paused his stirring to amplify the desired effects, adding in a pinch of this, a drop of that.

Nara slowed her breathing as her senses saturated with ethereal information. Her eyes were no longer needed, and words could not form inside her head. Only metaphysical emotions unidentifiable by consciousness flooded her perception.

When Matteus was satisfied with his brew, he extracted a silver metal stylus from his collection of arcane tools. He scraped up the infused mixture into the core of the utensil, then pushed the paste down with a metal rod until the potion poked out of the tip in a fine strip of pigment.

He then began tracing methodical lines over Nara's flesh, forming words long lost to modern society, words that expressed concepts rather than thoughts. He sketched out spirals of characters across her body, each stroke made with utmost care and precision.

As he continued his ritual, he hummed an ancient hymnal, a song of conflict and trial. A song of adversity and the struggle to overcome. With each note that passed his throat, the runes glowed a bright lilac warmth, scorching their image onto flesh. The light followed his stylus as he traced onward, the cinders trailing in soft wisps with each stroke he made.

The song continued with words of perseverance as he moved along her limbs, sprouting abstract concepts of guidance and healing through experience. An armored spirit entered the room from another plane of existence, enveloping the altar with a force of resilience as it warded off the anguish of the physical realm.

The room faded around Nara, the blue walls melting into a starry night sky. She submerged herself into the ether, no longer possessing a sense of physical presence. She became a passive observer to the trials of existence as the world around her slowly evaporated.

A field opened in front of her. A group of featureless, unrecognizable humanoid forms lived in contentment on the grass. She watched their carefree interactions from the sky above, a peaceful display of harmonious civilization.

Then, a few members of the clan spontaneously burst into flames, golden plumes swathed around their limbs and body. They glowed brightly enough to illuminate the daylit sky, walking the earth as living furnaces. But these individuals were not in pain and were comfortable with their physical predicament, carrying on with their simplistic lives.

But those who were not aflame grew concerned for their blazing brethren, guiding them to the lakes and streams winding over the land. When the enkindled individuals refused to comply, the unafflicted took matters into their own hands, pouring buckets of water over the flames and drowning them in rivers. Agonized screams resonated through the field as the flames were quenched, leaving behind the charred helpless bodies of the once vibrant clan.

Amity evaporated between the factions of the Ignited and the Unburned. The schism distressed the earth beneath them, and the rocky land ruptured, tearing itself apart with thundering moans of anguish.

Destruction broke out as the villagers warred. The Ignited fled as the ground beneath them shifted and quaked, and the Unburned hunted after them with no remorse. Casualties were numerous, and the sky's light dimmed with each fallen member of the Ignited.

At the climax of battle, the Burning soared up to the sky, escaping their pursuers as they sought out a new place to call home.

Space glittered with light as the galaxy became dotted with specks of living fire. The individual flashes formed a mechanical presence, a battered flotilla of starships heading off to an unknown destination. Dust and cinders trailed behind their engines, marking their path as they left their decaying world.

As the fires of the ships faded into the stars, the old world crumbled into a billow of ash. Desiccated soil swirled and evaporated into the void as a deathly stillness replaced the once peaceful celestial body.

Nara was presented with another world: warm and welcoming, its surface engulfed in flames as bright as the neighboring sun. It looked like home to her, but it was not home.

Conflicted feelings and images washed over her mind as she sat above the planet's scorching atmosphere, watching the flames dance harmlessly over rock and foliage.

Everything was as it should be.

##14.3##

Garrett glanced into Nara's bedroom, finding Cain curled up on his side, eyes staring vacantly into space. He shook his head and walked into the kitchen, waiting for his nerves to finally settle down after the evening's affairs.

The disorderly array of bottles, unwoven bandages, and open cabinets welcomed him with a suitable diversion. He began to put everything back in order, taking inventory of missing ingredients on a note in his NetCom.

But his deceitful brain replayed the image of Nara collapsed in front of an electrical minefield, and he couldn't help but feel like he was somehow at fault.

What would have happened if I hadn't pressed that button? he thought morbidly. *I could have killed her. Why did she trust me with that kind of power?*

He shook the feeling out of his head as he placed another bottle in the cabinet. All that mattered for now was that she had returned safely, and he resolved to discuss the issue later with Nara, perhaps even get a better feel of her opinion of him.

He dutifully continued his cleaning tasks, trying not to consider the innumerable possibilities that could have gone horrendously wrong. He rinsed the mess of Nara's blood and glass down the sink, absentmindedly watching the mixture disperse in hypnotic swirls.

Just as he allowed himself a moment of peace, the hairs on the back of his neck suddenly prickled with a disconcerting awareness, and his body was stricken with the compulsion to look over his shoulder.

As he turned his head around, a squeaky gasp escaped his mouth. Sparks erupted across his nerves as he met eyes with a clean-faced Cain, standing uncomfortably close to his personal space.

With a violent slosh, the bottle Garrett held slipped out of his hands, causing him to flail at the air. He snatched the vessel out of gravity's embrace before it could shatter on the ground, cradling it against his chest with both hands.

"Uh . . ." Garrett started as he slowed his heart, setting down the precious flask of medicine. "Can I get you some—"

"I know who you are." Cain only said five words, but his severe glowing eyes assaulted him with an encyclopedia of warnings.

Garrett's eyes widened at the implied accusation. Panic flushed his face as he wondered what the man would want of him in exchange for silence. Or his motivation to reveal him to Nara.

I thought I was being careful, he thought. *What the hell have I done wrong to let my identity slip?*

"Well." Garrett finally managed a nervous cough, staring down at his feet. "I'm sure I—"

But when he looked back up, Cain was gone.

Garrett stared at the front door in disbelief, the glowing light of the lock displaying its normal status. It had not been opened.

It was as if the man had vaporized into thin air, leaving Garrett alone to contemplate the volatile nature of his continued existence while his trembling nerves whispered the most violent outcomes.

##14.4##

NARA TRACED a finger over the purple runes scrawled over her hand, trying to make sense of the images that infected her mind during her sleep. Meditation was an elusive skill. She was never taught how to translate her garbled floods of incorporeal allegories. Anyone she spoke with or accounts she'd read about back at home described dramatically different experiences, much more tangible metaphors that could be communicated with ease.

She regarded each written character over her skin thoughtfully, but each inscription was part of a puzzle that she had no interest in deciphering. While she often buried herself in history books, language was a blind spot to her learning capability. She only had enough room in her head for the three tongues she utilized and had no interest in expanding her already overflowing brain with more alien syntax.

She moved her finger up her arm, admiring the stains the markings made on top of her armored plating, studying the fresh tattoos Matteus had taken the liberty of repairing while she was asleep.

"Would you like to talk about it?" Matteus' gentle voice dispersed the soothing air as he walked over with a steaming kettle.

"Not really." She slid over her stone cup for him to refill with fragrant hot tea.

"Any piece of conversation I can offer to distract you then?" he inquired, elegantly slipping inside the hanging netted cushion across from her.

She sat in silence among the tranquil scenery, gently swinging herself side to side in the hammock chair as she formulated a response. She focused on the flickering candles as she attempted to break down the night's affairs and the two unwelcome visitors who'd dropped on her doorstep.

Fate was not someone she often gave respect to, but this coincidental series of events started to make her feel like she no longer had control over her own path, like she was a mere observer hosting a body that didn't belong to her.

"I'm afraid I wouldn't know what would distract me. There are some ghosts from my past that have come back to haunt me," she finally admitted.

"Ahh. That's the troublesome thing about ghosts. They tend to want to tell you something very, very important," Matteus mused as he approached her, peeling away a bandage on her forearm. "But alas, they have lost the ability to communicate, their voices irreparably distorted after their passing."

She uttered a noncommittal noise as she watched him unwrap the glyph-coated gauze. The runes burned down to her skin underneath, staining the flesh with a deep plum cinder.

Cain and Bellanar are only fragments of the entire problem, she affirmed. *There is something else missing, something vital that I will be forced to deal with whether I want to or not.*

"It is frustrating, I know," Matteus said as he ran a finger down the void where an injury used to be. "They leave you alone with their enigmatic messages, making you bear the responsibility of deciphering them."

It always amazed Nara how astute the apothecary could be, as if he knew exactly what was going on through her mind, every detail and context. Even though his metaphorical musings could apply to many situations, he seemed to know the right string of words to etch away a mental riddle.

Her thoughts were interrupted by a notification alarm from her NetCom. Sentinel was calling her, most likely for a job offer.

"It is perfectly acceptable to say 'No', dear friend," Matteus pointed out.

"I could." She sighed as she glanced over to her coat hanging on the wall. "But those ghosts are very noisy. And I am not ready to answer them yet."

"Be careful," he warned, folding up the gauze. "Ghosts tend to have a limited window of time to communicate. And after their warning becomes obsolete, they vanish. Forever."

She mulled over the wisdom, rotating her cup around her fingers. She acknowledged the meaning of his words, but they did not sit well with her.

"Let me know what I used in your supply so I can reimburse you. I'm going to the markets again shortly," she said, changing the subject.

"The greatest payment you could ever give to me," he started, giving her a knowing smile, "is to take care of yourself. In all aspects. Do what is right for you, and the rest will follow. Perhaps even quiet the ghosts."

"I'm afraid I cannot promise anything," she confessed.

"I know you well enough not to expect anything different." The sage nodded. "I would like very much to tell you that everything will sort itself out in the grand scheme of life, but I am just a humble merchant."

"Yeah." She regarded the leaves at the bottom of her cup as the weight of the universe pressed down on her shoulders.

The two reclined in silence for the remainder of the afternoon, pondering the mysteries of the galaxy over their tea.

CHAPTER 15

##15.0##

"You do not appear well." Sentinel softened his face to a concerned frown as he watched the crimson giant drop heavily into the seat in front of him.

"I'd rather not talk about it," Nara evaded as she uncomfortably shifted her weight in the cushion.

"Very well." He glanced past her through his office door. "Your associate not here?"

"I did not want to take him out on this business matter," she stated flatly.

He nodded wisely. "That is for the better, I think."

"What is that supposed to mean?" Nara questioned as she scrutinized the otherworldly man's expression, internally clawing for shreds of fleeting data on the ubiquitous warlord.

Of all the organic lifeforms she had encountered on this planet, Sentinel's motivations were the most elusive to her. And the uncertainty fueled her already wayward paranoia.

"I am just concerned about who he is. Who he knows," Sentinel confessed as he eased into his own chair.

"If there is something you know," she breathed, letting impatience sharply roll off her tongue.

"I did not intend to cause distress, but I am afraid all I know right now is hearsay." He raised a hand. "And you are more than aware that I do not like to fan the flames of abstract rumor. It does nothing more than spread chaos. If I discover something more concrete, I will let you know immediately."

"I . . ." She forcibly exhaled out of her nostrils. "Fine."

Nara could not help but sneer at his enigmatic words as they prodded her brain with sharp implements. She was too exhausted to press further, and she knew it would be wasted effort against the man's impenetrable stoicism. But she could not help but feel like she was being toyed with, despite their amicable relationship.

"Is that all you wanted to see me about?" she inquired.

"No. I do have a job for you." Sentinel idly played with a stylus on his desk as he pulled up a file in front of him. "And this one, I trust, will be an interesting endeavor."

She raised an eyebrow. "What do you mean?"

"A client wishes the surgical removal of a Mr. Sedgwick Velonir, of the splinter corporation Skyward Robotics."

"Galavantier's media face?" She scoffed. "The one with an actual bedside manner?"

"Precisely."

"This . . . isn't a joke, is it?"

"I am afraid not." He firmly shook his head.

"Am I allowed to ask what in hell the client thinks this will accomplish?" Nara let out an exasperated sigh.

"There isn't much detail to give you, but in theory, the demise of this particular individual could pave the way for a power shift," Sentinel mused as he fidgeted with the stylus, twirling it between each of his fingers.

Nara pinched her temples with a hand, fuming internally about the predicament. She had asked for a distraction, and the universe had just slapped her across the face with one. Barely having time to recover from the disaster of the following night's events, she knew she didn't have the capacity to concentrate on such a crucial objective.

"I . . . I can't do this," she declared, rubbing her forehead distractedly.

"I wouldn't have brought you here if I didn't think you could," Sentinel countered.

"Velonir is one of Galavantier's legitimate clean-cut do-gooders. You never see him anywhere in the Undercity."

The man shrugged. "So you will have to go to the Uppercity to claim him."

"That's a problem. Disguise isn't my forte."

"You're not exactly built for stealth either, but you have managed this far somehow," he pointed out.

"That's different. It involves not being seen." Nara glowered. "Disguise means being plainly seen, but my features forbid me from traveling Upworld undetected. Especially since I am easily recognized by several choice corporate police forces. Galavantier himself, namely."

He pointed with the stylus. "Then you will have to sneak in plain sight."

Nara furrowed her eyebrows at the man, trying to discern his rationale. His persistence baffled her, and she wondered how much involvement he had with the client. There was another motive in the murk of his avoidant words he was hinting at, but she could not pluck the meaning from them.

"How much?" She groaned dejectedly.

"Thirteen million."

"That's not nearly enough for someone that high-profile," she scoffed. "No less than thirty."

"I'll see what I can do." Sentinel nodded with a coy smile.

"What sort of time frame are we looking at?"

"Technically, the contract will void after three weeks." Nara interrupted with a derisive snort, but Sentinel continued unmoved. "Conveniently, he is hosting a rather lavish regalia a few evenings from now."

"How convenient, indeed," she retorted. "And there is only a small chance of Galavantier himself making an appearance if his face is doing all the propaganda work."

"Precisely," the man agreed. "And I have even procured an invitation for you, which will make things all the easier."

"Wonderful," she snorted. "Is it legitimate, or am I going to have problems at the security checkpoint?"

"I assure you it is entirely legitimate."

"How can you, exactly?"

"The client was invited," Sentinel revealed.

"So, you know who is hiring me." A bitter sensation was beginning to corrode the back of her throat as suspicion soared through her head.

"To a point," he admitted. "And discretion was obviously demanded of me, so I cannot say any more."

"That is not comforting," she bitterly remarked.

"It is nothing to be concerned about. This was a matter that required an incorruptible character," Sentinel explained. "And you were the first that came to my mind."

"Your faith in me is perplexing," Nara commented. "And won't my actions discredit the employer?"

"Let's just say they are not concerned about whatever outcome you may choose to act on," the man assured.

"I am getting a very bad feeling about this contract."

She was being thrown in the middle of a colossal political struggle, to be used as a pawn that could start a city-wide war. With the severity of the strife, she had no idea how much she could depend on Sentinel to keep her out of any resulting fire.

As escape plans churned through her brain, the notion of declining the mission dissolved. She was past the point of no return, at least in her mind, and Sentinel had imprinted the importance of the contract into her deliberation.

Sentinel disrupted her concentration. "Don't overthink it. Take the trip Upworld as a practice session."

"What the hell do you mean by that?" Nara glared at him, wary of the abrupt topic change.

"Things are getting rather . . . tense in the atmosphere, both in Under and Upper," Sentinel explained. "Again, I don't know much for certain, but I sense a rift is about to erupt, and I think you may be in direct line of the backlash."

"We've discussed your ambiguous supernatural senses before, *Serr'Maht*," Nara warned. "Speak plainly."

His amber eyes flickered. "All I am saying is that you may want to consider leaving the planet, at least for a little while. And we all know it's easier to leave from Upper."

"What the—where the hell is this coming from?" she asked incredulously. "And what would I do, exactly? I can't just dump my life here and ship off to another godforsaken rock just for kicks."

"I can make arrangements if—"

"Out of the question," she snapped.

"As you wish." Sentinel bowed his head.

What exactly is he playing at? she simmered. *Something serious is about to happen if he is directly interfering in my wellbeing. But how the hell does he think that toying around in Upper is a reasonable course of action? Only one way to find out, I suppose, and see how many scars this will leave behind.*

"I'll contact you once the job is done," she announced curtly, standing up to leave the office.

##15.1##

GARRETT STOPPED himself from pacing in Nara's living room. It had been several days since her last mission, and she had still not returned. He was uncertain about the limits of their relationship boundaries, spending the majority of his solitude in her apartment deliberating on whether it was better to wait for her to return or to leave before she arrived. He considered sending a message on her NetCom, but even if she wasn't in danger, he was probably the last person she would want to hear from.

As time lingered, he grew increasingly apprehensive that Baran would summon him before he could be certain of Nara's safety. His restlessness exploded inside him as he ran out of menial tasks to busy himself with. The kitchen was spotless, and he'd read through most of the books in her computer library that were written in Trade.

He found himself staring at the front door, and a chill ran down his spine as his one-sided conversation with Cain scratched his memory. He couldn't comprehend how the ghostly man had easily disappeared in front of him. Playing the encounter repeatedly in his head, he focused on the door lock, assuring himself that it had not been opened as he recalled the flashing status lights once more.

Garrett began to investigate the apartment's interior, trying to piece together what his mind told him he saw. The few windows inside were barred with heavy metal girders, so there must have been another exit he wasn't aware of.

He wandered into the kitchen, standing in the exact spot in front of the sink the night of the unnerving encounter. He turned around and stared at the door, pondering the potential techno sorcery that might have occurred before his eyes.

Out of the room in front of him, the walls were covered in Nara's gun cabinets and ammunition stores, but moving them out of the way to get to an exit without Garrett's noticing was implausible. This left the remaining rooms behind the kitchen. He didn't feel comfortable pawing through someone else's place of sleep, so he continued his investigation in the bathroom instead.

The aesthetic was something appropriate for a starship interior, brushed chrome on every surface. It was a utilitarian space, with the fixtures and hardware mimicking a stripped-down machine with structurally organized piping. All basins were just large enough to serve their purpose, and nothing more. The flooring was grippy with rubberized safety tiles, the pattern broken by a circular drain in the corner of the room. A shower head jutted out from the paneled wall above the hole, no curtain or enclosure to be seen.

Having nothing else better to do with himself, Garrett examined the seams of the paneling, looking for abnormalities in the patterns or different widths or spaces for hinges. He knocked on the wall nearest to him experimentally, and to his disappointment, the other side responded with a solid thud. He continued his venture, assaulting each panel separately, straining his ears to extract anomalous data.

When he was through two meters of the wall and started to feel silly about the task, the acoustics shifted to a slightly softer tone. He stopped in his tracks, letting off harder strikes against the chosen panel with his knuckles. He paused between each beat, trying to determine if his ears were merely toying with him.

He slid a finger along the seam of the panel, trying to detect drafts emerging from behind. He spread his arms wide to reach a second panel for comparison, but the increased blood flow of his battered hands had warmed up the metal surfaces, throwing off his perception.

Before he could conclude his findings, he heard the lock cycle from the living room.

"Hey, you still here?" Nara called as she opened the door.

"Yeah, be right there," Garrett called from the bathroom, flipping on the sink to avert his suspicious actions.

A gargantuan weight was lifted from his anxiety as he heard her voice, relieved that she had made it back home in one piece. His brain immediately battered him with a flurry of questions about her whereabouts, but he restrained the urge to ask.

"Got a new job?" he coolly inquired, wiping his hands on his pants as he entered the room.

"Yeah," Nara breathed sullenly.

She traced her eyes over Garrett, mulling over Sentinel's arbitrary words of warning. But she could not find anything amiss with him, and it irritated her greatly. He was concerned and stressed, but after the previous night, that was nothing unexpected. She had grown accustomed to his quirks and antics, but now she wondered if she was becoming complacent rather than tolerant.

"What's the matter?" He furrowed his brow as he watched her thoroughly examine him.

"This one is . . . different."

"How so?"

"It requires . . ." She hesitated, barely believing the words coming out of her mouth. "Significant time in Uppercity."

"Ah." He rubbed the back of his neck as he searched for the appropriate response. "That sounds . . . lucrative?"

"To say the least." She slammed down onto her couch, resting her elbows on her knees.

"What's the issue?" he asked curiously. "Haven't you done jobs in Upper before?"

"Yeah, but it just involved creeping on the rooftops and dodging patrols," she stated. "This one's a little more involved."

"I see."

"I need a plan." She heaved a labored sigh.

"No." Garrett shook his head. "You need a persona."

"I have rather distinct features. You can fabricate all the history you want, but it isn't going to hide my face."

"There's ways around that." He rubbed his chin as an idea bubbled around in his mind. "Stand up for a second. Let me have a look at you."

"What?" Her lip curled in disgust at his request.

"Humor me, please?" he urged.

"I don't have time for games."

"It is not a game. If my plan isn't agreeable, you can find something else to do," he insisted, waving his hands up. "But you have to admit, I am probably your best resource on this subject."

He had a point, but Nara didn't appreciate his peppy outlook toward her situation. Against her better judgment, she begrudgingly stood up in front of him, scowling deeply as she made a show of the effort it took for her to rise.

"Well, you could pass as human up there," Garrett critiqued. "Height isn't a big issue. Everyone would assume you have had alterations."

He circled around her from a safe distance away, gnawing on a knuckle in contemplation, getting a perspective of her physique.

"Probably easier to keep covered," he continued. "But in general, many people who are well off can dye their skin, hair, and eyes to whatever the hell they feel like."

"The privilege of high society." She rolled her eyes.

"Yeah, we can make this work," he said as he ignored the remark, raising her elbows up.

"We?" she sniped as she disdainfully pulled her arm away.

"Dress can be arranged." He ignored her comment, pushing her arms higher. "Then all you would need is a forger to create some documents for you."

"And a plan to actually complete my task." She resisted the urge to swat at him.

"Not my specialty." He pulled out a digital ruler from his NetCom, laying the bright strip of light over her arm. "I'm just good at blending in, navigating through the sea of blue blood and acting how I'm expected to. The gritty bits are all up to you."

"This is absurd," she groaned, watching him weave around her.

"I have just the tailor to fix this up," Garrett continued despite her protests, concentrating on the measurements on his display. "They're Undercity, don't worry. It's where I got my gear to travel down here."

"And you are sure they can do the opposite world?"

"Of course. Now take off your coat and let me get the rest of your measurements," he instructed.

"And their discretion can be trusted?" she persisted, discomfort starting to crawl over her skin.

"Certainly," he assured. "And there's nothing to be secretive about. I am buying some clothes as a present for a friend."

"Wonderful." She grumbled a few indistinct syllables as she shrugged the coat from her shoulders.

"C'mon, arms up," he coaxed.

He darted around her, the strip of light illuminating his peculiar dance as he stretched his fingers, gathering data on the seams, height, and length of his reluctant model. Ignorant of her personal space, he slithered in uncomfortably close to her, brushing his shoulders with the insides of her arms.

Nara stifled a startled gasp as he suddenly wrapped his arms around her torso, instinctively edging away from the invasion. She gritted her teeth and slowly reset her stance, cringing as she resisted the urge to break from his fumbling embrace. She looked down at his mess of hair flitting about below her, shaking her head admonishingly as he struggled to make his fingers meet around her massive trunk.

Flustered by the obstacles in his task, he squeezed her tighter until the ruler clicked into place. He then traced the arc around the front of her, securing an accurate waist measurement. A quizzical expression plastered his face as he looked up at her chest, his next task hindered by her elevated stature. He stood up on his toes, flailing an arm at her as he reached up. As his balance got the better of him, he stamped a foot down to catch himself from teetering over, causing Nara to shoot him a disapproving glare.

"I . . . hmm." He scanned the room, eyeing the chairs in the dining area. He dragged one over, filling the once peaceful apartment with grating screeches as the legs scraped across the floor.

Climbing up on the seat, he resumed his intrusive data extraction with another awkward squeeze around her chest. As his ear was pressed against her pectorals, he became briefly distracted by the unusual sounds swirling around under her armored musculature. It was almost melodic, a line of delicate pulses gently pattering in harmony with her shallow breathing, contrasting a human's sharp beats.

She glowered. "Are you quite finished?"

"Sorry." He promptly released her and observed the numbers on his screen. "I have what I need. I'll be back shortly."

"Shortly, huh?" She dusted herself off, shaking the revulsion out of her nerves.

"My friend works quickly." He shrugged.

"You know, you seem to be enjoying this situation a little too much," she remarked.

"Don't you ever wish to be someone else?" He lowered his voice as he jotted down notes. "I, for one, would jump at that opportunity."

Nara pondered the notion and was confounded by how astute the question was. She frequently thought of what it would be like to shrug off her emotional burdens and live a simpler lifestyle. It was what she tried to do after she was ditched on this oppressive planet in the first place. As she dug deeper into the quandary, her ruminations inevitably took a more morbid, finite route.

"I'll be back!" Garrett promised as he walked out the door, leaving her to ponder through existential fog.

##15.2##

Garrett returned several hours later with a large black satchel and an eager grin plastered across his face. As he burst through her apartment door, he tripped over his feet, snatching the bag shut before it spilled its contents.

"Hey!" Nara yelled from her desk. "Calm your shit!"

"I . . . sorry." He plunked the bag on the floor and clawed excitedly through his prizes.

"Huh. That was fast," she commented.

"Like I said, friend works fast." He continued excavating through shimmery garments until his fingers closed in on his target. "Here, try this on."

He extracted a sharp tailored jacket, artfully crafted from satiny navy-blue fabric. A high collar framed the neck, ending with sharp tips that pointed at the mandible. The torso was slim-fitted, tracing over the figure until it met the hips, where it fluted out in long tails that reached below the knees.

He pulled out a waistcoat in a softer, coordinating tone of blue with swirling patterns embossed into the fabric, visible only in certain angles of light. Instead of buttons, the waistcoat had a thin strip of a pastel teal polymer that acted as a clasp, separating and reforming like an organic magnet. Digging deeper, he uncovered an ash colored undershirt to be worn underneath, accented with short, ruffled cuffs at the wrists. A pleated pair of matching dress slacks completed the ensemble, making a simple yet dignified statement.

Nara regarded it with a flat expression, feeling the slippery material in uncertainty.

"So . . . what do you think?" Garrett inquired hopefully.

"Well." She paused to find the words. "It's rather . . . frilly."

"But fashionable, without being too decadent," he pointed out.

"Hmm," she uttered as she continued her scrutiny, feeling the inside of the lining. She stuck her fingers through the various compartments sewn inside. Two large pockets took up the entirety of the front panels on both sides of the jacket, with several others of varying sizes sewn on top. "There are a lot of pockets here."

"I didn't know what you needed to smuggle, so I improvised." He shrugged. "Go on, try it on."

Nara gave him a stern glare as he enthusiastically motioned toward the back of the apartment, watching his showman-like grin widen the longer she stood in place.

"You are insufferable," she declared as she begrudgingly walked to her bedroom, roughly shutting the door behind her.

"And I will stay right here until you come out," he called after her. "So, don't think you can just hide in there forever."

"I think I could outlast you before you get either bored or hungry," she said through the door, leaving him smirking. "And I'll say it again—you are way too excited to actually be helping."

After a few moments of rustling and cursing, the bedroom was unnervingly silent, leaving Garrett wondering if he was wrong about the location of the escape route in the apartment.

"You okay in there?" he gingerly asked.

"Meh," she managed as she finally emerged from the room, sheepishly tugging at the hems of her sleeves.

"Let's take a look," he said, beckoning her with a wave of a hand.

Distaste contorted her lips as she approached, amplifying the regal air that the outfit exuded, bestowing upon her the aura of a ruthless feudal lord casting punishment on dissenters of court.

"So, how does it feel?" Garrett grinned in approval, astounded by the presence in front of him.

"Like I am a wolf trying on a sheep suit," she griped. "Is it normal to feel this hollow?"

"Yes, well, that fades a little with time as you get used to it." Garrett rubbed the back of his neck. He looked up and found himself marveling at the artistry in front of him, captivated by how well the ensemble suited her. "You do look quite striking, for what that's worth to you."

"Hmm," she muttered, distractedly brushing the tails of her coat.

"Ah, and there's one last detail I have forgotten." Garrett fished in his pocket and produced a silver circular pendant with a hexagonal ocean blue gem in the center. The focal was surrounded by five additional multicolored gems along the perimeter.

"What's that?" Nara asked as she regarded the trinket.

"A Holomask," he explained. "It's the cheater's way to hide your features without the use of genetic modifications."

"Interesting." She took the device in her hand, delicately swiping a finger around the buttons.

"Here, let me," he offered, waving her down to his level.

Nara bowed down with unintentional elegance, allowing him to fasten the chain around her neck. The pendant vibrated awake, glowing warmly as Garrett pressed the stones along its surface. It ejected a tiny flurry of needle-like beams as he held it up to her face, letting the miniature laser show zip eagerly over her features to analyze her.

"*Initializing*," the device purred into her ears.

The mask used advanced face tracking technology to project an image over physical features, mirroring the same expressions in synch with the wearer. Various guises could be selected by the user. Most popular themes involved personas of fantasy armor or mythological creatures. Many models also had voice alteration software, allowing for seamless identity alteration.

Garrett had chosen her the visage of a metallic gargoyle. The structure of the face was much wider than Nara's, chiseled in sharp angles and elongated into more of a draconic creature. The eyes were replaced with glittering silver faceted stones, taking up the entire opening of the sockets, no whites or irises on display.

Sharpened scale plates covered the bridge of the creature's nose, tracing up to the image's forehead. The lips were carved into a permanent grimace, with prominent fangs protruding from a slight underbite. The ears were exaggerated into sharp points, jutting out from a mane of artfully messy black hair.

"There, now you can tuck that in your collar, and it will take care of the rest," he explained. "How does it look?"

Nara found a reflective surface to examine her transformation. The creature's eyes widened in astonishment as she tilted her head, scrutinizing the details of her new face.

"Well, fuck me," Nara said, startling herself as a masculine voice laced with electronic cadence answered her.

"I wouldn't say that out loud if we go to Upper." He let out an uncomfortable chortle. "Mystery and intrigue are kind of a fetish, and many would literally leap on that offer."

"I'll keep that in mind." The gargoyle frowned. "You couldn't have picked something more low-key, could you?"

"Hmm, let me show you how it works, then you can play with the aesthetics," he offered.

She quickly picked up the controls and set to shrinking the jagged features of the demonic visage. With a few pulls and tugs of the shapes, the face morphed closer to a polygonal knight's helm from medieval lore. She transmuted the hair until it fused together, favoring a fabric hood effect. She kept the solid eye color, finding their image harder for observers to decipher emotional intent.

"I think I prefer this," Nara announced with uncertainty.

"Without knowing the situation, I'm sure it will be just fine," he commented.

"Fantastic. What else are you going to subject me to?"

"There's a set of gloves in that bag," he added, ignoring the mechanical spite in her voice. "That's a popular feature of Upper attire. They don't like touching things that other people, potentially lower class, may have touched."

"I see." She sighed.

"And there are four similar outfits in there as well," he continued. "In different colors, with slight alterations to the style."

"Why so many?"

"Well, I didn't know how long you need to be up there," Garrett explained. "And you wouldn't want to be seen wearing the same clothes, now would you?"

"I had hoped this would be like my quick in-and-out trips." She gave an exhausted groan.

"Again, I had no context, so I just prepared you for war." He shrugged. "A very fashionable war, I might add."

"I just . . . what? What does that even mean?" She shook her head in exasperated bewilderment.

"I'm not sure myself." He uncomfortably cleared his throat. "Now let me see you walk. You need the right motions to avoid sticking out."

"Are you fucking serious?" She irritably sighed. As she placed her palm across her face, the mask swallowed her fingers, giving off an unsettling illusion as her hand disappeared from this dimension.

"Presentation is everything," he pressed. "If you walk like a droid, people will know something is up."

The mask scowled at him as Nara took a few experimental paces across the room. She finished and turned to him, folding her arms across her chest while the mask amplified her disdain.

"No, too rigid." Garrett shook his head. "Your normal gait is far too aggressive. Relax, and casually stride like you have something to show off."

The mask raised an eyebrow. "I am not sure what you are referring to."

"Oh, come now, haven't you ever earned bragging rights for something? Kicking someone's ass publicly?" he suggested. "I am certain you know how to act haughty."

"Arrogance is a despised trait where I come from, and it is against my personal ethics," she said. "It's a sign of poor discipline and is almost punishable as a crime."

"I see, okay." His lips pursed in contemplation. "Let's try a different approach then. How about this? Cleverness is a trait commonly valued in the Upper city. Act as if you know something and everyone had better give you a damned good reason to share it."

"I don't see the distinction between that scenario and the previous one," Nara stated.

"All right, all right." Garrett pinched the bridge of his nose. "Bask in the knowledge you have then. People be damned if they know it or not."

"You people like to damn each other for sport, don't you?"

"Do you want to do this job unnoticed or not?" he chastised. "Loosen your shoulders, stand up straight, and . . . glide, for lack of a better term. Sneak like you are in an underground base. That, at least, should be familiar to you."

She sighed and made another attempt, practically slithering across the room as she unlocked her joints. She completed her disgruntled patrol with a skillful half-turn, glowering at her judge with animosity.

"Much better," Garrett praised with a clap of hands. "If you can get used to doing that in a crowded room, you would be in good shape."

"Great." Nara let her shoulders slump in defiance.

"All that is left is to discuss your language," he added.

"You don't think I can speak High Trade well?"

"I didn't say that," he said. "I was just going to mention your excessive swearing."

"It's not excessive if you mean it every time."

"Be that as it may, avoid it at all costs. And speak softly. A gentleman's voice should not radiate much farther than the person he is speaking to."

"Ugh. You humans and your genetic caste system." The mask warped in disgust. "Gross."

"And no matter how hard a person gets on your nerves, never lose your temper. Ever," he scolded. "Think decorum at all costs. Now you need a name."

Garrett circled her with a pensive look, folding his arms across his chest and pushing a thumb into his teeth as he considered what to call his creation.

"Patience and attention span fading," Nara murmured.

"Reaver." He rubbed his chin. "Mr. Elias Reaver."

"That sounds grossly unappealing," she retorted. "And so does this entire make-believe dress-up party."

"Well, if you can come up with something better," he countered.

"All that is coming to mind are various ways I can throw you off a roof," she growled. "How many times do you think you can bounce on the concrete before gravity intervenes?"

"We can calculate the physics of that over dinner."

"Excuse me?" His statement barely registered in Nara's ears before her suspicions soared.

"Well, you have to get used to the atmosphere and observe how people act." He knelt over the pile of clothes on the floor, folding them neatly before packing them back into the bag. "What better way than to have dinner up there?"

"You *are* enjoying this," Nara accused with a snarl.

"I've never had the chance to share my interests with someone else.

Come on, you are already dressed for it," he goaded. "Grab your gear, then let's head up. You'll be fine."

"Your certainty will be tested, I assure you."

##15.3##

"You going to be all right?" Garrett tested the covert neural link as they approached the elevator station. *"I know you may feel naked being up there without weapons, since the majority is illegal for citizens."*

"Everything can be turned into a weapon," Nara stated bluntly.

"I see." He cleared his throat in discomfort. *"Let's hope you don't need to utilize that skill, otherwise it would make getting back down a tad awkward."*

Garrett escorted her to one of the smaller stations to Uppercity, away from the clamor of the pseudomarkets. It was one of the more dubious hubs, a back entrance where Upper citizens sneak down to indulge in their semi-legal interests.

There was only a handful of corporate soldiers monitoring the area, owned by Tenshinn Security Tech, notable by their solid black armored suits. As one of the guards approached, Nara handed over the identification data she'd had Art update before they arrived at the station.

Being in his usual charitable spirits, Art had encoded the device for free, in exchange for letting him play with her shiny new holomask for an hour before they left the Undercity. As was his tendency, the device was not returned to her in its original condition, and she had to wade through a slew of extraneous features and configurations to restore the image over her face.

After a few passes with a scanner, the apathetic patrolman waved them into the elevator entrance, not even asking her to disengage the mask.

"My friend, you were right. The outskirts are way more exciting than the market fronts!" The inflection in Nara's voice amplified with the mechanical augmentation of her mask. "Thank you for showing me! I can't wait for our next escapade."

"Indeed." Garrett rolled his eyes. *"You're not funny."*

"Why, aren't you having fun?" The mask smiled wickedly.

"Eugh. I suppose it's only fair enough for what I've put you through," Garrett admitted defeat. *"So, Mr. Reaver, what kind of atmosphere would you like for dinner? I can show you what is considered haute cuisine up here, something gimmicky, or something quiet. The food I personally enjoy isn't up here, as you may know."*

"Quiet is preferable, but anywhere I don't have to learn a new language in order to eat my food," Nara remarked, watching the rising buildings through the window.

"Does 'don't use your face as a utensil' count as a separate language?" Garrett smirked.

"Is that the only rule I'm expected to follow?"

"Fingers are considered low manners as well," he added.

"I can deal with that, I suppose," she conceded.

"I think I can find something."

After a quiet ride up, they stepped out of the elevator into an office district of Upper, welcomed by the dimmed synthetic lighting reflecting the time of evening. Compared to the garish main circuits, the streets were paved with muted beiges, dotted with plain wrought iron-like streetlamps. Clean-cut topiaries and structurally grown trees dwelled inside matching concrete pots that lined the pathways, exuding a manufactured coziness to the damned souls who worked in the area.

Few citizens inhabited the streets, emerging from late-night shifts in a hurry to get home, paying no mind to the unusual pair of strangers meandering through. The reduced number of eyes decreased Nara's anxiety, but she had plenty of surplus to work through before she could consider herself relaxed.

"Hey, I want to show you something first before dinner," Garrett said. *"It's not that far. Do you mind?"*

"I mind every waking moment of my existence." Her bitterness lanced through his brain.

"Was that a yes or a no?" he confirmed.

"I don't care." She groaned.

"Well, fine." Garrett sighed. *"Do me a favor—close your eyes and follow my lead."*

"Excuse me?" The mask's nose wrinkled in disdain.

"The sight will have a greater impact if it's a surprise."

"Impact?" The mask eyed him suspiciously

"Yeah, okay, that was a poor choice of words." Garrett took her gloved hand and pulled her forward. *"C'mon, just humor me. If you don't like it, we can leave immediately."*

"Fine." With an audible grumble, Nara begrudgingly complied, shifting the sensor screen on the holomask to black. She analyzed the environment as the human guided her on, listening for the features of the street surrounding her.

The sleek pathways clicked a gentle chatter through their footsteps, conversing with the lamp posts and benches lining the road. The skyscrapers could not engage directly, their massive forms too far away from their trail. But they vicariously added to the discussion, the swirling winds of mildly shifting weather patterns flowing through the magnificent pillars, regaling the travelers with a trivial update. House servant drones bubbled and churned as they flew past, too self-absorbed with their tasks to stop and talk.

Her ankles compensated as Nara felt the path elevate over a ramp, and the prattling dialogue distorted as it bounced off a massive spherical surface in front of her. Upon reaching the end of the path, the air split apart, and a rush of warm, humid air combatted the tepid environment of the outside. As she was led on, the smell of the air shifted, and a moist, earthy scent trickled through her nose, accompanied by a green crispness. But it was still somehow different, clean.

The human's game continued for a short while as he dragged her on, turning one way, then the next, until he finally stopped her inches away from a tall, wide object. Life trickled over her senses, fervent, thriving.

"Okay," Garrett spoke softly, nudging her shoulders forward. "You can open them now."

Nara wiped the blackness away from her vision, and she was welcomed by a stalwart monolith of bark. She looked up in awe at the greenery that sheltered her. It smelled alive and welcoming. Her breath had left her as she delicately reached an arm toward the tree, feeling the grooves and knots of the surface through her gloved hand.

"It's not exactly native up here, of course," Garrett explained with an apologetic glance. "It's all lab created, but it's as real as it can get."

"I don't . . . understand," she tried to vocalize.

"I wasn't sure if you were aware of the Arboretums up here." He stuck his hands into his pockets and toed at a fallen acorn. "You said you missed foliage, and this is the closest thing we have in Upper."

Her words refused to leave her lungs as a torrent of conflicting emotions washed over her. She remained frozen in front of the ardent wood, decoding the human's intent with a focused stare.

"Come on, let me show you around," Garrett prompted as he watched the unsettling reaction. *I think I've made another mistake.*

The landscape was designed to mimic virgin deciduous forest. Every detail was taken into account, down to the colorful dots of tiny flowers and earthy fungal inhabitants. Tiny songbirds chirped delicate melodies as small mammals darted across the ground, arguing over the trees' fertile sustenance.

The plush grass yielded beneath their feet as they followed the path of a stream carved into the artificially sculpted earth, a miniscule current bubbling softly next to them. They settled down on the bank of a pond, where colorful fish painted an aurora of light in the gently rippling water.

"You okay?" Garrett asked.

"Why did you bring me here?" The tone across the neural link was cold, distant.

Garrett looked at the ground, uncertain of the answer. She had shown him fascinating sights in Undercity, despite the hazards, and he wanted to share the miniscule gems Upper had to offer within the safety of its plastic aura. But he'd overestimated her interest and caused discomfort instead.

"I just thought you might appreciate it." He shrugged. *"And that's as deep as you need to look into it."*

"I see."

Nara leaned back into the grass, longing to feel each cool, living blade on her bare skin instead of through the confines of her garments. The smell evoked memories of the lush forests on her home planet, the only place she could seek refuge from the thousands of staring eyes. The sensation filled her with an odd warm feeling as she drank in the atmosphere. For once in her life, she wanted to sit still and absorb her surroundings instead of sprint aimlessly toward nowhere.

"Let me know when you want to leave," Garrett offered, sinking down next to her. *"I've got a quiet place to go for dinner."*

"Sure."

They watched the satellites dart across the sky, feeling the slowing of time as the foliage soothed them with their lively embrace.

##15.4##

GARRETT ESCORTED Nara to an open-air concourse on top of a glass-paneled building. Plum canvas umbrellas provided shade from the bright spotlights hovering above the patio. Lush ferns and pastel flowering ivy bordered the perimeter of the sky bistro, trimmed just enough to construct an orderly net around its environment, forbidden from sprouting too far and inconveniencing the guests.

Delicate clinks of glass and silverware softly pitted the air as the few patrons dining conversed in hushed tones, absorbed in their own world. Even the wait staff communicated their specials in quiet reservation, creating a tranquil bubble of space in the wood smoke-scented atmosphere.

They were escorted to a free table, and after a brief pleasantry, Garrett placed an order for the both of them. Once the server left, the two sat in uncomfortable silence, both pondering what the other was thinking.

"How are you doing?" Garrett timidly asked through the neural link.

"I appreciate not being stared at by more than a dozen eyes," she remarked. *"But I still want to leap off the nearest precipice and freefall back to Under."*

"I'm afraid I don't know how to help with that," he sympathized, hiding his face in his wine glass.

"Neither do I."

Their meals shortly arrived, replacing their internalized nervousness with a smoky sweet aroma. They were presented with a white serving dish of beautifully seared red meat, glistening in a shallow pool of berry red sauce. Propping the protein up was a bed of lightly charred vegetables, arranged in rainbow order from most to least vibrant.

The two hesitated to dig into their meals, the flow of their conversation stifled by emotional resistance. Garrett wavered over his thoughts, knowing he was the one who always guided the discussion. Just as he gained the courage to speak, the words jumped back in this throat when Nara decided to initiate.

"Where did you learn to stitch skin?" she inquired, raising her head to meet his face.

"Necessity, really." He paused to take a sip from his glass, caught off guard by the blunt question. *"I've done quite a bit of research on worst-case scenarios that I'd rather not recollect, especially during dinner."*

"I see." It wasn't an unreasonable answer, but the failed data extraction gnawed at her. Sentinel's prophetic words were still ringing in her ear, and she would have to think of other ways to reveal the human's identity. Since direct questioning was ineffective, she considered picking his wallet the next moment he had his back toward her.

"Did I make a mess of it?" He looked up at her earnestly. *"You were pretty fucked up. I tried helping how I could. But I also didn't want to risk moving something out of place."*

Then again, she found herself developing a conscience toward the clumsy human. It wouldn't be fair to take advantage and violate his trust, but why did she suddenly care?

"No, you were fine," she assured, lowering her eyes to her plate.

"Oh, that's good then." Garrett was buried inside his own mental quandary. He tried to distract himself with the meal in front of him, but he could not shake the foreboding sensation as his identity was casually unmasked by someone whom he had never met personally.

But if that specter of a man operated similarly to Nara, how did he manage to find out about him?

"So," Garrett began, trying to keep his thoughts calm. *"Does Cain do a lot of work with biotech companies?"*

"Most of his business is in Upper." Nara shrugged. *"He's passable for a synthetic, so he can get into a lot of places here."*

Nara poked at her plate as she tried to hide her irritation. She knew he wasn't intentionally being malicious, but his meddlesome curiosity always seemed to tread on her most sensitive nerves. She was not surprised that Cain had not stayed in her apartment, but some show of gratitude would have been nice of him. But considering their conflict, she should have expected so much.

"I really don't want to talk about him," she finally declared.

"Sorry." He looked up at her to ask a less personal question but was sidetracked by the amusing spectacle of the holomask.

A smirk escaped from the corners of his mouth as he watched her fork disappear into the black void, only to reappear after she finished her bite. It chewed as she did, giving a disjointed illusion to anyone who paid close attention to her appearance.

"What's funny?" Nara demanded. *"Is the mask showing?"*

"No, no, it's just kind of unsettling the way it eats." He released a soft chortle. *"A little terrifying, actually, like a haunted doll coming to life."*

"Interesting imagery."

"Sorry." Garrett patted his mouth with a napkin as she spoke out loud. "So, what would you like to do after dinner?"

"Honestly, I am rather tired from all this excitement." She sighed.

"I think I can accommodate that."

When they had finished their meal, Garrett took her to a neighboring hotel, a destination primarily used for late-night shifters who were cursed to work early the following day. He winked at the desk clerk as he quietly requested a single, private room for the night, who in turn responded with a knowing smirk as they handed him the keys to a honeymoon suite.

Nara shot daggers through her eyes as they made their way to their room.

"Sorry, sorry, sorry!" Garrett cringed through the neural link. *"Just*

trust me."

Their room was luxurious, at least compared to Undercity's finest inns. The aesthetic cast a contemporary aura with shiny black marble floors reflecting the cool grey walls. A simulated fireplace sat in the center of the living area, tiled in the same black marble. Framed art dotted the walls in symmetrical arrangements, each displaying a cycle of digital projections from a local art museum.

"I had to make the strange room request," Garrett apologized as he made himself comfortable in the recliner. "But it was the only way I could guarantee there weren't any cameras in here. You should be okay to take the mask off in here, if you'd like."

"Yeah, I'd rather not." Nara firmly shook her head.

"Fair enough." He shrugged. "There should be a tram schedule and a route guide in the kitchen somewhere. Unless you plan on walking, then there should be a navigation directory on the room's NetCom if you can't or don't want to connect yours up here."

"Mmm," she halfheartedly uttered, still mulling over what was preventing her from rifling through his belongings. Perhaps she was softening with her chronic weariness and starting to consider the human a friendly associate. But ultimately, he was still a client, and violating that kind of trust did not sit well with her. It was the only form of control she had in her miserable life.

"You going to be okay?" Garrett broke her concentration with a question she had no answer to.

"We'll find out, won't we?"

Garrett's worry elevated. He knew the thickness of the layers of political red tape that wove itself around people that committed even the most minor infraction. He had only heard rumors about the existence of maximum security prisons. The news only mentioned the names of criminals who go there, but never a sentence length, or even where the compounds were located. His logic presumed they might be somewhere in Under, or worse, on an off-colony labor camp. The news never reported escapes, so security was either disproportionately ruthless or their inefficiency was covered up.

He thought about having to bail her out of prison, using his influence to bend a few guards' will. It would be lucky if she got arrested at one of Antonin's governmental compounds. It would be much easier for him to get her out. But then he would have to explain his actions to Antonin personally, effectively damning his future. Knowing the awful man too well, he would probably use her as a hostage, promising to keep her alive in exchange for Garrett doing whatever the horrid man pleased with his future.

"Oh, I suppose that's enough time spent without being suspicious," Garrett stated as he looked at his NetCom, shoving the morbid thoughts to the back of his head. "I'll see you later. Not sure where I will be at in the immediate future, so just contact me whenever you want to hang out again."

"You're not staying here?"

"Aren't you on business?" he queried. "Besides, my work here is done. I got you a basecamp set up for your mission. I'm sure you can take it from here."

Nara tilted her head as she regarded him, pondering his intentions. She was starting to appreciate his growing understanding of her delicate operation, though his omission of specific details still annoyed her greatly. Regardless, it was a drastic change from the few months they had hung out together, and she almost admitted to herself that she enjoyed his company.

"I, uh, well. Goodnight. And good luck." Garrett smiled warmly and left the room, leaving her with the realization that she was alone in an alien world.

##15.5##

GARRETT MOSEYED through the shopping districts, considering what he should do with himself. Baran still hadn't summoned him back to the estate, and he was increasingly worried for his well-being. Unease began to settle in as he considered the worst, what his guardian had found in his room after the unwelcome visitation.

The lack of scheduled activity sent his thoughts reeling, and he searched the street for a temporary destination. Going home was out of the question, and staying out in the open for too long was dangerous. He could camp out at another hotel and wait for Nara to message him in case she got into trouble, but she would probably handle everything herself, despite his connections.

He wandered to a beverage stall, purchasing a fruity concoction to steady his nerves while he deliberated his predicament. Soaking in the monotonous drum of pedestrian traffic, he made his way over to a bench and settled in. With a cleansing breath, he shed the apprehension away, focusing on the delightful flavor of his drink.

His ease drained away as he passed his eyes over the crowd, spotting the insidious Cordelia gliding through the road, searching the sea of faces for an unknown prey.

Aw, hell. Maybe she won't see me, he prayed, shrinking in his seat. *Please?*

But as his dread overwhelmed him, his throat tacked shut with dryness, inhibiting his ability to breathe. He took a sip to clear the sensation away, but the fizzy pops of the refreshment assaulted his windpipe, launching his lungs to a state of panic.

Fuck, he growled as he clamped his violent coughing, his face reddening with the struggle. He released a whimper as the dreadful woman looked in his direction, her satisfied smile exuding a sickly cloud.

"Why, hello there, Garrett." She purred as she slithered over. "Fancy seeing you here."

"Yes, hello." He swiftly wiped tears away. *Sure, this was a chance meeting. My ass.*

"I saw you in the Arboretum today," she informed. "But you probably didn't see me."

"Did you now?" he replied, keeping his tone neutral as he cleared the residual prickle from his throat. *All right, this is getting out of hand.*

"Who was your friend?" she probed as she slipped into the seat next to him.

"Hmm?" Her veiled curiosity sent alarms across his heart. *Shit, Nara. She'd better not fuck with her. I'll kill her myself.*

"That man who was with you in the garden," Cordelia pressed.

"Oh, him. He's just a study partner," he evaded, hiding his discomfort inside his beverage.

"Oh, how fun." She beamed.

"Indeed." He kept his answers vague and succinct, speaking with vigilance while she waited patiently for him to trip on his words and unwittingly spill what she desired.

"You've never traveled with anyone before," Cordelia said matter-of-factly, tilting her head with a practiced expression of interest.

"How observant of you," he responded with a calm tone, synapses firing in his brain as his suspicions amplified.

"It's a clever idea to walk around with someone of that stature. You can't be too careful, especially with the places you go," she implied with a hint of concern.

"I am not sure what you mean. Upper is quite safe." His eyes strained as he suppressed the dread from his face. *What the fuck is she playing at? Does she know about my trips to the Underground?*

"The galaxy ports, of course." Cordelia squinted coyly with her clever grin. "I bet a lot of kidnappings happen there."

"I suppose that could be dangerous," he said, forcing his jaw to open so the words didn't hiss through his teeth. "Was there something you needed?"

"Oh, I was just passing through." She pressed a finger to her cheek. "And I wanted to see if you would like to get together sometime."

"I'm afraid I can't speak for the foreseeable future," he denied with a disappointed sigh. "Between classes and the business, I don't have an availability for at least a month."

"I'd almost claim you were trying to avoid me." She winked.

"I am flattered you take the time from your demanding schedule to drop by," Garrett countered with a smile. "I cannot fathom how the COO of one of the pentarchic corporations of Arcadia can manage a social call."

"It's all about management and automation. How nice of you to take interest." She impishly wriggled her nose. "Perhaps I could tell you more."

"Perhaps at a later time." he glanced down at his NetCom. "For now, I must depart. I am being summoned elsewhere."

"Oh, what a shame." She tsked. "Would you like to be escorted to your destination?"

"I'm afraid I will have to decline. My security officer does not like unscheduled visits," he emphasized as he abruptly stood up. "My apologies."

"Well, I'm sure I could wait—"

"Do forgive me, but it is rather urgent," he interjected, absconding into the current of the crowd before she could react. He weaved through the gilded pathways, glancing over his shoulder as he navigated across the web of the city. When he was certain he was not being tailed, he slowed his pace and traversed through several more crossways, just to be safe.

His nerves demanded respite, tugging at his muscles as he paused in the center of a footbridge overlooking a laser tram rail. He obeyed their request and leaned over the railing, distracting himself with the colorful display. His lungs devoured the atmosphere, clearing out the murk of contempt seeping through his thoughts.

But as he began to settle, an unnerving chill ran down his spine, jumpstarting his heart with violent tremors. Before he gained the courage to turn around, a firm hand clasped onto his shoulder, sending spasm of fright through his body as he stifled a gasp.

"You should not be up here," an eerie voice whispered.

He glanced back to behold an imposing man dressed in a sharp black suit, perfect for blending in with Uppercity crème de la crème. His face was colored with a striking pallor but glowed with an otherworldly warmth. His eyes were both a bright sparkling blue that pierced directly into the soul of the observer. Garrett was taken aback by the spectacle, but his brain clicked pieces together as he recognized the stalker's facial structure.

"M–Mr. Cain?" Garrett recovered over the railing, heaving breaths to still his fleeing heart. "What are you—"

But as he turned to address the man, Cain had vanished, leaving nothing but the warning echoing in his ears. Garrett scoured the crowd for a trace of the peculiar being, but the specter eluded him, evaporating into the complacent populace.

His mind had made itself up—he would go back to Under immediately.

CHAPTER 16

##16.0##

Nara spent the past few nights awake in the hotel room, pacing about like a caged animal as she obsessively scanned through details of her objective. She had memorized the shortest route possible to the Velonir penthouse, electing to walk on foot instead of leaving a paper trail through the public transportation system. She mapped out a web of alternate escape routes, a network of side streets to lose patrols through should the mission go south.

It's not going to get any easier, she thought, heading out of her room. *The party is tonight. It's now or never.*

To her surprise, the journey to the penthouse proved uneventful. Barely anyone took notice as she sauntered along the glittering sidewalks. She even encountered a few individuals that were nearly as tall as she, but many of them were service droids escorting their masters to their destinations. The general disinterest in her presence perplexed her. Even the patrol drones whizzing by didn't see anything out of place.

The Upper world was beginning to seem less threatening, and she permitted herself to pause on a park bench to double-check the security detail planned for the evening. With the number of guests intending to make an appearance, the automated defenses would be turned off to prevent messy accidents should a drunk patron wander where they shouldn't. In place of this, the Velonir estate had hired a third-party security company to buffer the slack in their own personnel with additional soldiers.

While human guards were preferable to her, it also meant there would be more eyes to dodge while she was trying to complete her task. She took a deep draught of the sterilized air as she diverted her thoughts, clearing her head of the worst-case scenarios as she absorbed the scenery. Upper was a beautiful spectacle, for those who had the taste for it, but only the privileged got to see it that way.

Her duties back on home world exposed her to a limited amount of human culture, and she had never imagined such an extreme division of class like it was in Arcadia. Most humans she encountered were either smugglers trying to drop off contraband before heading to a GaPFed regulated planet, or military ships that stopped to refuel on the way to their next patrol station.

The natural order of this planet was illogical to her, the way it supported itself on the backs of those who were trapped below, never getting the chance to see the light of day. She was lucky, in a way. All it took was hard work to climb her way up the ranks and to choose her own path. To a point. It was a choice until she learned better, then it all disappeared.

Casting the bitter nostalgia aside, she inhaled a sharp breath as she rose from her seat, steeling herself as she headed to her destination.

The foyer of the Velonir estate reflected a tasteful elegance, a minimalistic design that still projected a luxurious aura, but not glaring into the observer's face. The room was large enough to be a ballroom of its own, bedecked with an inviting warm ivory tone. The slate tiles traced their way up to two curved staircases, each lined with a twisted wrought-iron banister. The vaulted ceiling was lit with grapevine sconces, casting shadows over the swirling carved molding bordering the room.

The host himself sat at the foot of the stairs, greeting each visitor that entered his estate. As Nara approached, he glanced over to her with curiosity, meeting her gaze with a warm smile. It was no wonder he was Galavantier's media representative. His warm and friendly demeanor radiated for miles.

The picturesque scenery of the entrance was disrupted by the obnoxiously bright security checkpoints and their jarring metal machinery hounding the arriving guests. Before Nara could formulate a formal impression of her surroundings, she was intercepted by a querulous security unit.

"Invitation, please," the officer demanded with an open palm.

She complied and handed over the document Sentinel had given her, waiting apprehensively as the officer hurriedly passed over the data with a scanner. He scrutinized the document, then looked back at her, raising an eyebrow of cynicism. He scanned the data again, swiping over the object in virulent disbelief.

"Is this some kind of joke?" he jeered after confirming the second scan.

"I beg your pardon?" she replied in confusion, keeping her mask neutral. *Sentinel, I swear to whatever celestial agencies you partake in, if you were lying about this invitation the entire time . . .*

"So, you're from Paragon?" The officer scoffed. "I'm sure of it."

Paragon?! Nara internally screamed. *What the hell have I gotten myself into?*

Paragon was the most clandestine force of the pentarchic powers of Arcadia. It was easily the largest corporation on the planet and an influential contender in the galaxy. The company had practically no media coverage after broadcast networks gave up trying to fabricate stories about the apocryphal super-complex. Their audiences grew bored listening to unoriginal lies regurgitated over data streams.

From what can be gathered by scraps of information littering the shadowy archives of the net, Paragon focused primarily on neuroscience and the behavioral health division of the medical industry. But their research methodology and their ascent to power remained a mystery to even the most discerning reporter. Their products were quietly released into the market, no advertising campaigns televised anywhere.

Inquiries regarding their procedures had the tendency to vanish from existence before they were able to come to fruition. Most records from GaPFed trade regulation reports were either tightly sealed, or nonexistent.

Several ethical councils had attempted to defame Paragon for potential immoral practices, demanding to see proof of their research procedures and claiming their use of involuntary test subjects. No resolution of complaints could be found in any legal entity or media network, leaving their business procedures an ambiguity to the mainstream populace.

Mr. Velonir approached the commotion after hearing the guard protest, his smile a beacon of excitement.

"Oh, what an honor." Sedgwick clapped his hands. "I have been contacting Paragon for years. I am absolutely delighted to have you here."

"Sir." The guard let his impatience slip. "I don't think this is authentic."

"Well, scan the invitation again," Sedgwick insisted.

Nara waited patiently with her arms crossed as the officer swiped several times over the data, letting a smirk crawl over the mask after his attempts.

"There's nothing wrong with the invitation," the guard begrudgingly confirmed.

"Then how else do you think this person received it?" Sedgwick insisted. "Considering Paragon's security measures, do you really think someone could have stolen it? Honestly, you should be ashamed for being so rude."

"I'm just doing my job, sir." The guard sighed as he motioned Nara closer with a weapon detector. "Please disengage your mask, sir."

"My employer forbids it, officer," she replied, raising a palm up in refusal.

"Oh, will you stop harassing the man?" Sedgwick blurted in irritation.

The guard grumbled as he waved his magic electric wand over Nara, disappointed to find a negative result.

"Come on through." The security man scowled as he waved her on.

"Good sir, would you mind accompanying me?" Sedgwick beckoned. "I'd love to be formally introduced to you."

"Certainly," Nara affirmed, clearing the nervousness from her throat.

The host led her up the stairs to an indoor greenhouse, the air thick with humidity from the environmental controls, perfectly adjusted for the comfort of the vegetative inhabitants. The foliage was permitted an unlimited level of chaos, giving the room the feeling of an overgrown ancient ruin. A pond bubbled at the center, dotted with large stones and artificially eroded statues.

"You may know me already," the charming man began. "But I am Sedgwick Velonir, the owner of this establishment. May I be permitted to know your name?"

"You may address me as Mr. R.," Nara replied.

"I will respect that." His smile widened. "And what is it you do at Paragon?"

"I am a security operative, of sorts. And unfortunately, that is all I am permitted to disclose," she explained. "To get into further detail would jeopardize myself, as well as the firm."

"Fair enough," he acknowledged. "I am very excited to have you here, and of course, you can trust me with discretion."

"I appreciate your understanding."

"I also just wanted to say," he started, staring at the pond as he searched for words. "I admire the work your employers do. To operate on such a quiet level, as well as releasing products for the good of society rather than creating a profit. It's fascinating how you have come so astonishingly far without the use of a marketing entity."

Nara watched the man curiously, discerning the deepest tone of sincerity in his voice. His honesty perplexed her, and his acknowledgment of social compassion settled heavily in the pit of her gut.

"The media can say whatever it likes, but everyone knows how much they engineer if they think it will earn them viewers. I think you are working for a noble cause, and maybe someday, we can work at dismantling the focus of living solely on material gain."

"Interesting perspective you have, sir," Nara mused, awestruck by his insight.

"Well, anyway. I do apologize, but I must return to my guests." He courteously bowed. "Please let me know if there is anything I can do for you. And I hope to speak with you again."

"Thank you. It was nice to make your acquaintance." Nara's conscience squirmed as she watched the man leave. *This job just got a whole lot heavier.*

She took in a few breaths of the heavy air as she shook the ethical implications out of her head. Whether he was earnest in his words or a highly skilled liar, she had a task to complete. She cycled through possible approaches in her head as she headed for the main ballroom.

A ramble of quiet chattering welcomed her as she stepped inside, the room barely illuminated by glowing halos of crystal chandeliers on the arched ceiling. The ambiance was accented with projectors displaying shifting patterns of stained glass, swirling above in hypnotizing rhythms.

Patrons wearing the finest natural fibered fabrics glittered in the subdued lighting, conveying the latest gossip to their cohorts and laughing at trivial matters. While the congregation mingled in the center of the room, the perimeter had plenty of lush seats and tables for those who wished to escape social fatigue.

Nara plucked a glass of amber liquid from one of the passing servers, trying to appear nonchalant as she headed closer to the crowd, as best as her stature would allow. She felt ridiculous and exposed in her surroundings, shoulder-deep in a sea of extravagant human puppets.

The crowd was generally disinterested in her presence, save for a few curious glances and reactionary polite smiles whenever she met their eyes. Security, in contrast, was rather interested in her movement, no doubt warned by the officer that accosted her to keep an eye out for trouble.

Taking a sip of her drink, she relaxed her shoulders and made a show of acting casual, scrolling through her NetCom impatiently to pass the time. She covertly scrutinized the room, pretending to look for someone while taking note of the exits surrounding the ballroom. With a shroud of feigned impatience, she waded deeper into the throng of idle faces, toying with the extraneous features Art had installed in her mask, unearthing an arsenal of sensory augmentations.

Visual settings that resembled the HUD of her armor readily reported to her command, as well as directional hearing that was eager to hone in on conversations of her choosing. A vision capture setting awaited orders to record video and stills of her current viewpoint. She had to hand it to Art. His unrestrained curiosity rarely did her harm. Rarely.

As she glided to the center of the swarm, she felt the sensation of two pairs of curious eyes fixate on her position. Glancing over her shoulder, she spied a set of fraternal twins dressed in rich blood-red suits and eager smiles, watching her every action intently. Nara experimentally shifted her course, observing their ravenous gaze moving as she did.

And what do we have here? Nara thought as she searched for an escape from the leering creatures, aiming for an empty lounge seat at the edge of the crowd.

Swiftly improvising her evasion, she let out a small cough and reached into her jacket pocket. With a flutter of fingers, she snapped her head down in masked surprise, watching an imaginary object drop to the floor. She let off a series of pardons as she dove into the regal crowd, pretending to chase the illusion rolling along the floor. The gathering hardly noticed her antics as she deftly navigated the sea of humans, leaving the widely spaced currents undisturbed.

When she reached the corner of the room, she rotated her hunched posture and slid into her targeted seat, remaining below the surface of the rabble. She then searched the room for the eerie interlopers, hoping to have evaded their curiosity.

To her discomfort, the two figures materialized from the edges of the throng, flanking her cushy shelter. Their eagerness to get acquainted with her radiated from their haunting smiles.

"My, you are a magnificent specimen, aren't you?" the female of the pair proclaimed as the duo admiringly eyed her over. "What do you think, Brother?"

"I beg your pardon?" Nara voiced as she shifted her gaze from one to the other.

"Yes indeed, Sister. Faustus picked a lovely individual," the other declared. "I think he will do just fine."

"Dear sir." The sister smiled as the twins sat on either side of her with a fluid synchronous movement. "You look like the kind of individual who enjoys the more . . ."

"Decadent side of life," the brother finished. "Without the consideration for consequence."

"I am not sure what you are referring to," Nara replied. *Oh, gods, where is this going?*

"Ahh, he is so modest as well." The two exchanged glances with a soft giggle.

"So how do you know I am the right one?" Nara questioned, playing along with a coy smile.

"We know everyone here," the brother answered.

"Except you," the sister added.

"I could introduce myself—"

"Tsk-tsk, no, my dear, hush." The brother raised a finger to his lips.

"That would ruin the intrigue." The sister winked.

"I see." Nara strained her cheek muscles as she feigned a smile. *Fucking hell, I have a goddamned job to do. I don't have time for human games.*

"Why don't you come along with us?" the sister implored, slipping an arm around Nara's elbow.

"Yes, we can show you where the real party is. Downstairs," the brother echoed, taking Nara's drink as he slithered under her other arm.

Nara's skin crawled as the foulness of the situation slathered over her nerves. While the disturbing duo were adamant about her attendance of whatever debauchery they hosted, downstairs would be much quieter, and she would get the chance to see more of the compound discreetly. But no matter what happened, she had to guard her clothing at all cost.

"You have me intrigued," Nara tentatively agreed, shaking off the urge to break from their grip as she allowed them to remove her from the couch.

"My, this one is *very* powerful," the brother commented, giving her triceps a fervent squeeze.

Nara implanted the hallways to memory, feeling increasingly ridiculous as she was ushered around by her enthusiastic captors, who were bursting with delight over the success of their ploy. She was unamused, finding this aspect of human behavior an annoyance.

She drafted her social evasive maneuvers as they progressed. Nobles often kept their vulgar trysts secret to keep gossip from exposing the participants. Bringing a hapless victim was their perverted way of amplifying the experience through mind games, rather than physical enjoyment. The degree of manipulative behavior disgusted her, but unpleasant as it would be, she hoped the real person she was replacing didn't find out before she could quietly flee.

They stopped her in front of a doorway to a dark room, nudging her inside. She expected to see a mass of sparsely clad gentry in compromising positions and sights she would have to burn out of her mind for centuries to come.

But she was wrong. So terribly, terribly wrong.

##16.1##

RED PILLAR CANDLES dotted the room, offering a meager, trembling illumination against the pitch-black room. Every surface was swathed in heavy black fabric, the walls, the furniture, turning the room into a miniature portal to an unholy void. The mechanical shades of the windows were drawn, blocking the skyline from witnessing the depraved actions that would transpire.

A sizeable gathering of people stared expectantly at her, their features obscured by heavy robes made of the same material shrouding the environment. A hushed silence filled the vacuous chamber as the audience examined her, intermittently broken by murmurs of approval.

And at the very center was an artifact that made her curse her knowledge of galactic history.

A dingy, aged bronze statuette rested in the center of a makeshift altar. The form was of a grotesque beast, a thick, larva-like body with six heavily muscled humanoid legs and four arms. Its back was studded with sharp chitinous spikes of a myriad of sizes. The beast had no neck. Its body ended at an elongated head extremity, with four curled horns on each side. It was devoid of facial features, apart from a jagged toothy grin stretching the width of the head.

Nara knew the monstrosity as Kraa'laanek, a bloodthirsty vile force whose influence thrived ten millennia ago to a small empire a solar system away. Known to be a pitiless ruler, worshippers would often engage in extravagant hallucinogen-fueled blood sacrifices to satiate the being's ravenous appetite for gore.

Its cultists would select prime soldiers to offer the deity, an attempt to win favor of their malefactor for upcoming wars, claiming the victims would continue their duty in the hellish afterlife. Ironically, the cultists were said to have been wiped out by a planet-wide power struggle, and many of their artifacts were destroyed from the aftermath of conquest.

You've got to be fucking kidding me. Nara cringed as she examined the materials strewn over the altar.

A leather holster was unfurled across the table, containing an orderly row of sparkling surgical instruments of various sharpness. A clear bowl sat next to the toolset, filled to the brim with a swirling purple concoction, fizzing and bubbling as its foul ingredients reacted to the air. A bizarre, aged tome sat at the feet of the sculpture, bound with suspicious leather.

Nara risked a glance down as a strange material crackled under her foot. The entire floor was covered in layers of black plastic sheeting, giving her insight on its intended purpose.

Disgusting hedonists. Nara fought to keep her scowl in check. *Where the hell did they get that book? It does not belong to them. Absolutely no respect for history or culture.*

The twins appeared on her sides again, grinning with pride.

"It seems you have not started yet," Nara observed, trying not to address the situation.

"We were waiting for you, my dear," the sister asserted.

"And now the fun can begin," professed the brother.

They cannot actually believe in this lore, Nara fumed as her eyes fixated on the surgical devices. *Just a bunch of mindless children playing with fire. People are merely playthings to them, existing only to fulfil their perverted boredom.*

"I must admit, I am surprised Master Velonir is party to this 'unique gathering'," Nara commented, keeping her anger contained.

"Oh, the blithering fool has no idea," the sister scoffed.

"He thinks we're all down here for an orgy," the brother added, returning Nara's drink to her hand. "No, my dear friend, this is something far greater."

Let me guess, Nara pondered, quietly sniffing the liquid.

>>*Analyzing vapors,* the holomask chirped into her ear. *Pharmaceutical-grade paralytic detected. Paragon brand, .028% concentration.*

Yep. Thought so, Nara griped. *Art, I could hug you, you magnificent little magpie.*

A heavy dosage, enough to quickly floor a massive human. But she was alien, and her systems often worked to her advantage. She weighed over the situation with her vast experience of chemical substances, both voluntary and involuntary exposure, calculating the risk if she consumed the drink.

"The cleaners will be here shortly," the brother announced. "Shall we get started?"

Cleaners? Nara thought. *How often do parties like this happen in Upper to justify a business model?*

The acolytes began to dispense the frothing beverage into tiny glasses stacked next to the altar, watching her with fascination as they passed the vile containers around the room.

Thirty or so in the room, Nara counted in her head. *There is no way I could subdue them all without attracting the guards.*

"A toast to our guest of honor, a new initiate," the sister proclaimed as she raised her own vessel.

I could just walk out. Not a whole lot they could do to stop me, other than get the guards to kick me out or get me arrested. Nara considered. *I'd have to either hide or find another way to get this job done.*

The twins maintained their frozen smiles as they synchronously swirled their glasses around, watching Nara intently. Silence overwhelmed the room as the throng of robed creeps stared at her in anticipation.

But a compulsion disregarded her audience as her eyes locked on the abhorrent grimoire beleaguering her from the altar. Her temper ignited her skin as her cultural binding to knowledge overshadowed her sense of self-preservation.

I need that book. Nara thought as she clamped her jaws. *It does not belong here.*

"The night is wasting, my good friend!" the brother pressed. "Join us!"

Go with the flow, she thought resignedly, *and dig yourself out later.*

She took a slow, shallow draught of her tainted glass, letting a thin trail of liquid slip from the corner of her mouth behind the mask. Lowering her chin, she caught the droplets into her high collar, the fabric slowly darkening as it consumed the toxin. As she felt the damp material brush her cheek, she made a mental note to thank Garrett for his unusual style preference.

Only when Nara lowered the glass did the congregation drink from their own refreshments, tilting their heads back in synch.

"Why not another?" The brother declared, raising his glass.

"Yes, the night will be long," the sister added with a wink. "No sense in spoiling the evening with one's own inhibitions."

You've got to be fucking kidding me, Nara groaned as she glanced at the remainder of her drink. She made a show to finish, arching her spine as she tilted her head back, letting as much of the poison discreetly spill as she could without drawing attention to the saturated spots of her clothes.

"Wonderful!" the brother cheered before draining his second glass.

"Why don't you come this way, my dear?" The sister shepherded her toward the center of the room.

Not too soon, not too long, Nara persuaded herself as she advanced.

"So, when . . ." Nara paused, displaying a wary expression on her mask. She took a step back, wavering from one side to the other as she played her part.

"Whatever is the matter, love?" the sister smiled sweetly.

"I . . . can't . . ." Nara choked out, sliding her hand around her throat. Glass shattered over the plastic flooring as she let her drink slip out of her hand. Gasping for air, she dropped her arms, lowering her shoulders as she staggered forward.

"My, my, someone is certainly not used to the high life," the brother tsked.

"Everything will be all right, dear." The sister patted her derisively on the back. "It will be over shortly."

You're despicable. Nara seethed as she projected a face of panic over the mask.

As she raised a foot, she unlocked her knees, then artfully tumbled to the ground, slamming her shoulder against the altar as she fell. She attempted to rise, playing with her limbs as she steadied herself on the floor. With a desperate cough, she loosened her grip and crashed into the furniture once more.

"That's it," the sister goaded.

"Nearly there," the brother echoed.

Members of the congregation approached and wrapped their arms around her, ejecting gauche grunts that disrupted the sacrosanct atmosphere as they struggled to heave her massive body onto a table. She resisted the urge to smirk as she pretended to fight against them, gently nudging her aggressors with noodly limp limbs and shakily outstretched fingers.

"My, you are a massive beast, aren't you?" the brother stared wide-eyed at the spectacle.

Yeah, you all brought this on yourself. Have fun hauling my 300-kilo ass. Nara internally grinned. *I am NOT helping you.*

As the gathering wrestled to keep her body steady, some of the hoods slipped off the faces of her audience, compromising their anonymity. Nara seized the opportunity to snap stills of the perpetrators, saving them for a devious use. Unsurprisingly, she did not recognize anyone in the congregation, but she knew a select few in Under who would.

With one final coordinated shove, they managed to pull her up, slamming her head on the solid surface as they dragged her into a flat position.

You fuckers. Nara stifled the urge to growl as twangs of pain lashed through her skull. She froze the mask's expression, allowing her to move her eyes freely to inspect her surroundings.

"Well, that certainly was a task," the sister sighed. "Grand Master, will you do the honors? I am starting to feel rather warm already."

All but two of the hooded figures gathered around the table, seating themselves on the floor as they gripped each other's hands. The twins had joined in the circle, bubbly smiles radiating from their faces as they eagerly waited for the ceremony to begin.

One of the standing figures nervously plucked the damnable tome from the altar, clumsily flipping through its crusty pages. After finding what they were after, they cleared their voice with a soft squeak and began to meekly recite the words on the page, struggling with each syllable as the foreign tongue passed over inexperienced lips.

"Louder, my child," the Grand Master barked.

The page timidly nodded in compliance, forcing the abominable sounds out of their lungs as they continued the incantation.

The Grand Master paced around the congregation, tossing a bitter, metallic-smelling liquid over the worshippers from a small brass pot. A tune rumbled from the orchestrator's throat, maintaining the base melody for their graceless recital.

As the vile ablutions continued, the audience began to repeat the words of the speaker, drowning out the poor disciple with unearthly monotone echoes. Each syllable intensified as the odious verses clawed their way from the organs of the congregation. The assembly began to sway with the abhorrent melody, gently rocking side to side in unison.

The effects of the elixir began to manifest inside the worshippers as the ritual progressed, the droning madness amplified as they released their grasp of each other, undulating their arms in the gloomy candlelight. Chaos filled the room as each member began to abandon the orator's words, babbling in raspy cries as their intoxication wrenched them away from reality.

The temperature rose with the fervor of the disciples, and they began to lose their ability to maintain their orderly circle. Woes and anguish reverberated across the walls as they dropped to the floor, crawling around the room until they found a place to sob undisturbed.

Through the cacophony of insanity, the Grand Master approached Nara's side, brandishing the largest knife from the collection. He reached a hand down to her, separating the panels of her jacket. Tracing a finger over the center seams of her waistcoat, he angled the knife in his other hand, deliberating his first cuts.

As he dug a nail under the clasp of the garment, a thunderous crack erupted in the chamber, and the Grand Master crashed to the floor with a startled wheeze. Streaks of blood trickled down his temple, tracing over the shocked expression frozen over his face.

The orator squeaked as they looked up from the tome, watching in stupefaction as the entirely mobile victim on the table sat up, glowering in their direction.

Just another day on the job, Nara grumbled as she slid off the table, rubbing her weaponized fist in aggravation. She cracked her knuckles as she advanced on the lucid performer, who began sputtering half-syllables as an attempt to plea for their life.

"That's mine now," Nara growled, snatching the tome from their trembling hands.

The hapless speaker yelped in fear of the creature in front of them, jumping back against the wall.

Nara gracefully knelt down and picked up a half-empty glass of the deplorable elixir, then took the quivering speaker's hand and wrapped their fingers around the vessel.

"I don't think it's fair that you don't get to participate in the fun. We will fix that." She leaned into the shrinking speaker. "Drink."

The poor page complied as best they could, droplets sloshing over the rim of the glass as they shakily imbibed the potion.

"Good," Nara purred. "Now have a seat and think about your life choices."

"Y–yes, s-sir." The quivering page slid to the ground, watching Nara move as she sauntered away.

Stepping over convulsing bodies, Nara headed for the door, letting off a few hearty kicks to the undulating wave of flesh as she traversed the room. A desperate hand stopped her retreat as it latched onto her ankle. The owner of the offending limb sobbed beseechingly at her, moaning about living without their lord's favor.

Feeling particularly savage, Nara lowered to one knee and grasped the sniveling mass by the chin. As she held their jaw up to eye level, she let the holomask disengage, revealing her demonic features and fanged scowl.

"You are not worthy of his favor," she snarled, her eyes burning a hole into the hapless soul's memory.

With a wail of anguish, the creature released their grasp of her ankle, and their sobs amplified tenfold.

Nara callously dropped the pitiful creature with a thud, then turned to leave the room, feeling only slightly vindicated. She wished she could encounter the dreadful twins in Under, then she could show them a few things about the decadent side of life down there.

##16.2##

NARA HEADED BACK into the hallway, flexing her hand experimentally as she began to feel a tightness over her fingers.

Fuck, running out of time, she thought as she glanced down the corridor, shoving the tome inside her jacket pocket.

She found the nearest door and pressed an ear against it, thwacking it with an experimental knock. Silence replied, to her relief. Her waning grip strength toyed with her as she fumbled with the doorknob, and she let off a barrage of agitated growls as she fumbled with the mechanism. When the barrier finally succumbed to her demands, she quickly slipped inside the empty bedroom, locking the door behind her.

Well, I guess we can see what kind of havoc I can wreak from here before bailing on this shitty adventure, Nara grumbled as she scrolled through her NetCom's applications.

>>*ACCESSING AVAILABLE NETWORKS. ANALYZING OPEN PORTS*, her device reported.

While she waited for her intrusive spells to cast, she made herself as comfortable as possible on the excessively sized bed. Her joints were beginning to rebel inside her body, stiffening up across her limbs as her muscles ached with a dull fatigue. Not having considered how she would get herself out of this predicament, she decided to send a message to a semi-amicable associate and ask for evacuation.

>>*Declan, my good friend!*

>>*Busy, what do you want?*

>>*Spot of trouble*

Nara struggled to type the message out, fidgeting with the touchpad as her fingers seized up.

>>*You mean you are actually giving me advance warning instead of just showing up on my doorstep?*

>>*Denzylhyrodoxine. Paragon brand. ≈100mg. 30 mins since dosed*

>>*What the hell have you been doing?!?*

>>*Haven't done it yet.*

>>*Where are you?*

>>*Velonir estate.*

>>*WHAT?!?*

>>*Just find me at this location.*

Nara transmitted him coordinates to a quiet location near the main entrance to the penthouse.

>>*Can you even *make* it there??*

>>*Gottagobye.*

She let her messenger bleep furiously as she swiped back to her invasion software.

>>*ANALYSIS COMPLETE,* the device reported. *FOUR ADMIN CREDENTIALS UNCOVERED. 14 ENCRYPTED MESSAGES INTERCEPTED.*

Nara sighed in relief, thankful that something on this awful mission was going her way. She passed a stiffened thumb across the screen as she scanned over the information her device faithfully retrieved.

Let's see, she mused. *'did you see so-and-so,' 'lookit what they're wearing,' ugh, 'Watch for odd masked man,' blah blah blah. Oh, here's something nice.*

Message sent 1130 on Today's date:

Part A Decrypted:

>>*To: Chief Forrester, Velonir Estate*

>>*This is Captain Garm from EsnaSec,*

>>*We're having some issues with synching up the camera audio and visual settings with the house. Can we get a temporary admin account made so we can patch up the connection?*

>>*TIA*

Part B Decrypted:

>>*To: Garm, EsnaSec*

>>*Sure, see attached. Expires in three hours.*

>>*-F.*

Nara glanced at the clock and blinked in disbelief. The root-level credentials were still active for enough time to be useable. She entered the stolen login to the root system, pleasantly relieved that it granted her entry. She then ordered her program to dig deeper into the network, weaving through gateways until she found the estate's defense system.

As she was about to fabricate her next attack, her arm suddenly jerked away from the device and a stinging sensation crackled through her elbow as she wrestled to maintain control.

Fuck, not now, she griped.

With shaking hands, she dug a finger under the restrictive cuff of her sleeve, tearing open the clasps with a controlled yank. As she pushed the garment up her arm, she brought the insubordinate limb to her face, pressing the skin side of her wrist to her lips. Taking in a cleansing breath, she clamped her jaw around her exposed flesh, biting down until her fangs broke through skin.

Ow, wake up, dammit, she scolded as she tasted the blood seeping into her mouth. Sparks burst through the perforations, lashing her digits with pain.

She opened a command browser with her uninjured hand, sifting through the global functions and variables referenced within scripts controlling the automated turrets. Amid the chaos of information, she found listings of family members, security personnel, and every staff member that resided in the Velonir estate.

Summoning a script editor, she spread out a fresh document over her screen. The program presented her with a toolset of color-coordinated boxes, colorful bubbles to piece together a draft of her assault. Each box contained fragments of code, functions, commands, and variables that were commonly used in the structures.

She slid her finger across the display, dragging bubbles into her workspace and composing a series of events that would, in theory, do her job without having to get close to Master Velonir.

Script "temp"{
On (system.time) at "0300" {
SetLogger(level.OFF)
Remove (user.biodata "svelonir")
Check (user.biodata)
If (user state [unknown])
Set lock at door.masterbed("all") to
Set turret.masterbed("all") to state "active")
If (turret.masterbed("all") "engage")
Wait for turret.masterbed("all") to state "inactive"
Remove (script.temp)
END
}

Is . . . is that all? Nara checked through the array of boxes spelling out the script. *Disabled the log tracker, deleted Velonir from the database, locked doors and activated turrets, removed function when completed. Yeah, I think I can leave now.*

But that was easier said than done. As she swung a leg over the side of the bed, her hips popped in protest, sending a thousand pins jabbing through her leg.

Fu-uck, she groaned as she heaved herself onto her feet.

The poison hurled her into a personal gravity well, a force on the floor yanking at her limbs as she strained to pull her back upright. Her skin was coated in iron and her plating was cast in lead.

Stings pitted her legs as she advanced with burdened steps toward the doorway. She leaned heavily on the frame as she cracked the door open, stretching out her rigid neck as she searched for occupants in the hallway.

She emerged into the corridor, leaning her back against the nearest wall. She paused to catch her breath, forcing air into her enfeebled lungs, the muscles in her chest constricting them against her spine. Her jaw clamped shut as she clutched the railing for support, the flesh around her throat prickling her vocal chords.

Fuck, I can't just walk out of the building, she thought as she let out a weak cough. *I'll attract way too much attention.*

As her mind raced through alternatives, a shadowy blur dashed around the corner. Before her brain could process the shape, a humanoid freight train slammed into her. She let out a pained wheeze as she reeled to keep her balance. But her body sided with the force of physics, and she crashed to the floor. Daggers drove their way through her nerves as her shoulder cracked with the impact, while waves of twitching prickles washed over her arms.

"I, oh dear, I am so sorry, sir. Are you all right?" A soft voice addressed her as a gloved hand stretched into her vision.

She craned her obstinate neck to get a look at the owner of the intrusive limb, a rather large human. Not as large as she was, but still quite impressively statured. Their features were also concealed by a holomask.

Wonderful, try and get out of this mess gracefully, she groaned. *No other option. This night is either full of coincidence, or I am about to make a very bad decision. Xannat, what say you?*

She accepted the figure's hand and let him hoist her up, trying to assist while failing muscles threatened to tear her down again. After managing to stand, she leaned into the human, bringing her mouth to his ears.

"Are you all right, sir?" the man asked uncomfortably, trying to pull away from her.

"Faustus," Nara forced through her teeth, recalling the name the deplorable twins had spoken to her.

"You know of him?" The man stared at her in surprise. "I was supposed to meet him here, but wait, are you—"

So the actual sacrifice finally decides so show up, Nara lamented.

"Trap." Her leg bucked underneath her as she pushed the syllable out. The man instinctively caught her, pulling her upright and wrapping her arm around his shoulder. "Poison. Help."

The eyes on the man's mask widened in horror with the realization of his folly, thoughts bubbling wildly in the victim's brain as he stared at Nara's incapacitation.

"I, oh, shit, I'll call the guard!" As he started to pull away, she summoned every drop of her strength into her belligerent arm, digging her fingers into the back of his neck.

"Need. To leave," she breathed into his ear. "Now."

"I, uh, okay, but I think it would be better if—"

"NO," the grating syllable burst from her throat.

"Is everything all right, sirs?" Another voice broke their conversation as a security guard approached them, encased in a heavily armored suit.

No, no, no, no, fuck, Nara repeated internally as she shot the man supporting her a severe glare.

"Oh yes, just fine. My friend has just had a bit much to drink," her new friend nervously explained. "I was just about to take him to a cab. He's feeling a bit under the weather."

"Would you like me to call one for you?" The guard offered, looking over Nara warily.

"No, it's quite all right, one is already on the way." The masked man hesitated, glancing around the hallway. "Um, is there a quieter exit we could leave? We don't wish to make a scene, and I want to spare him a little embarrassment in the morning."

"Certainly, sir." The guard ushered them forward. "Follow me."

"I, uhm, could use a little assistance, actually." The masked man shifted Nara on his shoulder. "He's, uh, quite heavy."

This is so ridiculous. Nara cringed as the security guard slipped under her other shoulder. *I'm going to end up in an Upper jail cell.*

She stared down at her feet as she was dragged further down the hallway, concentrating the remainder of her strength on her mutinous legs. Her awkward gait halted as her ankles locked in place. Pangs of numbness sliced through her legs as her knees crumpled from under her, her weight bringing her escorts down with her.

The armored officer dove under her body, wrenching her up with the assistance of their power suit. She tried to hold onto them as she was guided forward, but she had lost all connection to her extremities.

Can't feel anything.

Her lungs surrendered the fight, crushed under an invisible force. Dizziness began to swell inside her head as her air-starved brain demanded fuel. The hallway began to dim, and her vision faded as swirling clouds cascaded over the darkness under her eyelids. She felt herself gliding through the environment, her senses melting as she was carried off to an unknown destination.

"I'll take it from here, Officer." A voice echoed through the torrent inside her ears. Familiar. Apprehension. Anger.

A spectral force pierced through her senses, firing shocks through the back of her neck. The assault was followed by a cooling sensation, flooding her hardened veins with prickling reprieve. It wrapped her lungs with ice, cracking the chrysalis that bound her organs.

Her body separated from her consciousness, wrought with a disorienting awareness as she felt arms pulling her into an unknown metal container. She let herself unfurl across the hovering vessel, finding her support cushy and pleasant to lie on.

"You brought him out?" The voice inquired a distance away from her. "Please, come with me, sir. I'd like to know more about what happened."

CHAPTER 17

##17.0##

A charcoal-tiled ceiling greeted Nara as she peeled her eyes open. Her body felt as if it was extruded through a meat grinder then hastily compacted back together in some semblance of her original form.

"You are very lucky I had decided to show up for work in my Upper office during that incident," Declan's voice scolded. "And you looked like shit, so I kept you down for a while."

She sluggishly rolled her back toward the source of the voice, refusing to acknowledge his irritation.

"Found your hotel key in your pocket, so I took the liberty of checking you out. Your things are over in the corner," he informed. "Along with a gross ass book you were clinging to when I found you."

Nara grumbled several incoherent syllables as she unenthusiastically waved in his direction.

"Speaking of finding you, your helpful little friend who ushered you out will have a bit of trouble recalling the past few evenings."

She let out an evil smirk, mildly curious about what Declan had drugged the poor soul with. Memory tampering chemicals would be quite useful to her in numerous ways.

"Now, I don't want to know what the hell you were doing up there," he continued, "but *what the hell* were you doing up there?"

"Ask your master," she spat as she pulled herself upright.

Declan had taken her to his apartment in Under. The man never bothered to move places after all the years she'd known him. The confined space could be considered cozy if it didn't appear like an antiquated science museum. Drab, dark, and dry, just like his personality.

She slid off the medical table in the center of his converted living area and stomped to her feet, weaving slightly as her equilibrium teased her legs. Lurching to the corner of the room, she dug through her satchel, grumbling in frustration as she clawed through the mass of silky textiles.

"You mean to tell me Sentinel put you up to this?" Declan's face hardened in disbelief.

Nara ignored his conclusion. "You still have any of my shit that I left here?"

"Be careful," he severely warned as he opened a storage cabinet above him, digging out a pile of black Undercity attire.

"You know, I'm getting real tired of everyone telling me that," she hissed as she tore the garments out of his hands. "And no one telling me why."

"Because no one knows why," he said.

"What the fuck does that even mean? That's the most asinine fucking shit I've ever heard," she snarled as she hastily covered herself, flexing her aching shoulders under the comfort of rugged, loose-fitting, ordinary fabric. "Especially out of you."

"Shit's fucked. Is that better?" Declan threw his hands up in the air. "You're welcome, by the way."

A growl rumbled through her throat as she leaned on the counter, her head swirling around as it struggled to kick off the effects of whatever the medic had given her. She paused and permitted herself several deep breaths of cooling air, refusing to lose her temper around him again.

"Have you finished?" Nara fumed through her nose.

"I . . ." Declan clamped his jaw shut, restraining his bitter tongue. "I'm sorry. For what it's worth, I do care about you."

"You have a shitty way of expressing it."

"That part of me died a long time ago," he sighed.

"Yeah, I know."

The two stared at the floor in silence as they contemplated the root of their frustrations. They were both too exhausted to feel tired anymore, halfheartedly treading through life and burying their problems with work to drown out their belligerent neuroses.

"So, what now?" Declan softly asked.

"Now I turn this contract in," she said, taking his words literally. "Then I suppose I prepare for an imaginary war."

Declan regarded her as she gathered her belongings, a weight in his soul sinking to the pit of his stomach. He didn't know what he wanted to say to her, what was troubling him about her exploits, but he knew she would figure it out long before he could decipher it himself.

Nara met his eyes as she walked toward the front door, sharing a similar level of discomfort. Peace seemed so far away from her, and she wondered what kept her searching. Perhaps this contract would be a catalyst, and her inner turmoil would finally be brought to a head. The sooner, the better.

"Thank you," she murmured as she turned to leave.

##17.1##

Today was a dark day for some of the most powerful heads of progress. The charismatic leader of Skyward Robotics, Sedgwick Velonir, tragically died last night during an accident involving his automated home security. He was found by a staff member after turret fire was heard inside the master bedroom. The electronic locks in the room were activated during the incident, and security was summoned to tear down the doors in order to reach him.

According to reports, the Velonir estate hired Esna Security Corp to subsidize their personal guard force for a formal event. EsnaSec is currently under investigation for potential mishandling of protocol. The umbrella company, Galavantier Corporation, who annexed Skyward

Robotics twenty years ago, has yet to make a statement regarding the situation.

In a similar grim display, Alfonso Avis of Avis Organics was brutally murdered while attending a celebration held at the Rezzan Neurolytics estate. The two figureheads were celebrating the eve of a new merger, a momentous occasion that would bring new advanced technologies to both commercial and military markets.

The terrorist has not yet been identified by the Avis Organics police force, as they are having difficulties obtaining information on the incident from the Rezzan security force. More details will be posted as soon as we find out more.

A million thoughts burned holes through his brain as Garrett replayed the report, dumbfounded by the events that transpired during his absence Upworld. He didn't know Uncle Sedgwick well. As a child, the gentle man would infrequently visit Antonin, always regarding Garrett with a smile every time he had the audacity to interrupt the adults. It was a rare feature amid nobility, and he was ashamed to have taken it for granted.

The reports mentioned the inexperience of the security company, and accidents like this happen more often than they should, but he wasn't convinced the mishap could be reduced to coincidence. Even with his lack of computer knowledge, Garrett could weasel through the most intensive networks in both Upper and Under. All it took was the funds for the right programs.

What the hell was Nara doing up there? Garrett stared at the image of the vivisected corpse of the Avis lord, obscured by digital overlays the news editors plastered over the scene to protect the innocence of the populace. What gaps the censors tried to omit for the sake of decency, his imagination eagerly filled in with details from his Under experiences. *Is she capable of this?*

His heart already knew the answer. The display was a painful reminder of how privileged his life was, and how naïve he was to the world around him. He was nothing more than a pawn in a very dangerous political power struggle, and he found it unsettling to consider how much he was worth to sacrifice.

Cain's enigmatic yet terrifying warning shuddered through his ears, and he shook off the feeling of the man's hand on his shoulder. Now that man, he could certainly believe would kill in cold blood. The specter sent squirming tendrils across his skin, and he would love to forget ever meeting him.

But then again, why did he warn him?

It's all fun and games until you witness a coup, Garrett thought morbidly. *So which one of them did it? Or were they both up there for a different job altogether?*

"Hey, you all right, friend?" Darius scanned him with concerned eyes.

"Huh?" Garrett blinked.

"You've been staring at that newsfeed for two hours," the barman added, glancing down at Garrett's wrist. "That is not healthy."

"Oh, yeah. Just some trouble at home," he evaded, absentmindedly tapping his glass.

"Nothing serious, I hope?"

"That remains to be seen." Garrett sighed.

"I haven't heard from you in a while. Been worried about you," Darius professed. "Thought you might've been dragged off by wolves or something."

Just one wolf, Garrett thought.

"No, I've just been wandering." He dismissively shook his head. *I need to see Baran. He must know what went on that night. I need to know if he's okay.*

"Wandering, eh?" Darius raised a skeptical eyebrow at him.

"I should probably get going. Been down here a bit too long," Garrett declared. *But he hasn't called me yet. Maybe I shouldn't go home. What if Antonin set up a trap for my return?*

"All right, fair enough." Darius folded his arms, unconvinced by his avoidance. "Hey, what did you end up doing with that trinket? Did you get much for it?"

"More than I bargained for." He tossed his head back to finish his drink, then scooted out of the bar.

##17.2##

BARAN LEANED OVER THE COUNTER, motioning toward the keeper.

"Your usual," the man offered, pushing a glass in his direction. "And what brings you to this side of the Haze, friend?"

"Is Scorpio in? I need to talk to him."

"Yeah." He nodded. "I'll tell him you're here."

The barman pressed a button on his wrist, then stared at the wall across the tavern as if in deep thought. As the man conversed through his neural link, Baran glanced around the room for potential visitors who might have followed him down to Under.

Very few patrons inhabited the bleak-walled dive, and those who did were absorbed in their own universe of problems, depressingly drinking toward solutions until their recollections melted.

"Quiet night," Baran commented.

"He's waiting for you in the back." The barkeep nodded his head toward an imposing reinforced door behind him.

"Thanks." He downed his drink before heading to the back.

Baran unlatched the door and stepped into a dark room, lit by a single spotlight that cast over a small round table. A human male sat facing him, a sickly cloud from a smoldering cigarette shrouding him in mystique.

Like many of ill-repute in the Undercity, the man wore all black, only revealing his face through a loose-fitting hood. He was a handsome fellow, apart from the jagged scar stretching across his left eye, which glowed bright green from cybernetic enhancements. His straight brown hair obscured his real eye, leaving its color a mystery. A warm smile parted his wily expression as he watched Baran enter.

"Good evening, Sir," the man greeted. "Please, have a seat."

"How have you been?" Baran inquired, shaking his head admonishingly. "And I've told you many times, drop the formality."

"Well enough, Sir, and you?" His grin widened as he disregarded the order.

"Troubled." Baran sighed as he slid into a chair.

"Do tell," the man invited, pouring two drinks from an ornately sculpted glass bottle on the table, pushing one toward his unnerved guest.

"Antonin has disappeared," Baran revealed, taking the glass toward him.

"Well, that is troubling," Scorpio said through a smoky breath.

"Do you know anything?"

"He's moving," the man confirmed. "Where to, I haven't heard yet. But he is gathering enough resources to stop a small army."

"I see." Baran spun the glass in idle circles as he considered the report. "He hasn't said anything to me, just vanished."

"My field units haven't seen him in person." Scorpio shook his head. "We just know a lot of his allies are giving him a few extra 'toys' to play with."

"Such as?" Baran raised an eye.

"Artillery, and lots of it. Some even automated." The man paused to drain his glass. "Noisemakers, small clans that would have fun wrecking things just for some coin."

"What the hell is going on?" Baran furrowed his eyebrows. *And what is he doing making dealings in Under without my knowledge?*

"I heard someone took out Sedgwick," Scorpio idly commented. "A connection?"

"Most likely."

"How do you feel about it?"

"It's a shame and a waste. Sedgwick was a good man, very rare these days." Baran sighed. "But business is business."

"Spoken like a realist," Scorpio purred. "You know who was behind it yet?"

"My guess would be Chryansa. But that's just idle gossip." Baran waved a hand in front of him. "It was probably carried out by our friend 0975. She recently visited and stole some valuable tech. But as for who hired her, it could have been anyone with a deep enough pocket."

Scorpio regarded him curiously through a long drag of his cigarette, sensing a more complex answer to his friend's discontent.

"I thought you weren't supposed to worry yourself over 0975," Scorpio pointed out.

"I'm not. That blonde freak, Sebastian, took over jurisdiction a long time ago. Or at least was ordered to by his holiness himself," Baran spat. "And he hasn't done a good job of it so far. He's cocky and likes to play with his food too much."

Scorpio leaned back in his seat and watched his friend internalize recent events. Baran carried at least seven worlds on his shoulder, and he often wondered how long it would take before it broke the man again.

"And what has Garrett been up to?" Baran changed the subject, slightly irritated by the inspection.

"The boy has been a lot more slippery lately, as if he suspects he's being watched," Scorpio replied, amused by the observation. "He even spotted one of my agents recently."

"Interesting." Baran took another sip of his drink as he processed the news. "Where does he go?"

"Nowhere in particular, as far as we know. We lose him after he reaches Uncivilized Space." Scorpio shrugged as his guest shot him a stern glare. "My soldiers can only do so much, Sir."

"This isn't exactly comforting," Baran scolded.

"We do see him in the markets, accompanied by a presumable bodyguard," Scorpio offered. "A rather large fellow."

"Large fellow?" Baran narrowed his eyes at him. "That's all you have?"

"This guy keeps himself covered and doesn't like to be seen," Scorpio stated indifferently.

"That's not what I like to hear, coming from you." Baran scowled as he folded his arms.

"I'm not going to put my units under unnecessary risk. A favor only goes so far, Commander," Scorpio warned with a point of his cigarette. "We watch, not act. Besides, the guy doesn't trigger any warning signs. We've spotted him a few times fighting, and the guy can hold his own. Garrett is in good hands."

"I want you to find out more about him," Baran insisted.

"Trust me," Scorpio hissed in reprimand. "Garrett is fine. Leave it alone, Sir."

Baran was taken aback by Scorpio's reaction and annoyed that he was hiding something from him. But his friend's alignments had changed since they'd first arrived on this forsaken rock, and now it appeared he was overusing his influence on the shadow dealer.

"I suppose it's all right if you say so." Baran rubbed his forehead, releasing pressure on the futile argument.

"Garrett is fine, it's not him you need to be worried about."

"But you're not exactly being forthcoming on Antonin either." Baran stared down the empty glass.

"All I can offer is that my Shadows will keep looking," Scorpio assured. "But as of now, there's no point in speculating."

"I suppose you're right." Baran glanced at his wrist. "I need to get going again before anyone notices I've left."

"I do wish you would visit more often, Sir," Scorpio mused. "I don't hear much out of you ever since you've turned blue on us."

Baran let out a somber sigh. "The way things are going, I may soon have all the time in the world."

"That would be nice." The man folded his hands. "We could reminisce about our near-death experiences back on Vahrta."

Baran almost wished he could forget Vahrta and how many limbs he could have lost just to the ecosystem. Both he and his friend were careless daredevils, performing any mission recklessly just to see who could make it back to base camp in once piece. It pissed off their commanding officers to no end, but they were a duo that could always get the job done.

"Heh. Yeah, those were the days." Back then, he could always depend on Scorpio to have his back in the middle of a fire, but now it was different. Their paths spilt off, though it was mostly Baran's fault for abandoning him.

"Commander, you always claimed you weren't cut out for soldiering," Scorpio teased. "But I think you're lying to yourself."

"I still don't think I'm cut out for it," he grumbled.

"Then why are you working for a bloodthirsty general who is set out for conquest?" Scorpio's grin warped with wickedness.

"One of these days," Baran scolded, "Your mouth will dig you far too deep."

Scorpio saluted with a glass in hand. "And on that day, you'll come back to get me. Either to dig me out or bury me deeper."

"Goodbye, Scorpio." He shook his head as he stood to leave.

"Baran," the shady man called out after him, his faced cold, hardened. "Your emergency beacon always has observers down here. You may need it very soon. Be prepared."

He looked over his shoulder, considering the warning momentarily before silently departing.

##17.3##

NARA DIALED a call on her NetCom as she headed toward Sentinel's fortress. If she was getting toyed with by the fates, she would at least pass the favor on to someone else.

"How much do you love me?" she impishly inquired of her victim, slathering sweetness over her voice.

"I find your perverted humor deplorable, especially considering your recent capers," Annon sneered through the device.

"I'm on my way to turn in a job from another client, and I've done some extracurricular activities," Nara teased, ignoring his spite. "And I think they would interest you greatly."

"You have one iota of my attention," the agent announced. "Though I doubt whatever it is you have would make up a fraction of what you cost me."

"Oh, no, I need to hear it from you first," she egged. "How much do you appreciate me?"

"You are absolutely contemptable."

"Okay then. I'll just find another buyer for these photos then?"

Nara could hear the curiosity etching away at his resentment through the channel.

"I'm not hearing a 'No'," she continued with a vile grin.

"You are a valuable asset to my agency," he forced through gritted teeth.

"Oh, I suppose that is good enough," Nara conceded as she transferred the data of the disturbing ceremony.

Silence resounded through the device as she waited for the agent to flip through her gift, occasionally broken by stifled cries of disbelief as the man processed the subjects in the images.

"Are you still with me, Annon?"

"Where . . . how—"

"Whatever you do with them, I get half," Nara declared.

"You magnificent brute," the agent finally managed through a stunned breath.

"You are welcome," she taunted.

"Words fail me," Annon admitted.

"Don't make me hunt you down. I will get my cut," she threatened as she cut off the channel, entering her destination with a haughty smirk.

Nara slinked into Sentinel's office and quietly lowered herself into a chair. She was still not happy with the shadow games he was pulling over her, but she also wasn't entirely convinced that he was the one she should be upset at.

"I have heard reports that Mr. Velonir has suffered a rather embarrassing accident," Sentinel casually mentioned.

"I heard it was particularly messy," Nara commented, showing disinterest in the subject.

"You have done well," he praised. "I knew you could pull it off."

"Didn't make it any less unnerving."

"Existence is a continual erosion of the nerves." He stood up from his seat to offer her payment. "I was able to put a bit of a pressure on our client."

"Oh?" Nara raised an eyebrow as she took the offering.

"A mutual agreement was made." He nodded. "Especially considering your performance and discretion."

"How mutual?"

"Forty-five."

"That is agreeable." She shifted her leg onto her knee. "How did you manage to pull that one off? Brute force, or magic?"

"There are other ways, my friend."

"One of these days, you will have to tell me about them," she remarked. "Along with whatever mystical secrets you are withholding."

"In due time." Sentinel raised a hand. "Meanwhile, I would like you to consider my words regarding your future."

"I assure you, I have," Nara grumbled. "Every waking moment."

"I apologize for the distress," he sincerely expressed. "My resources are at your disposal, should you choose to act."

Nara regarded the warlord, his masked intent taunting her outside of her mental reach. Her conscience had not yet caught up with the consequences of her actions, her brain instinctively taking shelter behind the defensive walls that contained the cognitive mush infected with paranoia.

Her body was drained, and she wanted nothing more than a few nights' sleep, without chemical assistance. Perhaps after, she could consider Sentinel's words, or more likely, berate herself for accepting such a foolish job and putting herself in this perilous position in the first place.

"I'll think about it," Nara declared as she rose. "Call me if you have anything else."

"Be safe, child."

"No promises," she said over her shoulder.

##17.4##

A STRANGE DISSOCIATIVE feeling crept over Garrett as he stirred his coffee, and he found himself considering his immediate family line. Digging through the depths of his semi-principled soul, he came to the realization that he did not possess a single shred of concern about their safety.

As a teen, he had spent an unhealthy amount of time contemplating what he would do if they all simply disappeared, leaving him alone with the estate. He had never realized what the most probable cause of their departure would be until now.

The memories sat uneasily with him, and he began to think he had lost his humanity, willfully wishing death on his own flesh and blood. He was disconcerted by his sense of righteousness, and he wondered what would happen when he finally did take the throne, what he would do when the people he cherished were perpetually endangered.

He meditated over the concept, uncertain what it would feel like to have people under his wing that he would care for. Without current friends or amicable business contacts in the biotech industry, the only person in his life he wanted to protect was Baran.

Baran.

The man who fostered him was chief of security in Antonin's estate and an obvious target to anyone looking to wreak havoc in the Galavantier Empire. He was under constant gunfire every second of every grueling day.

Gunfire from people like Nara.

Having known her on a personal level, Garrett was unwilling to accept that she was a murderer, despite having seen her perform a number of brutal acts in front of him. But she always seemed to use lethal force as an absolute last resort, never raising the casualty count more than necessary to escape with her own life.

He argued with his conscience over what ethically defined a murderer. Even if she was the one who carried out the action, she wasn't the one who ordered it. In the end, he was not certain that made enough distinction to excuse her.

Guilt overwhelmed him for enjoying the adventure in Upper with her and showing her that it was easy to pass through the city without worrying over appearances. He was shamefully delighted to see her in regal attire. The suit fitted her exceptionally well, but he dearly wished that he had helped her prepare for a more jubilant occasion.

Oh, sweet, merciful gods. His eyes widened as a realization dawned on him. *I'm accessory to murder.*

"Garrett!"

The gods have no pity or mercy. He cringed as the overly sweetened voice clawed through his ears.

Cordelia slithered next to Garrett, her habitual seductive smile lacquered over with a coat of feigned concern.

"I just heard the news," she professed. "I'm sorry for your loss."

"Yes, it's come as a shock to us all," Garrett lamented, quickly wiping at his eye. *I'm sure your condolences are entirely sincere.*

"Your friend not with you?" she inquired, looking around the café.

"I wanted to be alone in my grief, actually," he said, a tinge of annoyance shading his tone.

"Oh, that's understandable." She looked at him curiously. "Remind me again, where did you find him? I've never seen someone quite so tall up here. Come to think of it, I rarely see you with him."

"I'm sorry, but why are you asking?" He was done with hiding his disdain for the sake of decorum.

"I'm just concerned for your wellbeing," she expressed with a soft twinge of recovery from the shock of the biting remark. "A man in your position should be very careful."

"Indeed." He stared into his drink, leaving her hanging in uncomfortable silence. *I do not have the energy to decipher her cryptic motives right now.*

"Well, I can see that this was not an appropriate time," she said as she stepped back. "Goodbye, Garrett. I will leave you to mourn. We will talk again soon."

She smiled sweetly before walking away, leaving Garret with a tightened jaw as he stared distantly at the café wall.

Fuck this. He swallowed hard. *I'm going to go find Baran.*

##17.5##

The penthouse was deathly quiet upon his arrival. Not a single staff member bustled about in preparation for the nightly routines. The kitchen was spotless, cutlery and dishes placed in their rightful homes, awaiting the next meal. The solitude amplified with Garrett's echoing footsteps across the shining steel floors.

As he moved into the foyer, the silence was perforated by the clacking steps of Baran's agitated pacing, distress stiffening his circular gait.

Oh, thank gods. Garrett cleared his throat, startling the man as his concentration shattered.

"Ah, young sir, can I help you?" Baran greeted him formally, frantically dusting himself off to make himself presentable.

Though Baran was already a lean-faced individual, his profile appeared slimmer. Swollen bags darkened his weary eyes, as if he had suffered from a week-long bout of insomnia. Even his clothing was disorderly, creased in all the wrong places, his tie inappropriately loosened and two buttons undone at the top of his collar.

"Are you all right?" Garrett eyed him uneasily. *What the hell happened to him?*

"Yes, sir, quite." The man forced out a presentable smile.

"You're bullshitting me, Baran."

"I . . ." Baran furrowed his eyebrows at Garrett's bluntness. "Language. And it's nothing for you to be concerned about."

"You can tell me."

"No." He firmly shook his head. "No, I cannot."

"Well, skip major details then," Garrett insisted, crossing his arms over his chest. "I haven't heard from you since I called about Cordelia. I won't leave this spot until I get an idea about what's been going on."

Baran narrowed his eyes at the impertinence, but Garrett was well-practiced with his endurance games. As a child, it would be the only way he could get the man to admit anything about his feelings, and he could sit still for hours. He had done it before, and he would do it again.

Baran gave in with a sigh as he anxiously ran a hand through his hair. "I don't know where your father is."

"Why is that a problem?" Garrett scoffed. "I would think that would be a relief. I can't stand it when the man is around, and I can barely tolerate knowing I am related to him."

He looked up at Baran and caught a flash of movement in the man's face, a distorted twitch of lips. A compulsory blink interrupted Garrett's scrutiny as the man quickly resumed his agitated expression, staring at the floor in dismay. He shook the ambiguous observation from his brain. His guardian was obviously stressed, and perhaps he had been hanging around Nara too much, overanalyzing meanings that didn't exist.

"I don't know why that's a problem," Baran finally admitted. "That's why."

"I still don't understand," Garrett said.

"He tells me everything. But I have been speaking with others. And he's plotting something. Something major. I don't know what, but it's a conspiracy so large that he didn't even want me to know." He looked over Garrett's face, then shook his head dejectedly. "All I am saying is, be careful. Wherever you go. There is a rift that is waiting to erupt."

Baran walked off, leaving Garrett to stew in bewilderment.

Well, I've had my fill of cozy home life, Garrett professed. *I'm going back to Under.*

CHAPTER 18

##18.0##

Blackened clouds cast over her as she stood on top of a mound of bones, physical remnants of the specters that haunted her. Her limbs were restrained by scores of twisted wrought-iron hooks, the metal buried deep into her flesh. Silent onlookers stared at her with featureless faces, a host of hapless beings that had no place being here.

The sky cracked open, cascading a blood-red light. A voice bellowed from above, unintelligible words from a voice she'd cursed eons ago. On its command, the barbs tore themselves away from her, ripping off her skin one sinewy strand at a time. She roared in agony, sinking to the pile of skulls as her knees collapsed, meeting the eyes of the souls that had fallen before her.

Her audience was not satisfied with the show, and the horde summoned a glimmering wall of cannons from the air, surrounding her with a battery of deceit. As another order echoed from the skies, they fired upon her, rhythmic thunder perforating the air.

Millions of shells ripped through the remainder of her flesh, tearing every scrap away until nothing but her bones remained. But she was still alive, feeling an ethereal warmth beneath her as her wrath manifested. Fire ignited at her feet, voracious and resolute. It licked over her skeletal form until her carcass was cleansed of her earthly form.

She descended the mound of bone, her scintillating manifestation sending terror through her executioners. She wanted nothing more than to shred them all apart.

She bowed to the ground, pushing her palms against the dirt. A voice rumbled from the void where her lungs once inhabited, a shout of rage that tore a chasm through the earth. Her war cry amplified as she strained against the rocky crust, wrenching it asunder with her slender metal hands.

Her destruction was interrupted by a shriek piercing the air, and she looked up to see gleaming metal bearing down on her from the sky. She couldn't move away from it. She was not permitted to react.

Agony cracked through her ribs as the monstrously edged sword impaled her, binding her to the fragmented soil. Mixed emotions bore through her, anger, pain, exhaustion.

She craned her neck to see a familiar hand clutching the pommel, driving it deeper through her until she was buried in the chasm that she had created. Darkness swallowed her as she let out a final anguished roar.

##18.1##

NARA SNAPPED awake in her bed, drenched in sweat. Before she could take comfort in the familiarity of her apartment, she felt a cold trickle of liquid crawl out of her nostril. She wiped it away, only to stare in horror at the glistening red ichor in her hand.

Not again, not like this. Her eyes widened as the recollections began to drown her consciousness.

Through the herbal sweetness of her blood, she inhaled the sharp green tang of humid forest air, heady fumes of weapon fire, and charred foliage. Her comrades shouted around her over the endless barrage of the assault party. They looked to her for orders between blasts of sniper fire, but they were surrounded. Nowhere left to run.

It was all too clean, too calculated. They knew she would be there and used her weapons against her.

"RETREAT," she roared, but it was too late for them. One by one, her squad fell, and she watched in stupefaction as the life drained away from their faces. Pain lashed against her shoulders, her ribs, her neck. She looked down to find her clothing soaked in blood.

Her limbs were frozen in place, her brain melted, refusing to let her escape this hellish melee. She could not just leave them there.

A shadowy figure lurked behind her, and she whirled around, heaving her arm in a tense arc until her fist met with a solid object. A wave of agony ripped through her knuckles, shocking the ghastly images out of her eyes.

She blinked, staring at the hand firmly planted against her bedroom wall, the cracks splintering across the dent she'd created. Her lungs caught up with her, forcing slow, repetitive gasps out of her chest as she slowly acclimated to reality. Her NetCom bleated from the kitchen counter, the alarm boring into her ears.

She sank to the ground, rolling onto the cold concrete floor as she brought her knees to her chest. She cradled her shins, compacting herself into a tight ball as the overwhelming need to flee saturated her thoughts.

I can't do this again, she murmured as tears began to stream from her eyes.

She let the alarm drone on in the background until it tired itself out, unwilling to acknowledge the outside world.

Something catastrophic was about to happen once more. It was just a matter of when. She could only hope that this time, she could read the signs.

GARRETT DIALED Nara's NetCom again, his concern magnifying over her silence. He had not heard from her since he'd left her in Upper, and the thought of her rotting away in a cell, or worse, passed through his mind.

Perhaps she didn't kill either of the victims in the news and was caught before she could do whatever job she was meant to accomplish. It would be a massive relief to his conscience, and he would be able to maintain their friendship without remorse.

He paused in his step, considering the use of the word 'friendship' to describe their affiliation. He had no other words to define it, but he wondered if her feelings were mutual. He severely doubted she would openly admit it to him, however.

He continued his journey through the Undercity streets, refusing to waver in uncertainty until he heard the answers directly from her mouth.

After several hours, Nara managed to pick herself up from the floor. She began to pace around the living room of her flat as her brain flooded her eyes with the daunting premonitions. Everything had been taken, her home, her dignity, even her flesh. She was cast down and forced to live like a criminal. What did she have left to lose?

The NetCom pierced through her unease, interrupting her internal strife. With a growl, she fidgeted with the settings, silencing the abominable machine.

"That's it. That's the end of me. What the fuck do I do now?" she lamented. Her eyes scanned over the massive arsenal encompassing the living room. *Keep your hands busy, that's what.*

She opened the nearest cabinet and extracted a multitude of armaments, scattering them around the room. She then began deconstructing her favorite pieces, covering the table with orderly lines of barrels, magazines, springs, slides, and frames, forming a micron of stability in her decaying world.

When the table was devoid of free space, she started her work of cleaning each individual component, focusing on her menial task instead of her damned future. She let the project fill her senses, the gunk of synthetic oil coating her fingers, the clicking of the components snapping into place. But her mind was a tenacious adversary.

Fuck, I wonder how long I can last in here, she thought as she counted charges of a chamber. *Two, maybe three months. I'll have to move to one of my other bases eventually.*

A knock on the door disrupted her preparation, and the startle flung the ammunition from her hands.

"Go away," she snapped.

"Hey, you all right?" Garrett asked from the outside hallway. "I've been trying to reach you for hours."

"Go. *Away.*"

Garrett staggered back by the force of her tone. She had never been this aggressive with him, not even when they first met. While it could have just been exhaustion, the nagging paranoia made him suspicious of her indignation, and he feared that she'd learned something he didn't want her to know.

He leaned against the door, letting out a weighted sigh. It was not an appropriate time to pester her, but with the eerie tension in the air surrounding him, he could feel his freedom shrinking away. Soon, he would be forced to stay in Upper permanently.

Baran's vague warning did not settle with him, the portends churning in his brain with swelling intensity the more he pondered. The man was a stone, always hiding his fear. Seeing him that visibly shaken troubled him greatly.

"How long are you going to camp out there?" Nara scorned from the inside the apartment.

"Till you come out and talk with me."

"You are such a child."

"A child who cares about his friend."

Silence replied from the other side of the door.

An impulsive idea poked its way through his head as he gazed at the impenetrable barrier of her front door. With his time fleeting, the only way he could subdue his unwavering doubt was to act with imprudence and sneak inside.

"Fine. I'm leaving," Garrett declared as he turned around. "If you need me, call me."

I am going to get violently murdered for this, he thought, heading into the street.

##18.2##

MAKING his way around the back end of the building, Garrett scanned the decaying fissures along the masonry, searching for a gap large enough to squeeze through. He stumbled upon a suitable hole torn in the once tidy pattern of bricks opening waist-high from the ground. Using the light of his NetCom to illuminate the area, he leaned into the chasm to survey the hazards inside.

As he rested his hand against the opening, his fingers propelled loose rocks into the building, pitting the cavernous interior with tiny echoes. His meager torch provided little assistance in discerning the purpose of the facility, and his view of the area was obscured by the destruction of the floor above. A jagged maw of flooring pierced through the center of the arena with its wooden frames and scarred linoleum veneer.

After making a superficial assessment of the risk, Garrett hoisted himself up through the hole and jumped inside, evoking a cloud of particles as he stamped his feet on the floor. As he dusted himself off, he glanced around to get a better look at his environment.

While he tried to appreciate the crumbling pre-war décor of the chamber, he could not help but stare in amazement at the centerpiece greeting him, a fully functional swimming pool and hot tub, filled to the brim with sparkling clean water. The water feature was surrounded by a mostly intact mosaic of blue and white ceramic, with only a few select tiles torn off the flooring.

Hoses led from the water into two contraptions of modern technology, quietly churning in the corner. Though crude and homemade in appearance, they performed their tasks superbly, filtering and heating the water to a comfortable temperature.

Huh. Fancy, Garrett mused.

Employing the tactics he'd learned from Sentinel's teaching, he quietly slinked around the perimeter, uncertain of Nara's capability to hear this far down the complex.

Apart from the caved in ceiling, the building was relatively undamaged. Holes were torn randomly around the area, revealing wooden beams and drywall patches. But there was nothing large enough for him to fit through. He checked over the doorways, but to his dismay, they were all blocked by debris, preventing him from accessing the hallways.

Just as he was about to give up and return to the street, his attention was brought to a suspicious pile of concrete in the corner of the room. He weaved around it, noticing that the stonework was a slightly deeper color and did not match the rest of the hotel. Large chunks were selectively piled on top of each other, as if intentionally put there by very, very strong beings.

Cain must have been in a hurry when he left, he thought. *He didn't put the rocks back where he found them.*

He shone his light into the crevasse, making its rays bounce around a gap that he could uncomfortably squeeze into. Having no other options, he slipped his sleeves over his palms and crawled inside, gingerly navigating his body around the sharp chunks of concrete and splintered rebar.

When he pulled his back end into the strange hollow, he looked up to examine the walls of craggy rock. The toothy surface stretched up about two floors, then transitioned into a pitch-black void. With a crack of knuckles and a twist of his wrists, he carefully rose to his feet, compacting himself in the center of the narrow channel.

He let out a gentle exhale as he began to scale the jagged footholds, taking soft, deliberate steps upward. He focused on shrinking his presence, the noises his clothing made as he adjusted his position, and the intensity of his breathing as he exerted energy on the ascent.

Through the convenient warren of strategically placed rock, the blackness above loomed over him as he ascended, threatening to swallow him in its emptiness. He reached up to brush his hands against the peculiar surface, finding it cool to the touch.

It was made of solid metal, with a similar rigidity of materials built to withstand ballistics. The coating was the deepest black he had ever seen, practically devouring the pathetic light his meager NetCom radiated.

He expected to hear his breaths echo obnoxiously against the empty column, but instead it absorbed the noise, creating an unnerving silence inside the corridor. He quizzically glanced up at the featureless void, attempting to decipher the secrets hidden in the murky surface.

So, what now? he thought as he felt around the smooth plane.

A sharp pain cracked through his hand as his index finger spontaneously bent backward, tangled on an invisible object during his sensory investigation. He stifled an outcry as he gnawed on the stinging knuckle.

With a flustered grumble, he carefully pawed at the offending area, unearthing a heavy wire bracket deviously protruding from the wall. The dastardly object blended into the abysmal black, and he had to squint to perceive the entire shape.

He ran his fingers up the wall, searching for another brace as he pulled himself higher. When he found nothing above him, he slipped his hand around the chamber, only to smack his pinky nail against another foothold hiding on the adjacent wall. A breath of frustration escaped his nose as he clawed at the new bracket, yanking his body up. A gentle swipe across the wall later, he found a third brace back at the side he started from.

To his annoyance, the footholds were arranged in an erratic pattern around the chamber, not in a straight line or spiral that most reasonable engineers employ when designing access to upper levels.He continued his labored hunt and peck game until he picked up a slow rhythm, adapting to the illogical order of the cunningly assembled ladder.

After what seemed like an eternity, the blackness rewarded him with a tunnel opening, painted with the same devilish shade of black. Steadying his breath, he took slow, placid steps forward, trying not to resemble a clumsy human as he crept onward.

He stretched his arms out, cautiously advancing to prevent the end of the hall from creeping up on him and ruining his invasion with an obnoxious collision. His blind fondling of the air was rewarded as his fingertips met with a solid barrier. He traced his hand around the perimeter of the surface, uncovering a tiny latch at the top of the panel.

He pressed his ear against the frigid wall, but he could hear nothing more than the rush of liquid swirling inside his head.

Well, now or never. He winced, hooking a finger under the latch.

When he felt the pin recede from the lock, he gently pushed against the panel. Light stabbed his eyes from the crack he created, and after several painful blinks, he was welcomed with the sight of Nara's bathroom, right where he thought it should be.

He strained his ears to listen to the apartment, detecting faint mechanical clicking coming from the living room. With a gentle push, he cracked the door open wider, thankful for the dampening powers of the rubber tiling. Lowering his body into a crouch, he slithered toward the nearest hallway, taking one arduous step at a time as he restrained his overeager lungs.

He stopped short of the kitchen, glancing up at the reflection on the cabinets ahead of him. He spotted Nara's distorted form, sitting with her back turned toward him at the dining room table, engrossed in the guts of a pistol.

Much to his disbelief, Nara remained unaware of his presence, distractedly fuming in a world of her own as she focused on her task. He watched her intently as she looked down the sights, shaking her head admonishingly at the device. As she abruptly bolted out of her chair, Garrett snapped back with a lunge. To his astonishment, she did not address him, giving him no indication that she had heard his messy retreat.

Why hasn't she noticed me yet? he thought with apprehension. *I have to be making noise. I haven't been training for long. Something isn't right.*

He heard a click of a cabinet latch, and he slipped an eye around the corner, watching her ease the gun back into its place. She stood motionless in front of the arsenal, frozen in a frantic train of thought. She began to mutter unintelligible words, but he understood the tone of stress and exhaustion. She was in a terrible state of mind, and it made Garrett guilty for trespassing.

"Need another shower," Nara mumbled as she rubbed her face in frustration.

Just as he deliberated on his escape, she angrily tore her shirt off her agitated self, interrupting his thought process. His eyes scanned over her sculpted form as his lips shrank with embarrassment.

This is wrong, he thought, feeling the heat of his flushing cheeks. *I need to leave. Now.*

But his legs refused to budge as he tried to tear his eyes away, her striking physique captivating his attention. With her chiseled muscle tone, she was comparable to a gargoyle that watched over a decaying building, waiting to strike on intruders with a medieval ferocity.

As his eyes moved up from her hips to her shoulders, his gaze was drawn to a grotesque disfigurement corrupting her form.

Three wide plates covered her back, highlighting the main muscle groups of the area, two above her hips and one on her left shoulder. The fourth that was supposed to protect her right was absent, and a jagged ravine of pale, winding scar tissue existed in its stead, a poor mimicry of its counterparts.

"Holy shit!" The words escaped the clutches of his throat, and he slapped his hand over his mouth.

Nara stiffened at the noise, whirling around at the stunned creature peeking through her kitchen doorway. She rumbled out an agitated growl, alarmed by the deceitful intrusion.

Seizing the fractions of a second he had left remaining on the planet, Garrett launched back into the bathroom, clawing the compartment open as fast as his terrified fingers could manage. His heart thundered in his chest as panic overwhelmed him, flicking his nerves across his limbs.

What have I done? He grieved as he bolted down the tunnel, his bare palms squeaking with friction as he slid down the dark metal column, immediately forgetting the orientation of the chaotic ladder. His feet slammed down on the rocky growths below, and he scrambled down the pillar, tearing his clothes on the concrete shrapnel in his flustered retreat.

He clawed his way out of the opening and burst to his feet, dashing into the city streets. His body was fueled with panic, refusing to stop until he was far away from the cursed place.

Despite his trepidation, his lungs threatened to burst inside his chest if he did not cease his flight. Gasping for air, he stumbled into an alleyway and plopped his pitiful carcass on a pile of concrete.

"What have I done?" he repeated. *I completely violated her trust. I have ruined a delicate relationship, just as it was beginning to strengthen.*

He wiped the streams of sweat from his face and seized control of his breath, staring out into the street as he waited for his pursuer to come. But only an unsettling silence greeted him.

What should I do now? he pleaded with his conscience. *I can't just walk away. I won't be able to live with this for the rest of my life.*

"Shit," he vocalized through a somnolent breath. He stared up at the hazy sky and considered his fate above-world. He loathed the busy life, the bright lights, and especially the politics, but now he was damned to live there forever, his fate sealed in an ivory casket.

What's done is done, he thought as he stood up, brushing himself off. *But I need to apologize to her at least, even if it costs me my life.*

Struggling to keep his heartbeat steady, he headed back to her apartment to explain himself, from the front door this time.

##18.3##

"Nara?" he called out as he knocked on the door. Silence. "Nara, if you're in there, please let me in."

He pressed his ear into the door, but only emptiness answered from the other side. Steeling himself, he poked at the handle, surprised to find it unlocked. With an anxious breath, he gingerly stepped into the living room. Silence.

An unwelcome feeling washed over him as he crept further, her absence disturbing his spasmodic thoughts as he stared at the pile of weapons threatening him on the table. The deadly contents advised him against waiting for her here.

He leaned back into the hallway, examining the fire escape access. The rooftop was a more peaceful place to wait, where he could sit and think about what he would say without the judgmental stares of a thousand instruments of war.

He clambered over busted walls and piping to get to the rickety rusted stairs outside. It had supported his weight several times before, but he supposed now would be the most acceptable time for them to crumble underneath his feet.

A few clanking steps commented on his ascent as he shifted up the structure. He emerged over the ledge and was startled to see Nara sitting on top of the parapet, dangling her legs over the precipice.

"I . . . uh," he started, unable to sort the mess of words frothing through his brain.

"You have bested me, so my promise will be kept," Nara declared, not turning toward him.

"I didn't mean to. I just wanted to . . ." he stammered.

"Oh, shut the fuck up, human," she scolded. "And come closer. I don't feel like shouting."

Garrett cautiously dismounted from the stairwell and approached, unsure of what she would do with him. He stared at her back as he quietly sank to the concrete, wishing he could see her expression instead.

"On my home world, I was known by two names, 'Sleepless One' and 'Eternal Red.' They are a constant reminder of my curse." She clamped her jaw shut as she extruded the words from her mouth. "I have a sickness that will consume me before my time is up."

"I had no family who would claim me, so when I was old enough to function, the council threw me in the army for lack of any better ideas. But everyone, even my commanding officers, were scared shitless of me. Never knew what I could be capable of should the Fever take me at any moment." She paused to recollect herself, staring down at the street as the memories trickled over her.

"I earned respect eventually, doing the only thing that could keep me sane—perfect myself as a soldier. I advanced quickly through the ranks, earned Warlord status, and commanded entire legions for the future of society. That made others even more on edge." She let out a pained sigh. "Even my squad was hesitant to follow me. It took a lot of work to subdue their discomfort. Until they left me for good."

She paused and stared up at the sky, blinking away a tear.

"We were patrolling an inactive zone, looking for rogue human outposts that have squatted on the land. Go to the checkpoint, then report back to headquarters. That's it. But it didn't happen that way." She cleared her throat to prevent her voice from choking her. "About a quarter of the way on our return trip, we were ambushed by a heavy weapons party. A human one. No reports had mentioned activity."

Garrett sat motionless behind her, absorbing each word as he watched her posture shift, rigid, cold. Each pained breath she exhaled deepened his remorse.

"They brought with them enough firepower to destroy an entire battalion, just to take out thirteen soldiers. Someone knew where we were going to be." She hesitated, each grievous syllable a strain on her lungs. "Where I was going to be."

The stillness of the air screamed at her as she dismantled her tale, her thousand-yard stare piercing the street below. She didn't want to disclose every graphic detail, but she relived each devastating second just to formulate a condensed reply.

"We put a major dent in their resistance, but one by one, the squad fell," she finally said. "I ordered a retreat, but they chased after us, picked us all off. I was the last one standing, but I eventually passed out from my injuries.

"They sent a scouting party after us when they lost contact." Nara shook her head. "There was no trace of the hunting party that assaulted us. It was completely clean. No bodies of the ones we killed, weapons, tracks, or charges. Nothing. So, they made the most logical conclusion: my condition forced me to kill off my own units."

Garrett restrained a hand from reaching out to her. He wanted to interrupt her so badly, to stop the torment. To give her a hug, for fuck's sake. If he had known the severity of her internal turmoil, he would have kept his fervent mouth shut.

"I was healed enough to stay alive and thrown in prison until they decided what to do with me." Nara rubbed a wrist distractedly. "Kept under heavy sedation should I have another episode and attack more citizens."

He blinked in astonishment, the awful scene playing through his elaborate imagination. She had never described the judiciary system of her culture, but he was disgusted by her treatment. He considered her logical, calculated mannerisms and wondered if all criminals were handled like this or if she was just a special case.

"The trial took ages to conclude, or so I think. I have no memory of it. I wasn't allowed to be conscious." She scowled. "Or defend myself. I never found out what the results were."

Nara shifted uncomfortably in her seat, rolling her shoulder in agitation. She shuddered as the familiar shadowy pain lashed itself across her memory, and she clenched her fists until it subsided.

"It was a punishment reserved for traitors and those deemed a danger to society." She tapped her scar. "It was rarely practiced in modern times, and outright execution had been outlawed generations ago. They bind the prisoner to two pillars as an incantation is said. Roughly translated: 'You have driven a knife into us, so we shall assist *Xannat* to drive one into you.' A poetic form of vengeance, I suppose.

"Then someone rips one of the plates off the back of the condemned, usually another Warlord. Like tearing out a fingernail, except they prevent it from growing back." Her face twinged as she controlled her composure. "They have to dig a bit to find the edge that's buried underneath flesh."

Garrett cringed at the imagery, his skin crawling from the gruesome narrative. He was too sickened to appreciate the symbology, feeling his resemblance to human garbage climax as he was regaled with the account.

"Should the prisoner survive the injury, they are reassigned, usually into the front lines to do menial labor or take out hostile ships so they die quickly." She paused, unhinging her scowl so her lips could continue to speak. "But they didn't do that with me."

Her skin flushed as anger swelled inside her chest. It had been thirty years, plenty of time to heal, or so she thought. She could begin to make peace if her brain didn't constantly obsess over every moment of the event and plague her dreams with twisted versions of reality.

But it doesn't matter anymore, does it? she thought, shaking the sensation away.

"Woke up in a cell on a strange ship, a shock collar on my neck," she mustered. "I don't really remember what happened, just ending up in an escape pod, a massive explosion behind me. The collar was in my hand. Well, a piece of it, anyway.

"Passed out again as the initial wave of the blast hit the pod, crash landed on this filthy rock, met Sentinel, and made a new life for myself. That's it." She brought her knees up onto the railing and clutched her arms around them. "The one good thing is, my brain lets me sleep a little bit now. Even had a few years where I could go down a full night. But as of late . . ."

As she trailed off, she considered what her next move would be from here. Every sign around her was telling her to flee, but she had nowhere to go. The past was tailing her, and the future was refusing to reveal itself in any tangible form. Whatever may come, she wished it would be swift.

"That's my story," she declared. "Satisfied?"

Garrett stared at the ground repentantly. He should have known better, the way she was so guarded and reserved whenever he brought up anything remotely related to her past. Despite seeing a large portion of Under, he had never experienced misery of this magnitude, and thus was blind to its existence. But her pained voice resonated through his sheltered soul.

"I'm so sorry. For everything," Garrett professed.

"Nothing to be sorry about." She shifted against the concrete. *Sorry is what that little worm Bellanar will feel if he dares to show his face to me again.*

Guilt overwhelmed him through her dismissive reply. It had become undeniably evident that she trusted him, but she had no reason to, especially after he had trampled all over her insecurities. He wanted to make it up to her and apologize for his impudence, but there was nothing he had to offer her that she would want. Except one vital piece of information that protected his existence in Under.

He had to reveal to her who he was.

"I . . ." Garrett started, voice quavering. "I think I should tell—"

Nara suddenly snapped to her feet, whisking the confession out of his lips. Her eyes furiously scanned the street below, fangs bared as she fervently searched for an obscure quarry.

"I fucking *knew* it," she snarled, vaulting over the parapet. "Stay here, human. It's going to get messy."

"I . . . okay." He trailed off as he watched her drop, following her descent as she bounded off jagged beams and busted balconies along the side of the building.

##18.4##

The ground shook as she landed, her boots announcing her presence with a clamorous thunder. Nara stretched her neck to the side, releasing tension with a sickening pop. She ground her teeth as a figure approached her, a man with shining golden hair and a wolfish salesman's grin.

Oh, Blondie, Nara spat. *Exactly who I wanted to see at this very moment. I'm going to put an end to all of this.*

A flash of silver twinkled across his jaw, revealing a patch of metal splitting his skin apart. The dubious man had procured new augmentations that he undoubtedly wished to break in. But Nara had no intention of giving him that pleasure. All she wanted was to swiftly beat his smarmy face in.

She listened to the voice of the street as she advanced, searching for his backup party. Four entities surrounded her, cowering in the safety of the buildings far away from their position, most likely brandishing scoped weaponry.

Was this the trap my dreams were trying to warn me of? she speculated. *I'll meet it head on. I don't care anymore. Let's get this over with.*

She took one step further before discerning an audial disruption to her left. Noise, fluttering, distress, a struggle. Silence. She kept her face neutral as she continued her approach, wary of the cocky man's next move. Another struggle. Silence.

What the hell is going on? she thought as another disturbance extinguished the soul on her right. Soon, she was surrounded by an unnerving stillness, no living creature around besides the irritant in front of her. *Fuck it, I'm done.*

"I'm in a very, *very* bad mood," Nara announced, looming in closer to her prey. "So, let's just skip the formality and go right to the part where I utterly annihilate you."

The haughty man flipped his hair over his shoulder, grinning wickedly as he raised a finger in the air.

"Well, actually . . ." **SPLORCH**.

Nara snapped a pistol in her hand as her eyes processed the gruesome sight before her.

The head of pristine, shiny golden hair had evaporated in a flash of crimson light, the man's stump of a neck revealing sinew and spine. The body, having realized it had lost its command center, slumped to the ground in a sickening heap, draining fluids onto the pavement.

Nara slowly craned her neck, glaring in the direction of the shot, spotting a familiar figure standing on a balcony with rifle in hand. Fury clamped her fists tight as her mind pieced the events together.

"Cain! You unholy cesspit of filth!" Her bellows resonated through the crumbling buildings. "I swear by the deepest frigid pit of Hell, if I catch up to you, I will tear you limb from limb until you are nothing but a mound of black ooze dripping over scattered wires!"

She held no regard of the impact of her personal attack as she punched her armor over her throat. Not waiting for the suit to fully form over her limbs, she bolted after her target, clawing up the nearest building to chase after the abhorrent creature on even ground.

Upon beholding the storm of ire barreling toward him, the ghostly figure took flight, clambering over the roof-paved path to gain distance away from the fury. The crumbling roofs shuddered behind Cain as he sprinted across the stonework, the living tank gaining distance on him. He tore along the path of the buildings, leaping from one to the next. With the pursuer dangerously approaching, he shifted tactics, sharply turning to head in another direction.

But the beast was just as reactionary, deftly revolving her weight with a grind of rock against heel. His problems magnified as the road in front of him began to diminish, the edge of the roof speeding toward him. With no other options, he charged forward, making one final attempt to break away.

He dove to the ground, scraping his hands along the concrete as he slid forward, halting his momentum. Flinging his arms forward, he caught himself on the parapet, his shoulders threatening to throw him over the ledge with his remaining inertia. He hurled a glare at the neighboring building, taunting him from across the street. Chancing a look behind him, he met the face of the armored beast closing in with enraged vigor.

His body bounded back as he channeled his strength for his getaway descent. He inhaled a desperate breath, then leapt on top of the parapet. With a measured step forward, he walked into the open air.

As he began to drop from the rooftop, a devastating force yanked him backward. A surge of pain cracked across his back as he was violently slammed against the ground. His eyes widened as the helmet of the creature looming over him receded, revealing the demon's glowering face etched with malice. Before he could rise to his feet, the beast snatched him by the throat and pulled him toward her.

"Who sent you?" Nara bellowed, hoisting him up to eye level.

"I was told to keep an eye on you," he coughed, prying at her wrist.

"By whom?" she growled. The man's eerie odd eyes avoided her gaze, and he meditatively ground his jaw as he considered his escape. "It was Sentinel, wasn't it?"

"No." Her ears barely had time to process his reply as he twisted away from her grip, darting off the nearest ledge and plunging to the streets below.

"You are a fucking terrible liar!" she shouted after him.

She belted out a violent roar as she stood alone on the roof, searing with animosity. Her quarry had escaped from her grasp twice in one evening. She was losing her touch. As the echoes subsided, she furiously ran her claws through her scalp.

Something was amiss in the air, and the uncertainty shredded the remnants of her sanity. She needed answers and another place to live. But the only person she knew who had a semblance of a clue was not a forthcoming individual. The unearthly warlord would not reveal why he had sent Cain after her, but she had to try and wrench a shard of inkling through his hidden psyche.

The human will have to be dragged along, she pondered as she stared back at her apartment. *Even if Sentinel avoids my questioning, he would at least keep him safe from my mess.*

"Come down and follow me," Nara ordered Garrett over the neural link. *"It is no longer safe in my house."*

CHAPTER 19

##19.0##

"W*here are we going again?"* Garrett asked through the link as he glanced around the marketplace quizzically.

"Sentinel's bunker," Nara stated, warily scanning the crowd.

"Isn't that in the other direction?"

"We're taking the scenic route."

It was a plan that made sense to her at the time, hoping a more populated area would be safer for them to travel. But something felt off, an odd creeping uneasiness that left her unable to distinguish between concrete threat or debilitating paranoia.

Garrett perked up as he watched her head move, relocating his attention to the spots she focused on. He spied a curious character loitering around a stall, making a terrible show of looking nonchalant as they halfheartedly inspected the wares. Their eyes shifted around, casually glancing in his direction while pressing a hand to their ear.

Their clothing looked expensive, which was not all that unusual in Under, but the way it hung over the voyeur's frame made them stand out. The leather on their coat was strategically scuffed on the elbows and trim, as if they'd attacked it with a belt sander. Tears scattered along the material were devoid of frayed edges, revealing the age of the destruction.

"We're being followed," Garrett announced, watching the interloper avoid his eyes and slither deeper into the crowd.

"Yep."

"It's definitely not Shadows."

"Nope." Nara counted several more similarly outfitted individuals swirling around them. *"We've got a problem. I can spot at least twenty."*

"What should we do?"

"We are going to have to separate."

"I'm not leaving you alone," Garrett protested out loud.

"The hell are you going to do to help in a firefight?" Nara scoffed. *"They're not after you, and I don't want to carry you around again after getting hit with a stray shot."*

"But—"

"No argument. Now this is what I need you to do—" Her plan was cut off by shouting at the other end of the market.

What the fuck? Nara swore as she furiously combed the street for the source of the disruption.

"Enforcers!" A voice split the air, initializing a wave of panicked shrieks as the crowd churned in a frantic mass.

An ocean of terrified faces and screaming surged through the plaza, the center rapidly draining as people emptied into the streets. Merchants frantically tossed coverings over their wares before scrambling to join the exodus. A swell of bodies shoved past the perplexed duo trying to make sense of the scene.

"Noisemakers," Nara hissed. *"Enforcers never reach this deep inside Civilized Space."*

"What? I don't understand," Garrett blurted, struggling to keep his footing as people shoved past them.

"It's a ruse," Nara affirmed as she snatched Garrett's wrist, pulling him into the crowd.

As she dove into the current, her eyes bounced between the instigators surrounding them. A score of armed humans appeared to be in less of a hurry, calmly moving outside the panicked swarm, herding them to an unknown corral.

There are way too many here, she griped. *There's too much noise. I can't pick all of them out in this mess.*

"Stay with the crowd," Nara ordered as she darted into an alley.

"Like hell!" Garrett charged after her, shoving bodies aside as he awkwardly carved a path for himself.

"I am not fucking around," she snapped. *"You will get yourself killed if you follow me."*

"Don't worry about me."

She was about to physically stop his insubordination when she sensed a shift in the air surrounding her. The hunters had changed tactics, altering their course to pursue her.

Fuck, they are definitely after me.

"In here," she directed, climbing through a window of the nearest building. She crept over to the far wall, leaning against the brick as she listened for movement. Countless footsteps surrounded them, above their heads, in the neighboring buildings, across the street. Heavy steps, machine tracks.

Fuck, there are so many here, she cursed, sliding pistols into her hands. *Has the crowd disappeared? There's practically an army outside.*

"Are we clear?" Garrett asked.

"Far from it," she reported as she edged her face out the window, exposing one eye to the street. *"There is a party waiting outside. It's only a matter of time until—"*

Her warning was cut off by thunder in the street, shadowed by a crack bursting through the wall she stood behind.

A bellow ejected from her lungs as a searing hot javelin impaled her shoulder, effortlessly piercing through plate and bone. She gripped the invasive artillery, glaring at the clean hole in the masonry as she staggered back. Her useless hand released the pistol from her grip, the weapon clattering to the ground.

"Nara!" Garrett shouted as he gaped at the horror protruding out of the back of her coat. The end of the lance had splintered into a glistening barb of iron, each point voraciously digging furrows into her flesh as she struggled with the sinister device.

"Get back!" she bellowed as she laboriously retreated to the center of the room.

A swarm of heavily armed thugs flooded the room, crawling through windows and holes, descending the stairs. Nara lurched toward the back wall, pushing Garrett behind her and concealing him with her hunched mass.

The crowd edged toward her, brandishing a diverse collection of weaponry of assorted calibers. A sharp whistle sliced the air as the congregation settled, splitting the attack party to make a path for their silent leader.

The man was dressed in casual Upper attire, stretching an arm out as he approached, pointing their NetCom in her direction. She didn't recognize the human, but she had a suspicion that she knew who had hired him.

"If you want something done," A condescending voice emerged from the device, "You have to do it yourself."

Fuck, fuck, fuck, Nara repeated in her head. *Not him, anyone but him.*

The source of the voice flickered into reality from the Upper thug's wrist, and the image of Antonin Galavantier grinned eagerly at her, clearly proud that his plan was properly executed.

Garrett's eyes widened as he heard the voice echo in the room, panic cinching his throat shut as his heart spasmed erratically in his chest. The precarious line between his two worlds had suddenly snapped in front of him, and the maw of Hell eagerly awaited below with open jaws.

Oh gods, oh gods, oh gods. Garrett's mind droned as he absentmindedly pulled his mask from his mouth. *This can't be happening. What the fuck do I do?*

He stared at the faces in the mass, not recognizing a single one from his view.

"I should commend you," Antonin continued. "It took me so long to get the resources necessary to bring you at my mercy. Though I find that more irritating than anything else."

Garrett's knees quaked as he lifted a foot, edging himself out of the safety of his towering shelter. He gathered the nerve to wrench his lips into an irate scowl as he leaned toward the projected image.

"Kid, you stay the fuck back," Nara warned.

"Who is—" The smile on Antonin's regal face shriveled upon meeting eyes with the youth. "What the hell are you doing here, Garrett?"

"I would ask you the same question—" He stopped himself short as his jaw twitched from dread.

Nara picked up on a missing word from the human's sentence. Her skin ignited as she was flooded with a sudden awareness of the situation.

'Father.' She gritted her teeth as the syllables jabbed at her mind.

"Human," she boomed over the communication line, *"you will tell me your family name. Now."*

Garrett hesitated, the dire coincidence freezing his heart. There was a catastrophic rivalry between Antonin and Nara, and he blindly stood in the middle of the warzone.

"My—" Even his thoughts quivered as he expelled the confession. *"My surname is Galavantier, heir to the Galavantier Corporation."*

The muscles in her eyes convulsed as the words dropped a hammer on her soul. This was what her mind was trying to tell her all along. Everyone around her knew, and she willfully ignored the signs in favor of her professionalism.

"You will pay for your omission," she threatened.

"I will only ask you once more, Garrett. What are you doing here?" Antonin impatiently demanded.

"Business, and you?" Garret retorted, ambling toward Antonin's image.

Don't you fucking leave me here, Nara thought as she hurled the human a venomous side-eye.

"Business? Is that the best you can do?" Antonin scoffed, gesturing at Nara. "What in God's name are you doing with this . . . outsider?"

As the familial quarrel mesmerized the grunts in the room, Nara scanned her surroundings for an escape route. But the sea of rugged mercs was far too thick for her to navigate, and exhaustion began to pollute her concentration as her wound tore at her chest.

Every exit is covered, she lamented. *Even if I could take a few of them out to clear a path, I can't move fast enough to get through. Fuck.*

"She is under my hire," Garrett stated.

"Oh, how endearing." Antonin laughed derisively. "And how are you paying for such an esteemed individual? Unless this one had become so desperate that it had to resort to charity work?"

"I don't see how I have to answer to you. We're not in Upper," Garrett fumed, irked by Antonin's bigotry. "You don't have control over me down here."

I have to get out of here, I need to find a place where— her thought process muddled to goo as a scorch of fire traced around her vision. She could feel her consciousness dissolving as the internal conflict blazed within her.

"Is that a fact?" Antonin bellowed. "We will discuss this later."

"No, we will discuss it now," Garrett interjected as he stepped toward the image.

Antonin ignored the rebellious outburst, waving a hand up to signal his posse. The gesture initiated a symphony of clattering and energetic beeps as the legion raised their weapons, taking aim at the wavering target.

Nara raised a shaky hand to the metal protrusion invading her shoulder. A peculiar force of strength took hold of her muscles as she latched onto the device. With a sickening crunch, she snapped the javelin in half, leaving a jagged shard protruding from her flesh.

I need to . . . Fragments of her voice dissipated as she clutched onto the offending metal. *I will . . . destroy . . .*

But just as the fire began to consume her vision, Antonin lowered his arm.

The room erupted with electronic sparks as the mob unleashed a barrage at Nara's form. Sickeningly wet thuds permeated the air as the party gleefully perforated her torso with their assault, her blood rhythmically spattering against the wall behind her.

Nara clamped her mouth shut as the agony ripped through her flesh, refusing to give the bloodthirsty general the satisfaction of hearing her pain.

"Enough." Antonin commanded the cacophony to silence, pleased with the degree of carnage.

With the force of the assault no longer supporting her, Nara dropped to her knees, the ground shuddering with the sudden force of her weight. She felt the warmth of her blood trail down her skin, pooling along the seams of her plating.

"Nara!" Garrett called out. He reached his hand out, but fear paralyzed him, his legs unable to approach.

She struggled to lift her arm, bringing her coat sleeve to her mouth. As she wiped the blood from her lips, she scratched the lining open with a fang. Through a feeble cough, she extracted a tiny black pill from inside the material. She let the object drop onto her tongue, feeling the embossed skull on its surface.

"Eh, heheh. Oh, you're dead, kid," Nara managed to taunt through the channel before she collapsed on the concrete.

"Hmph," Antonin tsked. "If it's still alive when you take it to the Foundry, strap it up."

Garrett stared in stupefaction at the unmoving body of his fallen companion. A cold fist yanked on his throat as a realization saturated his conscience. His secrecy had killed her, and he had vicariously fired each one of those shots himself.

"Take him to his room and make sure he stays there. I have other business to attend to." Antonin snapped his fingers. "Be as forceful as you need to, but don't leave anything permanent. And don't. Touch. His. Face."

The hologram flickered off as the stylish thug approached the carcass, hefting it brusquely over their shoulder and carrying it off.

"Hey!" Garrett tried to run at her captor when his flight was sharply halted by a cracking pain shattering against the back of his knee. He tripped on his feet as the propulsion shoved him forward, and he landed face first into the concrete. Before he could pick himself back up, two thugs flanked him and grabbed his arms, slipping manacles over his wrists. They hefted him to his feet and forcibly shoved him out the door.

His mind raced as he was violently ushered onward, fearing the punishment that would be cast on him. The slurry of predicaments melded into an unsettling stew as he considered the worst, the notion that he may not be returning to Upper. It would be well within Antonin's character to remotely berate him as he ordered others to have him executed.

The sound of the grunts' boot stomping reverberated across his ears as he calculated their gait, furiously scanning the streets for a getaway. His sense of self-preservation bubbled over inside as he imagined the gallows that awaited him.

Fucking, fuck, FUCK, Garrett sputtered, hastily examining the ruins up ahead. *I can bolt for that building, maybe? Can I react faster than them? For fuck's sake, Sentinel trained you for this shit!*

As he forced fragments of plans together, two soft thuds piffed behind him. The commotion was shadowed by a pair of startled moans and the satisfying noise of bodies falling, solidly hitting the pavement with a rustle of clothing and a clattering of guns. Before he could turn around and discern the commotion, he was snatched up by his wrists and yanked backward into an alleyway.

##19.1##

He strained his neck around to find a figure enveloped in black dragging him toward a sleek ground vehicle.

"Now hang on a minute," Garrett protested, grinding his heels into the pavement as he pulled against his captor. *Great, now I'm being kidnapped.*

But the stranger was not impressed, locking an arm underneath his elbows to steal away his leverage. His captor then wrenched the back door of the vehicle open and shoved him into the passenger seat.

Garrett kicked out at the man, but his captor's inhumanly fast reaction snatched him by the ankle. The abductor shoved his leg against the step of the vehicle and pinned down his calf with their boot. After a struggle to perceive the aggressor's movement, Garrett found himself on his stomach, cheek pressed against the leather of the car seat.

He felt the pressure of the manacles suddenly release around his wrists, the bindings dropping to the floor with a clang. Before he could turn around, the figure slammed the door behind him, locking him inside. Garrett watched in stunned fascination as the figure walked around the car, storming into the driver seat.

With a sharp, indignant exhale of air, the man snatched back his hood, revealing a shock of disheveled red hair. The pale, thin face glared at him with scornful blue eyes.

"Baran!" Garrett blurted. "What the fuck is going on?!"

"Language, boy," the man scolded as he punched the ignition. "I haven't got long to get you out of here."

"That doesn't . . . what are you doing down here?" Garrett stammered.

"I resigned. I thought that was obvious," Baran stated as he sharply turned the vehicle around, darting into the dreary street.

"Why . . ." Garrett's brain refused to keep up the pace as he braced himself against Baran's driving skills. "Why the hell would you do such a thing?"

"Kid, you don't belong in this life," he responded plainly. "You need to get off this rock."

"We were about to go to someone who could help with that, but then this shit happened," Garrett snapped.

"We?" Baran raised an eyebrow.

"Nara, my bodyguard, and me," Garrett added. "The one I hired a while back that you wanted nothing to do with?"

Nara. That alias, Baran pondered uneasily. *Wait a minute.*

...Rather large individual, likes to keep himself hidden...

...Leave it alone, Scorpio had said...

What little color the man possessed in his face naturally had completely drained as the gears ground at each other inside his head.

"Garrett, I need you to answer me straight," Baran warned with a terse inhale. "You wouldn't happen to know of an Agent RD, would you?"

"She told me her street name was Red Death?" Garrett furrowed his eyebrows. "Does that mean anything?"

"Oh. My. *Fucking*. Gods." Baran exhaled through clenched teeth, his knuckles whitening over the steering wheel. *0975. Scorpio, the next time I set foot through your door, I will flay you alive.*

"What? What's the matter?" Garrett asked in apprehension.

"Holy shit, kid!" Baran shouted in exasperation. "You kept that from me?"

"Of course." Garrett shook his head in mild irritation. "You didn't want to know anything about my trips."

"I suppose I should be thankful for that. You would have put me in a rather uncomfortable position." He let out a breath of relief, then looked up at the mirror nervously. "You didn't . . . tell her about me, did you?"

"Of course not!" Garrett snapped as he folded his arms across his chest. "I kept my family name a secret from her in case this shit happened. But look what fucking happened anyway."

"I . . ." Baran lost his train of thought, sighing in frustration as he navigated through the city.

"How the hell did you find me, anyway?" Garrett asked.

"Some friends told me to come get you," he explained.

Friends, Garrett scoffed. *Wait a minute.*

"You're the one who hired the Shadows!" Garrett blurted.

"Yeah, and a whole hell of a lot of good they did me," Baran scoffed.

Garrett's mind was spinning as he considered how many lies he was living under. If Antonin was dealing in the Underground without his knowledge, who knows what sort of repercussions were in store for either him or Baran. The questions nagged at him, elevating his fears as he considered the thick layer of corruption coating the corporate chieftain.

"Did you know where he was?" Garrett demanded, referring to Antonin. "On his business trips?"

"Yes."

"And you wouldn't tell me?"

"I obviously couldn't," Baran dismissed. "Look, there's no time for this. I need to get you someplace safe while I deal with the backlash of my actions."

"And I need to get her away from Antonin! I need to know if she's still alive!" Garrett insisted. "He said he was taking her to the Foundry."

"Yeah. That's one of the places he's got that contains holding facilities," Baran stated.

One of? Garrett's lip shriveled in disdain. A shudder ran through his spine as his imagination took him through a macabre ride, visualizing the sort of shady operation Antonin ran far away from prying governmental eyes. He found himself playing the gruesome machinations of Nara's escapades through his head and had no trouble picturing the despicable man ordering his army of minions to perform any act of horror for his profit.

Baran let go of the wheel to take out a cigarette from his coat pocket, lighting it up as he drove with his knees. He met eyes with Garrett in the mirror, who stared astonished at his vice.

"How the hell did you think I kept my composure with you galloping around the underground with bullet holes in you?" Baran retorted through a smoky exhale. "And your father doing what he does?"

"What exactly *does* he do?" Garrett jeered.

"Now is not the time for that. Perhaps your friend, his biggest annoyance, can tell you." Baran passed a data storage device back. "Here, this is a map of all the buildings your father has control of in the Underground. You need someone else to get her out. Don't be rash and do it yourself."

"Fine." Garrett squeezed between the front seats and punched in coordinates into the vehicle's navigation computer. "Head to this spot. I'll have a friend help me out."

"Is that . . ." Baran's eyes widened as Garrett confirmed the destination. "Is that the border of the Sentinel Clan Headquarters?"

"Yeah, you know him too?" Garrett asked.

"What the *fuck* have you gotten yourself into?" Baran shook his head in astonishment.

"What do you mean? He's a good man."

"He's fucking *untouchable*." Baran shook his head. "If you're on his good side, I have absolutely no problem dropping you off there."

"What about you?" Garrett asked grimly. "You could come with me."

"No, I could not," Baran insisted with a firm head shake. "Besides, I have quite a few loose ends to tie here."

Garrett leaned his head against the window as he watched the streets blur by, formulating an argument to make Baran consider his own safety.

The man was an enigma to him. All his life, he thought he knew the amount of integrity the security chief possessed. He was comfortable knowing Antonin was rotten, but he could not bring himself to consider what sort of dealings Baran had a hand in deep in the Underground, the people he might have hurt. The man was supposed to be his protector, and yet it was entirely possible that he had taken countless lives for Antonin's personal gain.

The vehicle slowed to a halt in front of the intimidating mountains of rust, cutting off Garrett's existential quandary.

"This is your stop," Baran declared.

"Yeah." Garrett hesitated, meeting the man's distant gaze.

"It's dangerous to linger," Baran warned. "I don't know how long it will be till the hunting party sniffs out my trail."

"I can't leave you," Garrett protested.

"I'm not dragging you down in my messes. That would not be fair," Baran pressed. "And you have your own to clean up. Do that quickly before you regret it. Every second spent here is closer to all of us getting killed."

"Promise me we can see each other again," he implored.

"I can't." Baran sighed dejectedly. "Please, Garrett, you have to go. Now."

It took every drop of his strength for Garrett to pry open the car door and clamber out into the rainy street. He took one last look at the man who'd raised him, trying to find the words to convey the storm of emotions he was always afraid to tell him, gratitude, fear, pride, despair, but nothing would surface.

"I . . ." His farewell lodged itself inside his throat. "Goodbye, Baran."

As he softly shut the vehicle door, the driver side window rolled down and Baran's severe eyes met his once more.

"Garrett." Baran hesitated, scanning over his face with a warm smile. "I love you. Make me proud."

Garrett's heart spasmed as the leaden words assaulted his ears. As he fought to unhinge his stunned jaw to reply, the vehicle glided into the street, disappearing in the hazy air.

In all of his miserable, angst-riddled life, this was the first time he had ever heard those words spoken to him. His father had never cared enough to consider his wellbeing. He was an investment and his property, after all. And Baran was contractually obligated to keep his relationship professional. Any sign of attachment was promptly and severely reprimanded.

The syllables reverberated through his mind, and his throat seized with emotion as he struggled to process them. Warm liquid suddenly seeped from his eyes, startling him as it mixed with the cold raindrops trailing down his cheek.

His legs rooted to the ground, and all he could do was stare at the empty, wet street.

##19.2##

NARA WOKE to the bright lights of a plain white room. The cold, hard slab she lay on sent shooting pains through her aching back. She looked down at herself, letting off a disgruntled sigh as her eyes traced over the innumerable lacerations scattered over her skin. The javelin, the bullet wounds, they didn't exist in this room.

And back to this hellscape, Nara thought bitterly, the awareness of her semi-conscious state filling her with irritation.

"Well, well, well," a voice invaded her ears, speaking to her in her native tongue. *"It's been a very, very long time. A decade at least, surely."*

Nara looked over to find the weird source straddling a plain metal chair, clutching the back of the seat as they rested their chin comfortably on top of their knuckles.

The creature was a bastard combination of both human and Ara'yulthr, grinning at her with an unhinged smile, brandishing their flattened teeth. A sleek, charcoal pinstripe suit covered their slender frame, tailored in a style of attire from a historical simulation, set in the golden age of pre-modern commercialism. Their hair was shaved on one side, the bare flesh decorated with a golden serpent tattoo woven across their skull. The rest of their head was covered in waves of back-length hair that shined with the iridescence of a murky oil spill.

There was not a single point in their features, and they could have been passable for Uppercity nobility if it wasn't for their pitch-black eyes and bright vermillion skin.

"I must admit, I am very surprised to see you here again." The creature stood, revealing a cape of smoky, swirling tendrils caressing their shoulders. *"You know very well that you don't need me. But you won't accept that, will you?"*

Nara grunted as she strained against her stiff body. She was not bound, and the door was in front of her. She could leave at any time.

"Those blackouts when your odds seem dire. You wake up, safe and sound in bed, the taste of someone else's blood in your mouth." The creature cackled. *"Very bitter, isn't it?"*

With an unceremonious heave, Nara flopped her shoulder over, plunging to the shiny clean floor in a messy heap. Her joints were crystalized, creaking against her efforts as she tried to propel herself forward.

"You're sick. Diseased. A danger to all those around you." The creature casually approached. *"And you know it."*

Nara ignored the creature's jeers as she struggled to rise to her feet, but her muscles would not carry her, the rebellious limbs clumsily flagellating on the ground.

"I, myself, am perfectly happy with the knowledge that I am a forbidden creature, something that should not exist within the vast, complex laws of metaphysics." The creature squatted down to her level, feigning a look of concern. *"Why can't you accept that as well?"*

Nara looked down as a sharp pain tore through her leg, finding her hand clutching the handle of a knife buried in her flesh, the blade identical in size to the slashes littering her body. Try as she might, she couldn't drop it. Her hand would not let her. The harder she pulled, the deeper it slid.

"But with all your impressive physical and mental endurance, you couldn't save yourself this time? Calling on me to bail you out instead?" The creature raised a finger to their lips, projecting a pensive gaze into the ceiling. *"There's something distracting you, isn't there? What is that, I wonder?"*

Beyond disinterested in the creature's mental games, Nara crawled away from them, pathetically dragging her useless, petulant body toward the door.

"The human?" the creature hummed, tilting their head curiously.

Nara hesitated at the suggestion, feeling her nerves rush with resentment.

"Ahh. What a curious mess of tangled emotions we have there." The creature moseyed toward her. *"It's nothing to be ashamed of. But it is very entertaining to watch."*

The door was deviously close to her, just inches away from her arm's length. Nara scrunched her body in, attempting to propel herself toward the exit, ignoring the agony tearing at her and the cackling taunts of the voice behind her.

"I just don't know what to do about you. Most people make a deal with me because they have the need to live. You, curiously enough, do not have this need." The creature was patronized as they met Nara's wounded pace with slow, exaggerated steps. *"Just a burning desire to make all those who have wronged you suffer. An amusing notion, but the fun is always fleeting in the long run."*

She was almost at the door, her body beginning to submit to her commands as she edged forward. The light through the crack underneath stabbed at her eyes as she endured the creature's prattling.

"But here's the thing—there is nothing I could do to you that you have not done to yourself already. You do more damage than I can ever imagine, not a simple task, I assure you." The creature tsked. *"I have never encountered a being with such a potent cocktail of self-loathing swirling around inside them. It must be a fascinating sense of inebriation. I can taste only a fraction of what you endure. But ultimately, that is not good for a business relationship. I have nothing to gain here, you see."*

Nara scraped a claw along the edge of the door, pulling herself closer to freedom. She weakly stretched an arm out, grazing the doorknob with her fingertips. As her palms brushed the handle, she heaved herself up to her knees, leaning her shoulder against the solid barrier.

"Well, I suppose there is work to be done now." The creature let off a bored sigh as they glanced at their extravagant gold watch. *"I don't say this to many of my customers, none of them, as a matter of fact, but while I do enjoy these little chats, I truly hope I never see you again. As soon as you're in the clear, I'm out. No more of this. I'd rather endure dissolving a thousand times than to help you anymore."*

Light drowned out her senses as the creature's admonishing words echoed in her ears.

##19.3##

Now is not the time, Garrett chastised as he slapped the liquid from his face. His desperation got the better of him as he recklessly stormed through the junkyard, the rusted shrapnel clawing furrows of reprimand over his skin as he charged to the fortress. But adrenaline had dulled his awareness, and his desperation fervently combated the pain.

When he had cleared the treacherous field, he bolted up the stairs to the entrance, stumbling over his footing as his nerves nipped at his ankles. The vault door relieved his spirits as he approached, releasing the vise in his throat as he frantically slammed his fist into the intercom button.

"Hey, kid! How's it—"

"Hark, I need to talk to Sentinel," Garrett blurted. "Now! It's an emergency!"

"Jesus, kid, come in and take a breath."

The lock cycle barely had time to finish as Garrett wrenched the door open, and he shoved his body into the corridor. His lungs ached as he barreled through the atrium, but he refused to stop.

"Whoa there! Hang on a sec." Hark snatched the flailing human by the back of the collar.

"Now is not the time, Hark! I need to speak with him right now." Garrett pried at the man's hand. Unable to break the adamantine grip, he twisted under his captor's arm, cinching the man's digits inside a garrote of fabric. Snatching the leverage away from his attacker, he wrenched his shoulders back, yanking his shirt out of the man's clutches.

"He's in a meeting right now," Hark scolded as he pivoted around the hysterical guest, wrapping his other arm around the visitor. "And you're bleeding. Take a breath and tell me what exactly is going on."

"Please! There is no time! Let go of me!" Garrett shouted as he twisted and pulled to escape the bear-like embrace.

"What is all of this commotion?" Sentinel's imposing voice broke the skirmish, emanating from the balcony above. He glanced at the combatants expectedly, eyebrows raised in suspicion.

"Sir! I need to speak with you right away! I—" Garrett paused as he choked on his own fluids, ejecting a string of coughs as his breath tore him down. "I have made a terrible mistake."

"Have you, now?" The warlord looked at him severely. "Come inside and let me know what is troubling you."

Garrett wrenched away from Hark's restraint and scurried into Sentinel's inner sanctum. Nothing had changed from the last time he had visited the man's office, but the room somehow felt eerily cold. A shudder ran down his spine as he edged forward, and an overwhelming sense of fear crept through his veins as if he were a condemned man approaching the execution chamber.

"Thank you, I just—" He feverishly snatched at the murk of thoughts darting around his grasp, trying to summarize the severity of the situation.

"Calm yourself. Take your time," Sentinel assured him, but the man's stoic gaze pushed him over the edge of dread.

"It's Nara. She's in trouble," Garrett finally managed. "And it's my fault."

"What happened?" The man's face remained a stone as he absorbed the account.

"We were headed over here when we got ambushed," he started. "By my f—"

Garrett's mouth spasmed as the word tangled over his tongue. Though he always struggled with admitting his relationship to the deplorable man, after the ambush in the street, he found the familial title exponentially difficult to extract.

"I need you to be honest with me." Sentinel narrowed his eyes.

"My father, Antonin Galavantier," he softly confessed. "I am the heir to his estate. Or at least was."

"I see." Sentinel folded his arms across his chest, his succinct reply expressing a score of mysteries to Garrett.

"Please, take anything you want from me. I will pay millions, billions," Garrett implored. "Fuck, my internal organs, take them all, I don't care. Just get her out. Please. I have maps of each of the facilities that—"

"Be *still*," the warlord boomed.

The warning jumped across his body, sending tremors through his limbs. He struggled to take control of his breath as he locked eyes with the fearsome man. The silence drilled into his ears as he tried to pick at any shred of expression in Sentinel's face.

His imagination ran in circles as he tried to conceive how the man's wrath would manifest. Baran was not someone who was easily shaken, and he was uncharacteristically anxious of Garrett's acquaintance with him. Perhaps he wouldn't personally take his deserved pound of flesh. Perhaps he would leave it to the legion of people under his roof who were fiercely loyal to him.

"We will discuss payment arrangements at a later time," Sentinel announced as he directed his attention to the corner of the room. "But I do believe I have just the agent to work on your case."

Garrett felt a chilling presence sidle in from behind, casting an imposing shadow in front of him. He turned to meet the piercing gaze of the pale man towering over his diminutive form, arms crossed in displeasure. Terror gripped his heart as his blood froze, dubious of what the spooky man would do with him.

"Mr. Cain," Sentinel addressed the specter, "Are you free this evening?"

##19.4##

Nara slowly peeled her eyes open, scanning the darkened room for her bearings. An odd feeling of euphoria swirled her head around as she drank in the air. She could move her neck of her own volition, but she was somehow distant from herself, immersed in a state of comfortable numbness.

She looked down at her torso, assessing the state of her injuries. The bullet holes that riddled her body had been sealed up with a chitinous black murk, expanding and reshaping itself each time she inhaled. The creature had settled inside her and was fulfilling its part of the bargain.

"Fucking symbiotes," she grumbled as she spat out remnants of the pill.

Devil's Pact, as it was known in Under, is a highly dangerous and an excessively illicit pharmaceutical. Rather than a chemical substance, the tablets contain a potent temporary synthetic lifeform that overtake the user's body, giving the host a second wind in a last stand situation.

The development of organic symbiotic creatures had been banned centuries ago by GaPFed regulation, making the distribution of the drugs extremely risky to any parties involved. Penalties were swiftly carried out, with the most lenient cases involving immediate execution, followed by erasure of the accused's personal records, effectively wiping them from existence. Galactic legal enforcement powers kept a tight fist on the case files of the drug in hopes to make it nothing more than a ghost story.

Upon ingestion, the creature flooded the user's systems, filling in veins, repairing tissue and bone, then coating the user in its inky black carapace. The creature then took control of the host's body, fighting any and all obstacles in the path to sanctuary, friend or foe.

The victim's consciousness is pulled away from the mind, forcing them to act as an observer to the horrors the creature wreaks with its newly found habitat. Survivors of the drug have claimed the creature takes on a nightmarish persona that taunts them while under the influence, versions of themselves that terrify them the most. It is said that this is to distract the user from the trauma the body is subjected to while the creature fights on their behalf.

It also leaves an imprint on the user, making it exponentially difficult to break away from its influence after repeated use. Eventually, the creature refuses to relinquish control, continuing a rage-fueled warpath until outside forces annihilate it with enough firepower to decimate heavy artillery.

Declan had warned her about taking it, even going as far as showing her recordings of humans who had completely lost the ability to control the synthetic creature inside them. They became horrible black-encrusted ghouls that terrorized the vicinity, demolishing streets and violently brutalizing any unfortunate soul that neared the havoc.

But she found his observations to be quite different from her experience. Perhaps she was too alien for it to take her over completely, or she had done the unthinkable and built a tolerance to it. Or worse, the creature was simply refusing to cooperate.

As her eyes adjusted to the dim lighting, she examined the contents of her cell. Human-sized indents traced along the wall, metal clamps situated at the arms and legs of each well. The room was otherwise empty, apart from a neat row of storage cabinets adjacent to the door.

A chafing sensation scraped against her limbs as she moved around, and she eyed the metal clamps binding her to the seat she was occupying.

Let's see if they're good on their word, she grumbled as she flexed her biceps.

With a focused inhale, she pulled up against the metal. With an ear-splitting refrain of scratches and grinds, the cuffs popped off her arms and the metal flaps crashed to the floor with a satisfying set of thunks.

The clamps over her legs effortlessly yielded as she slowly stood up, cracking open with little resistance. She stretched her arms out, absent-mindedly brushing her fingertips against the ceiling as she loosened her muscles. A cacophony of pops ejected from her bones as she nonchalantly sauntered toward the exit.

A maddened grin curled over her face as she traced a finger around the crack of the door, judging the integrity of the material with a series of vigorous pokes. Her merriment elevated as she pulled back her fist, stifling a chortle as she hurled a jab at the barrier.

The metal crumpled under her assault, caving in around her hand as if it were made of thin-gauge sheet metal. Wires fizzled under her knuckles as the lock mechanism busted, the pins torn out of their sheaths as they surrendered to the unnatural force.

She delicately slid the door open, letting a drunken giggle pass her lips as she walked through the opening. A melancholic tune hummed between her vocal chords as she casually strolled down the corridor, filling the chamber with eerie notes. She traced her fingers along the wall as she traversed, contemplating her state of being.

The rush filled her with such delight, and she could not recall a time where she felt more alive. Though the creature's silence told her the sensation was fleeting, she would not let it dampen her mood, drinking in the affliction as the seconds ticked by.

Her musings were interrupted by a set of booted footsteps approaching.

"Ahh, visitors!" She clapped her hands together with glee, and a sadistic grin bared her fangs at the intruders turning the corner.

"Whoa! How did—" one of the guards blurted as they snapped up their gun.

Nara belted out a deranged cackle as she loomed in on her prey, deliberating how she would handle the perpetrators. Her laughter intensified the closer she crept, the blackness creeping over her eyes until her sockets were imbued with a hellish void.

The grunts backed away as they discharged their weapons, showering her with scintillating laser fire.

The black chitin pulled itself out of her sealed wounds and crawled over her chest, swathing her in a vile shell as it anticipated the assault. She lit up the corridor with violent sparks as the volley ricocheted harmlessly off her body, scorching the clean walls with each shot.

"Shit, we need back—" The grunt's observation was cut off by an anguished shriek as Nara lunged at her quarry, whirling around them with frightening speed.

Bone snapped with a sickening crunch as she nimbly snaked around the hapless grunt's limbs, forcibly contorting their arms against the direction of their joints. She cut off the human's agonized cries as she stretched their back over her knee, moving to assault their ribcage with a vehement fist.

Their companion barely had time to process the voracious onslaught as they were suddenly pulled off their feet. They opened their mouth to let out a scream for help, only to be silenced by blunt trauma across the jaw. Unable to endure further brutality, the second grunt dropped limp in the predator's grasp.

"Oh, what a shame. My toys are broken." She cackled as she released the body.

Her ears perked up as she heard a faint electronic rustle across the way. She stepped over the writhing bodies, edging closer to the sound.

"Another one?" she purred creepily, winding back her fist as she waited for her next victim. "That's it, come to me."

The gentle mechanical hum tickled her ears, her impatience eating away at her as she gauged the distance of her new game. When the itching sensation grew too unbearable to endure, she lunged from the corner, hurling her fist around a tight arc at the intruder.

A rending screech jittered her knuckles as her strike met with a solid object. She felt cold mechanical fingers wrap around her hand as the intruder connected with her attack, pushing against her savage might. She looked up at the owner of the offending extremity, passing her eyes over the helmet of an armor-clad individual, comparable in stature to herself.

The figure strained against her augmented blow, taking a step back as she maintained her pressure. As she forced her fist through the intruder's defense, the armor over their palm splintered away, revealing corpse-white flesh underneath.

"Cain!" Nara blurted as the fog of inebriation tore away from her senses, the blackness receding from her corneas. "What the hell are you doing here?"

"I . . ." The armored creature hesitated, struggling against her fist. "I was sent here."

"By whom?" she demanded, slowly withdrawing her hand.

"I have not been granted permission to disclose that information," he reported.

"Of course n—" She suddenly let out a wail of agony as a thousand daggers tore themselves away from her flesh.

"My work here is done," a sinister voice trickled through her brain.

"I—" Nara tried to formulate words as a stream of black ooze crawled out of her mouth.

She staggered back, looking down at her body to find the black crusted scabs softening to sludge. Trails of ichor seeped from her wounds, evaporating to mist as the creature willfully broke away from its host. Her knees buckled as gravity hurled her weakened form down.

Upon watching the horror unfold, Cain snatched her into his arms, catching her as she sank. He tore out a badge from his belt and pressed it onto her collarbone, activating it with a swift flurry of commands.

Nara felt cool metal plates gently slide across her body as the armor deployed, encasing her in a soothing carapace.

"Medic unit online. Emergency protocol engaged," the device chirped into her ear.

A sharp prick bit down at her neck as the suit injected stabilizers, filling the fragments of her veins with a rush of cold liquid. The chemical sensation drowned out the pain of synthetic fillers as they expanded inside her wounds, sealing the damage the symbiote had created.

Cain scooped her up and draped her over his shoulder, delicately adjusting her positioning as he headed back down the hallway.

"You could've asked . . . me nicely," Nara slurred indignantly through the cloud of pharmaceuticals infecting her clarity.

She watched her surroundings dissolve around her as she floated down the corridor, giving up the protest against her escort as he ushered her into the unknown.

CHAPTER 20

##20.0##

Waves of ache swelled inside Nara's brain as the light invaded her skull. The surge traveled down her body as she strained to look around the room. She was in familiar territory, lying in one of Sentinel's med bays.

She ejected a labored groan as she fought with her muscles, attempting to flip herself on her side. When she managed to shift around, she spotted a figure lurking in the corner of the room, staring off into space.

"Cain? The hell are you still doing here?" she asked. The man shrugged his shoulders dismissively. "Ugh, fine, I'm too fucked to listen anyway."

Letting off a series of disgruntled mutterings, she slid her legs over the edge of the bed. With a heaving shove, she thundered to her feet, doubling over as her injuries lashed at her with admonishing pangs.

Cain dashed to her side, gesturing to offer assistance, but she smacked his hand away, holding up a finger of warning as she caught her breath. With a cringing inhale, she slowly uncurled her spine, wincing with every movement until she stood at her full height. She trudged toward the exit with her apprehensive shadow creeping behind.

The door slid open as she approached, and she looked down to find an irritable medic sighing in exasperation.

"I take it I don't need to lecture you on your predicament." Declan pushed his glasses up the bridge of his nose. Nara shot him a cold glare in reply. "Good."

As she stepped around the puny man, he matched her gait to intercept her path, pressing a hand on her chest.

"I really, *really* don't think it's a good idea for you to be walking around right now," Declan explained.

"Bite me," Nara growled.

"You know what? Go right ahead," he announced with a step back, gesturing toward the hallway. "I want to see how this plays out."

"I am too tired and pissed to be dealing with your bullshit right now, Declan."

"And that makes it so much more interesting." He beamed.

"Fuck *off*," she snapped as she shoved him aside.

She had made it about nine steps before her body demanded her to cease, the combination of tearing pain and heavy medication sapping the energy she thought she had. She leaned against the hallway as she caught her breath, muttering a series of curses to the unnatural forces of the universe. All she wanted was to have a nice quiet think in the atrium, and maybe some tea.

Cain uncomfortably edged over to her side, meekly offering a helping hand.

"Yeah, fine, come here." She surrendered as she grabbed onto his shoulder, leaning her weight on him as she dragged herself up.

She let him lead her on as she controlled her pace, mustering the force to move her exhausted limbs. But her concentration shattered as he suddenly halted, pulling against her teetering balance as they approached the entrance.

"Cain, I am not fucking around," she warned through gritted teeth. "I just want to sit down while the shit Declan put in me runs its course."

Discomfort contorted his lips as he hesitated, considering an internal predicament outside of her perception. He gave her a pained expression before stepping forward, ushering her into the room against his will.

"Thank you." Nara glowered as they entered. "How long was I out?"

"About eight d—" Cain cut himself short when her grip on him suddenly tightened, her claws digging into his clavicle.

Nara abruptly stiffened as her eyes passed over a disheveled looking human sitting in one of the recliners. Adrenaline coursed through her veins as her brain processed the features of the wretched creature, her muscles tremoring as a need for violence overtook her senses.

As Cain struggled to pull her back, Hark stepped in from his gaming table and assisted, blocking her path with his colossal width.

"Easy there, friend, you're still pretty beat up." Hark coerced as he grabbed onto her free arm, propping her shoulder against his. "You can rip into him all you like after you've healed a bit more."

A throaty roar reverberated across the room as she strained against her captors, the ache in her body waning as her wrath bubbled over.

"Hark, you will release me this instant," she warned through gritted teeth, keeping her eyes locked on her target.

"No can do." He shifted his weight to gain leverage. "You know the boss's rules on blood in the office."

Garrett looked up at the commotion, untangling his fingers from his greasy hair. His bloodshot eyes spoke volumes without context, and the sickly purple bags swelling underneath them revealed days of sleeplessness.

"You have three seconds to give me one reason not to tear you apart," she bellowed at the pathetic human.

Garrett stared at her blankly, the relief of her recovery barely registering through his muddled brain. He weakly shrugged his shoulders, shaking his head dejectedly as the response refused to surface.

"How *dare* you show your face to me after what you have done," she snarled. "What the hell were you thinking, hiding that information from me?"

"I wanted you to know me, not my family line." Garrett shifted his glance, staring at his feet. "I didn't know Antonin was your mortal enemy until now."

"How in nine hells could you be that blissfully unaware?" Nara scoffed, the sound trailing into a rumble.

"I'm locked up in a goddamned tower whenever I go back to Upper!" Garrett snapped his arms up. "I'm just a piece of property, an asset. I'm not allowed to know anything about his shitty business matters."

"I don't believe you," she hissed. "Was it his money that paid for all that equipment?"

"No, I told you, that was mine. From my side business," he explained. "I have enough funding saved up to last me four lifetimes."

Nara growled as her inhibitions dissolved, causing her captors to pull her a step back.

"I know. I thought I was protecting the both of us. I'm sorry." He let out an emphatic sigh. "Now that I know you are safe, do what you must. Kill me, maim me, whatever. I have nothing left to give a shit about."

The argument began to drain her, gravity pitching her toward the ground as she rested against her living obstacles. She was losing the battle with her emotions as her blood began to cool, the raw energy of her ire dying down as her bones screamed for relief.

"Get. The FUCK. *Out*," she snarled as she fought with her equilibrium, her bodyguards struggling to keep her still.

"I'm sorry," Garrett professed as he stood up. "For everything."

He tried to express his thoughts clearer, unsatisfied with the leniency of her wrath. He looked up at the two men to sense their feelings, but Hark had averted his eyes, and Cain was practically a machine. Through the tension of the atmosphere, Garrett stepped out to wander in the unwelcoming streets.

When the gate shut behind him, Nara submit to her body's wishes, collapsing as the source of her anger dissipated. Her entourage ducked down to lift her off her feet, carrying her over to the nearest couch. As Cain propped her into a comfortable position, she latched onto his wrist, glaring at him coldly.

"Please tell me you didn't know all along," she breathed. Cain shifted his gaze uncomfortably, distracting himself with his task as he evaded the question.

"*Nice*," she hissed. "I'm going to have a nap. Right here. Then I'm going back to my place and decide what to do with all of you fuckers."

"I think it's best if you abandoned your primary base," Hark suggested as he fluffed up a cushion behind her head.

"Ugh, yes, I will." Nara growled. "I just need to grab some shit first."

"In due time." Hark patted her hand. "I'll send Declan over to check on you."

"Tell the fucker to share his popcorn." She raised her voice to address the doorway. "I heard you back there!"

A thunk followed by a sharp pained shout announced the presence of the eavesdropping medic.

"Yeah, well it wasn't worth it, I'll tell you that right now," Declan snapped as he walked to her side. "Now go the fuck to sleep."

"Eat my entire . . ." Declan's drowsy sorcery claimed her functions, leaving her snide remark incomplete.

##20.1##

CORDELIA SIGHED as she surveyed the monitors, twirling a frosted glass knight piece between her fingers. A focused glare flattened her face as she avidly absorbed the images on the wall in front of her.

Her bookcase was butterflied open to reveal a flat screen divided into sixteen segments, each panel cycling through views of the streets of Uppercity. The monitors led her through a virtual tour of roughly sixty percent of the entire city, thanks to her remote access of the camera drones stationed through Vaylenuran territory, as well as the allied forces utilizing her father's optics technology.

She pondered over the new treaty negotiations with Tenshinn Security, pleased that it would broaden her jurisdiction. The company was enthusiastically interested in procuring Vaylenuran surveillance tech to modify their equipment, and it would only be a short wait before she could break in and open a new district of Under for her entertainment purposes.

But the playground would do her absolutely no good if Garrett was simply elsewhere. His recent sporadic behavior was beginning to irritate her greatly, and he seemed to avoid walking around in Upper altogether. Then there was the blasted security chief stifling her reconnaissance.

She would dearly love to hire someone else to monitor Garrett's routines and analyze her insurmountable collection of prerecorded data, but finding someone trustworthy enough to keep their discretion was too risky a venture. It was safest to observe herself, despite her limited free time, and leaving it to chance to find him personally. The tactic had served her well so far.

"Miss?" her office NetCom interrupted her snooping session.

"Yes, Octavia?"

"Your father has had a new breakthrough in the Echo project, and he would like to show you its progress as soon as it is convenient."

"I'll be there momentarily," she stated.

She absentmindedly set the game piece back down on the table, shaking her head in displeasure. Garrett simply wasn't in Upper, and that so-called study partner was certainly not an Upper citizen. But perhaps she could use that as an advantage and scrape up a scandal on both. He seemed to care quite a bit about his companion, at least enough to actively evade her questioning.

"Well, this won't do at all," she mused, extracting a book from her shelf. "It seems I have to extend my reach again."

She delicately plucked out a transmitter from a compartment inside the pages, turning it in her fingers as she dialed in an address. It was a piece of technology from several generations past, its software support had been abandoned, and the data format no longer used by modern devices, making it an ideal means of communication for her delicate subterfuge.

"What can you possibly want this time?" a gruff voice crackled from the device.

"My dear friend, I have someone I need you to find for me," Cordelia pleasantly elucidated.

"My costs have tripled," the voice muttered.

"Why, of course." She elevated the tone of her voice. "Is the usual means acceptable?"

"Fine. Just send the details."

"It's so nice to do business with you again," she cheerfully remarked.

"Save it for the amateurs you kill off."

##20.2##

SENTINEL FOUND Nara sitting alone in the darkness of the observatory, staring solemnly at the planets drifting over the walls. Her exhausted face was flecked with hundreds of projected stars and galaxies, giving her the appearance of an omniscient divine presence encumbered with the woes of the universe.

"May I speak with you?" he softly requested.

"Depends. Do I already know what this is about?" she responded curtly.

"Most likely. But since time is not on our side in the matter, I feel like it should be addressed promptly."

"Fine. Let's start off with you explaining to me why you lied." She turned toward him, folding her arms as she leaned against the glittering celestial wall.

"I am in an extremely delicate position," Sentinel explained, resting his shoulder against the doorframe. "It is very difficult to judge when and when not to interfere with relationships, business or otherwise."

"That tells me absolutely nothing," she snapped. "Your work seems to interfere with quite a few powers down here."

"My work is only a fraction of the entire picture." He paused. "A picture you are not ready to see quite yet."

"Goddammit, *Serr'Maht*," she snarled, rubbing her face irritably. "I am too fucking exhausted for these games. Speak plainly, for fuck's sake."

"I simply can't." He shook his head. "There is a time and a place for you to know more, but that time is not now."

"But everyone else is in on this . . . picture?" Nara scowled.

"Not as many as you think," Sentinel assured her. "But right now, you have more pressing matters. Your time on this planet is expiring, and you need to consider where your journey takes you next."

"I simply have nowhere to go."

"I don't think you have convinced yourself that's true just yet," Sentinel countered. "Consider all the people you have met here, all the places they have been. All the places you haven't even heard of. Somewhere, there has to be something for you to see."

"I'm weary, I'm drained, and I have no interest in seeing anything. I just want to rest." She sighed, glaring at the ground.

"Then search for your place of peace," the man offered. "The galaxy is vast. Your kind lives far too long to sit and wallow in stagnation."

"My kind also does not move around," she retorted.

"And that, my dear child, is where you are wrong," he pointed out. "There are quite a few members scattered about the stars, living their own lives away from the traditions of their home world. I've met a number in my time. Why not be another?"

Nara was uncomfortable with his persistence, speaking of matters she did not want to hear. It gave her struggles a physical presence, a life she'd tried so hard to snuff out inside her.

"I will leave you to think. But do know that I am willing to assist in any means you need. All you have to do is ask." As he turned to leave, he called back over his shoulder. "He is a good person, and at the core, you know it as well. It was the primary reason I did not wish to interfere."

Nara watched the man leave the room, questioning the truth in his words. The depth of the conversation shadowed her. She did not want to think about the future. She wanted to stay in the present. And presently, her home had been compromised.

Shoving back the muck infecting her thoughts, she set out to her apartment, preparing to pack her life away and move to another base of operations.

##20.3##

BELLANAR PACED around the base of the apartment complex, gesticulating madly as he recited a passionate conversation to himself.

"Do you know what really irritates me?" a voice softly hissed into his ear. *"Besides you, of course."*

He vaulted forward with a gasp, startled by the invasion of his personal space. He whirled around to meet the icy gaze of Nara, who had crept under his distracted radar. A frightened wheeze escaped his chest as he backed into the building wall, and he pawed at the masonry for an escape from the ominous creature.

"The uncertainty." She glowered, casually leaning her hand on the brick above his head. She cast a shadow over him as she loomed in, edging uncomfortably close. *"How did you find me?"*

"The ship you were put on," he started, slowing his breath as he edged away, pressing his back against the concrete. *"It was from an emissary of GaPFed, and they had put a price on your head."*

An ethereal bolt cracked down on her soul as the man divulged the story, a million pieces clicking together in her brain as the stage play revealed itself. GaPFed was a ghost that was supposed to have been assuaged under her power, and the pawns colluding with them should have been relieved of their influence. Her claws dug into the concrete as the implications drove nails into her brain.

"Another emissary came back to us after tracking the signal of their wrecked ship, demanding compensation for the destruction of the transporter." He firmly shook his head. *"The council refused, obviously, forcefully ejecting them from our space. But before they left, I had heard that the ship was headed to this solar system."*

"And you somehow managed to find me here?" She narrowed her eyes.

"There are only four habitable planets in this system. Two of them are inhabited by humanoid civilizations, the others by non-sentient animal lifeforms," he informed. *"And after thirty long years, I finally found you here."*

"Why?" she venomously breathed. *"Why are you here? Truthfully."*

"The people have fallen," he lamented. *"Your exile was the catalyst to a long, slow-building tension amid the powers."*

"That's it? Your entire motivation?" She scoffed. *"And what makes you think I would change that?"*

"Personality aside, you were a brilliant leader." He managed to squeeze a shrug from his confined quarters. *"But now, no one trusts anyone. The council has divided, and it is only a matter of time until blood is shed."*

"Let it," Nara spat.

"Then Loremaster was right. I should not have come," he professed, letting his posture slump. *"I tried to bring it up to the council, but he insisted I desist. So, I took matters into my own hands. Someone had to."*

Nara lowered her arm at the mention of her mentor's name, taking a step back to process the truth in the man's words.

"His life is in danger," Bellanar added. *"He is the last remnant binding the council together, his silence on the matter prohibiting any further action. Many are waiting for his opinion, but they are growing impatient."*

The account drove daggers into her ears, and she felt the burden on her shoulders drag her further into the conjectural hole she was already drowning in. Of all the problems she wanted to ignore, planetary war was the one she despised the most.

"He has still not named a successor." Bellanar's eyes dimmed. *"And at this rate, he never will. If he were to perish now, the world would erupt into chaos."*

Amid the sticky bureaucratic web of bickering, *Loremaster* was the only voice of reason. She attributed her cynicism to his teachings and upbringing, though gratitude was not an appropriate descriptor of her emotions. It felt wrong to abandon him, even though she was not the one responsible for his position.

"Because of who you are, I cannot believe you," Nara announced, bearing down on her victim with severe eyes. *"I will only consider giving my effort if Loremaster himself stands before me and tells me the same."*

"But, that's absolutely out of the question! He can never leave the

planet." The man's eyes widened at the proposal. *"If word were ever to come out that he had left his post—"*

"Then civilization will crumble anyway," she pointed out. *"But at least he would have the chance to survive it."*

"I simply can't—" He stopped himself as he considered his options, letting out a sigh of acceptance. *"I've come this far."*

"Let me make one thing absolutely clear," Nara proclaimed, jabbing a finger of warning in his direction. *"I don't care about your people. They can fester in their own filth, every last one of them. I care about Loremaster. He is the only reason you are not drowning in a pool of your own blood right at this moment. I suggest you show him gratitude when you return."*

She turned away from him, heading off into the street.

"I'm glad that made it back to you." He smiled, glancing up at her neck.

"Pardon?" Nara stopped in her tracks, turning her head to the man.

"The medallion. I had it with me in hopes of offering it as a reminder, but I made a rather unfortunate encounter with a couple of ruffians," Bellanar confessed. *"I can't recall how many arms I had broken, though admittedly, some of the metal ones were harder to snap. But I managed all the same. It must have fallen out of my pocket in the middle of the brawl."*

The chain around her neck tickled her skin as she brought a hand to her collarbone. She pressed a thumb on the coin underneath her shirt, grinding her jaw meditatively.

"This place is so unnecessarily hostile. No wonder you feel at home," he commented. *"I had the strangest encounters down here. People kept accosting me and demanding to know if I was 'Red Death', then attacking me before I could respond. But in the end, it helped me out. I learned that I was searching for you by the wrong name."*

Nara couldn't help but smirk at the insouciant attitude of his anecdote.

"I found your Sentinel friend, but he was rather short with me. He said he wouldn't tell me where you were even if he knew." Bellanar rubbed his chin pensively. *"That one had to have been lying, but he was so hard to read."*

You have no idea, Nara internalized.

"Then this bizarre ghost of a human tried to kill me. On more than one occasion, actually. It was as if he was trying to keep me away from you. Scary eyes." He stared off as he recollected the encounter. *"I had no idea what his problem was. You seemed to have made a lot of unique enemies down here."*

She had no more words to speak to him, only shaking her head as she turned the corner, heading up to her apartment.

"It was nice seeing you again," Bellanar called after her. *"For what it's worth."*

##20.4##

Darius quietly unlatched the door, peering inside the bedroom at the disheveled human mess passed out in the center of the floor. Bottles were scattered around the young man's contorted body, which had somehow managed to get comfortable using a fifth of rotgut as a pillow.

The innkeeper shook his head as he stepped inside, setting a tea tray on the night stand.

"C'mon, Garrett, up and at 'em," he coaxed as he rolled the snoring log over.

"What—" The lump ejected an agonized groan as the inebriation burned its mark on the poor soul.

"That's no way to deal with your problems," the innkeeper chastised. "I've been there, and it does no good whatsoever. Just delays the inevitable, and you get a bonus headache."

Garrett croaked out a few noises of dismissal as he messily propped himself against the bedframe.

"Now I know I said that you are welcome to stay for as long as you need, but like hell I'm going to watch you silently destroy yourself while under my roof," Darius added as he poured out a hot elixir from the teapot on the tray. "No matter how much you keep trying to tip me. It ain't right."

"Sorry," Garrett managed.

"You've been sayin' that a hell of a lot too." He handed the floor lump the steaming mug. "I'm sure it's bad right now, but it can also get worse, and you should have your wits with you."

Garrett sniffed at the sludge in the cup, choking back a retch as the sour odor invaded his nostrils.

"It tastes better than it smells, and works fairly quickly," Darius commented with a smirk. "After you drink that, go have a shower and sort yourself out. I'll be downstairs if you need anything."

"Thank you," he meekly replied.

"Don't mention it," Darius said as he exited the room, leaving the human disaster alone with his thoughts as he sealed the door behind him.

Garrett groaned as he stood up on his feet, shrugging off the filthy textiles clinging to his pathetic form as he trudged to the bathroom. He fought with the controls of the shower as his coordination took its time to catch up to him.

The muddled swamp of his thoughts began to clarify as the hot water eroded away his lethargy and reality began to ease its way inside. Awareness of his current status started to trickle at a digestible rate, and he found himself considering his immediate future.

He was no longer an Upper citizen, but that was not a hampering obstruction. Navigating through both cities was easy enough, and he had enough resources to falsify documentation to get him to the GaPFed ports. But his lack of galactic navigational knowledge left him with sparse options.

Baran's warm farewell haunted his memory. The thought of leaving the planet without knowledge of his safety cast a guilty shadow over his conscience. He refused to accept that he wouldn't be able to see the man again, the remorse of all the unanswered questions pitting his brain. But with the immutable nature of their departure, reason told him that he might be dead already.

Then there was Nara. She was better off without him, but Antonin's refusal to accept defeat was a tenacious force. The corporate warmonger would make her life hell, toying with her until he fabricated another deadly ploy. Garrett cursed his ignorance, searching for the 'what ifs' that might have averted the conflict, but his brain abandoned him in a well of despair. There was nothing he could have done to protect her.

He shook the water out of his hair as he stepped out of the shower, wishing Darius' potion did more than just cure a hangover. He barely had time to wrap a towel around his waist when his NetCom vibrated on the nightstand. His hopes soared as he bolted for the device, nearly losing his cover as he tripped over the material.

"Hello?" He cleared the exertion from his voice with a cough.

"Garrett, good. Haven't got much time. I'm being tracked," an unfamiliar voice reported.

"Who the hell is this?" Garrett demanded.

"A friend of a friend."

"Friend of . . . hey, can you tell me if Baran is—"

"No time," the caller cut him off. "Are you in a safe place now?"

"For the moment," Garrett replied, confusion tinting his tone.

"Good. You and your cohort need to see this. They've been pumping it through the Upper city billboards all day, and they will have it running through the Undercity pirate channels in a matter of hours."

A hologram projected from Garrett's wrist, displaying a rotating rendering of Nara standing up straight, alternating between her casual dress and her armored suiting. A circle of text traced around her feet as a soothing female voice narrated the news report:

"An alien terrorist, known simply by the alias 'Red Death', is wanted for trillions of credits in damages to valuable assets of the Galavantier Corporation. Reports claim that they may have a connection to the recent demise of the Skyward Robotics CEO."

"Ohh, SHIT!" Garrett blurted.

"Indeed," his shadowy companion agreed. "There's more."

"They are also responsible for the kidnapping and death of Mr. Antonin Galavantier's only heir and son, Garrett Galavantier."

"Death? What!" Garrett fumed, watching the projector shift to stills from his adolescent self.

"Oh, yes. Your father has deemed you a lost cause. He's putting on a nice display for you, however, making you seem like a pure, innocent victim," the voice explained. "But that's not the only troubling part."

"The Galavantier Corporation is offering a generous sum of 1.8 billion credits to anyone who can confirm the death of this criminal. The station would like to emphasize that this is an extremely dangerous individual, and any sightings or other reports may also be rewarded. Please contact your local Galavantier Police Service Desk for further details."

"That's . . ." Garrett's eyes widened as an extensive train of zeros flitted across the display. "Holy shit, I've never seen such a high bounty before."

"Which means everyone down here will be clawing at your friend's front door at any moment's notice," the Shadow added. "And if anyone notices you are in the area as well, things could get a bit sticky for you."

"Fucking . . ." He ran his hand through his tangled hair, plucking at knots in frustration. "What the fuck do I do now?"

"You have been advised to leave the planet. But what you do is ultimately your decision," the voice replied. "I have to go."

"I . . . thank you, whoever you are."

"Just following orders." The mysterious voice cut off the channel.

"Fuck!" Garrett exclaimed.

As he slapped the grimy clothing back on, he felt around for his wallet. He pulled out his identification card, staring at it in bewilderment. He had no use for it anymore, and carrying it on his person would be more of a danger to him than a tool.

"Fucking hell," he muttered as he stuffed the device back into his pocket. *I'll get Art to fry it. I can't leave now, while Antonin weaves the news how he wants to get his way. But what the hell am I supposed to do?*

He headed out of the room and down the stairs, hurling resentment at the steps as he descended.

"Feeling any better?" Darius asked as he caught his flustered gaze.

"Nope, you were right," Garrett declared. "Things got worse."

"I'm sorry to hear that."

"Regardless, thanks for dealing with my sloppiness," he added apologetically.

"Again, don't mention it. I'm just glad you stopped by," Darius said. "You're a quiet drunk, and those are the ones you gotta worry about the most."

"Yeah." Garrett's mind was still on the issue of the bounty. *No mention of Baran at all. Had he already been killed?*

"So, where you headed?" Darius broke his train of thought.

"Not sure. Trouble is tailing me, so I'll figure that out when it gets here. In the meantime—"

Garrett's wrist vibrated again, and he picked up a call from an unfamiliar number.

"You will help me get out of this mess," a deadpan tone that resembled Nara's echoed from the device. "Meet me at these coordinates."

The channel cut off before he could verify the identity of the caller. He lowered his quaking hand as it chirped out a notification.

Darius raised an eyebrow. "Well, that sounded serious."

"Yep," Garrett stated as he produced a flask from his belt. He knocked the clasp open and tossed his head back, consuming a hearty draught of the contents.

"Remember your wits, dear friend," Darius scolded.

"I'll give them a proper burial," Garrett remarked as he tossed a slice on the counter.

"That isn't even remotely amusing," the innkeeper said scornfully.

"I'm not sure it was supposed to be," he admitted as he walked away.

##20.5##

GARRETT DOUBLE-CHECKED the coordinates from the message, perplexed by where they led. He was standing in one of the more decayed areas of Uncivilized Space that edged a little too close to the Fringe for his comfort.

While there were plenty of places to hide during a firefight, not a single building around him provided enough shelter to accommodate a living space. The crumbled fragments of a paved road divided quadrants of jagged concrete formations, remnants of skyscrapers that once fraternized with the lower atmosphere. Desiccated husks of long-dead foliage creeped out from the glass carpeted earth, a morbid reminder of what once was.

As he searched around for his destination, his wrist beeped out a notification.

>>*Look down,* the message displayed.

He glanced at his feet and spotted a curious circular metal slab slightly elevated from the disintegrating ground. The portal was bordered with a ring of industrial piping, rusted over from decades of weather erosion.

He knelt down and grasped the handle, finding it surprisingly mobile despite the oxidation. With a heavy grunt, he heaved the slab upward, only to be welcomed by a pitch-black chasm beneath. Waving his trusty NetCom in front of him, he shoved his apprehension behind him and gingerly crept down the track of metal steps, shutting the hatch with a resounding clunk.

The dank cavern echoed with each step, and a sense of uneasiness swirled around inside him as he edged forward. His knees began to quiver as he advanced, and an unwavering sense of dread saturated his bump-riddled skin. He was uncertain if his feelings were a result of the spookiness of the environment or the apprehension of what was waiting for him at the other side of the corridor.

His adventure was soon halted by an imposing blast door encompassing the entirety of the hallway. A massive vault wheel stuck out of the center with a multitude of reinforced spokes, tempting him with access. After a quick search for alternatives in the hallway, he clasped onto the handles, bracing himself to test his strength against the formidable barrier.

To his surprise, the levers unlatched with ease, only taking half of his weight, and two heaving grunts, to heft it open. He leaned around the opening he made, finding an unnaturally welcome sight inside.

The chasm was brightly lit with rustic piped wall lamps, flooding luminescence into a rather cozy living space. A wooden dining table sat at the center of the white-walled pit, surrounded by a set of matching chairs. Cushiony couches lined the perimeter, and familiar-looking weapons lockers were intermittently stashed between each sitting place. The room looked like a pre-war-era bunker, converted into something more habitable with modern technology and environmental controls.

Nara was stretched over one of the recliners, legs casually sprawled across the arms as she read a ghastly leather-bound book.

"Hi," she greeted, looking up from her tome with a flat-faced expression.

"Hi," Garrett cautiously echoed, steadying his thumping heart.

"Let's go for a walk," she declared and snapped the book closed. She hefted herself up from her seat and slipped on an immaculate leather coat that was draped over one of the chairs.

"S–sure," Garrett breathed as he followed her out of the bunker, disoriented by her reaction.

The cool night air chilled his lungs, becoming an icy pestilence against his attempts to stifle his agitation. Nara was intentionally elusive, hiding her expressions from his comparatively sub-par observation skills. She wasn't going to drag him outside just to kill him. She would have done that already if she wanted. And that wasn't the issue that terrified him. Death would have been his preferred solution to their quarrel.

"So," he started, avoiding the obvious consequential subject matter. "You live in a hole in the ground now."

"It's *my* hole in the ground," she rebuked. "And I like it."

"Oh." He tried to hide his discomfort as he let his eyes wander their surroundings, growing increasingly anxious as they trekked deeper through the Uncivilized Zone.

It was eerily quiet and peaceful. Unusually peaceful, in fact, to a point where Garrett anticipated an ambush of bounty hunters, or Experimentalists, at any moment. He deliberated over which he would prefer to encounter, distracting him from the multitude of thoughts flitting through his mind.

He searched the air for a way to break the tension between them. A million fragments of expressions threatened to spill out of his mouth, but his voice had no idea how to jam them into phrases of effective communication.

"Why . . .?" he started, stifling the fluttering inside his throat.

"I don't know, that's why." She sighed. "There are about twenty-seven voices telling me to gut you right about now."

He looked up at her solemnly, uncertain of how to react to her admission.

"But I'm getting real tired of constantly being told what to do." Nara fidgeted with the lining in her coat pocket. "And I'm sure you feel the same."

Garrett glanced up at the Haze above as her comment evoked a new revelation. He was engrossed by what he had lost since his citizenship was revoked, but he had never considered what he'd gained. In their disjointed sendoff, Baran told him that his future was his own now, and he had the whole galaxy waiting for him to explore. As a child, he had always dreamed about possessing even a sliver of freedom like this, and now that he had it, he was devoid of all aspirations.

"Yeah." He let out a sigh. "Everything happened so fast, I still have yet to process it all. Even on my terms."

"Life doesn't allow you time to process," Nara opined. "Change is swift. And brutal."

He contemplated her poignant words, their brevity striking a chord in his thoughts. While her bitterness was overwhelming on his palette, the random spurts of intelligent conversation sweetened the interaction. Nara had nearly died right in front of his eyes, and the thought of losing a kindred spirit like her tore a void in his heart.

She was just as tired as he was of life's fateful games, maybe even more so, but after all that had happened between them, he wasn't sure if it was possible to reclaim their relationship. There were still facets of her character that were unsettling to him.

"All right, now that I have determined we are on fairly stable speaking grounds," he sharply steered the conversation, "and on the subject of the frailty of existence, I have one or two things that I would like answers to."

"I see." Nara let out an apprehensive exhale.

"Did you kill my uncle?" Garrett bluntly asked.

"You're going to have to be more specific." She snorted. "I've killed a lot of people."

"Velonir."

"Yep," she answered plainly. "That was me."

"Great. Now that that is settled . . ." He exhaled a distraught wisp of air. Despite her blatant admission, Garrett could not find anger or grief inside his thoughts. Instead, he was overwhelmed by a cloud of cold apathy, which disturbed him greatly. "I have no idea how to begin to feel about it."

"I'm an assassin. It's what I do, and you have known the entire time we have been speaking." Nara glanced over her shoulder at him, interrupting his ethical self-analysis. "Or does it not matter until I do something that directly impacts you?"

"I . . . am not sure," he admitted. "When you put it that way, nothing sounds justifiable. Where is the line?"

"I said I was an assassin, not a philosopher."

"If you had known who I was," Garrett countered, trying to absorb the entire perspective, "would you still have taken the job?"

"Most likely. I wouldn't have known you long enough for you to interfere." Nara shrugged. "I would have booted you out my door the minute you told me."

"I don't mean right from the beginning. I'm talking about after we had been traveling around Under for as long as we did," he pressed. "You must have at least a few amicable thoughts toward me to keep me around this long. And it's certainly not because of contractual obligation."

"You are treading a fine line," she growled.

Garrett clamped his jaw at the warning, vexed by her chronic emotional evasion. Her mental defenses were beyond infuriating, and considering the circumstance, he was entitled to at least a diminutive explanation behind her motivations.

"From what little I saw of him," Nara began, startling his internalized ire, "he was a good man. And there was some hesitation on my part."

Garrett blinked at her divulgence, not entirely convinced he had heard the words correctly.

"What made you do it in the end?" he whispered.

Nara thought of a number of reasons—her fear of failure, of the corporation that hired her, and her general apathy and displacement from the entire Uppercity political scene that shielded what little moral compass she had.

"That is an answer I am not certain of myself," Nara finally disclosed. "I'm sorry."

He thought over her words, slightly grateful that she'd expressed sensitivity. But it didn't change anything.

"I'd like to say it's okay," Garrett replied, "but it isn't. Though I am also struggling with the reason why."

"Don't pressure yourself to forgive if you don't want to. I'm not asking for it, nor do I want it," she said plainly. "Do what you will."

"If I knew what that was," he mused, "I wouldn't be wandering aimlessly in Under for kicks."

"Same."

They walked in silence as they pondered their separate definitions of morality. But the unsympathetic streets offered no help in their plight. Only the echoes of their footsteps chattered noisily away with no regard for conversational decorum.

"On another note, while we are digging through skeletons," Garrett began, "my guardian nearly had an aneurysm when I mentioned your name. Why?"

"Name?"

"His first name is Baran." He bowed his head remorsefully, ashamed that he didn't know anything about the man who'd sheltered him. "But I don't think he has a surname, as far as I know."

Nara stopped in her tracks, suppressing a twitch in her eyeball. With a sharp inhale, she buried her head in her hands, letting go of a string of garbled foreign obscenities that resonated across the barren street.

"You okay?" Garrett questioned uneasily.

"Fucking hell," Nara breathed, scrubbing her face.

"Do I want to know?"

"A whole hell of a lot of things have just clicked into place," Nara commented. "Fucking *hell*."

"Can I have some context?" he pled.

"Not right now."

"I guess that's fair enough." He shifted uncomfortably in the deathly quiet street, feeling invisible eyes peering at him. "Regardless, I don't know what your plans are for the immediate future, but I am leaning toward leaving the planet. As soon as possible, and before I get killed by an army of lackeys. Same as you? Maybe?"

"Where the hell would I go?" she scoffed.

"If that guy who keeps dropping by is any indication, your home planet seems pretty welcoming to you now," Garrett stated matter-of-factly.

"I will kill you later for making that suggestion."

"I am just saying." He raised a defensive hand. "A planet with impressive giant soldiers seems like a logical step at the moment."

"Where the hell did you get those presumptions?" she growled, pressing a palm to her forehead. "No, there has to be another solution. I need a shred of a moment to think about my options."

"What options?"

"I could kill your father," she said casually.

"I don't know how I would feel about that, either." Garrett scrunched his face in contemplation.

"I was joking."

"I didn't say 'No'."

His association with the deplorable man sent a shudder across his back. While he could distance himself to the furthest edges of the galaxy, he could not shake off the bindings of their shared genetics. Whether he liked it or not, the man was still a part of him, wherever he went. He twitched as his skin crawled, a vile slime itching his brain as he was overloaded with discomfort inside his own flesh. He scorned his mind for making the connection, scratching at a forearm uneasily.

The man must have been terrified to plot such a detailed trap for Nara. It was impressive how many people the man had managed to scrape together to fight for his side and how many resources had to be wasted just to get to one person. The scenario was laughably overkill, but apparently, Nara had forced the man to take any and every precaution.

"I'm not going to lie," Garrett began, "but I'm surprised you didn't just grab me and take me hostage back there or use me as a meat shield."

"That would have done absolutely nothing," she scoffed. "He had no intention of letting me go, or any issue with letting you die. I would have had to pull that trigger, and he would have gladly watched your corpse fall to the ground."

"That's a warm, fuzzy feeling inside me right now," he muttered. "Thanks for not doing that? I guess?"

"Sorry, but your father doesn't give a shit about you." She shrugged.

"Yeah, I am aware. I've had plenty of time to figure that out," Garrett grumbled. "What exactly did you do to get him so pissed, anyway?"

"Well, let's see here." She stretched her arms out and slowed her pace, letting off a deep, reflective breath as she stared up at the sky. "There was the time I stole plans for Project Artemis, then Centauri, and Cetus, Agamon, Quanti, Aphelion, then a few prototype organs and tissue samples—thirteen, actually."

"I, uh, wow, I—"

"Then breaking and entering into every single facility he owns just for the fuck of it. Hiding out for a few days in one of his especially secure ones just to piss him off." Nara began counting off on her fingers.

"I think I get the pict—"

"Giving his Chief of Security several nervous breakdowns that caused Antonin to pull him from leading the hunting pack against me." She ejected a wistful sigh. "Pity, though. He was tremendously fun to play with."

Garrett looked up at her in horror when he realized whom she was referring to. He tried to interject and ask for clarification, but she was not nearly done with her tale.

"Kidnapped a few of his high-rank scientists, helped a few of his scientists sell secrets to another company . . ." She let out another sigh as she continued her list. "Messing with the security cameras in amusing ways."

"Amusing ways?" He raised an eyebrow.

"I had them loop hardcore pornography from the net." She smirked. "Weird alien shit too."

"Oh, dear gods, you didn't!" Garrett clapped a hand over his mouth.

"He brought it on himself when he started attacking me." Nara shrugged. "He's got a giant chip on his shoulder."

"Tell me about it."

Disrupting the hint of revelry in the environment, Nara snapped a pistol in her hand and whirled around, firing off a shot into the street.

"It is *rude* to eavesdrop!" she shouted at the air. Before Garrett could question, she shoved him to the ground just as a crackling net of blue light whizzed past his vision with a hissing shriek.

CHAPTER 21

##21.0##

"Didn't think assholes would start showing up so early," Nara muttered as she punched her armor badge on her throat.

A humanoid blur charged at them, their arms sparking viciously as arcing energy ignited their flight path. As she stepped in to intercept, the living missile swiftly altered their course, heading straight for Garrett's bewildered form.

Oh, I see what game you're playing at, Nara commented as she grabbed a large chunk of concrete from the ground.

She dipped her shoulder and lowered her arm, swinging the chunk behind her as she analyzed the curvature of the speeding humanoid. As the being passed her line of sight, she twisted around and lobbed the fragment at the speeding merc.

The makeshift shot-put thumped its mark on the back of the being's head and the force of the blow abruptly shoved the humanoid off course. Giving them no chance to recover, Nara charged at the intruder, hooking an arm around a synthetic bicep and hurling them away from Garrett, who had just stood up after the initial attack.

Clouds of chalky concrete whirled around the attacker's feet as they braked, recovering in an assertive stance as they diverted their momentum. The merc glared at Nara as they recalculated their strategy, giving her the chance to assess her opposition.

The humanoid was impressively statured, almost reaching Nara's chin as they stood their full height. A torn sleeveless shirt hung loosely over their lanky frame, baring a sleek pair of shiny silver synthetic arms, the musculature an impeccable mimicry of its organic inspiration. The merc raised their fists in a tight defensive posture, revealing two curious seams bisecting each arm.

Though their legs were obscured by their garments, the merc moved in shallow, calculated bounces as they sized Nara up, revealing their synthetic nature. The person appeared to be unarmored, apart from a segmented metal gorget extending from collarbone to mandible, obscuring their face below their brightly lit violet eyes.

Having determined that they needed to enervate Nara before reaching their target, they shifted their stance, jutting their shiny chrome arms away from their sides. With a synchronous flick of their wrists, the augmented arms split apart, each unit separating into two independent limbs. A refrain of mellifluous clicks emitted from the partial joints, and additional digits telescoped out of their semi-wrists, forming a complete hand on each of the four arms. The auxiliary appendages gave the merc the likeness of a mechanized mythical demigod.

In an ostentatious display, the two upper arms arched behind their back while the lower pair reached behind their waist. After digging around their obscured personal storage, each limb snapped forward, brandishing a pistol in the palms of each hand.

All right, not fair, Nara griped, darting around the merc before they had the chance to aim.

Flashes of light piffed against her armor as she charged, her systems obsessively reporting energy depletion with each strike. She let off a few counter shots as she closed the distance between them.

The merc dashed behind a concrete slab, extending two of their arms around the edge of their cover to continue their barrage.

Dropping the pistol behind her, Nara rushed the obstruction, weaving around her opponent's wild assault as she sped up the jagged surface. She swiftly scaled the peak and vaulted over the precipice, pouncing on her foe underneath.

Upon hearing her drop, the merc bolted forward, narrowly avoiding being crushed by her weight. As they reset their stance, Nara lunged forward, bringing herself closer as she tore out a dagger from her arsenal.

Snatching an open opportunity, she thrust the blade inside the gap between the set of half-arms facing her. As she took another bounding step forward, she drove the blade into the merc's torso, feeling the resistance of soft tissue.

So, you still have some squishy in you. She smirked. *Built for speed, not for strength. Respectable.*

The merc recoiled and clamped the two halves of their arms together, compressing Nara's limb inside their mechanical spring trap. Before she could free herself, the merc yanked her back, dragging her off her footing.

As she tripped back upright, the merc stamped down on her boot, pinning her in place with their mechanical hoof as they wrenched her around their torso. She strained to pull her arm back as they continued to torque her body over theirs, tearing pangs shooting through her shoulder as her armor began to submit to the onslaught. With one final twist, a sickening pop burst through the air as her arm tore out of its socket.

Nara burst out a bellow of flustered anguish as she snatched back her balance, snapping upright as she kicked out the knee joint of the leg entrapping her.

All right, that's it, she hissed as she hurled her scorching shoulder back, dragging the merc with her as they remained latched to her flimsy arm. Ignoring the screaming inside her bones, she wrapped a leg behind the merc, twisting around the augmented limb until she pulled them back against her.

Reacting to the grapple, the two free arms on the other side of the merc pivoted around the axis of their shoulder, flipping the orientation of their hands. Reaching behind their back with their new freedom, the two arms wrapped around Nara, latching onto the back of her helmet and her waist with jagged talons.

Warning sirens screeched in her ear as the claws bored into her armor, digging through until they tore into her skin. Before she could pull herself out of the snare, a surge of scintillating energy shattered across her vision as the merc released a debilitating shock into her flesh.

She gasped for air as her knees caved beneath her, her contracting muscles dragging the merc down with her. As she struggled to regain her footing, her armor countered with its own electric countermeasures, the surge flinging the invading claws off her back in a spasming tangled mess.

When her nerves permitted her to move again, she tore out another dagger and dove under the merc's twitching elbows. She plunged her blade into the gap of their shoulder socket, right where the artificial limbs split. Sparks flew as shrieks of rending metal pierced the air, showering the pavement while she twisted the dagger inside her foe. With an adamant pop, the connections severed, wilting the two half-limbs.

Fuck, this hurts. She snarled as she tugged at the arm immobilized inside the merc's grip. *Let's see if we can even the odds.*

Snaking her functional arm around the merc's slender torso, she stuck her dagger into the maw of their opposite arm, sliding it in between her trapped limb and the jaw of the vise. The merc wriggled in her grasp as she hugged them tighter, scratching the blade against her own armor as she held them steady.

Using the dagger's edge for leverage, Nara wrenched on the merc's arm, widening the gap that restrained her. She continued to pull up until the shell of the mechanical limb cracked in half, channeling her strength into the device as it split. She gripped onto the damaged pieces, yanking upward until the plating broke away, leaving the forearm dangling by a bundle of wires.

As she rolled her shoulder out of the binding, the merc twisted their hips around, slipping out of her step while she recovered. Before she could lunge after them, a thunderous crack split the air, halting the fight.

Nara watched in bewilderment as her foe took a staggering step back, spotting a sizeable exit wound on the merc's spine steadily trailing synthetic vital fluid down their shirt.

"I have had *just about enough* of this shit," Garrett snapped, holding out a freshly discharged pistol.

The merc lifted a foot to step toward him, but the human's tolerance had run dry, and he fired two more rounds into the attacker.

"Not one more *goddamned. Step*," he growled through clenched teeth. "My aim is shit, but so help me, I will get you down eventually."

But he didn't have to make good on his threat. Nara slithered from behind and launched a violent hook from her good arm, slamming her fist into the merc's temple.

Reeling from the impact of the strike, the merc dropped to one knee, stabilizing themself with their remaining functional arm.

"I . . ." the merc began to teeter over as they tried to announce their intent. "I have a . . . message from my . . . employer."

The merc weakly raised their hand up, gesturing at the NetCom in their fingers with a shaky head tilt.

"I don't think you are taking this relationship seriously, Garrett," Cordelia's voice grated through his brain like coarse-grit sandpaper.

"What the hell do you want?" He scowled at the noise. "You can't seriously expect me to believe you are still interested in me."

"Oh, but I am," Cordelia mused. "And your empire."

"Watch the news," he jeered. "I no longer have it."

"The thing is," the cheery voice perked up, "it would be very interesting to see what the world would think if Garrett Galavantier suddenly came back from the dead. Your father would have a field day trying to patch that PR nightmare up."

"Go to hell," he snapped. "I want nothing to do with you."

"I am giving you one more chance to redeem yourself," the voice offered, ignoring the jab. "If you won't come to an arrangement with me, your father will. He would love to know where you are right this very minute."

"Choke on your arrogance," Garrett snarled.

"Ahh, well. Such is the plight of the fortunate. They think they have choices." The voice paused to sigh emphatically. "Well, I suppose it was nice to know you. We could have been something admirable. I will be sure to have someone tend your grave after the hounds catch up to you."

"Yeah, I've heard enough," Nara intervened, snatching the device from the merc's hand and crushing it in her palm. She then let off a reprimanding kick to the merc's side, sending them crashing to the ground.

Garrett stared at the busted device venomously, his mind soaring a million miles away from reality.

"Old girlfriend?" Nara jeered.

His face contorted into a scowl so deep that he could have borrowed it from her. Words would not pass through his lips. The animosity that frothed inside his brain corroded the connection between it and his throat.

"Come on, let's go before the cavalry arrives," she said as she scooped the battered humanoid up, hefting them over her shoulder. "Go back and wait at the shelter."

"Nara?" Garrett questioned uneasily. "What are you doing with him?"

"I'm going to see Declan," Nara stated as she walked off.

"Alone? With that guy?"

"Yes, alone. They need a new boss." Nara shifted the body around. *All right, buddy, don't make me regret this.*

##21.1##

NARA LAY on her back on the medical table, smoking a heady cigarette as Declan scrutinized her shoulder, occasionally shooting her an irritated glare as the smoke curled in his direction.

The medic delicately rotated her elbow around, bending it up as he gingerly positioned the limb. After a sequence of light adjustments and delicate movements, the bone obeyed his command, slipping back into its home with a sickening pop.

"Ahh, *FUCK*!" Nara exclaimed in agony as the ligaments vehemently rebuked her for her carelessness.

"That should do it." Declan dusted his hands off. "Compared to recently, you don't look that bad."

"I wasn't the target," she groaned as she sat up.

"For once," the medic scoffed, grabbing a salve from his stores. "And your friend over there—what's their story?"

"Dunno, didn't get it out of them before I pummeled them into submission."

Declan groaned at the sardonic account. "I meant why did you bring them here instead of killing them?"

"Last I heard, you didn't specialize in psychiatry," she jeered as she cradled her arm, wincing from the pain.

"For *fuck's* sake." He pinched the bridge of his nose. "What am I supposed to *do* with them?"

"Whatever you want? Pick a favor out of them? Bring them to Sentinel? I don't care." She absentmindedly shrugged, then immediately snarled at her carelessness as the joint stabbed at her.

"You're insufferable, you know that?" Declan slammed a cabinet closed.

"Speaking of, I need your help with another plan."

"Oh? This sounds promising," he jeered, slapping a medicinal patch on her wrist.

"Those, eh, 'spare parts' . . ."

"Yes . . .?" Declan raised a suspicious eyebrow as he smeared salve over her back.

"You still got 'em?"

"What are you planning?" He emphatically sighed, wiping his hands clean on a cloth.

"Something that might take the heat off a little bit," she evaded, gingerly slipping her shirt back on.

"I think I know where this is going." Declan shook his head. "You want the legitimate ones or the human botch jobs?"

"You've kept *all* of them?" She cringed.

"You never know when you need practice," he argued. "Or shitheads come at your door demanding them back."

"Gross." Nara scrunched up her nose. "The botch job, I guess, as long as it will pass through detectors."

"You're doubting my work?"

"I lost all faith in everything years ago." She slid off the table. "You should know this by now."

"Delightful." Declan rolled his eyes. "Yes, they will do just fine, especially if you just need it long enough to clear the air until you get off the planet."

"Works for me."

"You sure you are capable of executing whatever your mysterious plan is?" He folded his arms across his chest. "And you're sure it will work?"

"No, but it will be extremely funny." She carefully shrugged on her coat, the painkillers beginning to cast their soothing spell over her nerves. "Especially if I can con some money off him too."

"I think you will be the only one who appreciates the humor," Declan remarked. "They're still plain, by the way."

"I'll have Matteus decorate them for me." She shot him a vile grin.

"Now who's being gross?" Declan grimaced.

"I'll be in touch. Hopefully conscious," she commented as she headed for the door.

"Hey," Declan called after her. "Be careful."

"No promises." She shook her head.

"I'm serious." Declan met her gaze with an austere expression, his lack of coarse language impacting his tone.

She had no hopeful words for him, letting silence speak in her stead as she walked out of the building. She was beyond the protection of caution, her existence a beacon to all those who wanted to tear off pieces of her. She would see this through till the end, but how the end would reach her depended entirely on fate Themself.

##21.2##

Nara leaned back in the cushiony seat, blowing the sweetly spiced steam from her teacup. She focused on Matteus' fluid hand motions across the table as he delicately plucked a series of polished emerald colored stones from a black velvet bag. Gentle plinks dotted the meditative silence as he arranged them on the surface in front of him, turning them over one by one to reveal the golden symbols etched on their faces.

Matteus rubbed his chin pensively as he pieced together the divination. His expression morphed as structures connected, and his features flattened into solemn understanding as a quiet murmur rumbled inside his throat.

"Would you like to hear what they have to say?" Matteus offered, gesturing at the casting.

"Not really." Nara avoided his gaze. "I just like to hear the clicking of the rocks."

"As you wish." Matteus regarded her with a knowing smile. He brought his hand on top of the arrangement, ushering them into a pile as he swept them back inside the drawstring bag, leaving their portents a mystery.

"You sure you're okay with this plan?" Nara inquired through a sip of tea.

"Would you believe me if I said I've performed more odious tasks before?" he countered, knotting up the drawstrings.

"I would be skeptical at first," she began, setting her cup on the table. "Then I would wisely keep my mouth shut."

"Does this mean you finally found a place to go?" he asked hopefully.

"No, nothing has been decided." She rapped her knuckles against the chair arm. "I've only just recently opened up to the idea of leaving."

"Ahh, it will be bittersweet to see you leave then." Matteus shifted his wide frame in his seat. "But I am sure I will see you again in my travels."

"You're leaving too?"

"Not permanently, just a vacation per se," he explained. "I haven't embarked on a research expedition in a while, and I've got a tip on an interesting ritual near the Oaexotl cluster."

"I wish you a fulfilling journey, then," she bade.

"I wish you the same." He smiled. Nara hummed in acknowledgment, comprehending the sage's subtle intent.

"I suppose I should leave before Garrett explodes from panic." She sighed, slowly rising from her seat.

"Please take care of yourself, no matter where your travels take you."

"I can't promise anything," she stated. "I can only promise that I will try."

"That is all anyone can ever ask of themselves," Matteus affirmed.

A weak smile flitted over her lips as she regarded the mystic. While she did not share his belief of the metaphysical, there were far too many coincidences in his words that left her with a disquieting feeling. She took one last look around the cozy plum-walled den, wistful nostalgia already seeping into her thoughts. The smoky sweet-scented sanctuary would still be here, even if she moved on.

"I'll be in touch," she bade as she headed for the streets.

The muggy air enveloped her in doubt as she traversed the road, swirling around her mind with its offensive density. Her ploy would never work, but the act of plotting out strategy was just enough of a distraction for her to briefly ignore the uncertainty that loomed over her.

She walked a different path to her bulwarked home, teetering over the edge of the Fringe to find solace in unfamiliar surroundings.

But she was not alone in her venture. A presence was shadowing her, faint. Very faint. An eerie aura cast around the apparition as she sensed it shift through the haggard rooftops above her. She pinpointed the projection and raised her pistol in the direction of the source.

As if on her command, a massive humanoid form dropped in front of her, quaking the crumbling ground as they landed. The ghastly being stood silently in front of her, a wide grin scrawled across their pale lips, displaying a flash of pristine white fangs.

Nara pinched the bridge of her nose, sharply inhaling a deep draught of the humid atmosphere.

"Uuuuuuuughhhhhhhhhhhhhhhhhhhh," she vehemently expressed, steadily releasing the air in her lungs in exasperation. She scanned the grinning foe up and down, shaking her head in defeat. "I don't suppose there is *anything* I could say or do to prevent this from happening?"

The being kept their cold gaze on her, their massive form unnaturally still.

"Fi-*ine*," Nara groaned. "Let's just get this over with. Or whatever."

The eerie humanoid's smile widened at the challenge, edging toward her with glee. As Nara backed away to evaluate the antagonist, they quickened their pace, cutting off her retreat as they swiftly closed in. The being dipped a shoulder down, pulling the force of a fighter jet with their rocketing fist.

Nara snapped an arm up, catching the ballistic strike on her armored forearm. Shockwaves reverberated across her bones as she strained against the impact, forcing her to shift her weight to stabilize herself.

She caught a flash of movement from their other side as they set up for another strike. Impulse forced her movement, and she ducked down to hurl a jab into their abdomen, her knuckles meeting with tough, reinforced artificial musculature.

Fucking synthetics, she griped as she twisted behind the being.

Grinding a heel into the rocky ground, the humanoid revolved around and snatched the distance between them, sending a rapid volley of blows in her direction.

She dipped and weaved against the flurry, fighting to count the pacing of her foe's augmented reaction. Between a hooked blow, she snapped her shoulders back, giving herself enough room from the assailant to extract her armor badge from her belt. With her free arm, she snaked around an incoming fist, twisting her elbow around theirs while she raised the device to her throat.

But the being would not permit an unfair fight, curling into her side as they executed an aimed strike at her opposite hand, smacking the device from her fingers.

Ahhhhh, fuck you. She snarled as she cut the spooky creature in the jaw, releasing the ghoul from her grip as she tore after the device. As she leaned down to grab at the badge, the humanoid stepped in, cutting off her path to the ground. She let off a kick to their kneecap as she darted back, snapping upright to face the challenger again.

The skirmish morphed into an antagonistic waltz, the foe forcing her to react with each movement as they whirled around each other. Nara grew frustrated with keeping up, gaining no edge on her adversary. With every attack there was a parry, then another counter, smoothly followed by another. The being delivered blows meant to wear down her endurance, taking advantage of her organic limitations.

Eyeing her exposed flesh, the foe began to direct their attacks on her throat. But her phyletic combat training was hard-wired to her brain, and she snapped her arms up to her neck. Shifting her weight back, she launched another sharp kick to their knee, knocking them aside.

The grinning foe swiftly recovered their footing with a mechanized pivot of their hip, charging in again with another battery of strikes. Nara maintained her distance, leaning back as she wrapped her neck with her arms, raising her knee up to force space between them.

One, one, two, one, two, she counted. She focused on her breathing as she observed the attacker, patiently waiting as she uncovered an opening in their attack.

After calculating a small window of respite, she waited as the attacker lowered their arm. Bracing herself in the crumbling concrete, she fiercely uncoiled her leg, launching her heel across their temple with a sickening crack. She retreated a hasty step back as the force of her strike sent the humanoid reeling sharply to the side.

Synthetic fluid trickled from their forehead as they vaulted back upright, their grin widening at her successful hit. They broadcast a new posture, changing tactics as they pivoted their balance, twisting in wide arcs as they began to weave around her sides.

Nara edged back with the sudden movements, distrusting the openings presented to her as they tried to snake toward her squishy vitals. But their tactics grew more erratic, and she began second-guessing their chaotic movements.

Her eyes rapidly scanned their form as she watched them gyrate, protecting her chin from an incoming missile as they dramatically leaned over, presenting their floating ribs to her. With a snap of her wrist, she accepted the bait, hurling a fist at their exposed side.

She barely had time to enjoy the satisfying impact of her blow as a piercing sensation tore through the nerves above her hip, sending her synapses through an agonized frenzy as a foreign object invaded her flesh. With a painful growl, she violently wrenched herself away, glaring at her opponent's hand. Her anger elevated as she traced over the barbed spikes jutting from each of their knuckles, glistening with the shiny varnish of her blood.

She had little time to scowl as their relentless assault quickened, her flesh gradually tenderized with perforations as they hunted for the seams in her plating. Her muscles screamed for respite, her punctured flesh demanded attention, and her mind was beginning to tire. Each tearing movement seared across her skin as she felt the warmth of her fluids seep into her clothing.

Shit, come on, hang in there, she pushed herself, crunching her abs together, half to brace against the incoming strikes and half to cringe in pain.

As the humanoid wrenched upright, she instinctively raised her elbows up, gritting her teeth through the pain as she clasped at her neck in anticipation. But a last-minute twitch of the being's shoulder broadcast her grave miscalculation.

Her eyes widened in shock as she felt a force of a jackhammer slam into her chest, a volley of jagged pangs shredding across her muscles. Through the intensity of the impact, she could feel her chest plates crack as the foe punched straight through them, the thorny knuckles boring into the vital organs behind her ribcage.

The shock had barely processed in her mind as her hand clutched the invading wrist, her claws digging through their pale artificial skin.

"ENOUGH." An unholy voice reverberated through her vocal organs.

She felt her quarry attempt to tear away from her grip, but her stance remained unmoved, anchoring their spiked fist inside her flesh. Her other arm found its way to their shoulder, her knees locked as she pulled the being closer to her.

Her strength slipped from her control as her thoughts coagulated into murk, displacing her consciousness outside of her reach.

Fire began to creep across her eyes as the pain began to subside. She felt herself rise and push through the shadowy entity in front of

CHAPTER 22

##22.0##

The meek associate at the front desk gave the imposing visitor a startled look, bolting up from his seat as the frightening being advanced.

The eerie guest wore conservative Upper attire, concealing every shred of skin in black textiles. Their face was obscured by the swirling galactic void of a holomask, loosely sculpted around their head, obscuring their identity. They clutched a large messenger bag by the handle, their ample height preventing the strap from dragging along the ground.

"W–welcome to Galavantier Technologies. H–how may I help you?" The clerk gave a valiant attempt to keep a warm smile on his face.

"I am here to speak with Antonin Galavantier," a ghostly mechanized voice reverberated from the creature, speaking with a sharp, yet slow emphasis of each syllable.

"Do you have an appointment?" The clerk inquired, fidgeting with the scheduling panel.

"No," the visitor asserted.

Anticipating a troublesome confrontation, the clerk slowly moved toward the security beacon on his desk. The guest spied his movement, shifting their stance to a less aggressive form.

"I have something he wants," they coaxed as they turned to the two guards sauntering into the foyer.

"Well, I am afraid there is nothing I can do If Mr. Galavantier is not expecting you," the clerk explained, scraping up as much of his courage as he could muster in his quavering voice.

"I assure you, he will want to talk to me," they softly pressed as the guards edged closer. "I have something very important of his."

"If you do, please leave it with me, and I will take it to him the next time he is available." The clerk pointed an open palm at his desk.

The being's head tilted curiously as their holomask warped over their face, materializing a deranged grin through a projection of twisted lips, clearly pleased with the permission. The guards drew out their weapons as the visitor slowly raised the satchel.

A puff of rancid air laced with the sickly-sweet taint of death violently escaped from the opening as they unzipped the latch. The unsettling guest slid their hand inside, slowly extracting a cold severed arm for the clerk to witness. The rigid appendage was bright crimson in flesh and delicately tattooed with a serpent motif coiled around the skin. The golden detailing glistened in the bright lights of the lobby, revealing the artistry over the darker chitinous protection tracing along the limb. The visitor messily plopped the trophy on the associate's desk, sending loose chunks flinging from the unit, splattering onto nearby paperwork.

"Dear gods! Security!" The associate gagged at the stench, fearfully backing away from the show of callous brutality.

The guards approached the intruder, attempting to subdue them with restraints. Anticipating the assault, they made slight adjustments to their stance as the soldiers reached for their shoulders. Using the guards' inertia against them, the creature swooped and weaved, disabling the assailants with calculated motions.

After a swift altercation, the imposing visitor wrapped their arms around the guards, binding them with the cuffs they had dropped. The humanoid then delicately sat the guards down on the floor behind them and calmly approached the clerk once more.

The agitated receptionist frantically flailed his arms over his desk until his desperate fingers clawed over a set of controls. Upon his fearful command, two auto turrets popped out from the ceiling behind him, slinging a hiss of electronic chattering as they powered up and aimed at the ghastly creature.

"Mr. Vallah? What is all that noise?" A voice from an intercom on the desk irritably interrupted. The clerk craned his neck over to the source, horrified to discover that the finger of the severed arm had depressed the call button for Galavantier's private office.

"Mr. *Vallah*?" The voice barked at the hesitation.

"N–Nothing, sir, just getting rid of an unwelcome guest," the clerk stammered.

From the corner of the room, a small surveillance device whirred around its perspective, examining the scene. The camera panned around, tracing over the intruder, then fixated on the repulsive specimen on the receptionist's desk.

"Send him up," the voice commanded.

"Y–Yes sir." The clerk looked back at the grinning creature, shakily pointing at the elevators behind him. "M–Mr. Galavantier w–will see you now. The elevator will . . . take you there."

The guest wordlessly slung the bag over their shoulder and slithered into the opening doors, leaving the shaken receptionist alone with the gruesome trophy.

The guest let out a gentle shudder as they stood in the chamber, restraining an impulse as they were transported through a digital security checkpoint inside the shaft. Flashes of orange light passed over the being, scanners attempting to analyze their composition as they traveled through the secured areas of the Galavantier complex.

After a short wait, the elevator opened to an opulent waiting room. Bronze and black metropolitan themes coated the moody lit environment, the still environmentally controlled air hovering at a comfortable temperature. Black velveteen lounge chairs bordered the room, and impressionist paintings made with traditional materials dotted the walls, giving visitors a pleasant view while they waited for their appointments.

A display drone floated over to the being, compensating its elevation to meet their eye level. The monitor portrayed a dignified nobleman standing behind a wall of reinforced glass, showcasing a breathtaking view of the city below.

"Please excuse my appearance." Antonin gestured. "I was in the middle of a rather important meeting, and I am currently at a remote location. I believe you have some news for me, Mr. . . .?"

The ghostly man remained eerily still, their gaze fixated on the hovering projection.

"Not the conversing type, I see. Respectable." Antonin paused to size up the stoic creature, taking in their formidable presence with a curious smirk. While he formulated his opinion of the spectacle, he extracted a portable computer from his pocket, glancing through the security footage on the display.

"You have some formidable cloaking defenses built over your hardware," Antonin commented, not looking up from the screen. "Quite impressive."

The creature gave no indication of acknowledgement, their stance mimicking a statue.

"Forgive me if I express a bit of . . . skepticism toward the evidence you have brought to me," Antonin began, putting the device down. "An arm, though an admirable trophy, is not exactly the most convincing proof of death. Many people live full lives while missing an appendage, you see."

The being took the remark as an invitation and dutifully fished around their bag. Another gust of foul air tainted the atmosphere as they produced an alien looking organ, much too large to be considered human. The being situated the gushy device in their grip and stretched their arm out to the drone.

"What is it?" Antonin raised an eyebrow

"It was extracted from the chest." The ghoul shrugged emphatically.

"Interesting." Galavantier's smirk widened, amused by the unflappable man handling gore. With a series of commands, the drone popped out a metal tray from its chassis, offering itself to the creature. "May I?"

The man plopped the viscera on the plate, lowering their arm while making no effort to wipe the fluid remnants from their fingers.

"I haven't seen you much around the city," Antonin said as a probe ejected from the drone, poking and prodding the mysterious organ curiously. "You are a hunter, I take? From Under?"

The being maintained their silence, letting Antonin come to his own conclusions.

"How did you do it?" he asked as he ordered the probe to extract a sample. Squelchy slurping noises curdled the air as a set of needles extracted fluids from the posthumous tissue. The display on his portable device flashed with a volley of figures and calculations as the drone reported data on the specimen.

"Stun rounds," the being curtly explained. "Removed what I needed while the target was down."

"That's quite a simple explanation." Galavantier wrinkled his face, perplexed by the inconclusive analysis on his screen.

"You didn't ask for details," the being countered. "There was struggle from both parties."

"But you somehow managed to overtake it?" Antonin raised an eyebrow suspiciously.

"I have a considerable advantage regarding physical endurance," the being added. "Though the incursion was rather time-consuming."

"So, it felt everything as you performed the extraction?" Antonin asked, amusement curling his lips.

"I don't know. I never bother to ask."

"Fascinating. And barbaric," Galavantier admitted. "What happened to the rest of it?"

"Enforcers."

"Hmm. That is unfortunately convenient." Antonin switched off his scanner with a nod. "Well, I thank you for your contribution. I will reach out to you with payment once the specimens you have provided are verified."

"I do not agree with those terms." The creature glowered. "The encounter proved a taxing confrontation. Some form of compensation is in order to make up for collateral damage."

"Ahh, you are quite the informed businessman." Antonin regarded the hunter with a smirk, considering the bold proposition. "I just have one more question for you. Was my son with it?"

"I thought he was killed." The being tilted their head in confusion. "The target was alone when I tracked them down."

"I see." Antonin hummed, keying in a series of commands into his computer. The drone reached out a wiry hand to the hunter, offering a slice. "Five percent, as a down payment. But since you are quite the discerning gentleman, I think I have one or two tasks that would be fitting for your skills."

"You have my attention," the being announced, pocketing the offering.

"My son is, in fact, not dead." He paused to judge the being's holomask, which still remained expressionless. "But, should you encounter his body, I will most certainly make it worth your while. Be as gruesome as you need to. The media loves a tale of savagery."

"I will see what I can . . ." The holomask contorted into another unhinged grin. "Discover."

"Excellent." Galavantier nodded in approval. "It was a pleasure doing business with you."

The eerie hunter wordlessly departed from the office, bringing the meeting to a cold conclusion.

##22.1##

A SWELL of throbbing pain coursed through her sinuses, scolding her for the audacity of opening her eyes. She swallowed a buildup of fluid idling over her tongue, feeling the acrid, chemical tang of synthetic vitals cutting through her taste buds.

Fuck, Nara thought bitterly. *Not again.*

"That was very entertaining to watch." An unfamiliar voice pierced through her disorientation. "We had to follow you for miles through the Fringe before we could get close enough to bring you in."

She rotated her limbs in a preemptive check on her surroundings, finding herself unrestrained. After recalling the fight that downed her, she felt unusually revitalized, apart from stiffness in her bones and a sickening sensation swirling her senses around. She found no evidence of any injuries from the demanding altercation.

Letting out a heavy sigh, she craned her aching neck around, examining the contents of the room she was in. The area was barren, devoid of furniture, apart from the utilitarian cot that Nara was lying on. The walls appeared to be constructed out of a hollowed block of concrete. No doors or windows revealed an obvious point of entry, and no seams traced around the floors or ceiling.

She spotted the source of the voice leaning against one of the corners, a curious man dressed in a heavy black cloak. An all-knowing smile cast an eerie beacon over his face while a glowing green eye gazed at her with amusement.

"A former foe requested us to help," the shadowy man informed, not waiting for her inquiry. "He says he'd like to apologize and asked us to emphasize that this won't even begin to fix the past, but he had hoped it would be a start."

"So, exactly how many buttons need to be pressed until Shadows start breaking their neutrality contracts?" Nara buried her face in her hands, not in the mood for the strange man's enigmatic revelry.

"It took us quite a bit of convincing to assist you, admittedly, especially with the charged political issues surrounding your existence," the man continued, smirking at her perception. "But that's not your concern. You're not the one who owes us. My name is Scorpio, by the way."

"Where am I?" she irritably croaked.

"A bubble inside No Man's Land," Scorpio imparted.

"That clears that up then," Nara remarked scornfully. "Well, Scorpio, how the hell did you fix me?"

"We know someone, who knows someone, who knows someone who hangs out at the ports. And they happen to be a galactic medic." The playful dance trickling over the man's tone irritated Nara greatly. "But you didn't require much treatment. Intriguing."

"I fail to see the amusement." She glowered, ignoring his implication. "And where is this 'former foe'?"

"He is . . . indisposed at the moment." Scorpio approached and handed her a warm flask of an unknown elixir, bearing down on her with a wry smile. "If he recovers, I am sure he would apologize in person. He is a good man. It's just unfortunate that circumstance brought you on the wrong side of him."

"I am sure of it," she rebuked, sniffing the contents of the flask. She was surprised to find a familiar medicinal aroma wafting inside, a concoction that she hadn't partaken in years.

"Ah, yes, and I do believe this is yours as well." The Shadow produced an armor badge, delicately handing the battered device to her.

"You will forgive me if I do not trust this magnitude of charity," Nara jeered. "Especially considering I am sealed off in a cell with a stranger of your caliber."

"It is entirely understood, and I will reiterate that you are not in debt with us." He bowed. "Someone else is taking these matters personally."

"Joy," she muttered.

"I would also like to say that watching your story unfold here was quite fascinating." Scorpio folded his arms over his chest, releasing a wistful sigh as he recited his nostalgic narrative. "I enjoyed watching you grow here, and it will be a shame to see you go. Perhaps another time, you can come back and tell us all about where you have been."

"If you're so well-informed, you should be more than aware of how much I hate one-sided accounts," she hissed. "And how much I hate those who withhold information for the sake of sport."

"True enough." His smile widened. "But a curious mind is never satisfied. No matter what species possesses it."

"Am I permitted to leave?" Nara abruptly changed the subject, uncomfortable with what the shady man hinted about her character.

"Certainly." Scorpio stuck his hand in his pocket, fidgeting with an unknown device inside. "This way, if you please."

A section of the concrete slid open, revealing a dark corridor leading into nothingness. Nara stood up and leaned into the cavern, then turned to glare at the man disapprovingly.

"I assure you, this will return you home. Trust may not be your strongest attribute, but you should employ it more often," the crafty man jabbed.

Inhaling a deep sigh, Nara shook her head and entered the blackness, stifling her internal warning signs flaring across her skull.

"Safe travels, and do come back. We will miss you down here," Scorpio called after her.

She turned around to address the man with a biting remark, only to find that he had disappeared. In fact, so did the concrete room and the tunnel that led her here. A chilling breeze fluttered the tails of her coat, the streets of Under greeting her with its harsh atmosphere. The landmarks of the Uncivilized Zone began to process through her brain, and she found herself a few blocks away from her home base.

"Fucking Shadows," she muttered with a disgruntled head shake, walking toward her bunker.

She pushed back the obnoxious encounter, shedding the uneasiness that seeped through her skin. With the entirety of Under hunting for her flesh, she had no time to analyze the motivation of the irritating little man.

Utilizing the remainder of her mental power, she tried to scrape together a strategy for escape from her dismal predicament. But no solutions wanted to present themselves to her bedraggled mind.

I simply cannot hide for the rest of my days, Nara thought as she heaved the vault door open, sliding down the steps to her shelter. *I need to leave the planet, but where the fuck would I go?*

Her thoughts a murk of exhaustion and grief, she crept down the corridor and pulled open the airlock door, only to find an unexpected guest in her dining room.

A venerable member of the Ara'yulthr sat with folded hands, casting a pensive gaze at the table. His heavily greyed navy hair was tightly woven into a thin braid that curled around his lean neck. Bright emerald eyes shed a beacon of experience, wordlessly expressing a tale of a hard-fought era. A considerable number of creases dashed along his face, but he appeared years younger than a human of comparable age.

"Loremaster," Nara cautiously greeted.

##22.2##

The answer to her trials had come to her home, making himself comfortable over a steaming cup of tea.

"Greetings, my child," the aged visitor responded.

"You're okay! You–you were gone for so long, I had sent Sentinel after you and . . ." Garrett stammered, bolting up from his seat. He traced Nara's gaze to the guest, whom he had immediately forgotten about upon her arrival. "I . . . he stopped by the door and I let him in. I couldn't just leave him outside. I—"

"Stop babbling," Nara ordered. A movement caught the corner of her eye, and she spied the anxious form of Bellanar lurking in the shadows.

"Warlord," the man addressed her apprehensively.

"Get out of my sight," she growled at him. After an agitated bow, Bellanar hurriedly slipped out the airlock to linger in the dark hallway.

"You shouldn't be so hard on him," Loremaster chastised.

"He's a spineless thorn with the weakest arguments," Nara spat.

"He stole a ship from the scientists to get you back."

"Uncharacteristic of him," she scoffed, sitting across from her guest. *"But I see he somehow managed to convince you to come to my pit oj misery."*

"He is passionate about his culture. But I am here for different reasons," Loremaster affirmed.

Garrett sat down in a chair between them, looking at Nara desperately through the exchange of foreign words.

Nara sighed, switching to Trade. "I suppose I should hear what happened from the beginning."

"That is probably for the best." *Loremaster* nodded, sipping on his tea. "After your removal from society, I took a hands-off approach to politics. This formed a rift between the three parts of the Council."

"That doesn't seem like an extraordinary series of events," Nara commented.

"It made trade complicated with the outside universe, but all in all, it was a peaceful resolution, for a while." *Loremaster* delicately put his cup down. "That is, until Warlord Abberon seized power of the Present."

"Pestilence." Nara's claws found themselves buried into the surface of the dining table.

"Yes, well. That's not the leading concern," *Loremaster* added.

"Oh?" She unclamped her jaw as she waited for the rest of problem to crash into her lap.

"If you can recall back when you were still in power, the Council of Future had been working on building starships to form a navy for planetary protection and enforcing trade matters."

"I think I see where this is going." Nara sighed, turning to Garrett. "The Council of the Future is the science division of government."

"I see." The human marveled as he latched onto the conversation.

"Yes, they have decided to use it for their own purposes," *Loremaster* continued. "They want to leave the home world and continue their research peacefully on a new planet, away from political strife."

"What's wrong with that?" Garrett chimed in.

"The Council of the Present, which is our military power, is not in agreement." *Loremaster* regarded him warmly. "But they are also dealing with internal conflict. Abberon wants to use the navy for exploration, but more than half of the Warlords want to resolve the issues with the Future and keep the fleets close to home world."

"But why is that a problem?" Garrett asked innocently. "Seems like you have enough resources to settle it peacefully and make both parties happy."

"There is no such thing as 'conflict resolution' to Abberon," Nara scoffed. "And he thinks 'exploration' and 'conquest' are synonymous."

"Yes. Unfortunately," *Loremaster* softly breathed. "As of now, the navy is still in control of the Council of the Future. Violence has not broken out yet, but I suspect it's only a matter of time."

"But that still doesn't give me the reason you are here," Nara reproached him.

"Abberon has become intoxicated with all of the negativity of Human thinking, and thus lost sight of *Ötmarr*. Without that, he has no discipline. One of us, as strong as we are, without discipline is an extremely dangerous force," *Loremaster* enlightened them. "I am not asking you to return for our sake. We can solve our own problems or condemn ourselves while trying. I am asking for the sake of the civilizations he will destroy in our name. He will taint us further into being the very ones we have spent generations fighting against."

Nara closed her eyes in vexed deliberation. He had an extremely constructive argument, and she weighed it against whether she could conjure enough energy to show concern anymore.

"Does anyone else know about your departure?" she asked.

"No. And every second I am gone brings us closer to total chaos, should that information should be discovered."

"And what makes you think they would listen to me?" Nara jeered.

"You were the most respected and successful Warlord in quite a long time," *Loremaster* replied.

"You forgot feared." She let the venom wisp through her teeth.

"Yes." He nodded in agreement. "But it was from superstition, rather than brutality."

"Regardless. What was done is unforgivable." She folded her arms, staring through the wall across from her.

"That is most true," the aged man added sympathetically.

Nara remained in silent contemplation as the discussion pressed on her. It took every shred of her will to keep the events of her banishment suppressed enough to allow her mind to consider the invitation, but her mental barriers could not block out her visceral anger.

Thirty years in exile, she seethed, *and now they want me to come crawling back.*

"I don't think anything could evoke enough passion in me to care," Nara finally spoke.

"Then perhaps you shouldn't do it as a patriot," *Loremaster* offered, "but as a mercenary."

She brought her gaze to the floor, ruminating over the shifted perspective. Mercenary more appropriately described her identity, as opposed to Warlord, but the distinction still made her feel like a pawn for someone else's gain.

"My prices . . ." She hesitated, internally reprimanding herself for considering the offer. "Are not cheap."

"You have an entire planet of resources at your disposal," *Loremaster* replied. "All you need to do is name your price."

"What I want is to be free of your kind." She swallowed as much poison from her breath as her throat would allow.

"And if you leave this issue as it is, that will never happen," Loremaster warned. *"If you don't encounter more of us in your travels, then your nature will always keep you awake at night. Wondering."*

Her lips curled in disdain as she stifled an angry tear. He was right, but all that pain . . . she refused to forget.

"When I first arrived at this place, the visions had left me. I was able to rest for the first time in decades," she admitted, looking down at the table. *"But ever since this human came into my life, the visions started returning. And I have a feeling they will not leave me for quite some time."*

"You were never one to have good portents, were you, my child?" Loremaster sympathized.

Nara looked over to Garrett, who was watching her reaction with a pained concern, his willingness to offer help shadowed by his uncertainty. Even though her current predicament was partly his fault, it was unfair of her to leave him on this rock to suffer. It was also a crime to let one so willing to learn waste away.

"My price," she began, preemptively formulating her escape plan from her home planet. "A ship. Advanced for its generation, and constant upkeep. When I am finished sorting your mess, I will pursue my objectives elsewhere."

"I am sure the Council of the Future would be more than willing to work with you for this payment," *Loremaster* affirmed.

"So, it is decided," Nara admitted reluctantly.

"I will return immediately. Your arrival will be disclosed to only a couple of the remaining loyal generals and a few heads of the Council of the Future. Preparations will be made, and they will be ready for your orders," *Loremaster* explainedas he stood up from his chair. "Haste is important in this matter. Will you be leaving with me?"

"No. I have a few loose ends to tie up here."

"As you wish." *Loremaster* bowed politely.

"I also have a submission to the Archives." Nara walked over to her desk and picked up the ghastly book from her dreadful escapade in Upper. She handed it to *Loremaster*, who regarded it with fascination.

"This is a very interesting piece," he marveled as he delicately flipped through the pages. "Where did you find it?"

"I'd rather not get into that, actually," Nara professed.

Garrett watched in adulation as he observed how *Loremaster* treated the book in his grasp. With such a gentle touch, the man held a high respect for knowledge, no matter how vile the source.

"Bellanar!" Nara boomed at the corridor, summoning the nervous man back inside. "Take *Loremaster* back home. He doesn't belong here."

She advanced as he entered, bringing herself uncomfortably close. He let out a sharp grunt as he backed away, colliding against the pointy vault door handle.

"And you'd better take care of him," she warned with a rumbling echo. "*Or so help me, I will track you down and make you know the meaning of suffering."*

The man slowly nodded as he waited for her to leave his personal space, taking the counsel to heart as he hastily shifted away from her.

"When can we expect your arrival?" *Loremaster* asked, ignoring the scene as he headed for the door.

"For safety reasons, I cannot tell you that either," Nara stated.

"Understood. I have a communication line for you to use so that you may reach planetside discreetly." *Loremaster* nodded and handed Nara a transmitter. He glanced over at Garrett, who was wide-eyed at the interaction. *"I like that one. He knows how to learn. Reminds me oj you at a younger age."*

Garett looked at Nara in bewilderment, watching the aged man scan him. *Loremaster* suddenly regarded him with a warm smile, and his heart raced with anticipation.

"I do hope we can speak again. Your company is most enjoyable," *Loremaster* declared.

"Thank you, sir." Garrett blushed, bowing in reverence. "I will anticipate our next meeting."

"Take care of that one, Elam," Loremaster said as he exited to the dark corridor.

Nara leaned her arm against the doorway, sighing in exasperation as the severity of her promise slapped her across the face. Her fate was sealed, her destination selected for her. Apprehension soared through her veins, closely tailed by her self-loathing.

"I'm taking a walk. Alone," she grumbled, stuffing a few select armaments into her pockets. "Need to clear this filth out of my head."

"You sure that's a good idea?" Garrett questioned uneasily. "You've only just returned from what I assume was a hellish week. Should probably at least tell Sentinel that you're okay."

"No, it is not a good idea. Which is why I am walking around in the middle of the Fringe," she replied flatly. "Least it would be my own damn fault if I died, instead of waiting for the parasites to come to my own goddamned doorstep."

CHAPTER 23

##23.0##

A creaking sequence of ratcheting clunks announced Nara's arrival. The haggard giant slung mutterings of frustration as she shut the vault door behind her, adjusting an unfamiliar assault weapon across her back as she leaned against the crank wheel.

Her coat reflected with the sheen of a mixture of blood and an unknown silvery blue fluid, a frayed tangle of dripping wires draped over her shoulders. She glared at the hallway with a distracted fury, her ignited expression amplified by three gruesome furrows stretched across her face. The open wounds trailed crusted drips of liquid down her neck, cracking apart in scabbed chunks as she ground her jaw.

Garrett's lips contorted into horrified revulsion as he witnessed the spectacle, his wide eyes meeting with the shredded remains of a clawed cybernetic arm she dragged behind her, the mass of split wiring and circuitry jittering within her grasp.

"What?" Nara retorted as she dropped the twitching mess. "They aren't going to need it anymore."

Garrett stared at her blankly, his mouth agape at her callous remark.

"I am going to get something to eat," she declared, unraveling the mess across her back. "What do you—"

She stopped when she spotted two additional figures hovering around the far corner of the room, scanning over her with worry.

"Aw, *hell*." She let out an exasperated sigh, glaring at Garrett accusingly.

"I . . . you said you were going through the Fringe. I told Sentinel I was worried and—"

"I was on my way over here anyway," Sentinel assured. "I have some input regarding your travel plans."

"Ugh, come the fuck *on*." Nara slumped into a chair, narrowing her eyes at Declan. "And I suppose you were 'just in the area'?"

"No, I was dragged along to fix your sorry ass," the medic snapped, tossing a damp rag in her direction.

"Wonderful," she grumbled, wiping the dried blood from her face. "I suppose now I can—"

Her words devolved into a rumble of irritation as a new visitor sidled up to the table from the airlock entrance. A swirling void of a holomask sheltered their features, but Nara immediately recognized the visitor.

"For *fuck's* sake, is this a goddamned intervention?" Nara flopped her shoulders forward, slamming her head on the table with an emphatic thunk. Refusing to acknowledge the visitor's face, she continued the discussion by addressing her lap instead. "I know I had asked to meet with you, but I hadn't told you *when*, and I certainly didn't say *where*."

The mask shed from the face of the intruder in a flutter of light-bending petals, unveiling the ghostly features of Cain. He cast her a wounded expression as he extended an arm, offering the slice he secured from Galavantier.

Nara rolled her forehead to the side in reaction to his reserved silence, letting out another sigh as she met his pained eyes.

"I'm sorry," she softly apologized. "I know that was a shitty thing for me to ask you to do, and I'm glad you're okay."

The eerie man shrugged his shoulders, suppressing a shudder as he kept his arm raised.

"Great, fantastic. Now that I have brought you all here . . ." Nara scowled, delicately plucking the slice from Cain's fingers. "I suppose we can discuss my getaway from this cozy planet. That *is* why you're here, right?"

"We can certainly draft a strategy whenever you are ready," Sentinel agreed.

"Good. Glad I have a say in the matter," she expressed. With the nimbleness of a card shark, she juggled the slice between her fingers, splitting the single note into four identical pieces, then laid them in a row in front of her. "Nice to see we were able to scrape something off that asshole."

Cain looked over at Garrett, who was visibly uncomfortable with the ghoul's scrutiny.

"Is everything all right?" Garrett hesitantly inquired.

"He is after you still," the man revealed.

"Yeah, I know. Why is that pertinent?" Garrett scrunched his forehead.

"He wants you found in the most gruesome manner possible," the herald continued. "Told me the media likes a bloody display."

"Ah." Garrett swallowed hard. Having Antonin's cruel intent spelled out in front of him sent his stomach reeling. "I don't feel well."

"Could have been expected. I was wondering how he was going to handle the problem of your continued existence," Nara remarked, then looked over at Cain. "He's going to go after you next."

"Let him." The hunter shrugged.

"Regardless," Nara began as she slid two slices in the direction of Sentinel and Declan, then took a third and placed it into Cain's still open hand.

The man looked at her and shook his head, pushing the offering back in her direction.

Sentinel perked up. "I share similar sentiments."

"And why the fuck are you trying to pay me for taking my garbage?" Declan snapped as he approached her, waving a scanner over her face. "That's fuckin' weird."

"Listen here, I've had a bad night, or week, I don't fucking know. I haven't seen a clock in a long time." Nara swatted at the medic.

"I'm not dealing with any of your righteous bullshit right now. Take it."

"Then I will hold on to it for later," Sentinel affirmed.

"What the fuck would I do with money on a planet that has no monetary system?" Nara threw her hands up. "I-ow! For *fuck's* sake, Declan!"

"Get bent. You're not going anywhere till I fix those holes in you first," the medic spurned.

"Ugh, you are insufferable!" Nara tore her coat off, revealing a score of gashes crossing her torso, the hatched pattern over her skin occasionally broken by the odd bullet wound. In an irritated huff, she slipped the shredded remnants of her shirt over her head in one smooth motion, the gesture startling no one in the room except Garrett, who instinctively turned around.

"You are very helpful," Declan goaded, dragging a chair next to her.

"Human, what are you doing?" Nara raised her hand to her forehead as she addressed Garrett's back, ignoring Declan's patronizing.

"I, uh, thought I would, uhm. Well . . ." He sheepishly rubbed his neck.

"I assume you are part of this discussion, are you not?" she challenged.

"Yeah, I think, but you, uh . . ."

"Oh my fucking . . ." She grumbled inaudibly as she dragged her nails across her scalp. "Turn the fuck around and leave your weird body hang-ups somewhere else."

"Right." Garrett slowly slid into the closest chair, averting his eyes.

"All right, does anyone *else* want to show up, or can we begin?" Nara scowled at the room. "No? Good. Then how the fuck are we reaching Uppercity, much less anywhere near the starports? I don't particularly feel like climbing it again."

"I can arrange transport to Upper, but after that, I'm afraid I cannot provide further assistance," Sentinel offered.

"Oh, really now?" She eyed the man suspiciously.

"It does require some discretion on your part," he added.

"Of course it does." Nara scowled. "Then there is the issue of finding a pilot who would transport fugitives."

"I have a ship," Cain softly mentioned.

"Won't this little escapade impede your business travel?" She scoffed. "A black mark in the GaPFed archives isn't exactly the easiest to scrub off."

"Chassis mod. ID scramble. No problems." He shrugged.

"Well, that's just lovely. Glad that everything is piecing together smoothly. I—" Nara's train of thought was interrupted by a strange sensation coursing through her veins. The cooling effect energized her as she gained an inexplicable mental clarity. Her trepidation toward the scenario began to trickle away, as if evaporating from her skin. "Declan . . . what did you just slip me?"

"Don't worry about it."

"I hate you so much." She rubbed her temples irritably. "What's next? Getting through the city?"

"I know the area well enough. It shouldn't be a problem," Garrett piped in, setting his NetCom on the table. With a few button presses, an image projected in the room, displaying a bird's-eye map of Uppercity.

The circular plane was divided into separate territories, with major sections color coded to represent the jurisdictions of the leading corporate powers. Intermittent dots of contrasting hues clawed their way through the scenery, representing the diminutive technopowers that tenuously gripped the scraps of the remaining airspace.

The star ports edged the eastern rim of the diagram, shaded in grey to indicate a neutral zone. The ports were run by GaPFed embassies in order to maintain the neutrality of interstellar commerce amid the corporations. It was a forced establishment that prevented underhanded bureaucratic machinations, as well as sparing the lives of traders who would have been caught in the inevitable struggle for space routes.

Garrett pressed a finger on two of the largest splotches, amplifying their luminescence as he brought the sections to the attention of the room.

"We should be okay if we dress nicely and avoid Galavantier territory, obviously, as well as Vaylenuran. Plus, all subsidiaries." He highlighted several more areas with additional prods. "We should have a clear shot to the ports. Probably best to go through Tenshinn. They don't have ties, as far as I am aware."

"Worst-case scenario, what are we up against?" Nara asked.

"They'll start with human police guards and try to disable us," Garrett began. "They won't do much in the way of crowd control, especially if there is a significant civilian number in their way."

"*That's* the worst case?" Nara repeated.

"If he decides that casualties are inconsequential . . ." Garrett hesitated, inhaling an uneasy breath of air. "I've heard that pre-war riot suppression is always ready for deployment. Remote-controlled drones and robotics. I've never seen any of them employed, but then again, I haven't seen much in the outside world apart from the odd drunken nuisance getting arrested."

"Wonderful," she sighed. "Cain, would you be able to get us out of a messy situation?"

"Depends on how close you are to port," he reported. "Send me a signal. I'll get there."

"How will we know when you're on your way?"

"You'll know," he said coolly.

Nara shook her head admonishingly, sighing at the absurdity of the proposal. The anticipation of the abrupt exodus mingled with the unnerving silence swirling around the room. Much to her disbelief, she had almost spent the same amount of her life on this planet as her home world. While she had no intent on spending her old age on Arcadia, she had hoped to at least witness a sociopolitical change for the better in this accursed city.

She glanced over the faces that had supported her all these years, wondering where their lives would lead. Sentinel was the closest being that attempted to understand her, apart from *Loremaster*. She was grateful to him, though his elusive motives filled her with unease. The man had never talked about his past, and after a few disconcerting incidents, she had stopped asking. She was certain nothing would change with him. He would continue his charitable ways, seeking the estranged of Under and helping them stay on their feet.

Declan, well, he was Declan. The guarded man wouldn't admit it to her, but she knew somewhere through his snarky defenses, he would miss her. She couldn't help but feel the same. He shared a similar macabre humor with her, and he was enjoyable company, despite his neurotic tendencies.

Then there was Cain. Their relationship was a complicated issue for her, and the one thing she detested in life was complication. She still harbored discontent with the whole scenario, and his very presence irked her to no end. But for now, all she could hope for him was the same thing she desired—a sense of peace.

Ultimately, it didn't matter. Nothing did. People leave their impressions on others, then they move on. There was not a single force powerful enough to stop the chaotic reign of Nature.

In the end, Ötmarr always loses.

"Well." Nara inhaled deeply. "Shall we begin?"

##23.1##

THOUGH THE MAJORITY of the Fringe could be described as a vacant wasteland, it was a vivacious forest of ruin compared to the featureless desert that Sentinel had directed them to. A barren plain met the two travelers, the ground beneath them a sea of finely milled sand of powdered glass, crushed concrete, and rusted metal shavings. To the far west lay the edge of No Man's Land, its swirling sky-blue mist curling and creeping past its boundaries with caustic tendrils.

"Ah, good. You have arrived safely," Sentinel's voice manifested from behind. "I must say, *Serr*, you look quite distinguished."

"Thanks, I think?" Nara regarded the man oddly, tugging at the sleeves of her hunter green Upper suiting.

"Shall we depart?" Sentinel asked, gesturing in front of him.

"I'm not going to ask the obvious about our surroundings and just wait for you to do whatever it is you were about to do," Garrett commented.

Sentinel let out a soft chortle at the observation as he walked ahead, ushering them through the nothingness. He stopped after several paces and shifted his glance around, hovering a hand in front of him.

Upon his command, the air swirled in a murmur of electronic static, splitting apart to reveal a modest elevator access. The pillar that carried it remained obscured by cloaking technology, giving the chamber an eerie disjointed feel as it bent around reality. With a soft hiss, the doors opened to reveal a drab, steel-walled chamber.

"Follow me, if you please." Sentinel waved.

"Yeah, I suppose I should have expected that," Garrett replied as he edged toward the vehicle, with Nara shaking her head behind him. "Though I am surprised that no one else has unwittingly smacked into it."

"It is highly improbable anyone would," Sentinel explained as he stepped in the chamber. "Paragon contributes a considerable amount of resources to both the Shadows and the Cartographer's Guild to keep onlookers away."

Nara snapped the ethereal man a cold look as the elevator doors closed behind him, the mention of the ubiquitous company sending a twitch up her neck.

"I'm sorry, I don't think I heard you properly." Garrett raised a questioning finger. "Did you just say Paragon?"

"Indeed." Sentinel nodded. "I have a mutual working business relationship with Paragon."

"Huh." Garrett shifted uneasily, slipping a hand over the railing along the wall.

"One reason I mentioned discretion in our last conversation," Sentinel added.

"I see," Garrett managed to reply through his astonishment.

A muted hum whispered inside the elevator, harmonized with soft clicks of the mechanism's nearly silent engine churning to life. Garrett braced himself as the gentle pressure of gravity tugged at his knees, feeling the chamber rise at an indiscernible pace. The lack of glass panes on the walls added to the disorienting atmosphere, depriving the travelers of their sense of visual navigation.

"So, where will this lead us?" Garrett asked as he pulled up the

Uppercity map from his NetCom, trying to gain his bearings in the ominous setting. With a swipe of a finger, he spotted the shining pointer surrounded by a blank canvas, flickering outside the city borders.

"An old shipping district," Sentinel explained. "Even when it was active, it was only inhabited by automated drones, so you should have a quiet entry into a calm segment of the city."

Nara leaned against the wall, slipping her hands into her pockets as she took mental inventory of her equipment. She had to leave her lethal weaponry behind, most of it too bulky to be concealed in her restrictive garments. Keeping her loadout simple, she carried a handful of her most dependable gadgets, giving herself room to pick up more devastating armaments from a police grunt if the situation demanded it.

I'm in deep shit, she stewed, scratching a nail over the clasp of a folding knife to keep her fidgety hands occupied.

She flipped through her voluminous mental library of strategy manuals, choreographing disarms and breaks as she considered her potential combatants. Uppercity was a complex arena, and while she was used to being thrown against the odds, the consequences of her mistakes were far greater than on the battlefields of Under.

She wouldn't be executed, at least not right away. She would fester in the blinding lights and artificial recycled air of a corporate prison cell while her life was auctioned off to the highest bidder. And that was only if her captors didn't want to thoroughly vivisect her for the sake of science and amusement. She would be kept alive for centuries while her sentience was violently extracted by the abhorrent acts of corporate research practices, if her sickness didn't destroy her first.

Fucking bureaucracy. She scowled, bitterness crawling up her throat. *It's all the same, no matter the planet.*

"Nara, are you doing all right?" Garrett cracked through her meditation. "You haven't said a word this entire ride."

"Yeah," she lied, keeping her eyes on the floor. "Fine."

A grimace bent Garrett's mouth as he regarded her stiff posture, getting a sense of the inner turmoil infecting her thoughts. While the chains of his cursed future had been broken off his wrists, she was the one who had to pay the price. Words were not the most effective way to express the intensity of his gratitude, but with the calamitous perils that awaited them above, he might not get another chance to do so.

"Hey, I, uh, just wanted to say," he began, "that even with all the fucked up shit that went on out there, I'm glad to have experienced it with you. I appreciate what you've shown me these past months. If I don't make it, I want you to know that, in a sick and twisted way, it's been fun."

The corners of Nara's mouth creeped up at the profession, the irony settling into her features.

"Yeah." Her smile widened. "I'd say the same thing. It's been fun."

Garrett met her eyes as her wry smile infected his lips, the ridiculousness of their situation pushed back by a glimmer of revelry.

"Our destination has arrived," Sentinel announced, handing Nara a transmitter. "Should, for some reason, you wish to return to Arcadia, here is a communication line for you to utilize and get a sense of the political climate."

"It is within the realm of possibility. I can only tolerate my kind for so long," Nara commented as she took the device in her hand.

"Safe travels, *Serr*," Sentinel wished with a warm smile. "May you find peace in your endeavors."

"I'm not holding my breath," Nara retorted as she slid through the doors.

Icy air greeted them as they emerged, their breath misting into clouds as they beheld the desolation in front of them. They could see the brightness of the skyline ahead, outshining the stars as it drained the life force of the environment, casting its surroundings in darkness.

As they stepped into the night, the elevator departed with a flickering murmur, leaving them in solitude as it disappeared beneath its transparent shroud. The atmosphere pressed against them with a soft droning hum. Hollow winds brushed past with a gentle shove. The ground beneath them was divided into a grid of floating pathways, thin sheets of a translucent material that reflected the night sky above. The roads darted in every direction, leading to nowhere.

"Well," Garrett breathed, staring down at the black abyss below. "This is a sight."

"Yeah." Nara took a few steps forward, absorbing what few details the environment presented her.

"Only one way to go, I suppose," he commented, trailing behind her.

As they walked along the eerie path, a curious sensation began to tug at Nara, like an otherworldly presence enveloping her with an ethereal cloud. She felt her trepidation being pulled away from her skin, leaving her with a strange rejuvenation, a mental focus that bestowed a will to fight. She was about to question the peculiarity, but an overwhelming need to persevere edged her forward, pushing her toward the city.

A sense of wistfulness washed over her as she reflected on her time in Under. She pondered over her experiences, realizing that she was a different person from the one that crashed on this haven of suffering.

Over the years, she had lost her ferocity and the ability to feel the thrill of a dicey mission, finding the stimulating chemical reactions in her brain replaced with an overbearing cloak of weariness. It was as if she had grown a sense of maturity during her adventures here, or perhaps it was nothing more than reinforced cynicism.

As the tone of her thoughts mimicked the words of a millennia-old veteran, she snapped back into the present, scolding herself for having no comparable scale of their perspective. After all, she had hardly experienced a fraction of what other established warlords had before her.

"Where are we heading to?" Nara asked, chasing the bizarre spirits from her mind.

"Looks like the border of a business district on the outskirts of Tenshinn space," Garrett replied, looking down at his NetCom. "Should be a fairly uneventful walk there."

Nara made a noncommittal noise as they ventured on, her pessimism taking the report with a surplus of salt.

The travelers remained silent as they drank in the darkened serenity. They distractedly gazed up as the stillness was broken by a murmured chattering, spying the shiny oblong chassis of a transport drone idling by. It made no notice of the two as it rotated in soft arcs, drifting to its objective elsewhere in the tranquil vacuum. In better circumstances, this would have been the ideal place to wander and think, far away from sentient life.

Their journey came to an end as they approached two skyscrapers, the path between them pinched into a tight alleyway that extended into the Upper border. The golden smoldering light of the city abruptly halted at the edge of the path, refusing to illuminate the haunting surroundings behind them.

Garrett edged forward, bringing a hand through the enigmatic barrier. He stared in awe as his sleeve split with a harsh divide of shadow and light.

"Any last words?" Nara asked, engaging her holomask.

"Uh. Fuck the establishment?" His voice cracked as he uttered the halfhearted war cry.

She shook her head as she stepped into the glow, the still warmth breathing an unwelcome greeting over her.

##23.2##

NO SOULS WERE present to witness their approach into the quiet thoroughfare. Any potential observer was locked inside the towering monoliths surrounding them, sustaining the onerous corporate machines with their wretched life force.

"This thing still connected?" Garrett asked through the neural link.

"Yeah," Nara replied, adjusting the visual settings in her holomask to neutralize the judgmental glare of the ambient lighting. *"What's the plan?"*

"We have a bit of a walk to get to the ports," he reported, sharing his map data with her. *"If we can make it to a tram, we can cut a more direct route."*

"Lead on." Nara nodded her head.

They walked through the drab artificial landscaping, their footsteps slowly fading out as they approached an inhabited district. The scenery here was far from glamorous. The main Upper tourist centers outshined the modest concourse from the horizon. The boundaries were reinforced with a sleek steel-blue ambiance that gave off an oppressive, totalitarian feel.

No floating advertisements polluted the uniformity of the suspended gunmetal paved paths, the bright flashy lights replaced with the glinting status signals of hovering security drones buzzing through the air. Squads of black armored police officers patrolled the perimeter, casting an authoritarian shadow over the indifferent crowd.

Citizens milled about in fretful contemplation, their troubled thoughts intermittently drowned out by the occasional tram zipping by beneath the hovering roads. Even the vendor stands exuded a dreary palette, contrasted by the imported goods on display that cracked the dismal mood with extrinsic colorful packaging.

"This is Tenshinn Commons, mostly food and sundry vendors," Garrett explained. "*To be honest, we're probably a little overdressed for the area, but tourists come by here and there to conduct business.*"

"Wonderful," Nara commented.

The populace was disinterested in the newcomers as they eased into traffic, their dismal attitudes a dark contrast to the blissful pep from citizens of more grandiose districts. Here, the people were overtaken by a consuming inner turmoil, a shadow of worry that ate at their souls as they drifted through existence. Their tired faces reflected a dispirited world weariness as they engaged with the merchants, laboriously withdrawing their money to pay for necessities.

Tenshinn Security's commerce focused on militarized technology, and their territory ran as a reflection of the CEO's hard-edged systemic ideologies. While the district was considerably more comfortable than Undercity's squalor, it was exponentially difficult to stay afloat amid the rampant corruption and unnecessary complication of the bureaucratic system. The inhabitants, primarily Under citizens who had managed to scrape enough resources to live in Upper, often found themselves managing a tenuous financial balancing act as taxes were known to fluctuate based on the mood of the patrolman walking by.

Nara moved her inspection away from the common folk, counting off each armed officer in the vicinity. Her attention drifted to the sky as she spied a jagged miniature aircraft gently gliding above the crowd. Its sharply angled wings flitted in brusque motions as it navigated its flight path, sweeping its scanners over the street. With flashy lights and chattering bleeps, it eased along the crowd, murmuring approving reports.

"Hey, what's the tech on those things?" Nara indicated at the floating nuisance.

"I'm not sure. I've never seen them before," Garrett replied. *"They are branded as Tenshinn, but it doesn't look like anything they've produced."*

"Let's move away."

They glided from the main marketplace, moving over a bridge deeper into the city. A trail of featureless skyscrapers bordered the open walkway, dark metallic spires casting a daunting impression over the observer. A swell of wind whirled around them as they traversed, dancing around the modest steel railing that offered meager protection from mishap.

As they continued, Nara spied a roguish man slithering toward them, disguising his predatory eagerness behind charming eyes. His clothing was of higher quality compared to the surrounding citizens, but he blended with the gloomy ambiance of the region. A rapacious grin beamed across his handsome face, radiating a feigned sense of welcome as he advanced on his quarry.

"Hello, traveler!" the stranger addressed Garrett. "Are you lost?"

"Do not engage," Nara ordered. *"Watch your pockets."*

"You think this is the first time I've encountered a con man?" Garrett retorted.

"My, you are a rather large fellow." The rogue brought his attention to Nara, marveling at her stature as he passed his eyes over her. "Those augments must have cost a fortune!"

The duo kept their eyes on the road, silently wishing for the man to get bored and play with someone else. But the predator had not finished with his discourse, latching onto his unwilling subjects with voracious pleasantry.

"You gentleman going somewhere important?" the man pressed. "I must compliment you on your fashion sense. Splendidly dressed individuals such as yourself must be attending an event tonight. What's the occasion?"

As the trickster continued to antagonize them, Nara sensed

another human closing in, matching their pace as they traversed the bridge.

"Well, aren't you the quiet type?" the man prodded. "Not feeling well?"

Nara abruptly stepped to the side, glancing over her shoulder to identify their shadow. A lithe figure slinked back a pace, biding their time as they reassessed their approach. They nonchalantly raised a silvery augmented hand up, making a show of checking the time on their NetCom while pulling their hood over their eyes.

"It's awfully rude to ignore a friendly face, you know." The man's tone sharply morphed, a subtle lace of hostility. "You think you're better than me, or something?"

Nara feigned insult to the challenge, shooting the con artist a piercing gaze as she listened to the movement of the shadow.

The stalker made another brazen approach, quickening their pace to slink into Nara's back. Cognizant of their target's spatial awareness, they hastily edged an arm out, diving toward Nara's side pocket.

Sensing the motion, Nara whipped her arm around her back, snatching the offender by their cold metal wrist.

"No go, huh?" the stranger commented with a wry smirk. "Tough crowd."

The pilferer leaned past Nara, signaling to their companion with a nod.

"Help!" the showman shouted, waving his arms up hysterically. "Police! Assault!"

"Okay, well, this is, however, the first time I've encountered a con man that called the cops mid-stunt," Garrett announced through the channel.

Upon hearing the commotion, two security officers perked up, scanning the street for the source of the outcry. They set eyes on Nara's towering frame, weaving their way toward them.

A hissing pop cracked behind her, and she felt an abrupt release of pressure in her wrist as the shadow slipped away, abandoning their cold skeletal hand inside her grasp. She glowered at the dastardly companion, watching his insidious smile fade into the crowd. With a scowl, she flung the appendage behind her in annoyance, the populace behind barely acknowledging the morbid arsenal with a few disgruntled grumbles. She then raised a hand to her ear, fiddling with the audio settings of her holomask.

>>*Transmission signal intercepted,* the device reported.

"Skol brothers at it again?" one of the approaching officers said to the other.

"Yep. Fancy ones too." Their companion let off a whistle into the audio channel. *"Guy must be loaded if he can afford lifts like that."*

"Yeah, shake 'em down for whatever they got."

"Oh, good, officer! I am glad you are here." Garrett feigned exasperation, pointing off into the street. "These two scoundrels were harassing us. One of them tried to pick my associate's pockets—"

"Nice try," an officer sneered, folding their arms over their chest.

"I . . . excuse me?" Garrett blinked.

"They're going to demand a bribe," Nara clarified.

"Figures. Well, it'll get them off us quickly anyway."

"What I saw was two tourists making a scene in my streets." The other officer pointed derisively at them. "And damaging personal property. We ought to bring you in for disturbing the peace."

"I apologize if I have offended, officer," Garrett soothed. "If there is anything I can—"

"Ten thousand."

"I'm sorry?"

"The fine for wasting my time and to let you off with only a warning is ten thousand," the officer clarified. "If you can't manage that, then I am sure you would rather explain at the station why your companion was hurling body parts into the street."

"Despicable," Nara seethed into the neural channel.

"Oh, I , uh, certainly. I'd be happy to oblige." Garrett made a show of patting down his pockets before fidgeting with his NetCom, nervously digging out a slice from the device. He gingerly stretched out an arm to the officer, amplifying his befuddled expression as he timidly offered the payoff.

While Nara watched the interaction, a mechanized voice invaded her ears as the holomask captured another transmission:

>>*UNIDENTIFIED CITIZEN. OBSERVATION PROFILE 35% CONFIRMED FOR CLASS-1 SUSPECT. DETAIN AND TRANSPORT TO STATION 559786 FOR QUESTIONING.*

A squadron of scouter drones swooped over to Nara's eye level, encircling the two travelers as they ignited the area with their searing spotlights. Blaring sirens ejected from their audio ports, echoing warnings to the vicinity. The stream of nearby observers steadily shied away from the percussive disruption, eyes passing over the scene as they distanced themselves from repercussion.

"I thought you said Tenshinn was safe!" Nara rebuked through the feed.

"Tenshinn WAS safe!" he blurted. *"Unless a new treaty went into effect in the past few days."*

Before the officers could grab for their weapons, Nara snatched Garrett by the waist, squeezing a startled wheeze from his lungs as she lifted him from the ground. She darted to the side of the bridge, the combat drones rushing after them.

>>*PURSUING SUSPECT*, the drone bellowed into her ear.

Maps flickered across her vision as she leapt onto the railing, balancing her stunned cargo over her hip as she calculated her next move. With the buzz of the drones looming in, she stepped off the ledge, freefalling into the heart of the city.

"What are you—OHFUU—" The expletive extruded through his vocal chords like rope as Garrett felt his stomach plunge. He desperately clawed onto Nara, coiling his limbs around her torso as she navigated through the rushing winds of the atmosphere.

His eyes widened as she pitched downward, watching his horrified reflection speed down the glassy surface of a skyscraper. Nara edged them closer to the sleek monolith, and he felt the skin on his cheek crawl in revulsion, anticipating an abrasive burn over his face.

Sparks showered over him as they began to slow their descent, the chilling shriek reverberating through his teeth. He looked up to find

Nara defacing the building with a gauntleted hand, gaining traction with each inch as they decelerated to a manageable speed.

>>*ENGAGING SUSPECT*, the squadron leader of the entourage reported, charging up weapons with crackles of static.

Nara paid it no mind as she surveyed the city behind them, keeping one eye focused on the maps over her holomask. She locked on her destination, scrunching her body in as she brought her knees up to her chest. With a quick tap of her feet, she sprang from the wall, executing a skillful back dive into the abyss.

Plumes of blue energy soared above her, the drones igniting the sky as they miscalculated her reaction. They sharply pitched down to pursue her, slicing the air with a grating hum.

Garrett forced his eyes shut, refusing to witness the descent. Fear paralyzed his body, the muscles in his limbs seizing up as they tightened their grip on his acrobatic vehicle. He tried to ignore the churning in his stomach as she adjusted her movements, cringing as gravity pummeled his organs around his body.

He was not a religious man, but his brain compulsively recited a score of pleas to any celestial being who would listen as the roaring winds of their descent tore at his flesh.

A squeak ejected from his throat as he felt Nara roll over. He had just barely mustered enough courage to crack one eye open when he felt her slam into a solid object. Before he could comprehend the scenario, he was tossed on top of a cold sheet of metal, his eyes staring up at the sky. A disconcerting rumble crawled over his spine as the world darted through his vision, the sky rocking side to side as the familiar sound of tram rails rolled through his ears. He glanced over to find Nara crouched in front of him, staring down the wing of drones descending upon them.

"I–wha—" Words were jammed inside his windpipes as the thundering of his heart flogged his throat.

"You wanted to take the trams, right?" Nara teased through the channel.

"Not what I had in mind!" he forcibly vocalized.

>>*HALT. FINAL WARNING.* The drones interrupted their conversation as they closed in.

Nara tore out a metal disc from her jacket pocket and hurled it at the flying pest. The device exploded into a mace of sparks, entangling the hapless squadron in strands of shocking blue light. With a pathetic screech, the drones fizzled out, their lights deadened as the unforgiving embrace of gravity claimed them.

"Fuck this constrictive shit," Nara growled as she snatched her inventory from her coat pockets.

The air echoed with the dissonance of ripping stitches as her gauntlet breached the confining barrier of the fancy accoutrements, coating her skin with its protective embrace. Shreds of glittering material fluttered into the wind as she shrugged the vestiges off.

Garrett raised his shoulders up to sit up, but inertia thrust him back down, anxiety demanding his body be kept in contact with the speeding tram. He craned his neck up, disoriented by the inability to see in the direction they were moving. His eyes widened as an ominous black structure raced toward them, threatening to swallow the train in its inky maw.

"Tunnel!" But just as Garrett squeezed the last syllable out, Nara had already jumped off the side, fixing herself to the car with her supportive technological exoskeleton.

Garrett flattened his body, pushing his back against the vibrating metal as he was consumed by the darkness. He rapidly blinked as spotlights zipped past his face, spelling out a missive of doom in signaled dashes.

Is this what it looks like to see your life flash before your eyes? Garrett lamented as his vision impulsively moved in time with the lights.

The dashes shrank into orbs as he felt the rumbling reduce, the hum of the engines churning gears as it decelerated. The subway fluted open behind him, and the lights on the ceiling ascended as the station neared. Before he could get comfortable with the decline, the armored beast slithered into his view, snatching his arm and dragging him off the vehicle.

"Let's go," Nara ordered, pulling him to the railing.

"Hey, wait—" His protest was cut off as his feet messily crashed on the concrete path bordering the rail. He flailed his arms out as Nara pushed him away from the tram, eyes wide as he watched it lurch past.

Nara wiped a hand along the wall of the tunnel, tracing her fingers over a beveled seam in the paneling. She barely had time to celebrate her discovery when the chamber erupted with another cacophony of sirens. A jarring performance of piercing red lights announced the arrival of a new squadron of drones, their chunky, reinforced bodies brandishing a collection of sparking barrels.

"Well, fuck," she declared, slapping a device on the panel with a magnetized thunk. The edges burst with a puff of smoke as the internal locking mechanism of the secreted access hatch released a dying whimper. She wrenched the panel aside as it propelled from the wall, revealing a tunnel of wires and tubes leading into darkness.

"Move," Nara ordered as she snatched Garrett by the wrist, dragging him in front of her as she squeezed inside the cramped passageway.

>>*SUSPECT NONCOMPLIANT. INITIALIZING LETHAL ORDNANCE.*

The automated emissaries of law funneled into the corridor, synchronizing their movements as they chased after the perpetrators. The billowing rush of their engines roared inside the confined space, drowning out the clicking of weaponry as their forms transmuted. Their warning beacons strobed through the tunnel, flickering in a violent rhythm as the squadron leader unleashed a torrent of fire on their fleeing quarry.

Nara felt the pattering of bullets raining down on her back, her armor whining a song of caution as she watched the depleting energy meters on her screen. She stuck her arms up as she ran, absorbing the rain of fire as she shielded her vulnerable companion from the attack.

Fuck, need to get out of this place, Nara muttered, tearing through the railway security networks in her helmet. *Not going to last much longer.*

>>*DEPLOYING ARTILLERY*

Fire boomed through the tunnel, shredding the air with ballistic force.

A tearing pain perforated Nara's shoulders as she was abruptly launched forward, her feet reacting with a haphazard sequence of staggers to maintain her balance. Frigid air danced over the skin of her exposed back, lashing across shattered nerves of the fresh shrapnel wound. Warning sirens of her armor screeched in her ears, throbbing in tune to the pulsing ache. She growled as she regained her momentum, gritting her teeth while she waited for her systems to numb her seeping skin.

"You okay?!" Garrett shouted as he glanced behind him.

"Don't worry about me, just run!" she scolded as she throttled her energy stores, redirecting power in her armor to heal the damage.

Invoking a legion of menus through her vision, Nara tore through the network, unearthing a map of the maintenance tunnels. She floated through the grid, tracing her eyes over the outline of an open shipyard nearby.

"Hard left," she barked at Garrett, who wordlessly complied, promptly pivoting his heels as he dashed for the branching path.

>>*DISENGAGING*, the squadron suddenly announced.

What? Nara's nerves spasmed as the sound of the droids faded behind her. She risked a look over her shoulder, noticing the two of them alone as they continued their charge through the corridor.

##23.3##

Garrett heaved a shoulder into the door at the end of the passage, releasing a blast of warm air as they charged into the vast facility.

The stars looked down upon skeletons of tram cars sleeping in an orderly grid over an expansive concrete floor. A battalion of floating maintenance drones tended to their every whim, chattering statuses and commands as they performed their duties.

Elevated steel structures stretched toward the sky, divided into six levels of massive-scale shelving units, each containing a neat row of cargo crates ready for shipment to their interstellar destinations. But an unsettling stillness swallowed the barren airspace, devoid of the waves of transport shuttles that routinely hauled goods out to port.

"We need to move. Now," Nara ordered, dragging Garrett into the maze of shipment containers.

As they slipped into cover behind a stack of steel crates, the air inside the repair field stirred, erupting into a storm of chaotic clacking and surging energy.

"Garrett! I'm so glad you are so predictable." A jarring female voice bounced through the shipyard, accompanied by a coy giggle.

Nara looked over to find the human halt in his steps, clenched fists twitching as his blood pulsed over white knuckles.

"Now, we don't have a lot of time before reinforcements arrive," Cordelia chirped through the audio feed of an observation drone. "So before things get particularly messy, I will ask you to come forward, and tell me where your lovely tall 'study partner' is hiding as well."

Mechanical pattering closed in on them as a throng of combat droids began to sweep through the maze of cargo containers.

"I don't have the firepower to handle this," Nara said, typing off a message to her NetCom. *"I'm calling Cain. He should be able to come get us if he can get away from port police."*

Several tense seconds passed as she glared at her message board, and she rumbled a growl of impatience at the silence.

Of course he won't reply, Nara seethed.

"You are starting to abuse my abundant patience, Garrett," Cordelia proclaimed. "You have to admit, I am preferable company to your father at this point."

"Fuck this shit," Garrett fumed as he crept away from Nara, ducking into another pile of cargo.

"Where the hell do you think you are going?" Nara demanded.

"I'm going to keep her talking," he responded, edging deeper into

the arena. "*You'll have a better chance of moving around without me holding you back.*"

Nara stared in his direction as he disappeared, suspicious of his intent. Given their history, it was uncharacteristic of him to openly betray her, but the logical voices of her conscience screamed for her self-preservation, imploring her to leave him behind.

"This is hardly the time for a white knight antic," Nara finally declared.

"Fuck that! I'm not enduring one second more than I have to with that succubus," Garrett snapped. *"Get me the fuck out of here when Cain arrives!"*

He clambered up a ladder hanging over the side of a shipment container, pulling himself to the roof. As he moved to the center of the platform, he let off a sharp whistle to summon the attention of the floating heckler.

Screeching clanks responded to his call, puncturing through the air as a spider-like machine crawled up the side of his perch, viciously hurling its long-clawed appendages over the top of the container. It launched itself up to meet the human, creeping forward on six legs as its neck stretched out to analyze its prey.

With a crackling puff of smoke, its hands burst from its wrists, stretching its limbs into metallic snakes that pierced through the air. Before Garrett could react, the appendages coiled around his shoulders, coaxing out an anguished yelp as the claws latched onto his skin. The creature then reeled its arms in, yanking him close with a shriek of zipping metal.

Air tore out of his lungs as Garrett collided against the metal creature, and he tried to wrench himself away from its serpentine clutches. But the creature paid no mind to the pathetic defiance, hoisting him into the air as it imprisoned him inside its jagged embrace.

"You're not a very bright one, are you?" Cordelia taunted.

Hearing the skittering of mechanical digits creeping toward her, Nara slinked out of her shelter. As she edged around a corner, a flash of silver darted past her vision, narrowly missing her back as she retreated.

"NO HOSTILES PRESENT," an insectoid automaton bellowed. "INITIATING SCAN."

Nara dove between a pair of containers as a bubble of light exploded behind her. The blast singed the crates surrounding the droid, which stood motionless as it waited patiently for a response to its attack.

"RECHARGING. CONTINUING SWEEP."

Where the fuck is Cain? she growled as she watched the droid zip in another direction. With an irritated exhale, she peered over her cover to search for an escape route in the shipyard.

A chill shredded her nerves as a human scream pierced through the neural link, echoed by a disjointed latency rupturing through the dockyard, the noise shattering through reality. Nara brought her gaze to the source of the sound to find Garrett blazing with crackling energy, his face contorted in agony as his captor sent its abusive payload through him.

"All right, so I don't know to whom I am addressing personally," Cordelia announced to the arena. "But let's cut to the chase. Reveal yourself, and I will stop this."

Another surge of electricity coursed through Garrett's body, a trillion daggers chipping at his bones while his muscles tore themselves away from his control. The pain was constant, yet erratic, an agony that burned holes through his brain.

As he was relieved of the torrent of energy, he felt his weight drop beneath him, his knees trembling as he struggled to kick away from the beast. Sweat streamed down his face as he frenziedly panted, his skin crawling with the ghostly sensation that lingered over his nerves.

Keep her talking, Garrett scolded himself. But words would not come out of his mouth. Instead, a soft chortle manifested inside his throat. It escalated, warping into a deranged giggle. His morbid revelry then erupted into bellows of maddened laughter that tore out of his abused chest.

"What is so amusing, dear?" Cordelia inquired with a curious head tilt.

"She's an alien, you festering wolf fucker!" He gasped drunken heaps of air to control his unhinged cackling, fighting to form a single sentence within the span of one breath. "She doesn't. Understand. Human loyalty. Friendship. Is unfamiliar."

The drone floated over to him, edging toward his face to assess his spite.

"Such uncouth language. How uncharacteristic." Cordelia tsked, letting off another shock into his quivering body. "And you don't honestly expect me to believe that, do you?"

Just hang on, he urged as the needles tore at every inch of his skin. His fight seeped from him as he tried to wriggle away from the current and his body collapsed in the grasp of the droid. The ligaments in his bleeding shoulders scolded him for abandoning control, forcing them to support his weight as he dangled inside the sentient metal snare.

"I don't have to. She's probably gone already," he wearily goaded, spitting out fluids at the antagonistic drone. "Left me alone."

Deep down, he feared that Nara would abandon him and leave him to his fate. He stared at the jeering drone, visualizing the reality of an existence chained up to a creature such as Cordelia. He tried to regain control of his speeding thoughts, but weariness engulfed his body, forcing him to bear witness to his brain's cruelty.

Nara enhanced the audio settings of her helmet, trying to ignore the conversation at the center of the arena as she listened for the patrolling droids. Their clacking gait pitted her brain as Garrett's words drove a nail through her thoughts. Logic dictated that she should bolt for the nearest exit into the city, as between the two of them, she possessed a higher chance of survival.

But the human's pitiful cries tore into a part of her she was not comfortable engaging with. It had nearly killed her several times before. She shook the unsettling feelings from her brain, accepting that neither of them would live if she permitted herself to be distracted by a moral impasse.

"Hang in there, kid. Cavalry's coming," she lied through the neural link, concealing her agitated impatience. *Where the fuck is Cain?*

She strained against the sounds in the arena, counting off the steps of the automated pests. Convinced that she'd uncovered a break in the pattern of patrols, Nara dislodged herself from her shelter, creeping toward the center of the arena despite her better judgment.

"UNIDENTIFIED HEAT SIGNATURE," a mechanized voice called above her.

Well, fuck. She cringed as she slowly pivoted around, spotting a faceless arachnid leering behind.

"ENGAGING." The droid dropped to the ground with a sparking screech, bounding toward her with eager claws. It jutted its arms out to its sides as it charged, summoning a searing blue glow from the tips of its talons.

The energy expanded, enveloping the beast's arms with bracers of sparking blue bubbles. The light intensified as the energy crawled over the droid's body, shifting in red swirls as the edges of the blobs smooshed into each other.

Sinister red light crept over Nara's shadow as she wrenched around to escape the beast. The air boiled behind her as she dove inside the shell of a tram car, snaking her body beneath its paneling. She snapped her arms over her head as she compacted herself into a ball, hearing a winding zap behind her as the magma field exploded, showering the surroundings with its scorching payload.

Slinky zipping noises echoed behind her as she slipped out the other side of the busted tram. She glanced back to watch the droid vault over the railcar, rappelling itself with its ropelike limbs firmly latched to the roof. It vaulted into the sky, recoiling its arms with a shining flourish as it executed an automated pirouette midflight. Nara staggered to a halt as the beast crashed in front of her, tearing at the concrete with its talons.

As the beast shot out its claws, Nara threw her arms up, sending a pulse of electricity into the projectile appendages. A shudder ran down her back as she punched the invading hands away, the memory of the Enforcers tickling her mind. She lurched back as the silvery snakes dropped limp to the ground, shaking the eerie feelings away.

Unhindered by the incapacitated metal noodles, the droid leapt forward, stealing her personal space with sequential stomps. It balanced itself onto the back set of its surplus legs, its insectoid frame swaying like a rising cobra as it elevated over her.

A flash of metal blinked through her vision as it lashed out a leg. She wrenched her shoulder away from the strike, snatching the soaring metal inside the palm of her hand. A growl rumbled from her throat as she strained against the force of the automaton, her arm quivering as she pushed the appendage away from her. As she moved her opposite hand to brace her grip, the beast hurled another leg, forcing her to intercept the oncoming weapon.

Her muscles groaned as the creature pulled its talons apart, stretching her arms away from her torso as she maintained her grip. Before she could release its pointed extremities, a crimson spark flared in front of her face, launching a deafening crack through the shipyard. A searing pain tore through her abdomen, and she looked down to meet a massive gun barrel projecting from the creature's trunk.

Ow. She disengaged from the talons and rolled around the beast, emitting a groan as her armor slid over her torn flesh.

"Doesn't understand loyalty, indeed," Cordelia sneered.

Garrett struggled to turn his head toward the commotion, watching a swarm of drones scuttling toward Nara's position. He struggled to push himself up, but his nerves deserted him, leaving him a numb mass of meat within his cold captor's clutches. The strength to warn her deserted him as he helplessly viewed the scene, his focus slipping from his consciousness.

The metal pack soared toward Nara, bounding over obstructions with their telescoping arms and leaping over obstacles with predatory coordination.

But as they edged closer, the sky erupted in a crackle of purple light. A percussive *PWANG* resonated across the horizon, shuddering the ground. A trail of darkness engulfed the lights of the neighboring star port, and the station disappeared from view.

As the droids recalculated their balance from the concussive disruption, Nara slipped around the horde, lashing out in a dance of sparking arms as she evaded the flock of swooping pincers.

Fucking showoff, she grumbled as she darted for the center of the arena.

The pack reclaimed their bearings and charged after their prey, deftly orienting themselves in an arrowhead formation as they pursued her. Electronic chattering perforated the air as they called off course calculations, the squadron stretching the width of the shipyard.

A rolling thunder quaked the towers of steel as a colossal shadow eclipsed the path of the hunting party. The stars above were snuffed out by a jagged spacefaring raptor, its wings sheathed as it loomed over the miniscule creatures. The descending beast swallowed the ambiance of the shipyard, its blackened carapace bending perception to its will.

Light cracked around the back of the ship as the cargo deck peeled open, revealing a heavily armed Cain brandishing a massive antimateriel rifle over his shoulder. He chucked an object down at the horde and dove to one knee, aiming for the droid restraining Garrett's unresponsive form.

The shipyard burst into a bubble of glowing amethyst, engulfing the bloodthirsty mass with its debilitating radiance. The leaders of the pack collapsed, warning the stragglers of the danger with a hideous cacophony of agonized shrieks. The surviving fraction of the collective darted away from the blast, running to the perimeter of the arena in lithe ripples.

"Oh, that is inconvenient," Cordelia hummed, steering the drone to the edge of the arena. "Sit tight, Garrett. I'll get help to deal with this mess."

Garrett ignored the mockery as a blast erupted behind him. He tried to move his neck to find the source, only to be shoved forward by a violent gust of energy. A flood of cold fire submerged his body, leaving him with a bizarre sense of reprieve churning inside his brain. He felt himself fall to the ground as the droid dropped him, barely registering the pain from the collision. His sense of gravity warped as he felt arms slide underneath his back, lifting him into the air.

The remnants of the fallen droids regrouped, chasing after Nara and her living cargo as the battalion of clacking appendages rumbled through the industrial playground. A jarring chant of metal screeching filled the air as the horde grew disinterested in controlling collateral damage, tearing furrows through the concrete and slicing across containers as they advanced on their target.

With the drove of robotic ghouls closing in, Nara ran for the nearest shipping crate, hefting herself on top and continuing her flight across a road paved with storage capsules. As she maintained her rhythm jumping and sprinting across the yard, she met eyes with the awaiting Cain. A small salve of relief coated her nerves as she tore after the hovering ship.

"Catch!" she called to Cain as she slid the body off her shoulder. With a heaving grunt, she hurled the limp human toward him.

The man dropped to the floor of the deck, seizing Garrett by the back of the shirt. He braced his grip on the body with his other hand and rolled back into the ship, dragging the unresponsive weight up with him.

"Get us out of here!" Nara shouted as she leapt up, snatching the edge of the cargo door with her fingers. On her order, Cain dashed for the cockpit, steering the ship out of the yard.

Nara steadied herself from the force of the flight, controlling her erratic swinging as she rose precariously over the city. As she started to hoist herself on board, a clawed arm rocketed toward her. The prehensile talons snaked around her leg, and she furiously scraped at the deck as the weight of the insidious machine pulled her down.

A squeak of friction slashed over her leg as the droid cinched its pincers shut, cracking her armor as it began to burrow its claws into her calf. Pain ripped across her limb as the vise squeezed, her plating giving away with unsettling crunches.

"*FUCK!*" she snarled as she kicked at the clawed appendage. A throaty bellow echoed from her chest as she hoisted herself onto the deck, dragging the mechanical anchor up with her. The ligaments across her limbs screamed at her as she crawled over the floor, chastising her as she reached an arm out to the shiny red button of the door control.

She felt the android shift underneath her, releasing pressure on her flesh as it lassoed its other arm on the airlock door. Seizing the opportunity of her limited freedom, she squirmed toward the button, hoisting her torso up as she slammed the petulant device with her fist.

The cargo deck hesitantly obeyed the command, raising the door with a slow, laborious churn. The droid pounced in reaction, hastily retracting its arms to slingshot itself into the ship's hold. Nerve chilling shrieks resonated across the deck as the beast rammed its trunk through the shrinking opening, its talons scraping obnoxiously over the metal gate.

The door mechanism groaned in ratcheting clunks with the obstruction, hurling argumentative squawks as the stowaway fervently clawed through.

Nara rolled over and snatched up the rifle on the floor, taking a haphazard aim at the flailing automaton. The creature lashed out in response, hurling a tentacled arm to smack the weapon from her grip.

"Fuck off!" she shouted as she scooted away from the beast's undulating arbalest. Slinging an irritated growl, she squeezed off a round into the droid, coating the creature in aqueous silver fire.

With a yowl of electronic dissonance, the beast succumbed to the ballistic, draping over the cantankerous barrier in a tangle of limp appendages.

Nara let out an irritated groan as she crawled over to the door control, hauling herself upright with the barrel of the gun. She punched the control, watching the deadened creature slip into the abyss below.

The rush of her victory quickly diminished as she peered outside, her vision flooded with blinding red light. She watched in stupefaction as a squadron of GaPFed enforcement ships sped toward them, their glinting armaments reflecting the cityscape.

"Nope! Fuck that!" she shouted, hurling another blunt strike at the door control. "Company's coming!"

Upon hearing the outburst, Garrett dragged himself along the floor, attempting to rise through the swirl of disorientation flooding his brain. Of all the grievous injuries he had sustained during his life, he could now confidently admit that he preferred gunshot wounds over the hell inflicted by that sadist.

Nara cut off his struggle and hefted him up, limping toward the cockpit. As she laid him on the bunk behind the flight deck, pulses of force flickered the lights inside the ship. The paneling shuddered as a barrage of energy spattered against the hull.

>>*SHIELDS DEPLETING. HOSTILES INBOUND*, the ship's computer reported as the GaPFed ships unleashed their assault.

"You sure you can handle this shit?" Nara shot Cain a questioning look.

The man didn't respond, his concentration focused on steering. The craft ramped into the air, speeding toward the stars. A rush of heat scorched the view screen as Cain pushed the ship out of the atmosphere, heading into the orbital traffic of Arcadia.

The airspace was teeming with ships of every class, size, and nationality. Battle-ready cruisers mingled with extravagant trade ships, idling around orbit as they waited for passage into Arcadia's ports. Their engines glinted every color in the visible spectrum, softly radiating against the darkness of space. Tiny starfighters buzzed around the motley fleet, performing daring acrobatics over the nearby transports.

Well, this is an entirely new realm for me, Nara mused as she marveled at the sight.

But she had little time to enjoy the view as a blockade of heavy fighters intercepted their flight path. An orderly line of gunmetal-coated wolves maintained an uncomfortably close distance to them, dots of green fire lining along the wing extremities of each ferocious starship.

A notification chirped on the control panel, and Cain acknowledged the hailing message with a flip of a switch.

##23.4##

"YOU ARE IN DIRECT VIOLATION OF THIRTY-SEVEN GAPFED PROTOCOLS. POWER DOWN YOUR WEAPONS OR YOU WILL FORFEIT YOUR—"

Cain promptly flipped the switch off, steering the ship away from the attack squad. He pointed the ship toward empty space, speeding away from the accursed planet.

"Hang on," he directed through a sequence of button presses.

Nara clutched onto the wall, using her armored hands to secure herself to the metal paneling. She was about to do the same with her boots when a disorienting weight tugged her away, forcing her to stomp back to maintain her balance.

The engines surged to a blazing roar as they charged up, the interior vibrating with an unsettling tremor. A cloud of violet gas manifested in front of the nose of the ship, lashing out tendrils of energy as it swallowed them inside its trans-dimensional grip. As the engine plateaued its clamor, a flash of white slashed through the cockpit, and the ships tailing after them vanished, along with the gleaming orb of Arcadia.

Moments later and the engines wound down, steadying the ship inside a tranquil starry void.

Nara unhinged her grip on the paneling, processing the events that transpired before her. While the starports were part of her jurisdiction in her early life, she had never traveled aboard a ship, at least not consciously. She had occasionally flipped through books detailing the evolution of hyperspace travel, but she never imagined the maneuver to be so smooth and instantaneous.

"That is not going to be easy to clean off your record," Nara commented.

"I did what they asked," Cain stated with a shrug. "My weapons weren't on."

Nara shook her head as she hobbled over to the empty bunk, slinging curses as she slammed into the adequately cushioned mattress. She winced as she dismantled her armor, tearing the controls of the medical bot off the wall. While arguing with her nerves, she fastened the device onto her wrist, muttering in agitation as the absurdity of her escapade settled into her brain.

Cain slipped out of his seat and approached her, taking out synthetic patches to place over her more severe injuries. He leaned down to assist, but her disgruntled growls deepened the nearer he encroached on her personal space.

"How long for the trip?" she asked, slapping his hands away.

"Few weeks on a leisurely pace," he reported. "Days if I push it."

"Let's not and say we did." Nara exhaled.

Thirty years, she bitterly mused as the chemical substances trickled into her veins. *And I find myself right back where I started.*

She wasn't in the mood to acknowledge her feelings, but inside the stillness of space, there was nothing left for her to do but contemplate what awaited her at home.

The thought of calling *that* planet home repulsed her. She never belonged, but moving around the galaxy in search of a place to call her own was a mind-numbingly unappealing venture. It took decades to learn about the people surrounding her well enough to trust them, and now that she left, she would have to start the draining cycle once more. There were only a few select individuals on Arcadia that she admittedly enjoyed interacting with, and abruptly severing her connections was disheartening.

She looked over to Garrett's sleeping form, thinking over his banter with the corporate viper on the night she was ensnared in his trap. Humans were very difficult to get along with, and their malicious tendencies made healthy relationships nearly impossible. She couldn't understand why people spent so much energy associating with their community if they did nothing but tear at each other.

"Melodramatic little shit." She breathed a sigh of exhaust.

Garrett stirred as he overheard the biting remark, barely processing her words as he pried an eye open.

"Is it over?" Garrett drunkenly slurred.

Nara stared out into the stars, taking in the sight as she considered the question. A twinge sparked across her lips as a wave of envy colored her thoughts. The life he'd known was no longer a burden on him. His world had opened wide, while her past was breaking down her doors with torches and pitchforks. Unlike her, he was truly free.

But what the both of them would do from here, only *Xannat* knows. And they are not forthcoming with their knowledge.

"Yeah. It's over."

##END TRANSMISSION##

COMING SOON...

Having escaped Arcadia, Nara and Garrett flee to the Ara'yulthr home planet to face a new political tangle.

Cursed by her ingrained sense of duty, she must confront the government that had betrayed her to stop a civil war. Will she succeed? Or will she submit to her simmering resentment and watch the planet erupt into chaos?

Want More Nara? Be sure to check out https://www.odinsmusings.com/ and sign up for email updates on the next saga installments. Get exclusive access to unreleased content, sample chapters, and more of the Sleepless Flame galaxy.

Find the Sleepless Flame Universe at most book retailers!

ABOUT THE AUTHOR

A chronically bored spooky creature, Odin dabbles in a strange array of interests to keep their wandering brain in check. When not writing under the influence of caffeinated drinks and sugary snacks, Odin can be found escaping reality with video games or getting their fingers tangled in a mess of threads and needles. Provided their cats do not scatter the contents of their workspace across oblivion, Odin also creates beaded jewelry and video lessons on YouTube.

Be sure to find Odin around the Interwebs and see more of their works:

Jewelry Persona Odin's Bead Hall:
http://odinsbeadhall.com/

CPSIA information can be obtained
at www.ICGtesting.com
Printed in the USA
BVHW04s0822250818
524806BV00011B/5/P